THREE
MILES
DOWN

TOR BOOKS BY HARRY TURTLEDOVE

THREE MILES DOWN

HARRY TURTLEDOVE

TOR

TOR PUBLISHING GROUP
NEW YORK

THREE MILES DOWN

Copyright © 2022 by Harry Turtledove

A Tor Book
Published by Tom Doherty Associates / Tor Publishing Group
120 Broadway
New York, NY 10271

www.tor-forge.com

Tor® is a registered trademark of Macmillan Publishing Group, LLC.

The Library of Congress has cataloged the hardcover edition as follows:

Names: Turtledove, Harry, author.
Title: Three miles down / Harry Turtledove.
Description: First Edition. | New York : Tor, a Tom Doherty Associates
    Book, 2022. |
Identifiers: LCCN 2022008301 (print) | LCCN 2022008302 (ebook) |
    ISBN 9781250829726 (hardcover) | ISBN 9781250844859 (ebook)
Classification: LCC PS3570.U76 T477 2018 (print) | LCC PS3570.U76
    (ebook) | DDC 813/.54—dc23
LC record available at https://lccn.loc.gov/2022008301
LC ebook record available at https://lccn.loc.gov/2022008302

ISBN 978-1-250-82973-3 (trade paperback)

Our books may be purchased in bulk for promotional, educational, or business use. Please contact your local bookseller or the Macmillan Corporate
and Premium Sales Department at 1-800-221-7945, extension 5442, or by
email at MacmillanSpecialMarkets@macmillan.com.

First Tor Paperback Edition: 2023

Printed in the United States of America

0 9 8 7 6 5 4 3 2 1

This one is for Alan Awane, for all the right reasons.

THREE
MILES
DOWN

Jerry Stieglitz sat cross-legged in front of the stereo on the bottom shelf of one of the bookcases in his apartment. The thick red shag carpet was nearly as comfortable as the nubby nylon that covered the sofa. His powder-blue cord bell-bottoms almost glowed against the crimson and scarlet background, but he was too used to that to notice.

He had two cassette tapes. One came from his advisor. The other he'd bought a couple of days before at the Westwood Wherehouse. Without hesitation, he put the commercial tape in first.

He brushed back his long brown hair so his headphones fit more snugly. Then he turned the volume up. Side two of *Pretzel Logic* filled his brain. He'd liked *Can't Buy a Thrill* and *Countdown to Ecstasy* a lot, and the new Steely Dan album was at least as good as the first two. Nice to find a band that didn't run out of ideas after a couple of records. Too many did.

"Parker's Band" and "Through With Buzz" . . . Jerry's head bobbed up and down, enough to make him straighten his wire-rimmed glasses on the bridge of his nose. He'd worn cheaters for a long time; sometimes he straightened them even when he wasn't wearing them. Anna'd caught him doing it once or twice. His fiancée thought that was hilarious. He just thought it was stupid.

After "Charlie Freak" ended, he hit the Stop button and took out the tape. For one thing, he didn't like the last two tracks as much as the rest of the album. And, for another, he really wanted to hear the cassette Professor Krikorian had given him.

Because Jerry'd been working with Hagop Krikorian for five years now, he had no trouble deciphering the scrawl on the tape's label. "Humpbacks," it said. "Northern Pacific, July 1973." Only the summer before. Hot off the press, or near enough in marine biology.

He turned the volume up some more. Steely Dan was electric guitars and keyboard and drums. Humpback songs—some people called them *vocalizations*, but Jerry thought *songs* was more descriptive and more accurate—put him in mind of sad trombones grooving with bassoons. They weren't, of course, but that was what they reminded him of.

In 1970, a couple of months after Jerry got his B.S. at UCLA, pioneering scholar Roger Payne had released an album called *Songs of the Humpback Whale.* It became one of the most improbable top sellers of all time. One of the tracks was sped up to fourteen times its actual speed, and sounded astonishingly like birdsong.

Jerry appreciated the accelerated version's different beauty, but he liked the whale sounds better at their true pace. He tried to find patterns in them, and to work out why the humpbacks sang the way they did. Were males courting females, as birds did with their melodies? Were they talking about where the krill was thickest? Or were they just . . . singing? Nobody knew. Looking for answers, though, was endlessly fascinating—to him, anyhow.

Since he had the headphones on and the volume cranked up, he didn't hear people coming up the stairs to the second floor—his floor—of the apartment building. He felt the footsteps, though, through his legs and backside. He was too focused on humpback sounds to notice that those footsteps stopped in front of his door.

He didn't notice the knocks on the door right away, either. But they got louder and more insistent. He glanced at the stereo. When he put on the headphones, he usually remembered to poke the button that took the main speakers out of the loop. But he wasn't perfect about it. He'd already irked the couple downstairs two or three times. Did they have humpbacks swimming through their ceiling at heart-stopping volume?

As a matter of fact, they didn't. The knocking kept on anyway. Muttering, Jerry stopped the tape, stood up, went to the door, and opened it.

Three men he'd never seen before stood on the walkway outside his apartment, one in front and two behind. They all wore suits. One of the men in back carried a briefcase. The guy in front was in his fifties, short and burly. He wore his hair in a greased pompadour, as if he'd decided he liked the style in 1946 and never noticed the times had changed.

"You are Jerome Samuel Stieglitz?" he barked.

"Yeah, that's right," Jerry answered automatically. "Uh, who are you?" He hoped like hell they weren't cops—he had a couple of joints stashed in a kitchen drawer.

Instead of answering, the burly man pushed past him and into the apartment's long, narrow front room. His two buddies followed. As soon as everybody was inside, one of the henchmen closed the door again.

"Who *are* you people?" Jerry repeated.

As if he hadn't spoken, the guy with the pompadour said, "I'm gonna need to see some ID, Stieglitz."

He had a good command voice. That was what Jerry's friends back from Vietnam called it. Jerry's hand started for his wallet before he even thought about it. He made the hand stop.

"Hold on, dammit," he said. "Who the hell are you? You want something from me, show me a warrant."

The stocky man snorted in annoyance. "You can call me John P. I'm with the CIA." He bobbed his head toward each of his pals in turn. "This is Fred, and that's Steve." Fred was the one with the briefcase. Steve had shut the door.

Things were happening much too fast for Jerry. He stared at John P., and at his friends. "You guys are from the CIA, too?" he blurted.

Fred nodded. Steve said, "Actually, I work for the RAND Corporation." He was about the same age as John, and looked like a professor. Jerry had no trouble believing he drew a paycheck from the big, fancy think tank in Santa Monica.

"Your ID," John P. said again. He was not only built like a boulder, he was as implacable as one rolling downhill.

This time, Jerry did pull out his wallet. He displayed his driver's license. John carefully checked the photo against his face, then gave a grudging nod. As Jerry stuck the wallet back into his left front pocket, he said, "Now let me see something that proves you are what you say you are."

John shook his head. "Sorry. Not gonna happen. People who work for a secret outfit don't carry cards that say, 'Hi, I work for a secret outfit.' You wanna call the cops, go ahead. We'll be gone before they get here, and you'll never find out what this was all about."

Jerry didn't call the cops. He'd had his car broken into a couple of years before. The Hawthorne police were no faster than they' had to be, and no smarter. Later, he wondered if he should have. But that was later. At the moment, he just asked, "Okay, what *is* this all about?"

"You are Jerry Stieglitz," John said. "You are a grad student in marine biology at UCLA. You passed your doctoral exams a few months ago, and you're working on your dissertation."

"That's me," Jerry agreed. Then a light went on in his head. "Professor Krikorian said somebody was asking questions about me a couple of weeks ago. That was you people, wasn't it?"

"Could have been," John answered, deadpan. Then he unbent enough to grin. He looked years younger when he did. He went on, "You speak Russian, too."

"Not real well. I read it better," Jerry said.

"Okay. And you know a little Swahili. How did that happen?" John asked.

"I wanted to study a language that wasn't Indo-European, just to give me a different slant on things," Jerry replied. "The more I learn about all the ways people talk, the more I can bring to whale songs. I don't think they're speech, exactly, but I'm sure they're more than grunts and barks."

John glanced at Fred and Steve. Fred looked back with no expression at all. Jerry wouldn't have wanted to play poker with him. Steve smiled and nodded. Jerry felt as if he'd passed some kind of small test.

He asked, "Why does the CIA need to know all this stuff about me?"

Instead of answering, John went on, "Along with an article, you've also published two science-fiction stories, one in *Analog*, one in *The Magazine of Fantasy and Science Fiction*. They have whales in them."

"Well, yeah," Jerry said. "I'm writing about what I know about. I'm not gonna talk about lizards or gophers."

Steve smiled again. Fred just stood there. John said, "Before we go any further, you have to agree to keep what your hear quiet from everybody. Everybody means *everybody*. Reporters. Friends. Your advisor, Dr. Krikorian. Your father. Your fiancée, Miss Anna Elaine McGowan. If you make that promise and then break it, you'll wish you'd never been born. Understand me?"

They'd know when he was sleeping. They'd know when he was awake. They'd probably know when he was bad and good, too. Jerry was Jewish, but he'd learned Christmas carols in elementary school along with everybody else. "I understand," he said slowly.

"All right. Do you agree?"

Jerry had no great love for the CIA. He also couldn't imagine why they wanted anything from him. That was the problem. His bump of curiosity itched. If he didn't scratch it . . . If he didn't scratch it, he'd spend the rest of his life wondering what he'd missed.

He took a deep breath. "Yeah. I agree."

"Good. Glad to hear it," John said, and then, "Fred?"

Fred hefted the briefcase, as if looking for somewhere to set it down. His eyes first lit on the table in the dining nook between the front room and the cramped little kitchen. Jerry worked at that table. His typewriter held pride of place. Papers drowned the rest of the tabletop. He had to shove them aside when he wanted to eat. Fred put the briefcase on the coffee table in front of the ugly couch instead.

Jerry didn't like that table. It bit him in the shin whenever he wasn't careful. To open the case, Fred worked what looked like a combination lock. He pulled out some papers and handed them to John.

John passed them to Jerry. "Confidentiality and nondisclosure agreement. You can read it before you sign. I already gave you the gist, though."

Read it Jerry did, or at least glanced through it. "What's Project Azorian?" he asked.

"It's what you're going to keep quiet about," Fred told him: the first words out of his mouth since he'd barged into Jerry's apartment. "Keep quiet about the name, too, whether you sign or not. Real quiet." Both the other intruders nodded.

Project Azorian aside, the agreement was what John said it was. The word *felony* popped up a dismaying number of times. "Boy, you weren't kidding, were you?" Jerry said.

"I never kid," John P. answered. From some people, that would have been a joke. Jerry got the feeling the CIA guy meant it.

Which had nothing to do with the price of beer. Jerry walked over to the kitchen table, grabbed a pen that was sticking out from under some of the papers there, and scrawled his signature on the indicated line. He handed the agreement back to John. "Here you go. What did I just sign my life away for?"

John answered the question with a question of his own: "Have you heard about the ship called the *Hughes Glomar Explorer*?"

"The ocean-mining ship? Yeah. Funny-looking thing! I saw it on the TV news when it sailed into . . . was it Long Beach or San Pedro?"

"Long Beach," Fred said.

"Yeah. Long Beach," John agreed. He glowered at Jerry. "Okay. Now you find out why you signed that paper. The *Glomar Explorer* doesn't belong to Hughes. It belongs to us: to the Agency, the CIA. We don't give a shit if it ever pulls up any manganese nodules off the seafloor. That's just the cover story for what it'll really be doing in the North Pacific, which is what Azorian is all about."

"Riiight." Jerry let the word stretch. He hated asking the obvious question, but he didn't seem to have much choice. "What *will* it be doing there?"

"In February 1968, the Russians lost a submarine in those waters—the K-129," John said. "It's a diesel boat, but it was carrying missiles tipped with nuclear weapons, maybe torpedoes tipped with them, too. The ocean there is three miles deep: a little more, actually. They searched for it after they lost contact, but they didn't know exactly where it went down. They looked for a while. Then they gave up and went home. *We* found it, though." He looked and sounded smug.

The next obvious question was, *How did you do that?* Jerry didn't ask it. Instead, he said, "SOSUS."

Fred jerked as if somebody'd stuck him with a pin. "You aren't supposed to know about SOSUS!" he yipped.

John was cooler. "Relax. He's a marine biologist, remember? A marine biologist who does whales, no less. He'll know."

"'Fraid so," Jerry said. SOSUS was the acronym for SOund SUrveillance System, the strings of hydrophones the Navy had laid on the ocean floor in the North Atlantic and North Pacific. They were there to listen for Soviet submarines and warn the brass if the Russians tried anything nasty.

They were there to listen for submarines, but they also picked up whale sounds. A lot of the material people like Hagop Krikorian and Jerry Stieglitz worked with came from SOSUS recordings . . . unofficially, but it did. In fact, SOSUS technicians had been the first people to detect low-frequency blue whale and fin whale vocalizations.

"Anyway, that gave us a pretty good location," John said. "Then we sent out a sub of our own, one with cameras on the ends of long cables, and it gave us the exact position . . . and these."

He took a big manila envelope out of Fred's briefcase and gave it to Jerry. Jerry undid the metal clasp. He pulled out a stack of photos. Very detailed, they showed the wreckage of most of a submarine on its side at the bottom of the ocean. It looked cruder, more squared-off, than modern American boats. All the same, the sub seemed amazingly intact. In one picture, a skeleton still in seaboots lay near the hull.

Jerry noticed that the photos began with number 79 and continued through 180. "What's on one through seventy-eight?" he asked.

"You don't need to know that," John said sharply.

"Yet," Steve added. John sent him a red-hot dirty look. Steve just smiled. A quarter of an inch at a time, John subsided.

"Okay, you found the sub, the, uh, K-129," Jerry said. "Now what, though? You said it's three miles down. Not like you can bring it up from there."

"That's what the Russians think, too," Fred said.

"You bet it is," John agreed. "But they're wrong. Or we hope they are. We built the *Glomar Explorer* to hook a giant lifting claw—Clementine, we call it—under that submarine and haul it back to the surface. Missiles to analyze, maybe codebooks to let us read Ivan's mail . . . Who knows what kind of goodies we'll find?"

"Wow. Oh, wow," Jerry said. The first thing that came to him was *You're out of your fucking minds.* But they obviously weren't. The CIA wouldn't have spent some large number of million dollars and cooked up this elaborate cover scheme if they didn't think they had at least a decent chance of raising the lost Soviet sub. But . . . "Where do I fit into all of this?"

"We want you to come along," Fred answered.

"This is supposed to be a research vessel," John amplified. "While most of the crew will be learning how to bring up manganese nodules, you'll be learning about whales out in the open ocean. You know, like what's-his-name on the *Beagle*."

"Darwin," Jerry said faintly.

"Yeah. Him." John P. nodded. It was somehow perfectly in character that he could call up the ship's name but not the scientist's. John went on, "You really will be able to bring on whatever you want and do as much research as you can. You'll make things look authentic, know what I mean?"

"You get paid, too," Steve put in.

"That would be nice," Jerry said. What he made as a teaching assistant barely covered rent, food, and gas. Any expensive emergency and he'd end up moving back in with his old man. They both wanted that like a hole in the head. Anna worked in advertising at a travel magazine. Her paycheck was a good bit bigger than this. When they got married, they'd merge their finances. In the meantime, he scuffled. Scuffling was a grad-school way of life. A beat slower than he might have, he found the right question: "Paid how much?"

Steve didn't answer. Neither did John. His eyes swung toward Fred. Fred said, "As marine biologist aboard the *Glomar Explorer*, your monthly salary would be two thousand nine hundred thirty-three dollars. Two months guaranteed, after that as necessitated by the project."

"Twenty-nine thirty-three?" Jerry wanted to make sure he'd heard right. That wasn't TA money. Two months of that would be more than he made all year as a TA. It wasn't junior-faculty money, either. It was full-professor money, maybe even department-head money.

But Fred just nodded and said, "Correct."

"When do I start?" Jerry asked. He was proud of himself for making it sound like an ordinary question. He wanted to yell and scream and whoop and bounce off the walls and ceiling as if he were in a Bugs Bunny cartoon.

"We expect the *Glomar Explorer* to leave Long Beach harbor on or about June twentieth," John answered. "There's only a narrow window in the North Pacific when we hope sea conditions will be calm enough to let us do what we need to do. We want to make sure we can exploit it."

"June . . . twentieth." Jerry winced. He'd be done with spring quarter. That wasn't the problem. "Look, I know you guys will have me checked out nine ways from Sunday. And if you've checked me out, you'll know—

"That you and Miss Anna Elaine McGowan plan to get married on June thirtieth," John finished for him.

"No, we didn't know that at all," Steve said, and chuckled. Of the three of them, he was, if not the Good Cop, at least the Best Cop.

"We can't delay sailing for anyone's personal considerations. You have to understand that." John's tone said he could go to hell if he didn't understand it—go to hell and not go on the *Glomar Explorer.*

"We've already made arrangements, though," Jerry said helplessly. "We've spent money. We've rented the synagogue. We've got the food set up. We've booked our honeymoon. We've—" He gave up. If he went, Anna wouldn't want to marry him. She'd want to murder him. He didn't see how he could blame her, either.

Steve sidled over to Fred and whispered in his ear. Fred looked like a guy who'd just bit down hard on a lemon. Steve gestured to John. They all put their heads together.

"We'll pay all the expenses involved in delaying your wedding," Fred said. "That includes covering your rent here for as long as you're away."

Jerry didn't answer right away. *They really want me,* he realized. The feeling was strange. It went to his head like champagne. Grad students had to be among the most chronically unwanted people in the world.

After a few seconds, he said, "I still don't think Anna would be real happy with that."

"Understandable. We're messing up plans you've already made. If we give the two of you, ah, two thousand dollars as compensation for the inconvenience, would that make the lady happier? Would it make *you* happier?" Steve said. "We can call it a wedding present or something."

John and Fred both opened their mouths, then closed them again without saying anything. *These people have more money than they know what to do with. Literally,* Jerry thought. It wasn't a problem he'd ever needed to worry about before.

"Can I tell her that that will happen?" he asked.

"Go ahead." John didn't sound happy, but he gave the okay.

"Call me tomorrow afternoon. I'll let you know what she says." Jerry didn't bother giving his phone number. It was unlisted, but they had to know it anyway.

There wasn't much talk after that. The three men left as abruptly as they'd pushed their way in. Jerry watched them go down the stairs and out the door to the foyer. As soon as they disappeared, he started wondering if they'd really been there at all.

He wrote that down on a three-by-five card and stashed it in the manila folder he called his idea file. Waste not, want not.

Jerry parked his beat-up old Rambler on the street a couple of doors down from Anna's apartment building. Her place looked just like his: a two-story Spanish-style structure with units surrounding a concrete courtyard centered on a pool. Tenants kept their cars in spaces underneath. A swarm of places like theirs had gone up in Hawthorne over the past five or ten years.

He climbed the stairs from the foyer to the security door and punched 2–6–4 on the keypad next to it. A moment later, Anna's voice came tinnily from the speaker above the keypad: "That you, Jerry?"

"Nobody else, babe," he answered. The security door buzzed. He grabbed the latch and let himself in before the noise stopped.

As he climbed the stairs to the second floor, he suddenly wondered how the CIA guys had got into his building. It used the same kind of security setup as this one. Maybe they'd followed somebody else in. That happened. Or maybe they'd talked to the manager, whose apartment was right there. If they claimed to be cops or private eyes or whatever, odds were they'd have badges or papers to back it up. The stuff might not be legit, but it'd look legit. Jerry was sure of that.

He hurried down the walkway to the door with the tarnished bronze 264 on it at eye level. He was about to knock when the door opened. "Heard you coming," Anna said, "so I baked a cake."

"Cool," Jerry said. He had to bend down to kiss her. She was only five two, a foot shorter than he was. She was blond, and carried ten more pounds than she wanted to. In Jerry's biased opinion, she carried them goddamn well, too. He'd given up trying to persuade her of that. Better not to start fights you couldn't win.

When he came up for air, the King of Siam was glowering at him from the hallway that led back to the bathroom and bedroom. Those blue eyes held more ancient evil than a cat had any business knowing.

"I swear that beast used to belong to Queen Berúthiel," he said.

Anna poked him in the ribs. She had long, pointed nails. That wasn't why he flinched, though; she'd found a ticklish spot. "So why did you want to come over tonight? Besides that, I mean?" She glanced toward the King of Siam and the bedroom beyond him.

He took a deep breath. This wasn't going to be easy or fun. "Hon," he said, "we need to push the wedding back a couple of months, maybe a little longer."

She stiffened in his arms. Then he wasn't holding her anymore. He didn't know how he wasn't, but he wasn't. "And why do *we need* to do that?" she asked, her voice dripping liquid helium.

"Because out of the blue this afternoon I got an offer to go on the ocean-mining ship that came into Long Beach last fall, the *Glomar Explorer*. Remember?"

"Not really," she said. He believed her; she paid more attention to people she cared about—and to that damn cat—than to the wider world.

"Anyway," he went on, "it sails on June twentieth, and that's firm. I really want to go."

Anna stared up at him. Her eyes were almost as blue as the King of Siam's. "More than you want to marry me?" She was taking it personally. Of course she was. She took everything personally. Most of the time, Jerry liked that. Every once in a while . . .

"Babe, it'll be really good for my career," he said. If looks could have killed, he would have been lying there dead next to the chair by the window. Then he told her how much they'd pay him.

Her face changed. "You're making that up."

"No way, hon. Swear I'm not." He raised his right hand, as if taking an oath.

"In that case, you've got to have Polaroids of the guy who asked you with a sheep," she said.

He laughed and shook his head at the same time. The gibe was funny, but it stung, too. She'd never thought he was ambitious enough. She'd spent a year and a half at Cal State L.A., then bailed for the real world. She'd done well in it, too. She'd said more than once she'd never thought she'd wind up with a guy slogging his way through grad school.

But here she was. With him. And they had a wedding date. Or they *had* had one.

"They'll pay our expenses for putting things off, too," he said.

"They *will*?" Anna sounded astonished and delighted at the same time. She and Jerry were footing the bill for the wedding themselves. Her folks had supported her through high school. After that, it was "root, hog, or die" as far as they were concerned. She'd worked behind a typewriter or a cash register to pay for as much college as she'd got.

"That's what they said. I'll get it in writing before I go. You bet I will."

"You'd better." Anna cocked her head to one side, examining him the way a malacologist would examine a sea slug that might be a new species. "How come they want *you* so much?"

Jerry had been wondering the same thing. "Maybe because I write science fiction. I'm not even lying, or not very much. They mentioned it when they talked with me."

Anna snorted. "There must be a reasonable explanation instead." His tiny beginning of a career didn't impress her much. The people who published in *Journeys* flew or sailed all over the world, wrote travel expenses off their taxes, and turned out polished prose about what they'd seen and done and eaten. Next to that, what were a couple of short stories in pulp magazines?

"I guess. I don't know what it is, though. I do know they'll also give me—us—two grand for putting up with the hassles of changing our plans, only they'll call it a wedding present."

"Two grand?" Anna silently mouthed the words. Jerry nodded. Then he was holding her again. He didn't understand how she'd come back, any more than he'd got how she moved away. Teleportation, maybe. He didn't have long to worry about it. She tilted her face up. Unlike the kiss when he'd stepped into her place, this one was the real deal and then some. After they finally broke apart, she said, "I don't know what they think you've got. I just hope it isn't the same thing I think you've got."

"What's that?" he asked.

Instead of answering, she walked back toward the bedroom. Jerry followed eagerly. He paused for a moment to scritch the King of Siam under his chin and behind his mouth. The cat accepted the adoration as no less than his due, and even deigned to purr.

By the time Jerry made it to the bedroom, Anna had most of her clothes off. He shut the door behind him. When they were in bed together, the King of Siam liked to jump up there and help. Jerry didn't think he improved things. There, Anna agreed with him.

It wasn't always great with them. Anna seemed more complicated than any other woman Jerry had ever known; the challenge was part of what drew him to her. So they had their ups and downs with their ups and downs. But when it was good, it was spectacular. Tonight . . .

Afterward, he mimed putting the top of his head on again. "Wow," he said, and leaned over to kiss her one more time.

"Yeah." She nodded lazily. "Wow."

She got out of bed and opened the door. The King of Siam meowed irately as he paraded into the bedroom—what had the humans been up to that didn't require a cat? Since he'd been fixed, he couldn't even imagine. *You poor bastard*, Jerry thought, and petted the top of the cat's head.

The King of Siam scratched his hand.

Jerry stuck his head into Professor Krikorian's office. His advisor was explaining something to an undergrad in words of one syllable. By the blank look on the guy's face, even words of one syllable might have been too hard. Krikorian nodded to Jerry without breaking his own train of thought. Jerry ducked back into the hallway and leaned against the wall to wait.

A couple of chattering girls sashayed by, one in jeans, the other in shorts. Jerry's eyes followed them. He was attached, but he wasn't blind. And if UCLA didn't lead the world in pretty girls, he couldn't think of any other place that would.

Out came the undergrad. He was scratching his head, with luck in wisdom. Jerry went inside. "What's going on?" Hagop Krikorian asked. He waved Jerry to the chair the undergrad had just warmed.

"I found out what was up with the people who were asking about me," Jerry said.

"Oh, yeah?" Krikorian leaned forward. His thick, bristly beard, black with just a little gray, always reminded Jerry of steel wool—and reminded him his own whiskers were still on the wispy side.

"Yeah. They're from the *Hughes Glomar Explorer*. They want me on it when it goes out toward the end of June. I may get some good stuff if I can trail a hydrophone far enough behind the ship to mute most of the engine noise. I may need a leave of absence fall quarter—I don't know just when I'll be getting back."

"Huh." Krikorian scratched his cheek. His whiskers rasped like wire under his fingernails, too. "You want to go, do you?"

"You bet I do. Good chance for fieldwork. The money's decent, too. Better than decent, in fact, and I can use some better than decent now."

"That's right. You're getting married soon. What does—" The professor paused.

"Anna," Jerry supplied.

"Thanks. What does Anna think of all this?"

"She's not thrilled about putting things off, but she sees what a chance this is for me. What do *you* think, boss?"

Krikorian scratched at his beard again. After a few seconds, he said, "I don't know whether to be jealous or to tell you you're out of your mind. The whole sea-mining story sounds like the world's biggest boondoggle to me."

You don't know the half of it, Jerry thought, and wasn't that the truth, the whole truth, and nothing but the truth, so help me, Perry Mason? With a shrug, he answered, "Howard Hughes has money the way Carter has Little Liver Pills. If he wants to give me some, I'm sure not gonna complain."

"Nope. In your shoes, I wouldn't, either," his advisor said. "You think grad students have it bad now, you should have seen things twenty years ago. They used to take better care of the lab animals than they did with us."

And they don't now? Jerry almost said that out loud. He swallowed it at the last moment, though. He could joke with Professor Krikorian up to a point, but only up to a point.

When he kept quiet, Krikorian went on, "Do what you need to do. If you have to take that leave of absence, I'll help arrange it. I hope you bring back some good data. Any which way, you'll have a story you can tell over cocktails at conferences for the rest of your life."

"Sure." Jerry wondered what would happen if he tried that. Maybe the CIA guys would just lock him up and throw away the key. Or maybe somebody with a scope-sighted rifle on a rooftop across the street would blow his head off as soon as he stepped out of the conference hotel. John P. didn't seem like somebody who kidded around about secrecy.

He said his good-byes and went up a flight of stairs to his own office. They crammed half a dozen TAs into a space no bigger than one professor got, separating desks and chairs with three-quarter-height walls made of varnished plywood and frosted glass. If you ever needed to be reminded of your status, academia knew how to do it.

A couple of other grad students were in there, either waiting for students or doing some work. After the usual greetings and grumblings, Jerry sat down to see whether anyone from his Biology 101C sections would show up. Nobody did. Having wasted an hour of his life, he headed to the parking lot and drove home.

The southbound San Diego Freeway turned out to be a lot more exciting than his office hour. Some idiot towing a big boat had managed to flip his car and the boat trailer sideways across three lanes of traffic. Along with half the other people in the world, Jerry had to funnel through the single lane that remained open. A good time was had by none.

He anxiously watched the needle on his temperature gauge creep up. The Rambler didn't like crawling along. If the radiator boiled over, he'd add one more stuck car to the freeway nightmare.

But he made it past the clog. After that, he sailed down to El Segundo, where he got off. He headed east, past Inglewood, past Hawthorne Boulevard, past Prairie, till he came to the little street he lived on. Two minutes later, he was parking his car. He affectionately patted the door when he got out. He'd got back again.

He checked his mailbox in the foyer. The new *Fantasy and Science Fiction* was there. That would give him something to kill time with tonight. And a bright green flyer told him a Mexican restaurant was opening on Prairie. He tossed it in the trash.

As soon as he walked into his place, the phone rang. He trotted into the bedroom. "Hello?"

"Are we on, Stieglitz?" That could only be John P.'s raspy voice.

"Uh, yeah," Jerry answered. The CIA guy hung up. More slowly, Jerry did, too. Big Brother really *was* watching him.

Jerry had the Thomas Brothers, open to the right page, on the front seat beside him. He checked the road atlas when he stopped at a red light. Yes, the address he was looking for should be in the next block of Ocean Boulevard. The light turned green. He got going more slowly than he might have, but before the guy in the pickup behind him could honk.

There it was! The Long Beach apartment building was an older cousin to the ones that had sprouted like toadstools in Hawthorne. Instead of adobe-colored stucco and a Spanish-tile roof, it wore white stucco with blue shingles on top. Maybe it was supposed to seem transplanted from a Greek island.

He found a parking space and, carrying a suitcase he got out of the trunk, walked back to the building. He walked straight inside, too; it didn't have any kind of security system. His head swung right, then left.

Apartment 127 was to the left. As he'd been told to do, he knocked twice, then once. It made him feel silly, as if he were in a bad spy movie. But evidently genuine spies did stuff like that, too.

The door opened. A man who looked as if he'd been a leatherneck not real long before eyed him with no expression. "Yeah?"

"My name's Jerry Stieglitz. John sent me." Jerry felt silly again.

But the tough-looking fellow stood aside. "C'mon in. Set your suitcase down on the couch. We'll check it out. Then go over to Vic at the table there. He'll take care of your paperwork."

"Okay." Jerry followed instructions one more time.

Another guy who looked as if he could take care of himself started to unlatch the suitcase, then paused. "Anything monogrammed in here? Shirt? Belt? Handkerchiefs, even?"

"Nope. Not my style," Jerry said.

"Awright. We'll look it over anyway." The man opened the lid and started inspecting Jerry's clothes.

Vic, behind the table, was older than the other two and seemed milder. "Give me your wallet." Jerry handed it to him. Vic extracted his driver's license, Mastercard, and Social Security card. Jerry felt a pang. You weren't really you unless you had the paperwork to prove it. Then Vic pulled a small envelope from what looked like a cash box. "Here you go."

The envelope had *Steinberg* written on it in a script a sixth-grade teacher would have envied. Jerry opened it. Inside were a California license with his photo and address but the name Gerard Sheldon Steinberg, a Social Security card with his number and the same name, and a credit card with that name and a number that wasn't his.

He held up the Mastercard. "Can I really use this?"

"Oh, hell, yes," Vic said. "Same credit limit as your real one. It'll work."

"What if I need to write a check? My ID won't match."

"You're two days from sailing, so don't, all right? You gotta get something, pay cash or charge it."

"I will."

"Good deal. Now—you've taken care of everything you need to do before you leave?"

"Yeah. I've said my good-byes," Jerry said. The one with Anna had been lusty and tearful, the one with his father more along the lines of *Well, I'll see you whenever you get back*. He went on, "I've graded all my finals, too, and turned in the sheets to my prof and my department. So I'm good to go."

"Fine." Vic nodded. "Gotta make sure, you know." He snapped his fingers. "Oh! One other thing. Before you go, leave your house key with somebody. Just leave your car key—they'll start it up every so often while you're away so it'll run when you get back."

"Cool!" Jerry'd been worrying about that.

Before he could say anything else, the fellow searching through the stuff in his suitcase went "Ha!" and held up a handkerchief with a red, machine-embroidered *J* on it. By the way he displayed it, he might have found Nathaniel Hawthorne's Scarlet Letter.

"I forgot all about that," Jerry said, embarrassed. "My aunt gave me some of those when I turned twenty-one."

"That's why we check you out." The CIA man threw the offending square of linen into a large metal trash can. Jerry wondered how many other people's clothes and key rings and such already lay in there.

Nothing else in the case seemed to be against the rules. Jerry closed it up. The hired muscle at the door politely opened it for him. He walked out into the courtyard and headed for the street.

An older man lugging a battered suitcase of his own paused inside the entranceway, no doubt also looking for apartment 127. Jerry pointed back the way he'd come. "It's over there."

"Thanks," the man said, and then, "Hi, Jerry."

"Oh! Steve! Hi!" Jerry hurried forward and shook hands. "Good to see you. I didn't know you'd be going along on this . . . whatever it is."

"Whatever it is, is right." By the way Steve glanced at the apartments surrounding the courtyard, he figured they were full of KGB agents waiting for him to tell them everything they needed to know. The scary thing was, he might have been right. He went on, "But yeah, I'm coming. I wouldn't miss this for the world."

"Okay. Cool, even." Jerry was glad he'd have at least one slightly familiar face on the *Glomar Explorer*. Being more social caterpillar than social butterfly, he didn't make friends easily, or sometimes at all. He wanted to ask Steve about a million questions. The man from RAND's worried expression warned him that wouldn't be a good idea, though. He just said, "I'll see you there, then," and went on his way.

He'd be back in Long Beach tomorrow evening. They'd told him to board the *Glomar Explorer* no later than six p.m. (actually, they'd told him no later than 1800 hours, but he knew what that meant). Since he was one of those people who were compulsively on time—maybe in reaction to his dad, whom he'd heard called "the late Hyman Stieglitz"—that wouldn't be a problem.

And then . . . a sunken Russian submarine? He understood he was only along for the ride and the cover story, but the idea intrigued him anyway. Could they really bring it up from three miles under the surface of the Pacific? Would they find anything worthwhile if they did?

Even if they did find something, he'd never be able to talk about it. He got that. But he'd know. And if knowing wasn't what it was all about, he didn't know—that word again!—what was.

He parked the his car in the lot closest to Pier E, got his suitcase and a hydrophone with a UCLA sticker on it out of the trunk, and trudged toward . . . *Toward whatever happens next*, he thought.

Not just anybody could get to the *Glomar Explorer*. A tall chain-link fence secured it from the annoying and the snoopy. As Jerry got closer, he saw that the fence was topped with razor wire. They were serious about not wanting company.

There was a gate in the fence. A sign on it said AUTHORIZED PERSONNEL ONLY in big red letters. A booth about twice the size of a phone booth stood on the far side. A security guard came out of it as Jerry drew near. He was somewhere between linebacker and lineman size and wore a pistol on his hip for good measure. He carried a clipboard in his left hand. His right stayed free.

"Your name, sir?" he said.

"Jerry, uh, Steinberg," Jerry answered. His first chance to use his new alias, and he damn near flubbed it!

The guard checked the papers in the clipboard. He had to flip up a couple of them before he found what he was looking for. Jerry'd long since got used to life toward the tail end of the alphabet. "Steinberg, Gerald S.?" the guard said. At Jerry's nod, the fellow continued, "Let me see some identification, please."

"Here you go." Jerry showed his phony license.

"Thanks." It satisfied the guard. He unlocked the gate and held it open so Jerry could bring through the suitcase and hydrophone. Once he got inside, the guard locked up again. That felt very final to Jerry. Then, as Jerry'd been told he would, the guard said, "Give me your car keys? You *are* in the lot across the way, right?"

"I sure am! Thanks!" As Jerry set down the suitcase and dug out his key ring, he went on, "It's a '65 Rambler American, light blue. License plate is ONR 541."

"A '65 American. Light blue. ONR 541. Steinberg." The guard wrote in a little notebook he pulled from his breast pocket. Then he looked up. "Okay. We'll take care of it. Hope you have a safe trip and everything works like it's supposed to."

"Me, too. Thanks again." Jerry wondered whether the guard knew the whole story or thought the *Glomar Explorer* was going to try deep-ocean mining. He would have bet on the latter, but had better sense than to ask.

As he walked down the pier to the ship, its sheer size smacked him in the face. He'd seen it before in a couple of black-and-white newspaper photos, and in news snippets on his twelve-inch black-and-white TV. Those gave shape, but not scale. The *Hughes Glomar Explorer* was 619 feet long, with a beam of 116 feet—bigger than some American battleships that had fought in World War II. The central derrick rose more than 250 feet above the keel.

If they'd put guns aboard her . . . but they hadn't. She carried pipe instead, more than three miles of pipe. They'd join it all together when they got where they were going, join it together and use it to lower the giant grabber to the lost K-129. Then they'd bring it up again.

How much weight did the sub, the grabber, and all that heavy-duty pipe add up to? Had to be thousands of tons. How many thousands, Jerry didn't know. But he could see why the Russians figured anything that big, lost three miles underwater, was lost for good. Anybody in his right mind would.

Which says what about me, exactly? he wondered as he came up the gangplank connecting the *Glomar Explorer* to the pier. At the pier end, another armed guard checked his name off a list and examined his counterfeit driver's license. It passed muster one more time.

A fellow in crisp whites waited at the other end of the gangplank. A steward—Jerry was pleased with himself for finding the right word. "Welcome aboard, sir. You are . . . ?" the man said.

"Jerry Steinberg." This time, Jerry brought out the name that wasn't his with assurance.

"Steinberg." The steward checked a list, too. He nodded to himself. "Okay. We have you quartered with Mr. Dahlgren in cabin 116." He pointed toward the stern.

"Dahlgren. Gotcha." Jerry added, "Oh. Thanks," as the steward handed him a key. He hoped it would work out all right. Except for nights with Anna, he was in the habit of sleeping alone. You couldn't get much further from that than sharing a cabin with somebody for a couple of months.

He made his way aft. There was a huge square opening beneath the derrick, covered over now. He soon found out everybody called it the moon pool. When they got where they were going, the cover would come off, the bottom would open however it opened, and they would start stringing pipe segments together and lowering the claw toward the K-129.

In the meantime, relatively narrow steel passageways skirted the moon pool to port and starboard. The pipe farm lay aft of the derrick, in front of the bridge near the stern. The pipes were painted in a rainbow of colors: red, white, blue, yellow, and green. The setup looked as if it came from offshore oil drilling.

He wondered if he would have to ask somebody where cabin 116 was. He didn't, though; signs gave him all the directions he needed. For a moment, he stood outside the steel door with 116 painted on it, gathering his nerve. Then he turned the key in the lock, worked the latch, and went inside.

His new roommate was lying on the bottom bunk. Fair enough—first come, first served. The man turned his head. He and Jerry both started to laugh at the same moment. "Hi, Steve. Long time no see," Jerry said.

"Yeah, we've got to stop meeting like this," the older man answered. They laughed some more.

"I don't suppose Dahlgren is your real last name, either," Jerry said.

"I have the papers to prove it is," Steve said. "Of course, you've got that kind of paperwork, too. They told me I'd be with a fellow called Steinberg. I wondered who that would be. Now I know. I hope I don't snore."

"Hope I don't, too." Jerry looked around. "This is a pretty nice hamster cage, isn't it?"

"Could be worse. I've stayed in hotel rooms I liked less." Steve waved toward a pair of tall steel lockers welded to the wall. "I put my stuff in the one on the right. The one on the left's all yours. They've got shelves and hangers and whatever you need."

"Sounds good." Jerry nodded.

"Bathroom is through there," Steve went on, pointing to a door in the side wall. "Shower, two sinks, toilet. Pretty plain, but it'll do. We share it with the guys in the next cabin over."

"Okay." Again, Jerry hoped it would be.

"Anyway, I'm glad they put us together. Nice to be with somebody I've at least met before," Steve said.

Jerry nodded once more. "I was thinking the same thing." He hesitated, then asked, "Do you mind telling me your real last name?"

"I shouldn't." Steve hesitated, too. "But I already know yours, and fair is fair. Who will you blab to? I'm Stephen Dole—Stephen with a *PH*. On the papers I have here, I'm Steven with a *V*. What do you want to bet I screw up signing my name at least once before I get home?"

Jerry hardly heard the last bit. He was gaping at the man with whom he shared a cabin. "You're Stephen Dole from RAND? *The* Stephen Dole from RAND? The guy who wrote *Habitable Planets for Man*? I've read that book three times. You can't beat it for world-building ideas."

"I'm that Stephen Dole, yes," his roommate said. "Thanks. I didn't expect you to recognize my name."

Jerry burbled on regardless: "This is crazy, man! I'd rather meet you than Becker and Fagen, even."

"Than who?" Steve plainly drew a blank.

"The lead guys for Steely Dan."

Steve went right on drawing a blank. He and Jerry eyed each other in perfect mutual incomprehension. *He's thirty years older than you are, maybe more*, Jerry reminded himself. *It'd be scarier if he did know who they were.* Steve would have been in his thirties by the time rock 'n' roll came along. *Poor guy* was what went through Jerry's head: the heartlessness of youth.

Then something else occurred to him: "If you write about worlds where we might live or where aliens might come from, what are you doing on a ship going after a Russian sub?"

"That's not all I do. If it were, I'd write science fiction myself," Steve said easily. "My job title at RAND is director of communications. If we bring up any of the submarine's codebooks, I go to work. No, *when* we bring them up. John P. wants everybody confident."

"He . . . knows how to get what he wants, doesn't he?" Jerry said.

"From everything I've seen, yes." Steve swung off the bunk and got to his feet. "Do you know where the messroom is? I just came straight here and threw some stuff in my locker, but it's getting on toward dinnertime, isn't it?"

Jerry looked at his watch. Sure enough, it was almost half past six. "Getting there and then some," he agreed. "I did the same thing. No, I don't know where it is, but I bet we can find it pretty easy. They've got this ship *organized*."

"You don't know the half of it," Steve said, which was bound to be true.

When they went out into the passageway, they quickly came to a sign informing them the messroom lay one level down. The steel stairway was narrow and steep. "Gotta watch it," Jerry said. "You can break your ankle here if you aren't careful."

"Or your neck," Steve agreed.

Eight or ten men were eating in the messroom when Jerry and Steve walked in. Several of them nodded to Steve. They eyed Jerry with more speculation. He understood that. He was the youngest guy there, and the one with the longest hair—most of them looked pretty buttoned-down. He sighed to himself. He'd hoped he was done with that first-day-of-high-school feeling forever. What you hoped for wasn't always what you got, though.

The food was great. He ordered a rare sirloin, with mashed potatoes and string beans. Steve had his medium, and got french fries and a salad on the side. They both demolished their dinners. Halfway through, Steve said, "A beer would go great with this."

"Man, would it ever!" Jerry said. "But they told me they'd clap me in irons or something if I brought any alcohol aboard."

"They told me the same thing." Steve winked. "Once we get hooked into the grapevine, I bet we can find some anyway. The crew is big enough, somebody will find a way."

"I guess," Jerry said, and then, "How big *is* the crew?"

"I heard about a hundred and eighty, counting everybody." Steve eyed Jerry. "They didn't tell you much, did they?"

Jerry shook his head. "Close but not quite. They didn't tell me *anything*." He wondered if that was because he was a longhair. He would have guessed most of the men in the galley were on the other side of the argument about whether Richard Nixon needed to be impeached. People who worried about national security first and democracy later mostly liked Mad Milhous.

But John P. and Fred and Steve would have known beforehand where he stood. He didn't make a secret of it or anything. They'd taken him on even so. That counted for something.

He had cherry pie for dessert. Steve ate vanilla ice cream. As they went back up to their level, Jerry remarked, "Gonna have to find some way to exercise or I'll get too wide to fit in this stairwell."

"You? You're young enough to burn it off," Steve said. "I only wish I were. There's a helipad behind the stern bridge. Maybe we can walk or jog on that."

"Yeah, I saw it. I don't know why we have it, though," Jerry said. Steve shrugged. Either he also didn't know or he wasn't talking.

Signs said there was a movie theater on this deck. Jerry thought about visiting it, but it wasn't going anywhere. He had *The Queen of Air and Darkness*, Poul Anderson's latest collection, to read till he got sleepy. On the first night aboard, he'd keep things simple.

Steve slept in plain blue cotton pajamas. Jerry wore sweatpants and a ratty T-shirt. Odds were that left them both about equally comfortable. Jerry scrambled up into the top bunk. The mattress was better than he'd expected. Goldilocks would have approved. It wasn't too hard or too soft, but just right. However many millions the CIA had spent on the *Glomar Explorer*, some of the money must have gone into keeping the crew happy.

He turned off his reading lamp a little before eleven. Steve's stayed on. It didn't bother Jerry. He fell asleep right away.

He woke with a jerk after what didn't seem very long. The rumble of the ship's engines had got louder. And her motion had changed—she felt like a ship on the ocean, not one peaceably tied up to a pier. They were moving! They were on their way . . . to a spot in the middle of the North Pacific. To a Russian sub. To bringing up a Russian sub, if everything worked the way it was supposed to.

Steve's reading light was still on. Jerry grabbed his watch off the little steel shelf by his head. The dim light from below was enough to tell him it was a quarter to one.

"You awake up there?" Steve asked quietly. The thrash must have tipped him off.

"Nah, I'm still asleep," Jerry said.

After a few seconds digesting that, Steve chuckled. "Okay. We're heading out now to take advantage of the high tide. We draw a lot of water. When the tide's low, we might not make it over the sandbars."

"That'd be embarrassing." Jerry imagined a swarm of tugboats trying to pull the grounded *Glomar Explorer* free.

"Maybe a little, yeah. Anyway, that's what's going on," Steve said. "But since you're still asleep, you don't need to worry about it. G'night." He turned off his lamp and plunged the cabin into darkness.

So there, Jerry thought. Pretty soon, Steve started to snore. He wasn't loud, but he was noticeable. Jerry noticed. He didn't mind Anna snoring when she lay next to him, but this seemed different. He couldn't have said how or why, but it did.

Having been startled out of deep sleep, he took a while to find it again. Just when he thought he never would, he did. He woke one more time when Steve went to the side door and used the head, but returned to sleep before his roommate came back. They both got up at eight o'clock.

Breakfast was as good and as copious as dinner had been. Jerry washed down two fried eggs, four strips of bacon, and crispy hash browns with two cups of coffee. Steve had his eggs scrambled, and sausages instead of bacon. He remarked, "Not everybody your age drinks coffee." He was most of the way through his third cup.

"I didn't till I started working hard getting ready for my exams, or not much," Jerry said. "But hey, it's brain cells in a cup."

"There you go." Steve nodded.

Neither one of them had much to do after breakfast. Later, when the *Glomar Explorer* got farther out into the Pacific, Jerry planned to string his hydrophone to a long length of coaxial cable and see what he could get, but they were still way too close to shore for him to bother.

Just how close they were got emphasized that morning, when the ship stopped and a helicopter thuttered in to land on the platform above the fantail. Ten businesspeople—nine of them men—got out and were escorted to the messroom. Curious, Jerry tagged along behind to see what was going on. Nobody shooed him away, so he went on in.

It turned out to be a ceremony formally turning ownership of the *Hughes Glomar Explorer* over from Global Marine to the Summa Corporation, which, he gathered, belonged to Howard Hughes. There were speeches. A photographer immortalized the occasion on film (Jerry suspected he wound up in the background on a couple of shots). The guys in the galley had even baked a cake. It was a good cake, too; Jerry got a piece.

Then the visiting firemen went back to the helipad, climbed aboard the chopper, and zoomed away again. Before they went to dinner, Jerry asked Steve, "What the devil was that all about? Flying those people out must have cost a ton. Why didn't they just sign the papers on dry land a week ago or something?"

Steve smiled a thin smile. "Because Philip Watson is a pain in the . . . neck." He seemed the kind of man who didn't cuss unless badly provoked. Jerry was much looser about it.

The name rang a vague bell, but Jerry said, "Who?" anyway. Then he said, "Oh," as he remembered.

"He's the county tax assessor," Steve told him anyway. "He wants to tax the *Glomar Explorer*. He wants to tax Summa because he knows Howard Hughes has money. It's more complicated than that, but that's what it boils down to. He has no idea the ship really

belongs to the CIA, and nobody's gonna tell him. Doing the transfer to Summa in international waters takes it out of his jurisdiction,
or we hope it does."

Jerry held his head in his hands. "The farther I stay from lawyers,
the happier I am."

"You sound like a sensible fellow," Steve said. "Shall we see
what's on the menu tonight?"

"Let's do it," Jerry said, and out they went.

Dinner was crab-stuffed flounder. If it was going to be like this for
however long the voyage took . . . Jerry was sure he'd never eaten
so well for as long as that before, and wondered whether he ever
would again. *Enjoy it while it lasts*, he told himself, which seemed a
good rule most of the time.

After he finished—he made himself skip dessert—he thought
about finding out which movie the little theater was showing. Before he could separate himself from Steve, though, the older man
said, "You want to come with me, see something that might interest
you?"

It sounded like an ordinary question. Jerry realized it was really
an order, though; his old man talked that way a lot of the time. He
nodded agreeably. "I'm putty in your hands. Silly Putty, probably."

Steve let out a small snort. "Whatever else you do, you should
stick with your writing. The left-handed way you think, I bet you
can make a go of it."

"That'd be nice." A beat later, Jerry added, "Thanks."

"I meant it," Steve said. "C'mon." He headed off like a man who
knew exactly where he was going. All of a sudden, he didn't seem
confused about where things were or need to look at signs. Jerry
followed, wondering what else the man from the RAND Corporation was sandbagging about.

The *Glomar Explorer* held a couple of dozen of what looked
like cargo containers, the kind that went on freighters and then
got loaded onto truck trailers to get where they needed to go.
They were maybe twenty by eight by eight. The only thing that
made them unusual for containers was that each had a door in the
front.

Steve stopped in front of one with SPECIAL MEASUREMENTS stenciled on to the door. Jerry eyed that. It might have meant anything

or nothing . . . which, he suspected, was exactly the point. Unlike most of the others, the door also had a keypad next to it that reminded him of the ones at his apartment building and Anna's.

But the code Steve punched in was longer than three digits. The latch clicked instead of buzzing. As Steve opened the door, he said, "I'll teach you the entry number. What's in here is a big part of why you're along. Memorize the number. Don't write it down, not anywhere."

"However you say. I can do that." Jerry followed Steve into the Special Measurements container.

"It's important." Steve flicked a switch. Bluish ceiling-mounted fluorescent tubes came to life, buzzing faintly. Only after the door closed did the older man say, "I mean it. We've got this whole story to keep the Russians from figuring out we're raising their submarine."

"I know," Jerry said. "I signed all those papers that promised I'd go to Leavenworth if I ever opened my mouth about that. Hell, you were there."

"That's right. I signed those papers, too. But that's nothing—I mean *nothing*—next to what's in here. It's a cover story under the cover story." Steve pointed to a chair identical to the ones in Jerry's TA office. "Have a seat. This will take a little while."

Jerry parked his behind on the chair. Steve set a tape player with headphones already attached on the Formica work surface in front of him. Then he went over to a safe in the corner of the container. Its door soon swung open. He took out a sheaf of papers and a cassette tape, then closed the safe again.

"You have to sign these before you can hear the tape," he said, handing Jerry the papers.

"What? Everything I signed back in my apartment wasn't good enough?" Jerry said.

"That just had to do with the Russian sub," Steve answered. "That was serious. This is *serious*."

Jerry skimmed the new paperwork. The man from the RAND Corporation wasn't kidding. A phrase jumped out at him: "Sanctions for violations of this confidentiality and nondisclosure agreement may include measures up to and including termination with extreme prejudice." He pointed at it. "What's this supposed to mean?"

Steve pointed at the typewritten sheet. "Oh. That." His laugh held nothing like mirth. "Funny you should spot that. I asked John the same thing. It means that if you talk, they'll kill you. And they'll probably kill whoever you talk to, just to stay on the safe side."

You're joking. Jerry didn't say it. Steve sounded, well, dead serious. Jerry did say, "What the hell have I got myself into?"

"You'll find out, and be part of the team, as soon as you sign that," Steve said. "You'd find out after we do what we do, of course—if it works. But you wouldn't be involved in any way. And I think you'd regret that the rest of your life."

"Fuck," Jerry muttered. "I've come this far. . . ." He signed the agreement.

"Okay." Steve handed him the cassette. "Now you can listen to this—with the headphones on. Always with the headphones on."

Before sticking the tape into the player, Jerry read the label out loud: "'Midlothian Pipe Band, Chicago concert, March 1966'?" He stared at Steve. "What the—"

"'Midlothian' is the code name for the operation inside Project Azorian, the sub-raising operation inside the seafloor-mining operation," the older man said patiently. "And dates inside Midlothian are shifted back two years to avoid any congruence with the time period in which the K-129 was lost."

"So it *does* still have something to do with the submarine," Jerry said.

Steve didn't answer. Shaking his head, Jerry fed in the tape, put on the headphones, and hit Play. He hadn't thought he'd hear Scottish pipers skirling away, and he didn't. He heard next to nothing, only a faint, rhythmic sound like a faraway washing-machine agitator, barely above the limit of what his ears could pick up. He knew what that was: the noise from a submarine's prop in the distance. He'd run into it before, on recordings mostly involved with whale songs.

No whale songs here. The noise went on, pretty much unchanged, for five or six minutes. Then, without warning, it sounded as if someone were frying the world's biggest pan of bacon right in his ears. After that, he heard what could only be the K-129 going down and collapsing in on itself as relentless water pressure crushed the boat's hull. Silence followed.

Jerry yanked off the headphones. What else could you do when you'd just listened to dozens of men dying? "Jesus!" he said. "What happened?"

Instead of answering directly, Steve stopped the tape and removed it from the player. He went back to the safe with it. "We never leave it out, even inside this container," he said, working the combination again. "Never. The same goes double for what I'm going to show you." The door to the safe opened. In went the tape. Out came a full manila envelope of the kind that had traveled in Fred's briefcase. Steve handed it to Jerry.

He opened the clasp. The first photograph inside was numbered 1. He went straight to the last. Sure as hell, the number in the upper right corner there was 78. Only then did he actually look at the pictures themselves. He went through them slowly. When he got done, he looked through them again.

At last, he said, "These can't be what I think they are."

"What do you think they are?" Steve's voice was gentle, as if he were trying to calm a spooked horse. Jerry was spooked, all right.

"They look like . . ." He had to stop and try again: "They look like pictures of a, a spaceship on the bottom of the ocean."

"That's what they look like to everybody who's seen them, which isn't very many people," Steve said, still in that gentle voice. "The camera trailing from the *Halibut* took them when it was searching for the K-129. This . . . thing is only about three hundred yards from the wreck of the Russian sub."

"It looks like it's all in one piece. Not a wreck itself, I mean," Jerry said.

The older man nodded. "It does, doesn't it?"

"Did it sink the K-129?"

"We don't know for sure. We don't know anything for sure. But that's the assumption we're making at this point in time."

How many people at the Watergate hearings had said *at this point in time* when they meant *now*, said it over and over again till the ugly phrase escaped into the language at large? Normally, hearing it would have annoyed Jerry a lot. Now he noticed and then forgot it. He had bigger things to worry about. "How do you sink something from three miles down in the Pacific?" he asked. His mind's ear replayed that horrible bacon-frying noise.

"That's an excellent question, Mr., ah, Steinberg. If there are no other questions, class is dismissed," Stephen Dole said. "Seriously, we have no idea. We're going to try to raise the spaceship and find out, though. People who get paid to figure these things out have decided that this takes priority over the K-129. I think they're right. Don't you?"

"I . . . guess so," Jerry said slowly. "But what if it doesn't like that? What if it treats us the way it treated the Russian submarine?"

"In that case, among other things, our beneficiaries collect on our insurance policies. The effort was deemed more important than the risk."

"Who decided that for me?" Jerry asked.

"This project has approval up to the very highest level. You can be sure of that," Steve said.

"You mean the President?"

"The very highest level," the man from RAND repeated.

Considering what Jerry thought of Richard Nixon, that didn't seem recommendation enough. He asked, "How did you guys pick me, anyway?"

"You're an expert on the ocean. You know several human languages. Your mind is loose enough to let you succeed at writing science fiction. Who's likely to be better qualified to communicate with aliens, if there are aliens inside the object there?" Steve spread his hands. He made it sound natural, even inevitable.

It didn't feel that way to Jerry. "My mind is blown, is what my mind is." He didn't smoke a lot of grass. He'd steered clear of acid and coke and uppers and downers. His mind was blown anyway. He added, "'*If* there are aliens'? You don't know? *We* don't?"

"No. The . . . the weapon that sank the K-129 could have been automated. It could have been the last gasp of dying machinery. One other thing we don't know is how long the object's lain at the bottom of the Pacific."

Jerry looked at some of the photos again. "Not much sediment on it. No more than is on the sub. Maybe even less."

"If it can sink a submarine three miles above it in a way we don't begin to understand, why can't it keep itself clean?"

"Because—" Jerry broke off. "You got me. We don't know anything, do we?"

"Know anything? Jerry, we don't even suspect anything. Except that it's there," Steve said. Jerry nodded. It was there, all right—and the world would never be the same.

Along with the movie theater, the *Glomar Explorer* boasted a pretty good little library. It had a decent science-fiction section. During the two-week trip out to where the fortieth parallel of north latitude met the International Date Line, Jerry read everything he could find there on dealing with aliens. He wasn't sure how much that would help, but it couldn't hurt.

The library's history section was much smaller. No surprise, that. It did have a book about the Spanish conquests of the American Indian civilizations, though. He made himself plow through it, even if history had never been his favorite subject. The settlement of the New World seemed about as close to contact with aliens as people had ever really come.

He spent a lot of time in the Special Measurements container, too. He listened to the tape that ended in the destruction of the K-129 again and again. He kept hoping he wouldn't hear that frying-bacon noise, but it was there every time. He did his best to imagine what might cause it. His best wasn't good enough. Nobody's was.

And he pored over the photos. The safe held many more than the seventy-eight in that envelope; those were just a representative sample. The ship was egg-shaped, or closer to that than anything else. It was a little smaller than the nearby chunk of Soviet submarine. One end had short tubes sticking out; the other was dimpled like a golf ball. The motor's exhaust and the weapons system? Possibly, but which was which? Jerry couldn't tell, any more than could anyone else who'd examined the pictures.

A circle was scribed in the hull about halfway between the tubes and the dimples. Jerry guessed it was the way into and out of the spaceship. Again, though, he was only guessing. If they raised the ship, he might find out. He wondered whether he truly wanted to.

"This is so frustrating," he told Steve. "All I can do is think up ideas I can't prove or disprove with what we've got. I bet all the other people who've seen these photos have thought of them, too."

"You can bounce things off other people, too," the older man replied. "I've given you the list of men cleared for Midlothian information."

"Yeah," Jerry said with no great enthusiasm. Like John P., Dale and Jack and Dave and Ernie had *intelligence officer* written all over them. They were polite enough, but Jerry got the feeling they thought he was a hippie college kid (they weren't altogether wrong, either). All of them except Dave were old enough to be his father. So was Steve, of course, but it somehow mattered less with him. Dave, in his late thirties, wore longish hair and a mustache that looked like something from a porn flick, so he was a little less uptight than his elder colleagues.

Steve's eyes twinkled behind his bifocals. "They're here for the same reason you are. They helped pick you to come along on what's liable to be the most important thing for humanity since Eve ate the fruit from the Tree of Good and Evil."

Jerry didn't think of Eve. He thought of Anna. More to the point, he worried about Anna. Yes, she'd come around on putting off the wedding. She still wasn't real happy about it, though. Part of why he thought she wasn't was related to the reason he was hinky about the CIA folks. She had trouble taking him seriously, too.

"The time may come when they need to listen to me, if I'm supposed to be the expert on aliens," Jerry said—he wasn't going to lay his fretting over Anna on Steve. "Will they do that when the heat is on, or will they just go ahead with what *they* want to do instead?"

"Well, I don't know." Steve didn't pretend there was no problem. Jerry liked him better for that. He went on, "*I* would, but I've seen you have a head on your shoulders. If you let them see that, too, before push comes to shove, you'll stand a better chance."

"How? Till we get where we're going, till we get the spaceship up into the moon pool and start knocking on the door—if that is a door—I really am just along for the ride. I haven't even picked up any whale songs," Jerry said. It wasn't so much that he would rather have been writing his dissertation: as far as he could tell, no one liked writing a dissertation. But he didn't like feeling useless, either.

Thoughtfully, Steve said, "Why don't you make a list of all the things that might happen when we do get the spaceship into the moon pool, and all the things we can do in case those things happen? Show it to Dale."

"Won't he already have a list like that? I mean, I don't know that much about soldiers and spies, but aren't they, like, heavily into contingency plans?"

"Now that you mention it"—Steve sounded amused, which he didn't do all that often—"yes. But I'll bet you a double sawbuck that you come up with some things nobody in the CIA thought of. *That's* what you're here for."

Terrific. I'm the designated weirdo, Jerry thought, riffing on the experiment the American League had begun the year before. It hadn't helped his Angels a bit. They stayed lousy even with the DH. He vaguely knew a double sawbuck was a twenty-dollar bill. He never would have called a twenty that himself, but Steve's slang came out of World War II.

"I guess I can give it a shot," he said. As he knew too well, he didn't have much to do till the *Glomar Explorer* raised the sunken spaceship. *Or till we loudly and noisily vanish away*, he added to himself. If that Snark *was* a Boojum . . .

"Good! I'll tell Dale he can look forward to it," Steve said. That told Jerry he really did have to do it. He made himself smile and nod. Hypocrisy had its uses.

The thesis was the first thing he'd ever tackled that was too big for him to carry all the data around inside his head. He'd made and cross-referenced more than a thousand file cards to help him organize what he knew. He went at his list the same way. When he asked, he found that the ship sure as hell did carry three-by-fives.

He made a file card in red ink for everything he could think of that might happen once the *Glomar Explorer* brought up the sunken starship. Then he made a card in black ink giving every response to each scenario he could imagine. If an alien came out of the airlock shooting, what should the people it was shooting at do? Should they shoot back? (*Could* they shoot back? He didn't know whether they'd brought guns aboard. Well, that was Dale's worry, not his.)

How fast the scenarios and responses mounted up surprised him. He had close to three hundred cards before he typed them on the correcting Selectric in the Special Measurements container— nothing but top-of-the-line equipment for this project. Jerry had heard that some of the computers in other containers had as much as thirty-two kilobytes of memory. No, nothing but the best.

Once he got the list typed, he stowed it in the safe. It would stay there till he worked up the nerve to beard the project director in his den.

"Dale Neuwirth, Project Director," said the neatly printed sign taped to the head honcho's door. Jerry suspected the man in charge of the mission really owned some other last name starting with N. That seemed to be how the people in that Long Beach apartment operated.

He carried the list in a manila folder in his left hand. No one unauthorized could turn his head sideways and sneak a peek at the typed pages. He gulped. He felt like a buck private reporting to a general. He gulped again, then knocked on the door.

A moment later, Dale opened it. He was a solidly made man of about fifty, his brown hair going gray. To nervous Jerry, his smile seemed somewhere between perfunctory and professional. "Come in, Mr. Steinberg, come in," he said, his baritone warm enough. "Steve said you'd have something to show me."

"Th-that's right." Jerry swore at himself for stammering.

As director, Neuwirth had a cabin to himself. It still seemed small to Jerry. Dale waved him to one chair, then sat in another, almost knee-to-knee with him. After pulling reading glasses from a leather case clipped to his breast pocket and setting them on his nose, he started in on the list.

He soon peered at Jerry over the tops of his glasses. "As a matter of fact, we *do* have guns on the ship," he said. "A few rifles and shotguns."

"Do we?" Jerry said.

"Afraid so. The CIA insisted on it, to fight off Russian boarders." Dale's mouth twisted in distaste, or maybe just in scorn.

The way he said that made Jerry ask, "Uh, you're not CIA yourself, sir?"

"Me? Good Lord, no!" Neuwirth said. "I'm a civilian under contract. I work at the Lawrence Livermore Lab up in Northern California. Nuclear physics. They wanted someone in that field in charge of things, both for what's in the K-129 and for what's in the . . . the Midlothian object."

"I guess that makes sense," Jerry said. "Will we really shoot it out with the Russian Navy?"

"Good Lord, no!" Dale repeated. "They'd slaughter us. We'll

try to hold them off with our fire hoses. If that doesn't work, we'll let them board—but we'll deep-six our secret materials first. You know about that, right?"

"Yes, sir. Steve showed me." A weighted steel-mesh box stood outside the Special Measurements container. In case of emergency, secret papers went in there. Then the box slid down a chute and straight into the Pacific.

"That's not how it reads in the contingency plan we gave the CIA," Dale said. "But the CIA is back on dry land and we're out here in the middle of the Pacific. They put me in charge. I'm going to do what I think has the best chance to keep us all in one piece. And if the CIA doesn't like it, too darn bad. You got me?"

"I sure do," Jerry replied. So a real, live human being lurked under Dale's bland exterior. Jerry wouldn't have believed it if he hadn't heard it with his own ears.

"Okay," the project director said. "Let's see what else we've got here." He went on through Jerry's list of scenarios and responses for a while, then stopped and looked up, his eyebrows rising like semaphore flags. "What do we do if there's a methane or ammonia atmosphere inside the object? There's one nobody worried about till you!"

"Steve said to list all the possibilities that occurred to me, so I did." Jerry tried not to show how pleased he was. Other people had been puzzling over this for years. He'd had only a few days. Maybe there was something to bringing along a left-handed thinker after all.

Or maybe not. Dale said, "Any which way, we're not set up to deal with aliens who don't breathe oxygen. If that turns out to be what's going on, all we can do is hope whatever's in there stays alive till we get to either Hawaii or the mainland."

"Fair enough. I thought I should mention it, though."

"That's fine. That's good, in fact. And when we do go home, I'll tell the guys back in Washington there may be more things in the heavens and earth than are dreamt of in their philosophy."

Jerry blessed a sophomore English Lit class for reminding him where that allusion came from. "So you're telling me Washington's just a little Hamlet in the grand scheme of things?" he said with malice aforethought.

Neuwirth started to answer, then stopped before anything came out. He eyed Jerry over the tops of his glasses again, severely this time. "Anyone who makes puns like that can't be all good," he said at last.

"Thank you, sir," Jerry answered.

"Hrmm." It wasn't really a word: more a rumble down deep in Dale's chest. He flipped to the next page of the typescript. "I do think someone back in DC also came up with the possibility that there's water inside the Midlothian object, not any kind of air. I don't believe that's likely—very hard to develop a technological civilization under the sea."

"I agree with you," Jerry said. "Hard, but not quite impossible. What if it's a technology based on biological engineering, for instance? What if they *grew* that spaceship instead of manufacturing it?"

"Where do they get the motors that let them cross interstellar space with biological engineering?"

"Beats me," Jerry said cheerfully. "Where do they get them with mechanical or electrical engineering?"

"A point," Dale admitted. "We don't even know whether the object got here from wherever it started faster than light or slower. Before I got involved in this project, I would have told you traveling faster than light was flat-out impossible. Now . . . Now I just don't know. That darn object is down there."

"It sure is." Jerry noticed that Dale didn't like to call it a spaceship or a starship. Maybe he was very security conscious. Everybody on the Midlothian project seemed to be, and had good reason to be. Or maybe, down deep, Dale didn't want to believe it. If he didn't, how could you blame him?

"I see you thought about sublight travel, too," the director said. "You're right—it may be an automated probe in that case, like the ones we've sent out ourselves, but more sophisticated. Or the aliens may have very long lives. Or they may be in there in some kind of suspended animation, waiting for the object to wake them, or for us to do it once we work out how to get inside."

"That last one interests me a lot," Jerry said.

"I thought it might. 'The Sleeping Beauty problem,' you call it. You like to joke about things that intrigue you, eh?"

"Yeah." Jerry felt oddly reluctant to acknowledge that. He didn't care for other people spying out the way his beady little mind worked. Dale might be old and as ordinary as vanilla ice cream, but he was nobody's dope. Well, he wouldn't be, would he, if he was in charge of what might wind up being the most important project in the history of the world?

He neatened up the stack of papers and set them on his left leg, which he'd crossed over his right. "This is a nice piece of work, Mister Steinberg, and I thank you for putting it together for me. A lot in here for me to think about. Has Mister Dahlgren seen it?"

"Not all of it," Jerry said. "I've talked with him about some of the things in there, though. I'm only an amateur at this stuff—I hope I'm smart enough to remember that. He's a pro, if anybody is."

"Yes, if anybody is," Dale said, as Montresor might have said, *Yes, for the love of God.* "I have the feeling, though, that finding the Midlothian object makes every one of us an amateur. Don't sell yourself short. You're here for a reason. When I show him this, I think he'll be as impressed with it as I am."

"Really?" Jerry wasn't used to hearing things like that. Professor Krikorian took it for granted when he did things right and let him have it when he messed up. He saw that as natural enough; his father had the same style. One of the things he especially liked about Anna was how open she was in her happiness. Of course, she was also that open about being unhappy. At least he always knew where he stood.

"Yes, absolutely." Neuwirth's brisk nod brought Jerry back to himself. The director went on, "Is there anything else?"

Jerry recognized dismissal when he heard it. "Uh, no, sir." He stood up. Dale did, too. They shook hands. Jerry got the hell out of there.

When Jerry let himself into the cabin that evening, Steve lay reading in the bottom bunk. "How was the movie?" he asked.

"Well . . ." Steve's voice trailed away. His ears heated at the same time.

"That good, you say?" Steve chuckled. "What was it?"

"Umm . . ." Jerry hesitated again. *I don't want to tell you* was the first thing that jumped into his mind, but it would have been rude. And he never had been any damn good at lying on the spur of the moment. So he answered with the truth: "It was *Deep Throat.*"

"Oh." Steve laughed again, on a slightly different note. "Yeah, I heard we had that along, to go with the Westerns and the war movies and the spy films and the sci-fi. How was it?"

Talking about a porno flick with a guy old enough to be his father didn't stand high on Jerry's Things I Want to Do list. "I don't think anybody in it will win a best-acting Oscar," he said, which was true enough. Then he trotted out a joke he'd heard from one of the TAs who shared the office with him: "They say Nixon watched it about a hundred times at the White House, though."

"Why did he do that?" Steve asked obligingly.

"He wanted to get it down Pat."

Steve winced. "That's—pretty bad." Now it was his turn to pause. After a moment, he resumed, saying, "You may want to be careful about who you tell that joke to."

"I noticed that myself, uh-huh," Jerry replied. Most of the guys who'd been in there watching Linda Lovelace do her thing and several guys' things were from the pipe-laying crew or divers. The guys who'd send the thick steel pipe string down to the ocean floor were Southern rednecks, and proud of it. By contrast, the divers—rent-a-frogs, they called themselves—were neat and quiet and watchful. Jerry didn't *know* they came out of the SEALs or some similar program, but he would have bet that way.

They and the men who worked with the thick steel pipe made no secret about believing Richard Nixon was getting railroaded. Jerry didn't see how any reasonable human being could think that way, but he did see they were liable to whale the snot out of him if he said so. He hadn't been in a fight since the sixth grade, and he'd lost that one.

For that matter, the roughnecks and divers seemed downright sane next to the Global Marine officer who skippered the *Explorer.* In the messroom, Tom Gresham informed anyone who would listen that Henry Kissinger spied for the Russians. Jerry hoped he had better sense about engines and navigation than he did about politics.

He peeled off the clothes he wore during the day and donned his elegant night attire. Steve paid no attention to that, but went back to his book. As Jerry'd seen since the locker room where he changed into and out of gym clothes for junior high PE, guys—straight guys, anyway—didn't pay much attention to one another's naked or nearly naked bodies.

Up to the top bunk he scrambled. He read *Have Space Suit—Will Travel* for a little while himself. It was the only hardback he'd brought. He knew it almost by heart—it was a birthday present to himself when he turned twelve. His dad had taken him up to Pickwick's on Hollywood Boulevard, back in the days when it wasn't the main Pickwick's but the only one. He'd taken care of it, too. Even the cover was still in pretty good shape.

When the bad guys caught Kip and Peewee before they could make it to Tombaugh Station, he turned off the light and curled up on his side. He fell asleep easily most of the time, but not tonight, despite the book that was an old friend. Yeah, *Deep Throat* was stupid and gross and badly acted, but it still reminded him how much he missed Anna, and one of the reasons why.

He hadn't told Steve he'd seen it before. When it hit with a splash a couple of years earlier, Anna'd bugged him till he took her to it. "I want to see a really dirty movie," she'd said, over and over, till she wore him down. Truth to tell, he hadn't needed all that much wearing down.

So they saw it . . . and she was much more grossed out than turned on. He was not a little grossed out himself, but he did take an interest in the proceedings. And when they messed around at his place afterward, he guessed she hadn't been altogether disgusted.

He had the sense not to tell her so. And she never asked him to take her to another porno flick.

Eventually, he did sack out. His dreams were . . . interesting. He woke up just when things were getting close to the moment of truth, the way he usually did when he had dreams like that. It left him more frustrated than ever.

He was grumpy when he got up, but he was often grumpy before he had his coffee. Two big mugs, plus eggs over medium, sizzling sausages, and hash browns improved his outlook on life, or at least gave him things besides that to think about.

After breakfast, he went to the Special Measurements container and punched in the key code that opened the door. Once inside, he made sure the door not only closed behind him but locked. He'd thought that kind of fussing over security was paranoia personified . . . until Steve showed him the photos in the safe. Now, like Paul on the road to Damascus, he believed.

What would the world do when it found out a starship lay on the bottom of the Pacific? *Besides go nuts*, Jerry added to himself. He had a pretty good notion that the Russians would want to do what the United States *was* doing. They'd want to see who and what was inside, and what they could learn from it.

One way or another, this may be the end of the Cold War, he thought as he worked the combination to the safe. If live aliens waited for rescue inside the sunken spaceship, the world would never be the same. Even if they didn't, the United States might learn enough from the ship itself and from what it held to gain a decisive advantage over the Soviet Union.

The lock quietly clicked. Jerry opened the door to the safe. He'd lived his life in a world where countries on both sides of the Iron Curtain knew how to destroy everything. Well, almost: he was starting to cut teeth about the time the Russians tested their first A-bomb.

What if the aliens knew enough to stop atomic explosions? Or what if they had weapons of their own, weapons that made H-bomb-tipped ICBMs seem like bows and arrows by comparison? Just for a moment, Jerry again heard inside his mind the frying-bacon sound that had doomed the Russian submarine.

And what else would they know about, besides bigger and better ways to kill? How to travel between the stars, obviously, whether faster than light or not. Other things? Things like medicine, for instance?

Jerry's mouth tightened as he took out some more of the photos the *Halibut*'s probe had taken of the egg-shaped spaceship on the seafloor. He remembered how his mother had smoked like there was no tomorrow. For her, there hadn't been much of one. She'd died of lung cancer when he was seven and she was in her early forties.

Which was how he'd been raised, erratically, by his father. He often thought he'd done most of the raising himself, though he realized his dad would have something pungent to say about that. Then again, his dad had something pungent to say about damn near everything.

And Hyman Stieglitz *was* pungent. He didn't quit smoking after Jerry's mother died. All these years later, he was still at it. He stank of stale cigarette smoke, and had for so long that he didn't even know it anymore. So did the house. Jerry'd argued with him, yelled at him, screamed at him. Now he'd given up. As far as he could see, tobacco was as bad a jones as heroin.

Steve had told him that John Graham, the naval architect who'd designed the *Glomar Explorer*, wasn't aboard because he was dying of lung cancer back in California. From what Steve said, Graham was, or had been, another chain-smoker. He'd quit for a while after getting sick, then started up again when he realized it was too late for him.

Jerry banged a fist down on his knee: not the knee the photos lay on, though. He was careful about that. But he remembered his mother doing the same thing. He hadn't understood it then. He thought he did now. Understand it or not, he hated the hooks nicotine sank into people.

At least half the men on the *Glomar Explorer* lit up. The air in the movie theater had been foggy with cigarette smoke. The pipe wranglers and divers seemed to think they weren't real likely to get old anyway, so what the hell?

He stared at one picture that had caught his eye before. He'd found a magnifying glass in a drawer—the people who'd outfitted this ship honest to God had done their best to think of everything—and used it to examine the photograph again.

"Fuck," he muttered. Even with the magnifier's help, he couldn't be sure he was seeing what he thought he was.

Someone outside stopped at the door and punched in the key code. That was quite audible inside the container . . . which implied that at least some of what went on inside could be heard outside, too. Jerry knew a certain amount of relief that he hadn't shouted his obscenity.

The door opened. In came Steve. Like Jerry, he closed the door behind him, making sure it shut securely. "How's it going?" he asked.

"Not bad. You?"

"Fine so far."

"Cool. Take a look at this for a second, will you?" Jerry held out the photo and the magnifier. "Between the second and third tubes in particular. Any chance we can get an enlargement of that area?"

"*We* as in 'you and me,' here on the *Glomar Explorer*? Probability zero." Stephen Dole shook his head. "It *may* be possible to get someone who has access to another set of these photos, or to the negatives, to have an enlargement done . . . wherever those things are kept. I'm not trying to hide that from you; I don't need to know myself."

"Might be worth doing. Have a look and tell me what you think."

Look Steve did. When he raised his head from the magnifying glass and the picture, he was frowning. "I don't know. It may just be some sediment clinging to the spaceship's outer skin."

"Yeah, it may," Jerry agreed. "But there sure isn't much clinging to the rest of hull, is there? I was thinking it might be writing, only with the characters too small to show up well on a photo of this size."

"What would it say, though?"

"Some kind of warning, is my guess. You know, the way jet fighters say 'Don't stand here or you'll get sucked into the engine' in front of the air intake and 'Keep away from the exhaust if you don't want to get roasted' at the tail."

The older man smiled. "That makes a lot of sense. You *are* a science-fiction writer."

"If I made a lot of sense all the time, I wouldn't be able to write sf," Jerry said. Steve laughed, for all the world as if he were joking. Jerry went on, "*Can* we get a message back to the mainland, to ask them to check it out themselves?"

"We can. It isn't easy or convenient, but we can if it's urgent enough." Steve paused, then asked, "Do you know what a one-time pad is?"

"Sure do. Only shows I've read spy stories along with my sf when I should have been studying. You can agree on, for instance, two identical copies of the same book. The guy sending the message goes two one six, one two, four, and the guy getting it goes to page two sixteen, line twelve, word four and sees that it's *uranium*. And so on."

"Close enough. The way we do it here is, we spell message words out letter by letter inside the text of something that looks innocent. The person writing the message and the one deciphering it both know which letters count and which are just camouflage."

Jerry thought about that for a moment. "Those innocent texts must be fun to put together. It's like Scrabble—you can't just drop in an *X* or a *Q* any old place."

"You know who's very good at it? Dave Schoals, the recovery director. He can write innocent-text poetry."

"No shit?" Jerry said, impressed in spite of himself. Steve nodded. Jerry went on, "Boy, talk about a specialized skill!" That made the older man laugh. Jerry was not only impressed but surprised, though he didn't say so to Steve. In spite of Dave's longish hair and that god-awful mustache, Jerry would have guessed him too tightly wound to write any kind of poetry, let alone poetry with the constraints innocent text imposed.

"I'll talk with him and with Dale. If they think finding out whether that's writing is important enough, we'll let people on the mainland know," Steve said.

"Why wouldn't they?" Jerry asked in surprise.

"Because even if it is writing, we can't read it or do anything about it right now," Steve answered. "And because the only way it will matter is if we can bring the spaceship up into the moon pool, and then we'll be able to see for ourselves."

"Oh." Jerry felt foolish. He hated not thinking things through, but he could see he hadn't this time. "Yeah. You're right."

"Accidents do happen," Steve said. Jerry probably laughed more than the joke deserved, but he was glad his boss could make cracks like that and didn't come down on him for messing up. He'd known a lot more examples of the other kind of boss.

Every couple of days, Jerry would put on his Blue Tips and go back to the helipad for a little exercise. A circuit of the landing platform was about a hundred yards, so seventeen or eighteen made a mile. Fifty or sixty circuits made him sweaty and virtuous.

He wasn't the only guy aboard the *Glomar Explorer* to put in some work there, but he liked it best when he didn't have any company as he went around and around. Sometimes he came out onto the helipad after dark, too. He was almost always alone there then. He didn't understand why. When he turned his back on the ship's lights, he could see a million stars, so many that he wished he'd brought along binoculars. City lights dimmed natural ones in Los Angeles.

Now, though, he was the sole person back there under watery sunshine. He was, anyhow, till some of the sailors who made the *Glomar Explorer* go came there with their arms full of wooden crates and metal drums. They dumped them at random on the helipad and turned around, probably to get more.

Before they disappeared again, Jerry called, "Hey, what's happening?"

One of the *Glomar* men stopped and turned back to him. "Well, we're almost where we're going," he said, as if that explained everything.

"Yeah." Jerry nodded. He knew that. A little more than two weeks out of Long Beach, they were indeed close to where the K-129 had gone down—been brought down. But . . . "What's that got to do with anything, Tony?"

For a smart guy, you sure are dumb. Tony didn't say it, but his face said it for him. He did say, "When we get there, waddaya wanna bet we have Russian company? If they fly a chopper off their ship, we sure as hell don't wanna make it easy for 'em to land on ours. Am I right or am I right?"

"You're right," Jerry answered, because Tony *was* right. A helicopter full of Russian sailors—or would they be marines?— carrying AK-47s was the last thing the *Glomar Explorer* needed.

"Damn right, I'm right," Tony agreed with himself. "Cap'n Gresham, he don't miss a trick. Not one."

Jerry didn't say anything more. Tony went off to get more junk to obstruct Russian helicopters. Captain Gresham might have John Birch Society politics, but he did try his best to keep the *Glomar Explorer* safe. That counted more, at least while he was conning the ship.

When Jerry told Stephen Dole about what was happening on the helipad, the man from the RAND Corporation just nodded. "Makes sense," he said. "When the *Glomar II* was out here a few years ago, the Russians harassed her like nobody's business. I wasn't along on that one. Dave Schoals was—ask him, if you want the gory details. The Russians don't know exactly where they lost their sub, but they don't want us anywhere close."

No one had told Jerry another American ship—let alone another Global Marine ship—had publicly poked around a few years before. He wondered what all else no one had told him, either because people figured he already knew or because they didn't think he needed to know. He also wondered whether some of what he didn't know would rear up and bite him in the ass.

Rather resentfully, he thought that a character in a well-written story wouldn't try to do something so important while being so ignorant. Then he remembered Frodo in *The Lord of the Rings*. So much for that! In *The Lord of the Rings*, though, at least people on Frodo's side hadn't lied to him about what was going on.

He couldn't even bitch about that. It was part of the way these people played the game. He did ask, "What kind of cover story did the, uh, *Glomar II* use for being in the neighborhood?"

"Our outer one: that she was prospecting for manganese nodules," Steve said. "She didn't just stop here—that would have made the Russians suspicious."

"Made them *more* suspicious, you mean."

"Made them *more* suspicious, yes," the man from the RAND Corporation agreed. "So she made several stops here and there in the North Pacific. And she actually did bring up some manganese nodules. Manfred would pass them out at ocean mining conferences—there are such things. That's why it makes a good cover story."

"Who's Manfred?"

"He really is an ocean mining engineer. Our public face, I guess you'd say. Nice guy. Interesting guy. Immigrant from Germany. He served in U-boats during the war. He and his family went to Chile first, then came to America."

"How about that?" Jerry said: a pretty safe response to almost anything. He'd had a high school friend whose father had got the family out of East Germany in the early 1950s. Before that, his father had fought on the Eastern Front till he lost half his left foot. They might have sent him back into action even after he did; he limped, but he still got around pretty well. The war ended before they could, though.

These days, his friend's father was a liberal Democrat. Jerry'd never had the nerve to ask what his politics were like under the Third Reich. He didn't suppose he would if he ever met this Manfred, either. The world had changed. Jerry hoped like hell it had, anyway. Some of the guys on the *Glomar Explorer* now might not care just how ex an ex-Nazi was.

Then Steve said, "Whatever Manfred did in the German Navy, he doesn't go around wishing his side won."

"Okay. Good, even." Jerry cocked his head to one side and sent the older man a quizzical stare. "You're reading my mind, you know."

"It's a question that does crop up. The Nazis did so many horrible things, people almost automatically wonder about anybody who was an adult in Germany before 1945."

"I guess so," Jerry said. "They did so many horrible things, we squashed fascism flat and we'll never have to worry about it again. So there's that."

"Good point." Steve nodded. "There is that."

IV

The *Hughes Glomar Explorer* got where she was going: an invisible spot on the North Pacific very close to where today turned into tomorrow or yesterday, depending on which way you were heading. She got there and she stayed there and nowhere else. Her engines, electrically powered side thrusters at her bow and stern, and some fancy navigational aids no one wanted to go into detail about with Jerry held her exactly in place, or close enough for sending down pipe and, with luck, raising a sunken spaceship.

They got there, they positioned themselves, and they proceeded to do nothing for the next several days. The *Glomar Explorer* had an elaborate system to keep the pipe-laying derrick steady even when the ship rolled and pitched. It featured enormous hydraulic cylinders and what somebody said were the biggest bearings ever manufactured.

And the system worked as advertised . . . in moderate seas. When the waves grew too large, even the best of mankind's ingenuity was fighting out of its weight. Everyone got antsy waiting for the waters to calm down.

"*If* they calm down," Jerry said to Steve. "Storms from the north and the south get a running start at us here."

"True," Steve replied. "It would have been a lot more convenient if the starship had landed in the middle of Times Square, wouldn't it?"

Jerry shut up. You played the cards you got dealt, not the laydown grand slam you wished you had.

They had a narrow window in which to do what they needed to do. What would happen if wind, waves, and weather didn't cooperate? Would they keep at it even if things got risky? Or would they give up and try again next year?

He asked Dave Schoals about that. The recovery director gnawed on his mustache before answering. (Jerry did the same thing when he was thinking hard.) At last, Schoals said, "I don't know what kind of chance we have for the ocean mining cover story to hold up that long. The Russians would be unhappy enough finding out we were going after their submarine. This other thing . . ." He didn't go on. They might have been within earshot for people who weren't authorized to hear the word *Midlothian*.

"Yeah." Jerry nodded. "Can we talk about that?"

Dave thought for a moment, then nodded. "Okay. C'mon back to my cabin."

Like Dale, he was important enough in the grand scheme of things to have one to himself. He put on an Everly Brothers cassette so no one walking down the passageway would overhear.

Jerry said, "Suppose we do have to come back here next year. Maybe we should let the Russians know all the reasons we're here. I mean, this isn't only about us and them. It's about the whole world."

Schoals frowned. "I don't make policy. I don't get to change policy, either. That happens at a level way over my head. Probably at the very highest level. Till it gets changed—*if* it gets changed—we keep going with what we have. I want to be real clear about that. I want to make sure you're clear about it, too."

He waited—ominously, Jerry thought. That phrase from the nondisclosure agreement went through his mind again. *Sanctions up to and including termination with extreme prejudice.* Nobody would invite the Russians to play till it was too late. Anyone who complained about that outside the tiny group who knew what lay on the seafloor near the K-129 was liable to come down with a sudden case of loss of life.

Jerry paused no longer than half a second before he answered, "Oh, yeah. I understand exactly what you're saying. I'm not gonna talk out of turn."

"Okay." Dave nodded. He smiled. He didn't push it. He went on, "With any luck at all, you won't need to worry about it. The forecast is for better weather soon. We can start lowering Clementine on the end of the pipe string and do the scoop."

People on the ship called the claw Clementine, as in "Oh, my darling." That was one more bit of security. A claw was a claw, no doubt about it. Clementine might be anything, even a tangerine.

"Suppose everything goes well with the Midlothian object. Suppose we get it fast, even," Jerry said. "Would we try to raise the wrecked chunk of the K-129, too? I mean, we're here, after all."

"I don't think that's been decided yet," Dave said carefully. "You're right—we'd still be here. It might be technically feasible.

But the thing is, this ship is doing an engineering job like nothing anybody's ever tried before. It's designed to do that *once*. If everything goes right, I think it can do that. A lot of smart people have put a lot of time and effort and skull sweat into giving it a decent chance. You with me so far?"

"Oh, yeah," Jerry said. Dave would have been one of the people who put in that skull sweat. A slide rule in a battered leather case lay on his steel desk. It would have seen hard use while he tried to work out how to bring a giant egg up from three miles underwater.

"Good deal. What you need to understand is, we're playing with humongous forces here. The pipe string itself weighs something like four thousand tons. It's lowering Clementine to the bottom, and Clementine adds another two thousand tons. All that weight means the pipes will stretch something like forty feet by the time everything gets put together."

"Whoa!" Jerry said.

"Yeah. Whoa!" Dave agreed. "Then there's the Midlothian object to worry about. As long as it isn't any heavier than Clementine, we should be okay. But if the pipe string breaks anywhere . . ."

When he didn't go on, Jerry asked the morbidly curious question: "What happens then? Do I want to know?"

"If that happens, the recoil force may break the ship in half. We made damn sure we have good, watertight compartmentalization fore and aft. That may keep the pieces afloat long enough for people to get into the lifeboats. It may."

"Oh," Jerry said, and then, "I'm not sure I did want to know."

Dave Schoals's smile was distinctly lopsided. "You aren't the only one who feels that way, believe me. So my guess is, we may just leave the sub down there even if we do have a weather window. We might get lucky once. It's a lot less obvious we can get lucky twice."

"Gotcha." Jerry said his good-byes and left. He was as sure as he could be without seeing it with his own eyes that Dave was writing on a file card or a sheet of notebook paper. *Steinberg. Will need special surveillance after mission completed. Spoke in favor of information sharing with USSR. Suspicion of political unreliability.*

They would already have investigated him. They'd know he'd demonstrated against the Vietnam War. They'd know he'd worked for Gene McCarthy in 1968, even though he'd been too young to vote. They'd know he'd circulated petitions calling for Nixon's impeachment, and that he'd got a thank-you letter from Jerome

Waldie, a California Congressman who'd helped lead the charge. Hell, they might even know he'd had a DON'T BLAME ME—I VOTED FOR MCGOVERN bumper sticker on his car till somebody—probably an irate Republican—tore it off.

They knew all that stuff. They'd hired him anyway. Now they were stuck with him, and they might regret it. In which case, maybe he had more to worry about than the *Glomar Explorer* breaking in half and sinking.

The fog came in, and not on little cat feet, either. Jogging on the helipad felt like breathing soup. Visibility shrank to less than half a mile. Jerry knew the ship's radar could still see clearly, and see farther than the Mark One eyeball could even under perfect conditions. Any other ship out here in the middle of the biggest ocean in the world would carry a radar set, too. They wouldn't collide, the way the *Titanic* did with that iceberg.

Jerry knew all that. He worried anyway. Though he liked *Mad* magazine, he wasn't Alfred E. Neuman. *What, me worry?* did not apply. He was a Jew. He was a grad student. Of course he worried, even if that made him a walking double stereotype.

Fog or no fog, the *Glomar Explorer*'s work went on. The pipe farmers or riggers or whatever the right name for them was had connected the red-painted pipe they called the Dutchman with Clementine. All the other pipes in the hold abaft the moon pool were doubles: two thirty-foot lengths attached to each other. The Dutchman was a single, and thicker than the white sections that would go above it. Since it had hold of the claw's immense weight, Jerry supposed that was sensible.

Even with the Dutchman attached, the capture vehicle remained connected to the docking legs at the front and back of the moon pool. Some of the divers kept going into and coming out of the water. They would detach Clementine from the docking legs when the claw made its long plunge to the seafloor. And, by some of the bad language floating out of the moon pool, that wasn't all they were having trouble with.

At lunch—corned beef and cabbage—Jerry asked Steve, "Should we be having problems with the sensors on Clementine's fingers or legs or whatever you call them so soon?"

Steve sipped from a can of Coke before he answered. "Ideally, we shouldn't have any trouble at all. Everything should go just the way we planned, and we should start the exploitation phase in a couple of weeks."

"Well, hush my mouth," Jerry mumbled. He was glad his long hair would keep everybody in the messroom from seeing how red his ears were. They felt on fire.

"In the real world, of course, not everything works the way you expect it to," the man from RAND went on, as if he hadn't spoken. "If things have to go wrong, I suppose it's better they go wrong up here, where we can do something about it, not down on the ocean floor."

"Yeah." Jerry made himself nod. *But what if the sensors break up here, we replace them, and then the replacement parts fail when we need 'em most?* He didn't ask the question out loud. He could see for himself that that would be doubleplusungood. And he was superstitious enough not to want to jinx anything.

Precise as usual, Stephen Dole continued, "And I'm not the right man to answer you anyway. Like you, I'm here for what happens after Clementine comes back to us. I didn't have anything to do with designing it. A good thing, too—I'm not qualified. If you want the details, Dave Schoals is your guy."

"Well, maybe not," Jerry said, reflecting that there were ways things could be worse after all. Putting Dave's back up again was definitely one of them.

Steve glanced around. No one was sitting close to them, and nobody seemed to be paying them any special attention. The older man still lowered his voice. "You aren't in trouble, in case you think you are. Dave understands that your perspective on things is different from his. He understands it's different from most people's in his line of work."

He understands you're not a professional spy, Jerry translated. If he'd been saying that to someone else himself, he would have gone, *Dave gets where you're coming from.* But, again, he and Steve didn't always speak the same kind of English.

All that came with working alongside—working for—people who were older and way more conservative than he was. In a way, he'd understood as much from the moment John P. pushed past him and into his apartment. In another way, every day brought new surprises, few of them pleasant. He looked across the table at Steve. The man from the RAND Corporation was no different from the others, not in any important way. He was just quieter and more polite about what he was.

As long as the *Hughes Glomar Explorer* stayed out here in the middle of the North Pacific, none of the frictions mattered much. They all had the same job to do, and they'd work together to do it till the starship down below got hauled up into the moon pool . . . or till raising it went irretrievably wrong.

But if they got it aboard the *Glomar Explorer*, if they knocked on the airlock door and somebody—or something—answered, then what? Jerry realized he'd left one scenario out when he was cooking up his list for Dale. What if the people on the salvage ship started quarreling about what to do next?

Yeah, what if? Jerry wanted to thump himself on the forehead with the heel of his hand for not thinking of that sooner. Some writer he was, if he didn't come out with plot twists like that as automatically as he breathed! Then again, Dale wouldn't have been happy to find that scenario on the list. Maybe not dreaming it up wasn't so bad.

Steve chose that exact moment to say, "A penny for your thoughts."

"Thoughts? I'm supposed to have *thoughts*? Man, are you over-paying!" Jerry said, looking as impressively blank as he could. Steve laughed, so he must have been impressive enough. And some clowning defused a moment that could have been awkward or even dangerous. Once more, Jerry contemplated the uses of hypocrisy.

They got Clementine down to about a hundred feet below the *Glomar Explorer*'s hull and thought about uncoupling the capture vehicle from the docking legs. Before they could, the weather went south on them again. Wind and waves picked up, and everything had to stop. Jerry'd never seen a literal tempest in a teapot, but he sure saw one in the moon pool. Waves beat on its steel walls with a fury he'd never dreamt of in such a confined space. He hoped the designers foresaw that kind of battering. They must have; the ship didn't break up.

Every lost hour made the CIA people and their contract engineers fidget and twitch. They had a schedule and wanted to stick with it. The Global Marine roughnecks, veterans of offshore oil-drilling platforms, took it all in stride. "It's the ocean, for Chrissake.

It's bigger'n we are an' stronger'n we are, so what the fuck you gonna do?" one of them said.

"Sing it, Leroy!" a friend of his said. Leroy just grinned, the way anybody would who'd just said something too obvious to need saying.

One of the engineers working with Clementine went into the sick bay. The *Glomar Explorer* had a doctor and a couple of paramedics aboard, along with equipment that wouldn't have shamed a small hospital on dry land. If anyone broke his arm or needed his appendix yanked, the medical staff could handle it.

Word soon got out that the engineer had had a heart attack. The onboard doc described it as mild. "I don't know about that, man," Jerry said to Steve when he got the news. "Isn't a mild heart attack a heart attack that happens to somebody else? Sounds like being a little bit pregnant."

"Oh, there is a difference," Steve answered. "If you have a bad heart attack, they bury you at sea."

"Mrmp." Jerry thought that over, then nodded. "Yeah, guess you're right."

Steve surprised him by smiling widely enough to show a gold crown on one back tooth. "I like it when people tell me that," he said. "Not because it makes me feel smart or anything. Because it means I'm dealing with somebody reasonable, somebody who doesn't have to think he's right no matter what the evidence says."

"You don't get far in the sciences with that attitude. When new evidence comes along, it'll falsify a hypothesis no matter how much you like it." Jerry paused for a moment. "Some people are stubborn anyway, though, aren't they? The evidence for plate tectonics and continental drift looks pretty damn good, but some of the older oceanographers and geologists don't want to see it."

"I was going to say that, in case you didn't," Steve replied. "I would have used the fight about evolution in the nineteenth century, but your example's a good one, too. Scientists aren't just scientists. They're human beings, and they do all the dumb things human beings do."

Two days later, Jerry came out of the messroom after lunch (some of the best veal cutlets he'd ever had) to find the ship in an uproar. He ran into Dave Schoals in a passageway—almost but not quite literally. Dave was wearing a plastic hard hat and a worried expression. "Everybody's running every which way. What's going on?" Jerry asked.

"We got a distress call from a British freighter heading to L.A. from Yokohama," Schoals answered. "One of their people has a history of heart trouble. They think he's had another coronary, and they don't have a doctor on board. They want to know if we can check him over for them."

"*Oy!*" Jerry said. "What did we tell them?"

"It's a man's life. Have to say yes to something like that." Dave looked as if he wished the *Glomar Explorer* could have answered no. "We'll send Doc Borden over to their ship to see what's up. If we have to, we'll bring their guy back here. It's not something we want to do from the security point of view, but refusing would blow our cover from here to Moscow."

"The ocean's acting all nice and friendly, too," Jerry remarked.

"Right," Dave said tightly. Waves were running at eight or ten feet, keeping things too rough to let the pipe farmers lower Clementine any farther. The bad weather was supposed to be coming from a tropical storm named Gilda. Wherever it was coming from, it was driving the technical types bananas.

Dr. Borden, one of the paramedics, and Jack Porter went over to the *Bel Hudson* in one of her lifeboats. Jack was another veteran CIA guy; his title on the *Glomar Explorer* was director of security. Jerry supposed he visited the freighter to make sure it really was British and not crawling with Soviet spies.

The *Bel Hudson* evidently checked out, because the lifeboat came back with the seaman who was having chest pains. Getting him out of the boat and onto the *Glomar Explorer* turned out to be another adventure. He couldn't, or said he couldn't, climb a rope ladder, so they secured him on a stretcher and swung him aboard with a crane.

That would have been fine if the crane operator, who wasn't used to handling such light weights, didn't slam him into the ship's metal flank a couple of times before finally landing him. Jerry figured that, if the guy hadn't had a coronary before, the trip up would have given him one.

He was white as a sheet when Dr. Borden and the paramedic escorted him to sick bay. The verdict soon spread: he hadn't had a heart attack, but he did have some banged-up ribs that didn't come from his exciting arrival. He also had a vague memory—which hadn't come out before—of getting into a drunken brawl with the *Bel Hudson*'s skipper in the ship's lounge.

"How can you be drunk enough to forget a fight like that?" Jerry asked.

"Talent. Talent and practice," Dave Schoals answered.

When they asked the sailor if he wanted to get swung back into the lifeboat, he climbed down the rope ladder, maybe not so nimbly as a monkey but nimbly enough. The *Glomar Explorer* sent back a case of frozen steaks with him to liven up the *Bel Hudson*'s larder.

Jerry expected that would be the end of it, but the freighter's lifeboat made a return trip with several bottles of scotch. At dinner that night, everybody on the *Glomar Explorer* got a finger of golden-amber fluid. Jerry wasn't much of a whisky drinker. He tried not to cough when he knocked his back.

"Tastes like medicine," he said.

Steve clicked his tongue between his teeth. "The younger generation is ignorant," he said. "That's mighty good medicine. Expensive medicine, too."

"If you say so." The last time Jerry'd knocked back neat whisky, he'd been thirteen. It was right after his bar mitzvah, and he'd gone to the synagogue to help make a minyan for a morning service. One of the old men who was a regular at such affairs gave him a little knock in the bottom of a glass—and then laughed liked hell when he choked on it.

Scotch? Bourbon? Rye? At a distance of almost half a lifetime, he had no idea. All he remembered was, it was fiery and nasty. This stuff seemed no great improvement.

"I'd say more for me, only I think we're going through all of it." Steve sighed.

"If it were beer, now . . ." Jerry said.

The older man made as if to push him away. "Philistine!" They had a good time sassing each other through dinner. Arguing about favorite tipples, they didn't have to take it seriously. Jerry knew, and knew Steve knew, it might not be like that once Clementine grabbed hold of the starship.

Another distant storm, this one tagged Harriet, roiled the Pacific. The people in charge of the claw had other difficulties, too. They didn't go into detail, not where Jerry could hear, but Dave ordered Clementine hauled up into the moon pool so the technicians could work on it more conveniently. The *Glomar Explorer* had held its place above the Midlothian object for almost two weeks now, but the claw was as far away as it had ever been.

A mimeographed newsletter circulated every day or two, reporting news picked up on the ship's radio. The latest edition told Jerry that the Senate Watergate Committee had released its final report. That didn't say whether Nixon should be impeached, which was the House's responsibility. It did note that at least thirteen companies had illegally contributed almost $800,000 to the president's reelection campaign. Senator Weicker of Connecticut also noted that some witnesses had probably perjured themselves when they testified before the Senate committee.

What else do they need? Jerry thought. *Stuff like this keeps coming out. Impeach him, convict him, and remove him, for God's sake.*

Then he saw one of the pipe wranglers crumpling up a newsletter. "Wish this paper wasn't so pointy and scratchy," the man told his buddy. "I'd sure as hell wipe my ass with it."

"You an' me both, Ray," the other fellow agreed. "It's all a bunch of bullshit, every goddamn bit of it."

How could you avoid seeing what was right in front of your nose? Too many people seemed to have no trouble at all.

What would the roughnecks think when, instead of the K-129, Clementine brought up the Midlothian object? What would Richard Nixon think, if he was still president then? If Nixon wasn't president anymore, what would Gerald Ford think? How about the Democrats? *Fear and Midlothian on the campaign trail* ran through Jerry's mind. He feared he was the only person on the *Hughes Glomar Explorer* who read Hunter Thompson.

And what *would* the Russians think when they found out? Find out they would. Jerry was sure of it. Some secrets were too big to keep . . . weren't they? The CIA men on the ship would have argued otherwise. They'd managed to keep the spaceship's existence secret since the *Halibut* found it. But that would get harder once the Midlothian object wasn't hiding under three miles of water. Wouldn't it?

Little by little, the waves began to ease off. The divers finished fixing things that had gone wrong with Clementine's video cameras and landing legs. The meteorologist said the seas and winds might soon ease to the point where they could take another stab at lowering the giant steel claw toward the bottom.

Sure enough, Jerry discovered fog outside a couple of mornings later. That spoiled the view, but it was good news: fog and strong winds didn't go together. The *Glomar Explorer* sounded her fog whistle every so often. As far as Jerry was concerned, that would scare any ship close enough to hear it out of a year's growth.

And evidently there was a ship close enough to hear it. Some of the sailors who worked for Global Marine said the radar had picked it up. Jerry peered through the swirling vapor, trying to spot it himself.

It stayed too far away to let him, till a few minutes past nine, when it loomed out of the mist like a ghost manifesting itself. It was lean and looked dangerous, unlike a squat freighter or the even squatter *Glomar Explorer*. Jerry's first alarmed thought was *Destroyer!*

But he soon realized it wasn't, or wasn't exactly, a warship. Instead of guns or missiles, it sported a variety of white radomes. It drew closer to the *Glomar Explorer*, close enough to let him see a name—*Chazhma*—stenciled near the bow in Cyrillic characters. As if he'd been in much doubt, that told him whose fleet it belonged to.

He wondered how its crew knew the *Glomar Explorer* was in the neighborhood. He doubted like hell coincidence had anything to do with it. Maybe they'd picked up the radio interchange with the *Bel Hudson*. Or maybe a Soviet spy satellite had spotted the American vessel and sent the *Chazhma* out for a look-see.

Like the *Glomar Explorer*, the *Chazhma* sported a helipad. Not only that, it also a carried a helicopter: a four-wheeled machine with two big rotors on the main hub and a triple tail instead of a vertical secondary rotor. The outer tail fins sported large red stars. Seeing the chopper, sailors hurriedly carried more barrels and crates to the landing platform. *Doing our best to make it an* un*landing platform*, Jerry thought.

Before long, the Soviet helicopter hopped into the air. It buzzed around the *Glomar Explorer* for about fifteen minutes, the guy in the copilot's seat snapping pictures all the while.

"Can it spot Clementine?" Jerry asked Dave Schoals, who was taking his own pictures of the helicopter.

"I don't think so," the recovery director answered, more calmly than Jerry had expected. "The decking and the superstructure hide it pretty well." Eyeing things, Jerry decided he was right.

Some of the *Glomar Explorer*'s crewmen flipped off the Russians in the helicopter. Some spun around, dropped their pants, and turned the other cheek to them. Then Captain Gresham's voice roared out of the PA system like an angry Jehovah's: "Knock that shit off, you people! You hear me? Knock it off! We don't want to piss anybody off!"

"That'd be great, wouldn't it? Let's give them an excuse for jumping us," Dave said, as the sailors sheepishly pulled up their jeans.

The copter flew back to the Russian ship It made another pass at the *Glomar Explorer* later in the day. This time, a photographer with a really long lens on his camera took pictures while leaning out of the open doorway on the chopper's port side. Jerry didn't think he would have wanted to do that.

Then the PA system came to life again. "Mister Steinberg to the forward bridge!" it shouted. "Mister Steinberg to the forward bridge on the double!"

Jerry needed that repetition to remind himself that he was Mr. Steinberg here. He hurried forward and then up to the bridge from which Tom Gresham controlled the ship. "I'm Jerry Steinberg," he said. "What do you need, uh, sir?"

"We have the *Chazhma* on the radio. Took some work, but we do," Gresham answered. "I'm told you speak Russian. Can you talk to them, tell them we're a private seafloor mining vessel operating in international waters?"

"I'm not real fluent, sir, but I'll try."

"Okay. Give it your best shot. They don't admit to having anybody who savvies much English," Gresham said.

Jerry soon found himself at a radio set. The regular radioman showed him how to use it.

"This *Hughes Glomar Explorer*. You hear, *Chazhma*?"

"I read you loud and clear," a Russian voice answered in his headphones.

"Talk slow, *pozhaluista*. My Russian *nye khorosho*."

"I understand." The *Chazhma*'s radioman or skipper laughed.

"Tell me what your ship is doing here." Jack did his best to translate what Captain Gresham had said. The Russian asked, "How long will you stay here?"

After Jerry relayed the question, Gresham answered, "Two or three weeks—maybe a month." Jerry passed that on to the *Chazhma*.

"Good luck with your work," said the Russian on the other end of the circuit. A few minutes later, the *Chazhma* moved off to the northwest, toward Vladivostok or maybe Petropavlovsk.

"Nice job, kid," Captain Gresham said.

"Thanks." Jerry let out a long sigh of relief.

Dave said the *Glomar Explorer* was designed to work once. If it worked twice, everyone would be amazed. Over the few days after the *Chazhma* sailed away, Jerry began to wonder whether all the complex systems the *Explorer* carried would work even once. They had trouble separating Clementine from the docking legs, and more trouble with the pipe-handling system.

"It's supposed to be automated, dammit," Dave grumbled. "We can sort of make it go, but we've got to have somebody keeping an eye on everything all the goddamn time. That gets wearing, you know?"

The pipe-farm guys and divers worked regular shifts, twelve hours on, twelve hours off. The engineers and CIA men were on call around the clock. They ate and slept when they weren't trying to smooth out problems.

And, just to make matters more delightful, another Russian snoop showed up to keep an eye on the putative seafloor mining ship. This one was a lot less prepossessing than the *Chazhma*: she was an oceangoing tug, maybe 150 feet long, with "SB-10" painted in fading Cyrillic letters on either side of the bow.

Jack Porter, the CIA man in charge of security, scratched at his beard—which was thicker than Jerry's, though not in the same league as Professor Krikorian's—as he scowled at the tug. "SB is right," he said. "The Russian use those bastards to spy all over the damn world."

"Not exactly hiding what they're up to, are they?" Jerry asked.

Porter's smile was thin to the point of starvation. "Now that you mention it, no."

The SB-10 had hung back at first, though its crew had to know radar would have picked it out. Now, though, it was making circuits of the *Glomar Explorer* at a distance of no more than a hundred yards. Crewmen pointed cameras and binoculars at the bigger vessel.

Jerry didn't need long to notice that not all the crewmen were. "They've got a woman aboard!" he exclaimed.

"Two, I think," Jack answered. "They do that sometimes. You ask me, it causes more problems than it solves."

Jerry hardly heard him. Except on the screen, he hadn't seen anyone of the female persuasion for more the month. Till he did, he hadn't realized how acutely he felt the lack. The SB-10 was too far away for him to get a good look at the women she carried, but they were bound to be the two most beautiful girls for a thousand miles in any direction.

He and the security director weren't the only ones to notice the SB-10's coed crew. Divers, pipe wranglers, stewards, and even some of the contractors and CIA people who mostly lived in their containers lined the rail to check things out. They whistled. They whooped. They yelled invitations Jerry hoped the Russian women didn't understand.

"Jerks," Jack Porter aid.

"I was thinking the same thing," Jerry replied. "I mean, looking is great, but this. . . . It's like construction workers when a pretty girl walks by." As soon as the words were out of his mouth, he realized a fair number of these guys might have worked construction at one time or another.

Porter eyed him. "You've got a fiancée back in California, don't you?"

"That's right." Jerry tried not to crack up at the *don't you?* Jack Porter probably knew Anna's home and work phone numbers, what size jeans she wore, and how much she'd spent on groceries at the local Alpha Beta last week. Or if he didn't know offhand, he could dig out a file card back in his cabin and find out.

But all the security director said was, "You must miss her."

"Oh, maybe a little."

One of Porter's eyebrows jumped. Then it lay down again as he recognized irony. "Hard to be a young man away from your special girl."

"Yeah." Jerry nodded. "But I knew I wouldn't get another chance like this, and that was before I found out about. . . ." *Midlothian* was itself a code word, but he didn't say it. Too many people who might overhear weren't cleared for it. It wouldn't mean anything to them, not yet, but they might wonder about it.

Jack set a hand on his arm for a moment. "You're learning the ropes, aren't you?"

"I guess maybe I am. It's kind of sink or swim—or maybe more like baptism by total immersion."

"Heh!" Porter said, more appreciatively than not. "Total immersion isn't required—or my church doesn't think it is, anyhow. I'm Catholic."

"Sure isn't required for a nice Jewish boy," Jerry said: one more thing Jack was bound to know already. He went on, "But ever since John P. knocked on my door, that's what this has felt like. I just hope I get to come up for air one of these days."

"Believe me, we all feel that way," Jack said. "And John can be mighty persuasive, can't he?"

"There's one word. *Overwhelming* is another one." Jerry could think of some more words, too. Most of them would have made the smut the crewmen were yelling at the Russian women sound like love poetry by comparison.

"It will work out all right." Jack sounded as sure of himself as the Jesus freaks who annoyed people at UCLA by going around and asking if they were saved.

"I sure hope so," Jerry said. "But even if it does, I'll never be able to tell anybody I had anything to do with it, will I?"

"Doesn't look that way right now. But *never* is a long time, so who knows for sure?"

Jerry suspected that was the security director's way of keeping him on the reservation. He asked, "What happens if I want to write a story that's sort of about this but I change things around so it isn't exactly?"

"You'll need to send it to us so we can make sure it doesn't violate national security before you submit it to an editor. You'll need to do that with anything you write for publication from now on, in fact. We won't be unreasonable—we've dealt with this situation before—but we may suggest changes to help keep secrets." Porter answered as if he'd been waiting for the question. Odds were he had.

"Happy days!" Jerry said. As if dealing with one editor wasn't hard enough, now he'd have two on every story. He did remember something about this in the nondisclosure agreements he'd signed, but he hadn't worried about it then. He wondered how big a mistake that was.

V

Over the next few days, the pipe string began to descend in earnest. Things still weren't going so smoothly as Dave wished they would, but they were going. And they were going right under the SB-10's nose, and the Russians didn't know they were. That made everyone on the *Glomar Explorer* grin.

Sometimes the Soviet tug would sniff around the *Explorer* like a puppy hopping around a grazing cow. Sometimes it would back off and hold station southeast of the much bigger ship.

That puzzled Jack and Dave and Dale and Steve, but only for a little while. The *Glomar Explorer* disposed of garbage by putting it into trash bags and chucking them into the vastness of the Pacific. The bags didn't sink right away. Wind and waves mostly carried them . . . southeast.

The Russians captured as many of the floating trash bags as they could and brought them aboard the SB-10 to paw through them. As soon as people on the *Glomar Explorer* realized that, an order went out: make goddamn sure you don't throw anything classified in the trash.

From then on, the crew had fun with the snoops. They put worthless computer printouts or even *Playboy*s in trash bags and gave the bags a shot of acetylene gas, which made them float better and scud along before the wind like Portuguese men o' war. The tug would hurry this way and that to make sure it caught everything.

But the printouts and the centerfolds were liberally smeared with Aqua Lube. Jerry had already had the misfortune of meeting up with the green goop. If it wasn't the slipperiest stuff in the world, he couldn't imagine what would be: it greased pipe connections deep underwater. And when you touched it, it wouldn't wash off for days. It ruined clothes, too.

"Aqua Lube, my friend!" he sang, as another bag of gooped papers went into the sea.

Dave looked at him. "Aqua Lube isn't anybody's friend," he said.

That meant he didn't listen to Jethro Tull. Jerry only wished he were more surprised.

The ship's newsletter reported that, on an 8–0 vote, the Supreme Court had ordered Richard Nixon to turn over the tapes of his two talks with H. R. Haldeman the day after the Watergate burglars got caught. Jerry worried that Nixon would defy the court. He'd already covered up so much—what was a little more? Wasn't doing whatever you wanted the whole point of the imperial presidency?

But Nixon did cough up the tapes. As soon as he did, everybody saw why he'd held on to them so long and so hard. People who'd supported him through everything up till now started saying he had to be impeached, convicted, and removed. It wasn't a question of if anymore. It was a question of when.

"I'm more relieved than I know how to tell you," Jerry said to Steve, back in their cabin after dinner, when the news broke.

"For the sake of the country, you mean?" Steve asked.

Jerry still wasn't sure how the older man felt about the president. All the same, he answered, "Partly that. But partly this, too. I mean, suppose we haul the Midlothian object up into the moon pool. Suppose we knock on the airlock door, or whatever it is. And suppose the aliens open up and say, 'Take us to your leader.' Do you really want to introduce them to Richard Nixon?"

"His name is on the moon—he was president when people first went there," Steve said. "He went along with this whole project, too. We've spent something like half a billion dollars running that pipe string with Clementine on the end of it down toward the . . . the object. Not everybody would have done that. Don't you think he deserves some credit for it?"

"Um . . ." Jerry didn't want to give Nixon credit for anything. "Do you really want somebody like that running the government, though? He said, 'I am not a crook!' But he was. He was all along!"

Stephen Dole sighed. "That . . . seems to be true. It's a shame, and it looks like he'll pay for it. But one of the things it does is show you that people are more complicated than the movies and TV make them out to be."

The part of Jerry that wrote responded to that. He knew he couldn't convincingly create a character as gifted, as complex, and as flawed as Richard Nixon. He wasn't good enough yet. He wondered if he ever would be.

But he'd despised Nixon as long as he could remember. He'd got it from his folks, who'd despised Nixon longer than he'd been alive. His father still did. Jerry and Hyman Stieglitz had banged heads over plenty of things while Jerry was growing up, but never about that.

"All we can do here is our jobs, and do them as well as we can," Steve added. "What happens back in Washington happens, that's all. It doesn't have anything to do with what we're up to—unless, like you say, we have to introduce the little green men inside the object to Gerald Ford."

"Wouldn't that be trippy?" Jerry said. Steve laughed and nodded. They both seemed to think that was a good place to leave it, so they did. They'd got out of it without screaming at each other or trying to slug each other. The cabin wasn't very big. If they couldn't get along . . .

But Jerry wasn't so sure the man from the RAND Corporation had it all straight. They weren't just doing their jobs. They were doing them for the CIA, and for the U.S. government of which it was a part. To say that the CIA and the government as a whole were morally compromised would do for an understatement till a bigger one roared down the freeway. So it looked to Jerry, anyway.

On the other hand, what was the alternative? Leonid Brezhnev's USSR? Jerry wasn't one of those people who thought, because the United States wasn't so great, Russia had to be. The Iron Curtain that ran down the middle of Europe was there for a reason. The reason wasn't to keep swarms of Austrians, West Germans, Frenchmen, and Italians from rushing into East Germany, Hungary, and Czechoslovakia. It was to keep the people in the Russian satellites from getting the hell out.

He sighed, changed into his nightclothes, and climbed into his bunk to read for a while before he went to sleep. This anthology had Damon Knight's "Cabin Boy" in it. He hadn't read that one for a long time. People didn't know it the way they knew Knight's "To Serve Man"; it hadn't been a *Twilight Zone* episode. To Jerry, though, it was a better story. And it was probably where he'd got the idea of a grown spaceship rather than a manufactured one.

He smiled his way through it. Yeah, that was first contact done right! But it was only a story, even if it was a good one. Here he lay, in the middle of the North Pacific, on a ship dedicated to the proposition that stories might turn real. And wouldn't *that* be trippy?

Deeper and deeper sank Clementine, on the end of a string of pipes made of the same kind of steel that went into naval gun barrels. When the claw got about 13,000 feet down, a sonar mounted on it detected the seafloor. Dave Schoals didn't seem surprised about that—"It's doing what it's designed to do," he told anyone who'd listen—but he did seem pleased.

Extending the pipe string came with adventures, some small, some larger. One of the larger ones was a cable snapping and a thirty-ton counterweight crashing to—luckily, not through—the *Glomar Explorer*'s deck. Even more luckily, no one happened to be standing under it when it did. While the crew made repairs, Clementine sank no deeper.

"Never a dull moment, is there?" Jerry said to Dave Schoals.

The recovery director looked at him—looked *through* him, really. "We want them all to stay dull," he said. "Most of them do. We try to keep the exciting ones from getting too far out of hand."

"Right," Jerry said, and quickly went off to look for something, anything, to do somewhere else. When people talked about the pipe string, they talked about thousands of tons. Well, thousands of tons were millions of pounds, and Dave acted as if he were carrying all of them on his shoulders.

Atlas of the CIA, Jerry thought. But it wasn't funny, or not for long. Dave had been busting his ass on this project for years. He wasn't a smart-mouthed Johnny-come-lately, the way Jerry was. He'd helped design something that could bring up a starship from three miles underwater: the kind of thing any sensible human being would call impossible. Impossible or not, the *Glomar Explorer* was getting close to doing it. No wonder Dave was under a little bit of pressure right now. Yeah, no wonder at all.

Assume Clementine didn't break with the starship halfway to the surface. Assume the starship didn't decide it wouldn't let itself be brought up, and that it didn't do unto the *Glomar Explorer* as it had done to the K-129. Assume it actually lay in the moon pool, with the gates closed under it.

Then and only then would Jerry and Steve become possibly useful members of the crew. Till then, the most they could do was stay out of the way and try not to act like too big a jerk or an asshole. Steve had worked that out a lot sooner than Jerry had.

True, he'd been with the project longer. True, he was older and more practiced at getting along with people than Jerry was. Most of the human race fell into that latter category, as Jerry was uneasily aware. Another of the reasons he loved Anna so much was that she put up with him when he did something stupid without meaning to.

When the SB-10 sailed off as the *Chazhma* had done, everybody on the *Glomar Explorer* hoped the tug was gone for good. But the pesky little ship came back a few days later, as bothersome as ever. Some of its lunges brought it within a hundred yards of the *Explorer*. Its skipper reminded Jerry of a teenager playing chicken.

Jerry asked Jack Porter, "Why did it go away and then come back?"

"Asking why Russians do what they do is a mug's game. That skipper wouldn't keep trying to ram us if what they did made sense all the time." Porter might have been talking about John Campbell–style aliens, who thought as well as men but not like them. He went on, "My best guess is, they needed something from a submarine, and didn't want us to watch them making contact."

"Ah." Jerry considered, then nodded. "Sure seems more likely than anything I came up with on my own."

"It's still only a guess. Just because it seems likely doesn't make it true," Jack said. "The Russians do all kinds of unlikely shit."

"You mean we don't? What's the *Glomar Explorer* doing way the hell out here in that case?"

"Who? Us?" Porter was unflappable, as a good security man should have been. "We're mining manganese nodules, of course. Hey, it's the next big thing. Lots of minerals there at the bottom of the ocean, just waiting to get vacuumed up. Howard Hughes thinks so, and he spent a ton of money building this ship to prove it. He's got Manfred and other people at ocean mining conferences spreading the word, so it must be true."

"*We've* got Manfred, you mean," Jerry said. *You've got Manfred. The CIA has Manfred.* And did Manfred know about the spaceship, or only—only!—about the K-129? Jerry didn't ask. Jack might not have the need to know. Even if he did, he wouldn't blab. He *was* a good security man.

The SB-10 kept hanging around. The Russian crewmen didn't

even bother to pretend they weren't photographing the American ship. Men on the *Glomar Explorer* watched the tug, too, to make sure it didn't slam into their ship—and because it had those women aboard.

One of them was a dishwater blonde, the other a brunette. So some of the pipe farmers and divers swore; Jerry was never sure there actually were two of them. "Oh, hell, yes!" a rent-a-frog said, when he questioned that. "They swap dresses back and forth, too. Ain't you noticed?"

"No," Jerry admitted, wondering how they could swap dresses if there was only one of them.

"Pay attention, for Chrissake!" By the way the diver said it, anyone who didn't pay women microscopically close attention was probably a queer and certainly not to be trusted. Jerry wondered how he was with women he actually knew. That might prove a different story.

Jerry had never seen the women on the SB-10 taking pictures of the *Glomar Explorer*. They didn't seem to do a lot on deck, but *nobody* on the tug seemed to do a lot on deck. The men went around in dungarees, and often left their shirts off. The foggy middle of the North Pacific didn't seem like a great place to grab a tan. Then again, next to Petropavlovsk or Vladivostok it probably felt like Palm Springs.

He knew something about the two Russian cities because they were both ports. Anything that had to do with the ocean bumped up against what he'd been studying till this mad venture turned his life upside down and inside out. He knew Petropavlovsk lay on the Kamchatka Peninsula because that *was* a peninsula . . . and because Kamchatka was an important province to hold when you played Risk. About what went on fifty miles inland from Vladivostok he had no idea.

He'd never figured he would need to worry about it, either. But that was before John P. banged on his door one afternoon. Now . . . Now everything was different.

This container was another one with a keypad next to the door. The sign above the latch said CONTROL. Every time Jerry saw it, he wanted to giggle. It made him flash on *Get Smart*, which he'd watched religiously when he was in high school.

If they had Barbara Feldon in there . . . That would be far out, as a matter of fact. She'd seriously carbonated his hormones back in the day.

Steve's voice returned him to the here-and-now: "Depending on what happens when Clementine grabs, you may have business in here." He didn't say what Clementine would be grabbing, not where anyone else might hear him. He did punch a code into the keypad. "I'll give you this string when we're back in our cabin. It's another one you need to memorize."

"I can do that," Jerry said, as Steve opened the door. People dealing with the Midlothian object put as little in writing as they could. What did get written down was often intentionally misleading, like the date on the tape cassette that recorded the K-129's last moments.

Inside, the Control container had a lot more electronics than the one called Special Measurements. Two guys sat hunched in front of computer monitors, each tensely maneuvering an image of Clementine toward an image of the sunken spaceship. Or were they images? They looked as realistic as anything you were likely to see on a TV screen.

They had to be images, Jerry realized. The actual Clementine wasn't on the bottom yet. But the operators seemed as intent on what they were doing and as worried about it as if this were the real thing. Jerry'd hardly talked with them and their buddies on the voyage. They hung together when they ate. When they weren't in the messroom, they stayed in their cabins or here.

Quietly, so as not to disturb them, Steve said, "They're simulators, of course. With models of the Midlothian object and Clementine, the computer can simulate the forces involved in the capture. Seems like the genuine article, though, doesn't it?"

"It sure does!" Jerry whistled, soft and low. "Beats the crap out of Pong, you know? And I've blown a lot of quarters on Pong. If you could make a video game with this kind of detail, you'd be a gazillionaire."

"Not gonna happen," one of the operators said, without looking away from what he was doing. Jerry thought his name was Paul, but wouldn't have sworn to it. "These consoles are way too complex and way too expensive for the civilian market."

"Yeah, I guess you're right," Jerry said and then, as a new thought struck him, "Is there anything in the simulator that lets you game out what to do in case the, uh, Midlothian object starts acting up when you grab it?"

"You mean, if it does something but doesn't zap us the way it zapped the K-129?" Paul said.

"Um . . . That would be good, wouldn't it?"

"That would be real good if we ever want to draw our Social Security checks, uh-huh," the operator said. Jerry had heard these guys were from the NSA, which, he gathered, was an intelligence agency even more intelligent or spookier or more secret than the CIA. He was learning all kinds of things on the *Glomar Explorer*, none of which had anything to do with whale songs. His hydrophone hadn't picked up anything interesting, either.

The other operator (was he Eric? or was Eric on the other shift?) spoke up: "No, that isn't in the program. Maybe they couldn't do it, maybe they didn't think of it, or maybe they just figured we've already got enough to worry about."

"Not like they're wrong," Paul said. A second later, he added, "Shit!" Something on his simulator hadn't worked the way he wanted it to.

"When you start doing the real thing, will it feel like this?" Jerry asked.

"I think so," Paul answered as he fiddled with knobs and levers to fix whatever had gone wrong on the screen. "It's supposed to. These are the views we'll be getting from the cameras on Clementine. The simulator is even set up to make things get blurry fast when you move farther away from them, the way they do underwater."

"I saw that. It's wild," Jerry said. All the memory in the Honeywell 316s (so the little plaques under the monitors named them) was working flat out.

If only you could get this kind of detail into a game, it *would* beat the hell out of Pong. But Paul was bound to be right. How much did a machine like this cost? Twenty grand? Thirty? Somewhere in that ballpark, Jerry thought. You couldn't stick a fancy computer like that in an arcade. Hell, a row of them would pay for an arcade, with money left over besides.

It would be amazingly cool, though.

"Oh, nice grab! So smooth!" Paul said to Eric. Jerry remembered how pumped he was whenever he got to twenty-one before Anna did. It didn't happen often; her reflexes were quicker than his. But that thrill of victory looked mighty small next to snatching a starship. Okay, it wasn't a real starship. Yet. But it would be.

When he got out of the container, he felt as if he were leaving the future and falling back into the mundane world of 1974, where Richard Nixon was still saying he wouldn't resign and where the Senate was getting ready to throw him out of the White House on his crooked ass in case he meant it. He would have felt the same way if Clementine really were just going after the K-129, not a lost ship from another world. The simulator seemed as much the stuff of science fiction as the spaceship did.

He said as much to Steve. The older man nodded. "The same thought's crossed my mind," he answered. "We're pushing the state of the art in a lot of areas as far as it'll go, maybe even a little further. What we've learned from doing this would be worthwhile even if we didn't bring anything up from the bottom. People will be building on it for the next fifty years."

"Oh, hell, yes," Jerry said. "That's how science works. You couldn't move forward if not for everything everybody who was working on stuff before did. Sometimes we find out the old guys were wrong, but so what? They were in there swinging. Those people fifty years from now will find stuff we're wrong about, too."

Behind Steve's bifocals, one of his eyebrows quirked. "What happened to 'Never trust anybody over thirty'?"

"That's politics and society, man. It's not science," Jerry said. "Where there's no real evidence, you can argue till you're blue in the face—and we do. But either the Sun goes around the Earth or the Earth goes around the Sun, and the evidence tells you which."

Steve took a couple of steps without saying anything. Then, slowly, he remarked, "You know, you just may do."

It didn't sound like much. Quite a few of the things Steve said didn't sound like much when you first heard them. When you thought for a second, though . . . Jerry felt warmed, as if by the summer sun that was having trouble getting through the ocean mist here. He couldn't remember getting a higher compliment from anybody who wasn't in love with him.

"Hey, man," he said. "Hey."

"You just may do," Steve repeated. "I'll tell you something else, too. Fifty years from now, I'll be long gone."

"Your book won't. That's the kind of thing I was talking about."

"Thanks. Your thinking so means a lot to me. But let me get

where I was going. I'll be long gone, but there's a decent chance you'll be an emeritus somewhere, still teaching a class every now and then and maybe with a grad student or two. And you'll show them some of the old dogs can still learn new tricks."

Jerry had trouble imagining himself in his thirties, much less his seventies. What would 2024 look like? The politics would have to be better than today's. They couldn't very well be any worse!

"Or," Steve went on in a low voice, "fifty years from now, you may find yourself the ambassador to Alpha Centauri A-IV. How would that be?"

"Insane," Jerry answered, from the bottom of his heart.

The big question, the one for which the men on the *Glomar Explorer* had no good answer, was how much the starship weighed. If it was too much heavier than the K-129, something disastrous would happen when the Americans tried to take it off the seafloor.

Maybe one or more of Clementine's claws would break, letting the spaceship fall back to the bottom. Or maybe the pipe string would snap, and the recoil would break the *Explorer*'s back. Jerry thought of a breaking rubber band biting his hand. But the forces here were unimaginably bigger. All those millions of pounds hanging from the derrick . . .

They'd never put anywhere near this much weight on the system when they tested it off the California coast. Even with nothing going wrong, it was straining the *Glomar Explorer* to the limit, or somewhere close. Some of the ship's welds—her seams, if you were a landlubber—sprang leaks. The crew watched them warily. Everybody said this was nothing serious. Jerry hoped like hell that was the straight skinny.

When he worried out loud, Steve said, "Worry about why the Russian sub is on the bottom, why don't you? Worry about why the Midlothian object decided to do that to it. Worry about whether it'll decide to do that to us. Don't worry about what we can do if it decides that way, because we can't do anything."

"You really know how to cheer a guy up, don't you?" Jerry said.

"You knew this job was dangerous when you took it," Steve retorted.

"Thank you, Super Chicken," Jerry said. The man from the RAND Corporation looked at him as if he'd started spouting some of his Swahili. Well, it wasn't as if Jerry'd watched *Super Chicken*, either; the cartoon first aired after he'd graduated from high school. But he had younger cousins who'd been crazy about it, so he knew the catchphrases. He added, "When I got into this game, remember, I just thought we were going after the K-129. You know—nuclear missiles, nuclear torpedoes. The ordinary kind of shit."

"We don't talk about that much, for obvious reasons," Steve said. "We talk about the other even less, for even more obvious reasons. Too many people would either say we were crazy or start shouting about it when we want to keep it quiet more than anything."

"I don't shout. Hell, a lot of the time I hardly even talk," Jerry replied, remembering how Anna got on his case for not opening up more. "As for the other, I've been into science fiction since I found the Miss Pickerell stories and the Mushroom Planet books in the third grade."

"Science fiction is one thing. When it turns into—well, into the *Glomar Explorer*, that's something else."

"Yeah, this is real, all right." Jerry drummed his fingers on the arm of his chair. He heard the small noise that made. His fingertips felt the nubbly nylon of the chair's upholstery. He didn't think any drug could give him such detailed and trivial hallucinations. "The other thing that's real is, we're going to try grabbing the . . . the object in the next few days."

"Depending on how much it weighs, everything ought to go well," Steve said. "Everybody in Control is confident we can make the pickup without too much trouble."

"Ought to be second nature to those guys, with all the simulator practice they've had." Jerry said not a word about frying bacon. If that happened, it happened. Everybody on the *Glomar Explorer* who knew about the possibility seemed resigned to it, Jerry hardly less than the men who'd lived with it longer.

His writerly part told him he ought to be making notes—at least mental ones—about the feeling. You knew it could happen to you, you hoped like hell it didn't, and in spite of the shadow you got on as best you could with what you had to do.

But his writerly part hadn't been working very well since he found out about the Midlothian object. Part of that was learning he'd need to get his stuff vetted from here on out before he submitted it. And part was sheer bogglement. You didn't, he couldn't, imagine himself playing a role in anything like this.

Only he was.

Steve had said something; Jerry realized he had no idea what. "I'm sorry," he said, feeling foolish. "Try that again. I was lost inside my own head."

"I *said*, we're lucky in a way to be raising the Midlothian object and not the submarine. The K-129 is on its side on the bottom. We'd have to dig into the sediments under it to break suction and lift. And we don't know how sticky or how hard the seafloor there is. The *Glomar II* was supposed to find out, but that experiment failed."

"Damn!" Jerry said—he was paying attention now.

"Uh-huh." Steve nodded. "But it matters less with the spaceship. Because of its shape, the front and back or top and bottom or whatever they are are raised off the bottom. The outer claws can get under them without worrying about the mud or rock. Only the middle one has to take the sediment into account, and it's thicker than the others."

"They thought of everything when they designed Clementine!" Jerry said admiringly. He broke into off-key song: "In a canyon, in a cavern / Excavating for a mine!" He wanted to change musical styles, à la Tom Lehrer, but consideration for Steve's eardrums persuaded him not to try it.

"We'll know what we'll know pretty soon, all right," Steve said. "Until we do, everything feels like anticlimax."

"It sure does, here and in Washington," Jerry said. The House Rules Committee had passed three articles of impeachment, while turning down two others. Next stage was votes on the passed articles by the whole House. Barring a miracle or a resignation, Richard Nixon would become only the second president to be formally impeached. If he was, the Senate would try him, and looked almost sure to convict him and remove him from office.

"Never a dull moment," Steve said. "Whoever the president is, though, he'll have to deal with what we do after we take the Midlothian object on board . . . or with what it does to us if it decides it doesn't feel like getting taken on board."

"Yeah," Jerry said. "Or that."

So the worry worm wiggled in Steve's mind, too, did it? The man from the RAND Corporation held his cards very close to his chest. Finding out that he *did* worry about what the sunken spaceship might do when the *Hughes Glomar Explorer* tried to grab hold of it made Jerry's own thumping heart and sour stomach oddly easier for him to handle.

Suppose it sinks us, he thought. *What does the United States do then?* He wasn't sure the USA would do anything. The *Glomar Explorer* had tried to hassle a ship not of American registry in, or under, international waters, when the ship hadn't done anything to America. Pretending the whole thing never happened might be the smartest thing to do.

Anna won't think so, went through Jerry's mind. Maybe half a minute later, so did, *Dad may not, either.* They'd split the insurance policy the CIA had issued for him when he joined Azorian and Midlothian. He was positive that would keep his father quiet. He wasn't so sure about Anna, who often got off on talking back to people.

Yeah, she'd want answers. Whether John P. and his buddies on dry land could come up with any convincing enough for her was an interesting question.

Another interesting question was what the USA could do if it didn't want to take losing the *Glomar Explorer* lying down. Could they drop an H-bomb on a target three miles underwater? What kind of range did the starship's bacon-fryer have? Those were the kinds of things you wanted to think about before you started writing an alien-contact story.

It occurred to Jerry that those were also the kinds of things you wanted to think about before you started living an alien-contact story. Naturally, that occurred to him too late to do any good. *I'll be smarter next time*, he told himself. But there wouldn't be a next time, not like this.

A lot of systems on the *Glomar Explorer* and extending down to Clementine through all that pipe were hydraulically controlled. Just about all of them went haywire at one time or another while the pipe string descended toward the Midlothian object. Several different kinds of oil leaked, sometimes at high pressure.

Jerry eyed his sneakers with sad resignation. After he'd walked through those assorted kinds of oil, they'd never be the same. If he'd worn Blue Tips when he was in junior high, he would have been one of the cool kids. Surfers loved them, for instance. He'd mostly worn Hush Puppies: his dad was the one with the wallet, and with the last word.

Now I've got the Blue Tips, and what are they? Just shoes, he thought. Some profound life lesson probably lurked in there somewhere, but it seemed too depressing for him to try to ferret it out.

And the sneakers weren't the only thing the hydraulic oil spread over. The *Glomar Explorer* had its very own oil slick. People wondered out loud how far across the Pacific it was stretching.

Another question occurred to Jerry. He asked Dave Schoals, "What can the guys in the SB-10 learn if they scoop up some of the slick and analyze the hell out of it?"

"Huh!" The recovery director sent him a thoughtful stare. "You do come up with the interesting questions, don't you?"

"I try," Jerry said modestly, adding, "People say I'm trying a lot of the time, as a matter of fact."

"Wonder why," Dave said with a grin. Then he caught himself. "Wait. You're writing your thesis now, aren't you?"

"That's right. I mean, I was till all this happened."

"You've got an excuse in that case. Doing doctoral work'll drive anybody halfway round the bend. More than halfway. Finishing my dissertation isn't the smallest reason I'm single again."

"Yeah?" Jerry said. Schoals nodded. That wasn't the kind of thing Jerry wanted to hear. Anna was much less enthusiastic about the academic life than he was. He hoped that would work out in time (he also hoped that making at least as much money as she did would give him more clout, or anyway more talking points, in the relationship than he had now).

Maybe his flinch was visible. Dave got back to the matter at hand: "I don't *think* they can find out too much. That we're using a lot of heavy-duty hydraulic stuff, sure. But not what we're using it for, even the K-129." He waited a beat, the way a stand-up comedian would have. "I hope."

"Okay. I'm glad," Jerry said. These guys did have veins of humanity streaking the hard, dutiful, secret rock of their souls. They had them, but the stuff could be goddamn rough to extract.

On the morning of July thirtieth, Clementine hung about a hundred feet above the Midlothian object. The *Glomar Explorer* maneuvered ever so slightly to position the claw just where the men in the Control container wanted it to be. Then those guys would do what they did, and things would either work or they wouldn't.

Lunch that day was a choice of lamb chops or sirloin tips. Jerry was working meat off the bone of a lamb chop when Dale Neuwirth stood up and clinked his fork against his glass till the crowded messroom quieted. Everybody eyed the mission director, for more reasons than one. Dale didn't usually act that way; he tried to be one of the guys. Not now. You didn't have to be Sherlock Holmes to figure out something was up.

He looked around the messroom. "Some of you will have a notion of what I'm going to tell you now. Most of you won't," he said. "When we bring Clementine back up into the moon pool—and yes, that's *when*, not *if*—she won't have a big chunk of a Russian submarine in her claws. She'll be holding something else. Yes, the sub is down there. Yes, it's important. But if everything works the way we want it to, what we bring up will make the submarine hardly matter at all.

"We're getting close. It didn't seem fair to spring this on you by surprise when you see what Clementine has. But I'm gonna tell you—what we're doing out here isn't just important for the United States. It's important for the whole human race. And you're part of it. It'll be something to tell your grandchildren about, that you were here for this." He chuckled wryly. "If you ever get cleared to talk about it at all, I mean."

He sat down again. Several people called questions. He ignored them. The messroom buzzed. "Hey, Mr. Steinberg, what's goin' on?" the sailor named Tony asked from the next table over.

"We'll all find out pretty soon," Jerry said. *Or we'll get fried like bacon, or the ship'll break in half even if we don't.* Not mentioning any of that seemed a good plan.

VI

Jerry wanted to watch the guys who'd spent so much time and hard work on the simulator doing their things with the genuine, gigantic Clementine. He saw that none of the other people who knew Midlothian nested inside Azorian made a beeline for the Control container, though, so he also stayed away. He knew he wouldn't have wanted kibitzers while he was doing something hard and important, either.

It turned out not to matter for the next couple of days. One glitch after another kept the claw from descending to the bottom and scooping the spaceship. And some of the replacement sensors on Clementine didn't want to work. The engineers talked among themselves and no doubt talked *to* themselves, too. They couldn't figure out what was going wrong.

Steve and Jerry found themselves with a mystery of their own. Steve said, "I hear the TV cameras down there are showing a hammer on the seafloor next to the Midlothian object. Do you remember seeing one there, Jerry?"

"I don't think so," Jerry answered. "It would have stood out, wouldn't it?"

"Just a little. But I don't remember it, either. If it wasn't there before and it is now, how did it get there?"

"Maybe the Russians brought it over from the K-129. Maybe that's what the dead guy who's nothing but a skeleton in boots was doing outside the sub," Jerry suggested.

Stephen Dole sent him a severe look. "I thought you wrote *science* fiction, not the kind of stuff that's supposed to make your hair stand up on the back of your neck."

"Well, I haven't tried horror yet. There's not much of a market for it," Jerry replied. "But who knows? There wasn't a great big market for fantasy till *The Lord of the Rings* made one. Now it probably sells better than sf does. Maybe somebody will come along and be, like, a Tolkien for horror."

"Fine." Steve held on to his patience with both hands. "That still doesn't explain the hammer, unless we missed it on the *Halibut* photos."

They went over them in the Special Measurements container, both separately and together. The hammer hadn't been there then. It lay so close to the egg-shaped Midlothian object, it might have slid down that smooth curve before hitting the bottom. The photographs from five years before surely would have picked it up. Only they hadn't.

"Maybe it really was that dead Russian. Maybe I can get a story out of it—if I make the spaceship into a freighter full of gold or something, I mean." Listening to himself, Jerry liked the idea. He wrote it down. Then he glanced over at Steve with a sly smile. "Or maybe whatever's inside the spaceship threw it out there."

"I hear it looks like an ordinary hammer, like the ones you'd buy at a hardware store," Steve said. "Either the aliens are just like us or there's a simpler story."

A little to Jerry's disappointment, there was. One of the men who worked in the pipe farm remembered that he'd fumbled a hammer over the rail a week or ten days earlier. The roughneck's comment was, "Who woulda thought it'd go straight down like that?"

"He's right," Jerry said when he heard the story. "Who would've thought that?"

"I wouldn't have," Steve said. "But now we know. No dead Russians involved."

"That's 'cause I haven't written it yet," Jerry retorted. He got a chuckle—a small one, but a chuckle—out of the man from the RAND Corporation.

The next day, Clementine went all the way down to the bottom and moved toward the sunken spaceship. The people who knew what the claw would be grappling, Jerry among them, went around with optimistic smiles pasted on their faces. They were the ones who also knew exactly what could go wrong, the ones who'd heard the hot-grease noise that doomed the K-129.

Jerry'd never before been in a situation where he knew he might die very soon. His father had fought in Italy during World War II; he had friends who'd come back from Vietnam. One of them had been on a river gunboat that hit a mine. Jerry'd asked him what it was like.

"It wasn't *like* anything," Bill told him. "One second, we were chugging along on routine patrol. Next thing I knew, I was in the goddamn Mekong with my pants full."

He hadn't understood that in his belly when he heard it. He did now. It wasn't something the writer in him wanted to analyze, not anymore. His balls kept trying to crawl up into his belly. Somebody'd fished Bill out of the Mekong. If he went into the North Pacific, who'd rescue him?

The Russians on the SB-10? Would he want that? Would it matter? Or would the starship fry them, too, to make good and sure not even one survived to tell the tale? Those were all questions he hoped he didn't have to answer. And he understood his old man and his buddies better than he had before.

Because of what the *Glomar Explorer* was doing, she had to hold her position above the Midlothian object very precisely. The SB-10 chose that moment to make run after run at and around the bigger ship.

We are maneuvering with difficulty, the *Explorer* signaled to the tug: another good-sized understatement. The SB-10 paid no attention and gave no sign of understanding. John Porter's comments had made Jerry imagine the Russians as intelligent aliens. Now the SB-10's behavior reinforced that.

Because John and Dave and Dale were up to their eyebrows in problems bigger than soothing an anxious grad student, Jerry asked Steve, "Do you think they know what we're up to right now?"

"They haven't shown any sign of it," the older man said. "Best guess is, they're just making pests of themselves. I've heard stories about Cold War ocean games that would curl anybody's hair."

Jerry had heard stories like that, too, mostly secondhand from oceanographers who'd got whale song tapes from Navy personnel. He hadn't known how much to believe. Now he had the feeling the swabbies were playing things down, not puffing them up.

"Let's hope you're right," he said. "Let's hope they don't run into us, too, 'cause I bet they don't have insurance." He'd got rear-ended like that himself, coming off the San Diego Freeway on his way to campus. The Rambler's trunk had a smoothed-out, Bondoed-over dent because he'd paid a fly-by-night guy twenty bucks to fix it instead of shelling out plenty more at a body shop.

By the way Steve's mouth twisted, he'd met at least one uninsured driver himself. "Yes, let's," he said, and left it there.

Just to delight everyone on the *Glomar Explorer* even further, the guys in the Control container decided they needed one final double added to the pipe string, to give Clementine's breakout legs more play when they rose up and broke whatever suction was holding the spaceship to the seafloor. The trouble was, the pipe wranglers had to disconnect the hydraulics to attach the sixty feet of pipe, then hook things up again once the attachment was made.

They were loudly unhappy about that, the way anyone would have been. Much bad language ensued. Jerry listened to some of it in slack-jawed wonderment. He was good with words, good enough to get paid for them (occasionally). He'd never dreamt the English language could be so creatively profaned. He scribbled *stupid whistleass chucklefucks* in his notebook, vowing to use it as soon as he found an editor who'd let him sneak it into print.

Getting the hydraulics disconnected from the pipe string, adding the new double, and hooking the hydraulics up again should have taken a few hours. To make things all the more delightful, one of the heave compensators, which shielded the string from the ship's motions, chose that moment to go on the fritz. The seas stayed moderate, but the engineers swore like pipe-farm guys as they worked around the clock to get the compensator compensating again.

Another day gone. Another month gone. They didn't try lowering the breakout legs till after noon on the first of August. Jerry still didn't go into the Control container, but he and Steve and a lot of the CIA guys hung around near it to hear the word as soon as there was word to hear.

"Like sitting around in the waiting room while your wife is having a baby," Dave Schoals muttered.

"Like sitting around in the waiting room hoping your wife *does* have a baby," Steve added.

Jerry topped them both: "Like sitting around in the waiting room hoping your wife doesn't have Rosemary's Baby."

Dave winced. Steve thumped Jerry on the shoulder. He thought both reactions were similar.

A few minutes later, Paul opened the door to Control. He came halfway out and said, "We have the object off the bottom! We've jettisoned the breakout legs from Clementine—well, we've jettisoned three of them. The fourth one doesn't want to let go, so we're leaving it on for now. Extraction went as well as though we'd been practicing for weeks or something."

He grinned a wide, foolish, relieved grin and started to duck back into his sanctum. Before he could, Dave held up a hand. "Hang on! Do you have any feel for the object's weight?"

"I'm not on the controls right now—obviously," Paul answered. "Eric says he thinks it's lighter than he was braced for, but he isn't sure. We haven't done much with it, and we have the whole pipe string and Clementine down there."

"Gotcha. Thanks," Dave said. Paul nodded and disappeared. The lock gave forth an authoritative click as it engaged.

"We have it. Dear God in heaven, we really have it," Steve said softly. His head swung Jerry's way. "And it isn't the Devil's kid."

"Or if it is, it hasn't started acting up yet," Jerry said. Steve stuck out his tongue at him. It wasn't the kind of thing the man from the RAND Corporation would usually have done, but they were all giddy just then.

Jerry wondered why the Midlothian object seemed relatively light—if that turned out to be true. Whatever it was made of, it wouldn't be anything earthly science was familiar with. The K-129 had taken a beating while it sank to the ocean floor. The Midlothian object looked as fresh and undamaged as if it had got there only a few minutes before. It also still looked to be airtight, gastight, watertight, whatever the right word was. How, under the crushing weight of three miles of water?

Force fields? he wondered. He'd never liked stories that used them. They seemed like hand-waving bullshit, not something that could really exist. But who could guess what kind of rules the vessel down there played by? Some Earthly physicists might go stark raving mad trying to work them out.

If we can bring it up here for a look, he reminded himself. *Yeah. If.*

No force fields aboard the *Glomar Explorer*. Jerry didn't think so, anyhow, though he still hadn't been inside a few of the containers she carried. But the *Explorer* did have thousands of tons of steel. Some of it began to lower: the docking legs forward and aft of the moon pool slowly descended into the Pacific.

Pointing, Jerry asked, "What's going on?"

"We're lowering our center of gravity," Dave answered. "We've got all that weight at the apex of the derrick. It makes us top-heavy. We don't want to capsize if the waves pick up."

"Ah. Cool." Jerry nodded and gave him a thumbs-up. With someone his own age, someone closer to his politics, he might have used a peace-symbol *V* instead. Here, not rattling anybody's cage seemed the better part of valor.

For the next couple of days, the SB-10 kept flitting around the *Glomar Explorer*. It would circle the American ship, often at less than a hundred yards. Or it would keep station a mile or two astern of the *Explorer*. Or it would quit doing that, run up till it was out ahead of the big ship, then kill its engine and let wind and waves shove it back again.

Another ship, a freighter called the *Bangkok*, steamed past, four or five miles north of the *Glomar Explorer*. The *Bangkok* didn't have any trouble getting in touch with the *Explorer*: she radioed, asking what kind of ship it was.

"They thought we were funny looking," Jack Porter said, not without pride, as he told the story at dinner. "And you know what? They were right."

"We told 'em we were scooping up manganese nodules?" Jerry asked.

"Sure. What else would we be doing way the devil out here?" As far as a veteran CIA man could, Jack radiated innocence.

And, while all that was going on, the pipe string started coming back into the ship. Things went slowly. The pipe-handling system was at maximum stress. Lowering the string had been easier, since gravity worked with the pipe crew then. Hauling the pipe up again, plus Clementine, plus whatever the Midlothian object weighed, took everything the system had.

Engineers and ordinary sailors prowled through the *Glomar Explorer*, making sure all watertight doors stayed shut unless someone was actually going through them. Opening steel doors and dogging them shut behind him every few yards annoyed Jerry. The idea that such precautions were important alarmed him.

"When we started doing this, I figured it would take a week—six days if everything went lickety-split." Dave laughed a self-mocking laugh. "Shows what I knew, doesn't it?"

"Welcome to Murphy's Law," Jerry said.

Dave laughed again, this time on a sour note. "Murphy was a goddamn optimist."

Jerry laughed, too, not least at himself. If the starship didn't come to life and sink the *Glomar Explorer*, and if the overstrained ship didn't break in half and sink herself, he was happy enough to have smaller things go wrong. The longer he stayed on the CIA's payroll, the better his savings account liked it.

"How much pipe have we brought up?" he asked Dave.

"About three thousand feet so far," the recovery director answered. "Doesn't sound like much for two days' work, I know, but we've been taking it real easy while we're near max weight. If everything goes right, we'll pick up steam from now on."

In lieu of knocking wood, Jerry rapped his knuckles on his own forehead. "And every double we bring in takes off more weight."

"You got it—something like twenty tons every time," Dave said. "Of course, when you have thousands of tons on the string, that doesn't seem like so much."

"Everett Dirksen said something like that, didn't he? A billion here and a billion there, and pretty soon you're talking about real money," Jerry said.

"He was a piece of work, Everett Dirksen was," Dave said. Jerry nodded. They could agree on that, even if they might not agree on what kind of piece of work the flamboyant Republican senator had been.

The next morning, the ship's newsletter reported that John Dean had got one to four years for his role in the Watergate coverup. It also said that John Ehrlichman had got twenty months for perjury and conspiracy a few days earlier. The paranoid part of Jerry wondered whether the people who put the newsletter together had held off on mentioning Ehrlichman's sentence sooner because they hoped it was only an isolated incident. With Nixon having to turn over more and more tapes, that seemed a forlorn hope, but who would be sure of anything in these crazy times?

Slowly but pretty surely, more doubles came off the pipe string. Operations did go better as the weight the system was pulling against shrank. People who didn't have to be there, though, were strongly discouraged from venturing anywhere near the moon pool.

"What the fuck you think you're doing, dumbshit?" a rent-a-frog yelled at an engineer who forgot or thought he could ignore those instructions. The guy with the slide rule clipped to his belt retreated in confused dismay.

There but for the grace of common sense go I, Jerry thought, as the red-faced engineer stumbled past him. He looked down at the industrial carpeting under his sneakers so the other man didn't have to respond to him. That was the only comfort he could give.

He was walking around the helipad the following morning, working off some of his high-calorie breakfast, when he noticed the docking legs had quietly come up forty or fifty feet. He took that for a good sign: the guys who knew about such things had to think the *Glomar Explorer* was less likely to turn turtle now.

Which left only the Midlothian object to worry about. Only! The spaceship was more than halfway up from the bottom. It hadn't done anything but lie in Clementine's claws. It might have been as dead as the K-129.

It might have been, but Jerry didn't think it was.

All hell broke loose the next day. Not on the ship; pipe kept coming up steadily, if still slower than people whose opinions mattered would have liked. Jerry wasn't one of those people. As long as Clementine didn't break and drop the spaceship back into the abyss, he wasn't complaining.

In Washington, though . . . Jerry didn't find out about it till the following morning, but he'd got used to that. There'd been a *Doonesbury* where one congressman at the Watergate hearings groused to his colleague, "If only he'd knock over a bank or something . . ."

"By George, we'd have him then!" the second congressman replied.

And Richard Nixon, it turned out, had knocked over a bank after all. The tapes the Supreme Court ordered him to turn over proved it, too. They showed that when he'd talked with H. R. Haldeman twice on June 23, 1972, about using the CIA to stop the FBI from investigating the Watergate break-in. The *Glomar Explorer* newsletter headline, surely not written by anybody who hated the president, read "Smoking Howitzer!"

Even a Republican representative like Orange County's Charles Wiggins, who'd led Nixon's defenders in the Judiciary Committee, said he would have voted for the articles of impeachment had he known. Three other Republicans on the committee joined him. The others announced they were "reassessing" their stance.

There was another *Doonesbury* where Mark chortled, *"Guilty! That's guilty, guilty, guilty!!"* Some newspapers refused to run that strip, calling it too one-sided. Jerry hoped their editors felt properly foolish now. He wouldn't have bet on it, though.

When he went into the messroom for lunch, he felt like waving the newsletter over his head and screaming, *"Guilty! That's guilty, guilty, guilty!!"* himself. Only the worry that some of the divers might baptize him with hot coffee made him hold back. He even tried not to look like somebody who was gloating.

He might not have done too well, because Steve greeted him with, "Seems you were right all along."

"Yeah, well . . ." Jerry shrugged. "The important thing is, we've gotta make sure nothing like this ever happens again."

"If we can," the older man said. "People aren't perfect. The things they make aren't perfect, either. Chances are we'll get ourselves another power-hungry president one of these years."

That felt more likely than Jerry wished it did. He'd been thinking about imperfections, too, in a different context. "Clementine and the pipe string have had plenty of problems, but the object is still coming up." He kept avoiding *Midlothian* where anyone not in the inner circle could hear, but with luck that wouldn't matter much longer.

"It is," Steve said with a small nod. "Getting close now. They should be hooking Clementine up to the docking legs this afternoon. If everything works the way it should, the rent-a-frogs will get the first live look at the object then."

"Alevai omayn!" Jerry exclaimed. Steve gave him a quizzical look. Sheepishly, he translated: "May it work the way you said." He wasn't sure he was the only Jew aboard the *Glomar Explorer*, but he thought so. No black guys at all, or Asians. The people pulling up the spaceship for the United States didn't look just like the country they worked for.

"Ah." Steve stayed smooth and polite, as he always did.

Something else occurred to Jerry. "The things those other folks built"—yes, he was staying as oblique as he could for as long as he could—"aren't perfect all the time, either, or what was the object doing on the bottom of the Pacific for however long it was down there?"

"That's a good point," Stephen Dole replied. "An important point, I think. We look at all the things the builders can do that we can't, and sometimes we feel they have to be gods."

"*Chariots of the Gods?*" Jerry rolled his eyes. "I read it. All it made me think was, von Däniken didn't have any real ideas himself, so he didn't believe ancient people could have had any, either. But what do I know? He's laughing all the way to the bank."

"Did you see the movie?" Steve asked.

"No, thank God."

"It's worse than the book."

"They said it couldn't be done!"

"Oh, it was." Steve's smile was lopsided. "It got nominated for a Best Documentary Academy Award, too. Didn't win, so there's a little justice in the world. Not enough, but a little."

"I didn't know that. I wish I still didn't. I mean, it's good that it didn't win, but it should have got laughed at, not nominated. Hell, it shouldn't even have got made."

"'No one in this world, so far as I know, has ever lost money by underestimating the intelligence of the great masses of the plain people.' H. L. Mencken was a nasty man in a good many ways, but you'd have a devil of a time persuading me he was wrong about that," Steve said.

"I heard it 'of the American people,'" Jerry said.

"I heard it that way, too. I used it in an article that way without checking, and my editor called me on it," Steve said. "Now I quote it the way Mencken wrote it."

"Good for you. Good for your editor." Jerry enjoyed being edited no more than any other halfway sane person did. When you were wrong, though, all you could do was tip your cap and thank the fellow who'd kept you from committing stupidity in public.

After lunch, some of the divers went into the Pacific to secure Clementine—and what Clementine held in its claws—to the *Glomar Explorer*'s docking legs. Jealousy stabbed at Jerry as they swam down to the moon pool. The more he thought about it, the more *he* wanted to be the one who first saw the Midlothian object for real.

Right after they went into the gray-green water, he and everybody else still on the *Explorer* had something else to worry about. The SB-10 buzzed around the American ship like an angry bumblebee, sometimes coming within fifty yards of her. Captain Gresham signaled to the Russian tug that the *Glomar Explorer* couldn't maneuver at all. As usual, the SB-10 ignored the signal.

Jerry watched the tug's antics from the helipad. So did Jack Porter. The bearded security director was biting his lip with worry. "If they put a diver in the water, they can find out what we've got here," he said, perhaps more to himself than to Jerry. "Wouldn't that just screw everything to the wall?"

"Oh, maybe a little," Jerry said. Jack sent him a startled look— yes, he had been talking to himself. More quietly, Jerry went on, "We have some guns aboard? Did I hear that right?"

"Yeah. Some of 'em are in a chest under my bed, in fact," Jack answered. "Only we can't use 'em. That would be an act of war, or close enough, and sure as the devil they'd get off a signal before we could take them all out."

"Uh-huh." Jerry made himself nod and smile. He got the feeling that, had Jack owned a death ray that could have vaporized the SB-10 without leaving a trace, he would have fired it without thinking twice.

If we get inside the starship, maybe he will *get a ray like that,* Jerry thought uneasily. *Do I want him to?*

While that was going through his head, the SB-10 hove to, still no more than fifty yards astern of the *Glomar Explorer.* Most of the crew lined the starboard rail, the one nearer the U.S. vessel. Jerry didn't see the woman or women aboard the tug. He understood why a moment later. In unison, the Russians spun around, bent over, and dropped their pants.

Laughing fit to bust, Jerry mooned the Soviet sailors right back. Jack Porter and the rest of the Americans on the helipad did, too. "Turn the other cheek," Jack said. "It's in the Bible, you know?"

"It sure is." Straightening, Jerry pulled up his cords.

The Russians also covered themselves. They waved to the Americans. "*Urra! Urra! Urra!*" they shouted. The SB-10's whistle blew three long blasts. The tug's engine growled to busier life. The little ship headed off to the northwest, as the *Chazhma* had earlier.

"Do you think it's gone for good?" Jerry asked.

"Christ, I hope so!" Jack answered. "But I hoped so the last time it disappeared, too, so we just have to wait and see."

"No divers, anyway," Jerry said.

"Yeah!" Porter crossed himself, whether ironically or for real Jerry couldn't guess.

Not having the pushy, annoying tug around felt wonderful. Jerry wondered if it would get boring after a while. Then he remembered how Dave Schoals had pointed out that the ideal mission was one where everything went the way it was supposed to. They hadn't had that, but at least they didn't need to worry about Russian snoops anymore . . . unless the SB-10 came back again.

Jerry ambled forward, toward the moon pool (and snickered when he realized that had a whole new meaning now). Most of the strain was off the derrick and the lifting system. Now it only—that word again!—had to support the two thousand tons or so of Clementine, plus however much the Midlothian object added. Compared to what it had been doing, that was a piece of cake.

Everything in the moon pool seemed calm and serene. The water inside it was as placid as the rest of the ocean—they'd finally got the mild weather they'd wanted all along. Things were going in a way Dave undoubtedly liked.

A rent-a-frog who'd been attaching the claw to the docking legs popped up near the edge of the moon pool. Treading water, he pulled off his mask and shed the mouthpiece that hooked him up to the tanks on his back. "Holy motherfucking shit!" he shouted. "How come nobody told us we were gonna grab Humpty Dumpty?"

As far as Jerry knew, no one ever said "Midlothian object" again. In the same way the capture vehicle had become Clementine, everybody aboard the *Glomar Explorer* called the spaceship Humpty Dumpty from then on.

The name fit. Jerry wished he'd thought of it himself. The spaceship *did* look like an enormous egg. It had had a great fall. And it wasn't even slightly obvious whether all the president's horses and all the president's men could put Humpty Dumpty together again.

All the president's men . . . He hadn't read the Woodward and Bernstein book; it came out only a few days before he'd parked the Rambler in the lot near Pier E. Events had outrun it now. But in a sense he, like everyone else on this ship, was one of the president's men himself. He didn't like that much.

Nixon had to resign now . . . didn't he? He couldn't hang on anymore . . . could he? Jerry had joked about taking aliens to see Nixon. Right this minute, the joke didn't seem so funny.

Other things didn't seem so funny, either. He'd done a lot of hard work trying to imagine as many scenarios as he could about what might happen when the spaceship—when Humpty Dumpty—lay on the leaky bottom of the moon pool. Easy to be glib when it was still three miles down.

Now it lay only about 135 feet down. The docking legs had hold of Clementine at either end. Raising them would help the derrick bring the claw and Humpty Dumpty the rest of the way up. The spaceship wouldn't be a scenario, a hypothetical, anymore. It would be right there, as real as a punch in the face.

Which was why, that evening, he got trained in donning a suit that would, with luck, protect him from whatever Humpty Dumpty brought with it from the bottom of the sea and from wherever it had been before it found Earth.

Dave Schoals, who gave the training, wouldn't take no for an answer. He banged on Jerry's cabin door and said, "You want to go down into the moon pool, you have to know how to give yourself a chance to stay safe. C'mon." He fixed Stephen Dole with a businesslike stare. "You, too."

"I had the training up in Northern California," the man from the RAND Corporation protested.

"That would've been months ago," Dave answered. "You can do with a refresher, or else you can let Jerry grab all the glory from meeting the Martians."

Steve said something uncharitable under his breath, but he came. There proved to be two layers of long johns that went over people's usual underwear, a papery outer garment over regular clothes, and booties and surgical gloves for feet and hands. Those got taped to the outer garment to make an airtight seal.

A hood fit over the hard hat everyone who went into the moon pool would have to wear. A face mask protected eyes, nose, and mouth. "If it turns out there isn't an oxygen atmosphere inside the spaceship, we can rig up air tanks," Dave said.

"What if it's a couple of hundred degrees below zero, though?" Jerry asked. Coming out of the mask, his voice sounded unearthly in his own ears.

"In that case, we try to figure out what to do with the next man who goes in," Dave said. Jerry was already warm enough, and then some, in the protective suit. He got warmer yet. Dave went on, "After contact with Humpty Dumpty, we'll check you out for radiation and have you clean off till you make the Geiger counters happy."

Jerry found another question: "How about checking for germs?" He couldn't have been the only guy on the *Glomar Explorer* who'd read things like Harry Harrison's *Plague from Space* and Michael Crichton's *The Andromeda Strain*.

"We'll do the best we can with that," Dave told him, and said no more. After a moment, Jerry realized there wasn't much more to be said. What could they do but their best?

The newsletter the next morning had a breaking bulletin: Ron Ziegler announced that Richard Nixon would make an important statement the following day. The president's press secretary didn't say what his boss would be talking about. As far as Jerry was concerned, that was just as well. If Ziegler said the sun was shining, Jerry would have gone outside to check.

Some people called the difference between what politicians and their flunkies said and what was actually true the credibility gap. A gang of L.A. satirists who styled themselves the Credibility Gap poked fun at such politicos, first on AM rock station KRLA and then on KPPC. Free-form FM fitted them better, no doubt.

Having read Orwell's "Politics and the English Language" at an impressionable age, Jerry had another name for politicians' verbal shenanigans. He called them lying.

Slowly, slowly, Humpty Dumpty rose from the ocean toward the moon pool. Along with everyone else, Jerry sweated out the last hours of the lift. If Clementine broke a claw now . . . That would be too painful to bear. All the way to the top (well, almost all the way) and then all the way down? No.

Please, God, no, went through his mind. It wasn't exactly a prayer, but it wasn't exactly not a prayer, either. It came closer than anything he'd tried since he was a little boy and his mother was dying. Petition the Lord with prayer? Years before the Doors sang it, he'd agreed with them that you couldn't do it. But here he was, out in the middle of the ocean, with Humpty Dumpty nearly close enough to reach out and touch. Nearly. Not quite. Not yet. *Please, God.*

Lunch was roast beef. Jerry'd enjoyed it the Thursday before. It was probably just as good now; the cooks in the galley knew their stuff. But five minutes after finishing, he had trouble remembering what he'd eaten. He'd gone into the messroom because it was lunchtime. Okay, he'd fueled up. That was what it amounted to.

He wandered forward and peered down into the moon pool. The sun was out, if hazily. A mackerel, three-quarters grown, flashed silver just below the surface, then vanished into deeper water. Jerry's gaze went deeper still. Was that a pale, smooth curve down there, with darker bands where the black steel claws still gripped? Or was it just his imagination?

"Running away with me," he sang softly, yielding to the Temptations.

But the longer he stood there, the longer he looked, the more sure he grew that he really was seeing the ship from another world . . . through the sea darkly now, but soon face-to-face. He stayed where he was, watching, and stayed, and stayed some more. He wasn't the only one, either. Some of the divers and roughnecks looked down and into the moon pool, too. Dale was there, and Dave, and Jack, and Steve. So were the guys from the Control container. They'd all worked longer and harder than Jerry had. They wanted to find out what they'd done.

Jerry stayed there till his feet ached. By dinnertime, Humpty Dumpty was in the moon pool, with the gates sliding together toward their imperfect seal beneath it. Steak tonight, but no one moved.

"Will you look at that?" Dave said. "Will you just *look* at that?"

Look Jerry did. Whatever the spaceship was made of, it wasn't metal. Still mostly underwater, with the sun dropping toward the horizon, Humpty Dumpty glistened and gleamed and shone, like mother-of-pearl. Jerry gaped. He'd expected all kinds of wonderful things, but never such beauty.

VII

At last, when full darkness came, he went back to the messroom. He put Λ.1. Sauce on his steak, the way he usually did. He remembered that the next day. He didn't recall much about eating. He shoveled in food as fast as he could so he could go back out again and see what was going on.

Big, noisy pumps were throwing water from the moon pool out over the side and into the ocean. Aside from that, the view was disappointing. The *Glomar Explorer* showed her usual running lights, but the spotlights that could light up the moon pool stayed off. Jerry'd wondered whether Humpty Dumpty would glow in the dark. No such luck.

Steve came forward a few minutes later. Like Jerry, he had only gloom to examine. "I wanted to see more," Jerry grumbled.

"So did I," the older man said, nodding. "Five gets you ten a Russian spy satellite's due to come over before too long. We don't want to light everything up and show the Kremlin what we've got."

"Oh," Jerry said, and then, "Could they really tell from that high up?"

"This isn't my area of expertise, you understand, but I think *we* could, and we don't dare assume their technology is any worse than ours," Steve said. "Jack could tell you more, and maybe Dave, too."

"They could, but would they?" Jerry answered his own question: "I don't think so. I don't have the waddayacallit, the need to know." If he sounded bitter, he did because he was.

Steve couldn't very well have missed that, but pretended not to hear it. "Well, neither do I," he said, mild as usual. "That kind of thing comes with the territory here. They like to compartmentalize information."

"Man, do they!" Jerry said.

"But we know the important thing." Steve waved down toward

Humpty Dumpty. "The most important thing since the bomb, for sure—maybe ever. Tomorrow morning, we'll be able to see what we've got here."

Jerry got his newsletter at breakfast the next morning. It announced that the president would resign that day. Jerry demolished his bacon and eggs, and enjoyed them, too. Whatever aliens might lurk inside Humpty Dumpty, they wouldn't have Dick Nixon to kick around anymore.

After eating, he went up to the moon pool again. The big pumps were still going, but spitting less water than they had the night before. The center well had to be nearly dry.

That didn't mean he could see in. An enormous tarp, not far from the size of the one that would cover the infield during a rain delay at a ball game, went over the top of it. One of the *Glomar* sailors waved to Jerry. "We'll take it off in fifteen minutes, soon as the satellite's gone again."

"Do we have to cover up every time one goes overhead?" Jerry asked. "That'll make working on Humpty Dumpty complicated."

"Orders," the man replied. Jerry had seen bumper stickers that read *God said it. I believe it. That settles it.* Could those stickers have spoken, they would have sounded the way the sailor did when he said *Orders*.

He and his comrades took off the tarp as neatly as groundskeepers would have. Jerry stared at Humpty Dumpty with an avidity he hadn't known since the very first time he opened a *Playboy* to the centerfold.

The starship's curves were different from that long-ago Miss May's. He marveled at them just the same. Now out in the open air, the outer shell still put him in mind of mother-of-pearl or opal or something like that. If it was metal, it was no kind of metal human beings knew how to make. If it wasn't metal, what was it?

He was looking at the end with the golf ball–style dimples. He went to the other end of the moon pool so he could see the tubes that stuck out. They were made of the same stuff as the rest of the spaceship's exterior. And yes, those marks he'd seen on the photograph were still there. If they weren't writing . . . then they were something else, that was all.

One of the men who'd dealt with the tarpaulin was snapping away with an Instamatic. "Do they let you do that?" Jerry asked.

"Nobody told me not to," the sailor said.

Nobody guessed you'd try it, went through Jerry's mind. He didn't push it. That wasn't his place. He suspected something would happen to the film before the fellow could get it developed. He wouldn't have sworn to that, but he would have bet on it.

A few minutes later, Dave Schoals came to the edge of the moon pool. He also had a camera: a 35-millimeter with a fancy lens on it. A leather case on his belt probably held more lenses, and maybe more film with them. He started taking pictures of Humpty Dumpty, too. Jerry figured he had a better chance of keeping his photos than the sailor did. He was sure Dave had a fancier security clearance.

As was often true, he had to look around for something to say. As wasn't so often true, he found something. "Congratulations," he told the recovery director. "We've got it, thanks to you."

"Not just me. Team effort all the way," Dave answered. "But thanks. I was sweating bullets all the way till we got the gates as closed as they get and started pumping water out of the pool."

"Everybody was," Jerry said. Anyone who wasn't nervous about Humpty Dumpty probably wasn't the brightest bulb on the Christmas tree, either. It could still hit the *Glomar Explorer* with whatever it had used on the K-129. But this was a different worry: fear of success, not fear of failure.

"Where's the airlock or whatever it is? I want to get some shots of that," Dave said.

Jerry pointed. "Starboard side. You can hardly see it. Clementine's big claw is kind of wrapped around it."

"Ahh, you're right. So it is," Dave said. "Eventually, people like you and Steve and the guys we'll be bringing in on the B crew will start working out how to go inside and just what we've got here."

"The B crew?" Jerry had heard the phrase at meals a few times, but he wasn't clear about what it meant.

"Uh-huh. We're the A crew. For most of us, getting Humpty Dumpty up from the bottom was the big deal. The B crew will come out and exploit it more after we get where we're going. You and Steve will be part of that, too—don't worry."

"Oh." Of course, Jerry did worry. More hotshot experts would come aboard the *Glomar Explorer* and not want to notice a lowly grad student (a redundancy, if ever there was one). He asked, "What are we doing now? Where are we going? We're not staying here, right?"

"We sure aren't," Dave said. "We sent out a message in the clear days ago, saying that something had gone wrong with the nodule collector and asking if we can go to an area near Midway to see what we can do about repairs. In case you don't know, the Navy runs Midway."

"I did sorta know, yeah. It's a big breeding reserve for albatrosses, isn't it?"

"That's right. And the Navy has generously said it'll let us use Site 126–1." Dave barked laughter. "The Navy did everything it could to keep the Agency from raising Humpty Dumpty. They wanted to do it themselves. If they'd tried, they'd still be yelling at each other about the design and the Russians would know all about it."

Jerry didn't argue. He did wonder what the Navy would say about the CIA. Since they were heading toward Midway, he might get to find out. He admired the way the CIA gave a plausible excuse for leaving the middle of nowhere and heading south.

"Can we do whatever we need to do near Midway or on it or however that works?" he asked.

Dave Schoals shook his head. "I don't think so. That's probably just temporary, to let us get started. We'll do most of the work in Hawaii. We've got a berth reserved in the harbor at Lahaina. You know, on Maui."

"I do know." Jerry felt a small pang. He and Anna had had—did have again, he hoped—a room reserved at the Sheraton near Lahaina for their honeymoon. When they eventually got there from Honolulu, he'd have to remember to act as if he were seeing everything for the first time.

He couldn't tell her what he'd been doing while they were first scheduled to get married. Past *out in the Pacific*, he couldn't tell her where he'd been. He didn't like the idea of polluting his marriage with lies and silences. Anna, a forthright person if ever there was one, would like it even less.

Why didn't you worry about that more before you said you'd do this? he asked himself. But he knew the answer: $2,933 a month, all wedding expenses reimbursed, and two grand of mad money. And a starship in the moon pool, even if they hadn't told him about that when John P. banged on his door.

The sailors brought in the two Waverider buoys whose electronics had helped position the *Glomar Explorer* as precisely as the job required. Each of the fancy gadgets was tethered to the ocean floor by a three-mile cable much less formidable than the pipe string that had gone down with Clementine to grab Humpty Dumpty. The men didn't bother bringing up the cable; they let it sink after securing the buoys.

"If the Russians in the tugs had taken one of the Waveriders, what could they have learned from it?" Jerry asked Jack Porter.

"We would have done what we could to stop that," the security director answered. "Our electronics are better than theirs— sometimes a little, sometimes a lot. They aren't better to the point where the Russians can't imitate our stuff if they get hold of it."

That was about what Jerry had thought. He and Jack were eating lunch in the messroom. He had salmon croquettes, while Jack was working his way through two slices of roast pork. "I wouldn't have been able to do this before Vatican II," Jack remarked.

"Hadn't even thought of that," Jerry said. He didn't keep kosher; he'd just felt like fish. Friday dinner was fried shrimp and fried oysters. He intended to pig out. The dinner menu might have been a reminder of the days when Catholics weren't supposed to eat meat on Fridays. A lot of restaurants still served clam chowder as their Friday soup, too.

As he ate the croquettes, his mind kept wandering back to Humpty Dumpty. There in the moon pool lay technology the Russians wouldn't be able to imitate. He wondered if his own country could. And, again, he wondered whether it should. That felt like cheating. Or did he think it felt that way because Andre Norton's *The Time Traders* and its sequels still echoed in his mind?

He went out to the moon pool after lunch. Dave was there before him, calling instructions to a couple of men in radiation suits who aimed Geiger counters at the spaceship from close range. "Any extra hot stuff?" Jerry asked him.

"Just a little at both ends—above background level, but not enough to be dangerous," the recovery director answered over the chug of the small pumps that took care of the imperfect seal be-tween the lips of the center well's bottom gates. Dave added, "Of course, we don't know how well the hull shields us from whatever's inside it."

"Uh-huh." Jerry looked down over the rail. Three or four dead fish lay on top of the gates. He pointed at them. "We ought to pitch those, or else we'll smell 'em all over the ship."

Dave Schoals burst out laughing. Jerry cocked his head to one side. He didn't think he'd said anything funny, but he'd cracked Dave up. "Sorry," Schoals said after a bit. "Oh, my. You weren't around for that."

"I wasn't around for what?" Jerry asked, more sharply than he might have. Every so often, he got tired of being reminded he was still the new kid. Not as if he didn't know it himself.

"They built—we built—Clementine inside this great big roofed, submersible barge. Hughes Mining Barge Number One, we called it, because Hughes is fronting this operation," Dave said. "It was made in Northern California, then towed down to a cove off Cata-lina Island and sunk there so the *Glomar Explorer* could get Clem-entine into the moon pool without anybody watching. You with me so far?"

"I think so," Jerry answered.

"Good deal. Just to make things extra secure, we made the transfer at night. That was when the bottom gates got messed up, too, and we never could quite fix 'em right. But I'm not talking about that. When we did the transfer, we had the inside of the moon pool all lit up, 'cause we needed to see what was going on."

"Uh-oh! And the lights drew fish?"

"Almost. They drew squid, thousands and thousands of squid. By the time we got the claw up there and the gates as closed as they were gonna get, ol' Clementine was ass-deep in calamari, just about. And the stink after they died . . . !" Dave shook his head. "Lasted for weeks. We hosed the walls down. We scrubbed 'em down. Over and over, I mean. Still smelled like dead squid. So now you know."

"Now I know," Jerry agreed, and wondered if he was being too prickly. To keep from dwelling on that, he pointed to Clementine's central claw, the thick one. "When will the guys in Control loosen that up some? If we're gonna get inside, we'll probably start trying with the airlock thingy, right?"

"Hmm." Dave scratched at one ear. Instead of answering, he said, "Your hair's a lot longer than mine. Don't know how you stand it. I grew mine out mostly so my ears would get covered over—ears are great identifiers on photos. But it tickles and makes me itch all the goddamn time."

Ears are great identifiers. If letting your hair get long to keep the other side's spies from figuring out who you were wasn't the most CIA thing in the world, Jerry couldn't imagine what would be. He replied, "It doesn't bother me. Guess I'm just used to it. Women wear theirs long most of the time. Doesn't seem to give them any trouble."

"Yeah, that's true." By the thoughtful way Dave said it, what women did hadn't occurred to him till that moment. Maybe that also explained a thing or two about why he was single again. Or maybe not. Before Jerry could decide if the thought was worth following, the recovery director came back to what he'd asked: "We *can* loosen the grip. The hydraulics are still hooked up and everything. When we decide to knock on that door, we'll be able to go inside once it opens."

"Any thoughts about when we start doing that?" Jerry asked. He suspected he might be the one they'd want to take the first whack at it. Making contact with whatever Humpty Dumpty held was the reason he and Steve were here. Wouldn't Dave and Dale and Jack figure a grad student was more expendable than a senior expert?

Wouldn't they be right? Sure they would. All the same, he felt like a *Star Trek* extra in a red shirt, doomed to die before the next commercial break.

"Right now, I think the plan is to wait till we get to the site off Midway," Dave said carefully. "I'm pretty sure we'll want to take a shot at it before we head for Lahaina. If anything goes wrong, better it goes wrong where there aren't many eyes around."

"That might be good, yeah," Jerry said. If a death ray incinerated the *Glomar Explorer* in Lahaina harbor, people would talk. And in case strange space bacteria started turning the crewfolk green with orange polka dots, they also probably ought to do it well out to sea.

Dave nodded. "Glad you think so."

Jerry raised an eyebrow at the tone. Said another way, the words would have been sarcastic enough to sting. But Schoals sounded as if he meant them. Jerry was no more used to getting taken seriously by older people than any other grad student—hell, than any other twenty-six-year-old.

I could start enjoying this, he thought, and then, *If it ever happens again, I mean.* He had trouble taking himself seriously, too.

Midway lay about 725 nautical miles south and a little east of where the Glomar Explorer had plucked Humpty Dumpty from the bottom of the Pacific. Jerry used nautical miles for some of his work, but he didn't think in them. A little slide-rule work told him they made 835 statute miles, more or less. That, he could wrap his head around.

The *Explorer* cruised at ten knots, so Site 126–1 was about three days away. Jerry thought he would sleep and relax on the trip: he couldn't do anything that involved the spaceship in the moon pool. Orders were to look but not to touch, no matter what.

"We mean that. We no-shit mean it," Jack Porter told him. "Remember the nondisclosure agreement you signed before Steve would clue you in on what we were really going after?"

"You mean the one that talked about 'termination with extreme prejudice'?" Jerry said.

"Yeah. That one." The security director nodded.

"Nah. Remind me again what it said."

Jack snorted. "Funny guy! Listen up, funny guy. This is like that. If anybody lays a finger on Humpty Dumpty before we're ready, we'll dip the stupid son of a bitch in ketchup and drop him into the Pacific for the sharks' brunch buffet. You get me, or do I have to make that plainer?"

"I hear you. I'll be good," Jerry said. "But if anybody's awake inside Humpty Dumpty, or even if that was a robot that fried the K-129, don't you think it might have suspected something when a giant steel claw on the end of a pipe string grabbed hold of it and hauled it up here?"

"Clementine's a tool, a thing. People are people. That may not make any difference. But it may, too. Can you tell me for certain that whatever's in there doesn't read minds if somebody touches it?"

"You sure *you* aren't the skiffy writer?" Jerry said. Jack laughed and waved away the compliment, if it was one. Jerry continued, "If it does read minds, I bet it doesn't need contact, though. The Russian sub was three miles above it when it did . . . whatever it did."

Jack grunted. "There is that. We don't want to take chances even so. Hear me?"

"I already said so once."

Jerry waited. If Jack got huffy about that, he meant to get huffy right back. Being expendable brought certain advantages . . . till expending time came, anyhow. But the security officer just said, "Okay, fine," and left it alone. Jerry felt deflated. He'd braced himself for a fight that didn't happen.

The weather got warmer as the *Glomar Explorer* chugged south. In California, 40 degrees north latitude was well north of San Francisco, about halfway between Fort Bragg and Eureka. Midway, on the other hand, lay at 28 degrees north. That parallel split Baja California into two equal parts.

He'd seen albatrosses while the ship was grappling for and grappling with Humpty Dumpty. The gooney birds had wingspans that put him in mind of light planes. However magnificently they flew, though, they were as avid for garbage as Hermosa Beach herring gulls. The farther south the *Explorer* came, the more of them there were to squabble over the uneaten food the ship threw into the ocean.

Steve pointed at one that rose now after skimming along the surface of the sea. "I think it's eating a big piece of cellophane."

"That can't be good for it. Probably figured it caught a jellyfish or something," Jerry said. "People throw all kinds of shit into the ocean these days. I wonder how much of it birds and fish and sea turtles try to eat. A lot, I bet."

"Whales and porpoises, too," Steve said.

"Yeah." Jerry scratched his head. "That might be interesting, y'know? I don't remember any research studies about it. Not saying there aren't any, but I've never run across one."

"Have you ever looked?"

"Not really, but I've pawed through a bunch of journals doing homework for the diss. If I'd seen an article like that in a table of contents or flipped past it going to something I was after, I'd know I had." Jerry was proud of his memory. It let him do things most people couldn't, or not so easily. It let him be right most of the time, too. Only very slowly was he starting to wonder if being right most of the time wasn't an overrated talent.

Steve didn't challenge him. He said, "My mind works the same way."

"Comes in handy," Jerry said. A fair number of people who went into the sciences had minds like that. *Able to leap tall mountains of data at a single bound!* he thought. Again more slowly than he might have, he was beginning to realize the wider world did things differently.

"What's that one got?" Steve pointed again.

"Half a hamburger bun, looks like," Jerry said—burgers had been on the lunch menu. "That won't hurt it."

"I guess not." Steve changed the subject: "Have you thought about what we'll do if we get inside Humpty Dumpty?"

"Never once crossed my mind," Jerry answered, deadpan.

Stephen Dole started to gape, then stopped and exhaled through his nose. He was more annoyed at himself than at Jerry, for he said, "I should be used to your sense of humor by now."

"Always nice to know somebody thinks I've got one," Jerry said. "The thing I really hope is that we don't do too much damage breaking into the spaceship. That could be bad all kinds of ways."

"Bad for us or bad for whoever or whatever's in there?"

"Yes," Jerry said. Steve started to give him a fishy look, but pulled his face straight in a hurry. It wasn't as if Jerry was wrong. Obviously, smashing a hole in Humpty Dumpty or breaking in through what everybody thought was the airlock could do all kinds of destructive work. Just as obviously, the starship could do a lot of that, too. Anyone who doubted it had only to look at the photo of the skeleton in seaboots next to the K-129.

After a moment, Steve said, "You pack a lot into a little, don't you?"

"Well, I try," Jerry said. That was a useful knack for a writer, perhaps less so when talking: speech had repetition and redundancy built in, because it was there and then gone. He went on, "What if we can't get in any easy way? Whatever goes into Humpty Dumpty's shell, we don't know anything about it."

"True. It can't be weak. It survived space travel and years three miles underwater. I've talked with Dale about that. I've urged him not to be too, well, heroic trying to break in."

"Good. That's good." Jerry silently clapped his hands together.

"You could have done the same thing, you know. You should have."

"He wouldn't have paid any attention to *me!*" Jerry said it as if it were a law of nature. To him, it was. Professors and other senior people never paid attention to grad students unless they needed something from them.

But Steve shook his head. "I think he would have. I think he still will, if you go talk with him. You know more about what's likely to be in there than anybody else on the ship. That's what you're here for."

"I don't know a goddamn thing. And c'mon, Steve! You're sand-bagging like a son of a bitch."

"Not me. I'm a reliable academic type who's thought some about extraterrestrial life. That's why *I'm* here. But you're the one who's done all the wondering and played things out in his head. I wouldn't have come up with half the scenarios you gave Dale."

"Sure you would. Only reason I spun them out in a hurry was, I was stealing from half the things I've read. That doesn't exactly qualify me to meet the first aliens, if any aliens are in there to meet."

"Nobody knows what qualifies someone to do that. A habit of thinking about it can't hurt."

He made a certain amount of sense, even if Jerry didn't want to admit it. To keep from admitting it, he said, "One thing I'm pretty sure of—if Humpty Dumpty does hatch little green men, the politicians'll grab 'em so fast it'll make your head spin. I've got a hundred bucks that says Henry Kissinger starts picking their pockets by this time next Wednesday."

"No bet," Steve said.

In spite of nerves that made his stomach knot, Jerry did go see Dale Neuwirth. He worked himself up to knock on the mission director's door, then found he didn't have to: it was open. Warily, he stuck his head inside. Dale was scribbling notes at his desk. When he looked up, Jerry said, "If you're real busy now, I can come back."

"Don't come back. Come in," Neuwirth said. "Shut the door behind you and grab a chair. I see so little of you, I worry. You keep to yourself even more than the guys in the Control container."

"I do?" Jerry said in surprise; he hadn't even noticed. But he realized Dale wasn't wrong. As he sat, he went on, "I was talking with Steve, and I just wanted to let you know I think he's right—we'd better not get too rough with Humpty Dumpty."

"We don't have flamethrowers or artillery. I'm not going to break out one of the rifles and blow the lock off the door—if it has a lock," Dale said. "We have power saws aboard, too. I won't use one of them, either."

"Okay. I'm real glad to hear it."

"Whatever's in there, it belongs to a civilization that can do all kinds of things we can't. Fly here from wherever it started, for instance. And sink that Russian sub from three miles under it. Getting all tough-guy with it doesn't seem smart."

"Not to me, either," Jerry said. "If we mess this up, we may not get a second chance." He thought of Inca sentries watching Spaniards rowing ashore from their galleons. They'd be freaking out. They couldn't build ships like that. What kind of powerful strangers could?

Before long, they found out.

Dale said, "What I will do tomorrow is have Clementine's central claw retracted so it doesn't obstruct the airlock . . . if that is an airlock. A day or two after that, we can find out whether there's any obvious way in."

"'We'?" Jerry echoed. *Waddaya mean, we, Kemosabe?* went through his head. He didn't come out with that, luckily. He just asked, "Do you mean me?"

"Are you volunteering?" Dale returned. "If you are, you're the logical person to try it first. If you're not, I won't order you to and I won't hold it against you. I wouldn't order any man to risk his life. I understand you'd be doing that here."

"I've been risking my life ever since I signed up to go after the K-129, haven't I?" Jerry said. He hesitated again. He'd known there was danger since he found out the sub lay on the bottom because it did something—nobody was sure what, even now—to piss off the starship that got there first. But the danger of just knocking on Humpty Dumpty's door seemed a lot more immediate. He sighed. "Yeah, I guess I'm volunteering. This is what I came along for, isn't it?"

"Nobody came along to be a victim." Dale was thinking along with him, all right. "The goal is to get inside and learn as much as we can. There are risks involved, sure. But we've run risks since we started lowering Clementine toward Humpty Dumpty."

Clementine. Humpty Dumpty. The names sounded innocent—comical, even. No one on the K-129 was laughing. No one on the *Glomar Explorer*, either. Yeah, this was for keeps. Jerry sighed again. "Okay."

Tape the booties over the protective outer suit. Feel all around each calf to make sure the seal was tight. Tape the surgical gloves over the ends of the suit's sleeves. Southpaw Jerry had no problem doing up his right arm. Using his off hand to secure things on his left was harder, but he managed. He nodded to Dave, who was watching as he and Steve put on the gear that might or might not save their skins. "Glad I had some practice."

"Good. That's good." The recovery director nodded back. No *I told you so* in his tone or manner. He was a pro. He helped Jerry with the straps that held the air tank on his back, then did the same for Steve. "Remember, start using them as soon as you go into the moon pool. You have forty-five minutes after that."

"Gotcha," Jerry said. Steve nodded. They both wore their watches outside their overgarments, Jerry on his right wrist, Steve on his left. Mask and mouthpiece should protect against a poisonous atmosphere, at least long enough for them to get away. The gear ought to keep out germs, too. But if superheated steam or frigid methane came out . . .

That was why Dale had asked for volunteers. And he'd got two. Why he'd got two—

Worry about it later, Jerry told himself. *If you can.*

"You guys ready?" Dave asked. Behind the mask, Jerry looked at Steve. The older man was looking back at him. Neither of them said no. Dave set his hand first on Steve's shoulder, then on Jerry's. "Good luck. I mean it, from the bottom of my heart."

He undogged the watertight door that gave access to the center well from floor level. Jerry stuck in the breathing apparatus's mouthpiece. It tasted rubbery, but not unpleasant. *Inhale through your mouth, exhale through your nose, just like you've practiced.*

As the door opened, he flicked the valve that started air flowing. He stepped out into the moon pool. Steve followed. Dave shut the door behind them. Jerry heard him secure it, too. They were on their own.

Humpty Dumpty seemed much bigger when you looked up at it, not down on it. *The enormous egg,* Jerry thought, and flashed on another of the very first sort-of-sf books he'd ever read. Clementine looked a lot more massive this way, too. A couple of thousand tons of steel? He believed every ounce.

People were peering down at Steve and him from the edge of the moon pool. Jack Porter was filming with a movie camera. Someone else immortalized the moment on videotape. Jerry couldn't see who; the video camera was bulkier than the 16-millimeter movie machine.

Since the mouthpiece didn't let him talk, he printed on a scratch pad and held it up for Steve to see: *Let's do it.* He couldn't wear his glasses under the mask, so he had to hold the pad close to his face to see what he was doing.

Steve gave him a thumbs-up. They walked toward the capture vehicle's center claw . . . and toward the circle scribed in Humpty Dumpty's nacreous shell. The claw had moved away enough to let a reasonably slim person slip between it and the starship. Jerry and Steve both qualified.

Jerry remembered every moment leading up to his doctoral orals the winter before. He remembered leaving the department lounge with Professor Krikorian and walking across the hall to the conference room where the rest of the examining committee waited. He remembered how tight his necktie felt. He didn't wear them very often, and got reminded why every time he did. And he remembered the dreadfully final click as the conference-room door closed behind him.

(Of the orals themselves, he recalled very little. They'd asked him things. He'd answered as best he could. He'd stood out in the hallway again afterward, this time with the door closed against him, while the committee decided his fate. Only when Professor Krikorian emerged with a smile on his face and with his arm thrust out for a congratulatory handshake was Jerry sure he'd passed.)

He knew he would remember this approach across puddled steel the same way he remembered that shorter trip to the other side of the corridor. If he lived to be ninety, both would stay vivid in his mind. And if he didn't live to be ninety . . . it was liable to be because he died in the next couple of minutes. He tried without much luck not to think about that.

He wrote on the scratch pad again and showed it to Steve. *Stay well back. If it's too cold or too hot in there, don't let it get us both.*

Steve held his pad out at arm's length as he wrote his reply. Where Jerry had trouble seeing at a distance, the older man couldn't focus in close. Jerry had to lean in to make out his words: *I want to be able to help you if I need to.*

See what happens to me before you get close, Jerry wrote. He nodded vigorously to emphasize that, and pointed at Steve to drive it home. Then he waited till Steve nodded. Steve wanted to be brave. Jerry didn't want him to be stupid—or to need to be brave.

He squeezed between the claw and the spaceship. The lower

edge of the circle ran at about the level of his waist. He looked for a doorbell or a latch or anything suggesting a way to signal or a way in. Finding none, he did what anyone facing a closed door might do. He knocked.

He heard the sound his latex-covered knuckles made. It didn't sound like knocking on metal—more as if he were hitting pottery or wood. It felt . . . odd. He wasn't sure he'd actually touched anything material.

After a minute or so, he knocked again. He waited one more minute, thinking hard. He'd done a lot of that since talking with Dale, and before, too. He found himself in the same pickle as Frodo, Gandalf, and the rest of the Nine Walkers in front of the Doors of Durin, with wolves closing in. Durin's doors stayed stubbornly closed, too.

They did, at any rate, till Gandalf solved their riddle. Jerry thought the same trick worth a try. The best thing it had going for it was, he didn't see how it could hurt.

Thinking friendly thoughts, he yanked out his mouthpiece and loudly said, "Friend!" Quick as he could, he stuffed it back in. By the time he drew his next breath, the doorway had opened.

VIII

O h, fuck me, Jerry thought. Since he was breathing through the mouthpiece, he couldn't say the words out loud, but he thought them at the top of his lungs. He had no idea whether the door had slid aside, irised open, or simply disappeared. Whatever had happened, the obstruction wasn't there anymore.

He also realized he hadn't been steamed, broiled, or turned into a Popsicle. He was damn glad he hadn't, not that he could have done anything about it if he had. If viruses were penetrating his suit and trying to infect him with the Alien Itch, he couldn't do anything about that, either.

He peered down the entranceway. It looked . . . dark and blurry. Maybe he should have thought about contact lenses before he signed up for this mad jaunt. Maybe he shouldn't have signed up to begin with.

But then somebody else would be looking down this tube. Or maybe the CIA would have got someone who didn't have *The Lord of the Rings* infused in him the way hot water had Lipton's. In that case, Humpty Dumpty might still be a closed book.

Steve came up, eyes wide and staring behind his mask. He held up his scratch pad. *How did you do that?* he'd written.

Clean living and no fried food, Jerry answered. Aboard the *Glomar Explorer*, at least, the second half of that was bound to be a lie.

Do we go inside? Steve asked. He didn't try to give orders. Jerry had easily done what he must have thought hard or impossible. To Steve, that had to mean Jerry knew what he was up to and deserved to decide things.

It'd be nice if that were true, Jerry thought. He'd tried it mostly because it was quick, simple, and nondestructive. When it actually worked . . . He still felt dazed. Too much was happening too fast.

But the answer wouldn't wait. *I guess we do*, he wrote. He showed Steve the paper, then tore it off, folded it, and stuck it in a pocket. These conversations were supposed to be preserved for history, assuming history gave a damn about contemporary maundering.

Gulping and hoping like hell he didn't tear the protective suit, he scrambled up into the airlock, if that was what it was. As soon as he did, the inner walls in the corridor—all curved and rounded, not with hard, human-style right angles—started to glow softly. Humpty Dumpty sensed it had company. That was beautiful and scary at the same time.

Jerry turned around and held out a hand to help Steve in. The man from the RAND Corporation wasn't so young anymore and might not be up to climbing into things. Latex met latex as Stephen Dole grabbed hold of him and scrambled into the spaceship, too.

One of the pouches on Steve's belt held a camera. He took it out and started using it. *How come I didn't get one?* Jerry wondered. But that was another easy question, wasn't it? The first red-shirt down on some new planet didn't have a prayer of lasting long enough to collect residuals.

He took three or four steps down the corridor. It felt as real and unreal at the same time under his feet as the outside of the entrance-way had to his knuckles. If this was an airlock, its inner door had disappeared at the same time as the outer one, and as completely.

Steve followed his lead. Stowing the camera, he wrote, *Wonder what the atmosphere is. Not too different from ours?*

Pressure seems close to the same, anyway, Jerry answered. There hadn't been any big whoosh of air in or out when the door vanished. Then again, who could say anything for sure about how Humpty Dumpty worked?

If the air the aliens who'd built the starship liked wasn't too different from Earth's, why not take off the masks, breathe it, and talk instead of writing? Why not? Jerry imagined spores, bacteria, and viruses, all waiting to chow down on a tasty human after going hungry for Lord only knew how many years. He left his mask on.

A glance at his watch told him he'd been breathing from the tank for six minutes. It only *felt* like six months. *How brave do you want to be?* he asked Steve.

I don't want to lose sight of the way out, the older man wrote.

Jerry nodded. *Sounds like a plan.*

We should've grabbed some bread crumbs from the galley so we could leave a trail, he thought, remembering "Hansel and Gretel" from some long-vanished kids' book of fairy tales. What would eat the crumbs in these corridors? *Do I really want to find out?*

Instead of bread crumbs, the next time they came in they'd bring a roll of nylon twine or something that they could unspool behind them as they went. That had worked for good old What's-his-name in the Minotaur's Labyrinth. It ought to do the trick here, too.

Down the passageway they went, Jerry leading, Steve a pace behind. He hoped they would find more writing, if the stuff on the outside was writing. No such luck. For all Jerry knew, the stuff on the outside was an advertisement. If buses had them, why not spaceships?

They came to the end of the stretch of corridor that led in from the entrance. It branched there, going left and right. On the wall of the left branch was a yellow line—not a straight line (Jerry had started wondering if the aliens believed in straight lines), but a line. A little beyond it was an opening in the wall. Another corridor? A way up? A way down? He couldn't tell.

Steve took more pictures, facing into both branches. Then he stashed the camera in his belt pouch. He wrote on the pad again: *Let's go.*

Jerry didn't argue with him. They'd got in. Nothing had tried to kill them. For a first try, that would do. They retraced their steps, Steve in the lead this time. He turned around and got down, awkwardly leaving Humpty Dumpty tuchus-first. Jerry jumped down, feet thumping on the steel of the gate with a good honest thud.

Steve was staring and pointing. Jerry spun around. The airlock door was back in place. How it had got there, Jerry had no idea. Chances were, no one else on Earth did, either.

The *Glomar Explorer* didn't have a conference room. Dale Neuwirth's cabin did duty for one now. The mission director was there, along with Jack and Dave and Steve and Jerry. There weren't enough chairs. Jack and Dave sat on the bed.

Dale shut the door and locked it. He put on a Bing Crosby tape to make sure no one going down the corridor could overhear anything that went on. Jerry let out a resigned internal sigh—it was his father's kind of music. The other men in the cabin seemed to enjoy it. *They would*, he thought.

"Doc Borden says you guys both check out clean, as far as he can tell," Dale said. "You feel all right?"

"Fine," Stephen Dole answered.

"I guess so," Jerry said. After getting out of the suit, getting checked for radioactivity, and taking three showers with hot water, harsh soap, and a brush, he'd fallen into the doctor's hands. He'd breathed over culture medium. He'd spat into another flask of it. Then he'd had his mouth cleansed with nasty antiseptic, his mouth and as far down his throat as a swab would reach without making him puke. After that, he'd had to turn the other cheek for an enema. He'd enjoyed none of it.

"Good. We have to be careful, you know," Dale said. Jerry grudged a nod, wishing he could take everything in stride like Steve. The mission director went on, "I want to congratulate you for finding a nondestructive way to get into Humpty Dumpty. Your cleverness will be noted in the report."

"Uh, thanks," Jerry said. By the way Dave and Jack looked at him, they thought that was a bigger deal than he did. Well, they were career CIA guys. *What if you're a career alien-relations guy all of a sudden?* he asked himself. Yeah, what if?

"How did you think of something so simple and so brilliant?" Dale asked.

"You really wanna know?" Jerry laughed. Then he told him, and the others.

Dale, Jack, and Dave all wore identical *Am I really hearing this?* expressions. Steve said, "Gentlemen, I'd like to remind you John P. chose Jerry for a reason. Now you see what the reason was, and that it's a good one. I've thought so all along."

"It worked. Hard to knock stuff that works." Jack then proceeded to do just that: "But how did it work? Why? You're not going to tell me Humpty Dumpty understands English?" By the way he stuck out his jaw, he'd get mad fast if Jerry tried telling him that.

"Humpty Dumpty doesn't understand English," Dave said decisively, before Jerry could answer. "Paul went out there and said 'Friend' at it over and over, and it didn't open up."

"When Gandalf did it in *The Fellowship of the Ring*, he said, '*Mellon!*' That's Elvish for 'friend,'" Jerry said. By the looks on the older men's faces, they didn't want to hear about Elvish. Jerry went on anyway: "I don't think Humpty Dumpty speaks English, either. Or Elvish, for that matter. But when I said 'Friend,' I wasn't just saying it. I was thinking about everything friendship means, and that I wasn't dangerous to the starship. My guess is, it picked up on that, not on the word itself."

"A spaceship that *does* read minds?" Jack rolled his eyes. "Give me a break!"

"Could explain why Jerry got the door to open and Paul didn't," Dave observed. "Far as I know, Paul was going through the same motions Jerry did, but without the feeling behind them."

"Sounds . . . pretty wild," Dale said. Jerry guessed he got as much mileage with that as one of the pipe-farm guys did with ten minutes of inspired cussing.

"Maybe it isn't. We can measure brain waves and stuff," Jerry said. "If Humpty Dumpty's sensitive enough and smart enough to do it at a distance and analyze what it means . . . It wouldn't be telepathy or anything."

"It would be about as good, though," Steve put in.

"Doesn't seem likely." Jack thrust out his jaw again and looked stubborn.

"Nothing about this seems likely," Dave said. "How likely is it that we've got a spaceship lying in the moon pool? Based on everything we thought, everything we knew, before the *Halibut* took those photos, unlikely as hell. But Humpty Dumpty's there. Likely or not, that's *true*. We've gotta deal with it."

"That is a scientific attitude," Dale said.

"Engineering attitude," Dave replied. "Scientists worry about how and why things happen. Engineers don't care. We just want to know *what* happens. Then we go on from there."

"I've heard engineers at Livermore talk the same way," Dale said, his voice dry as a martini wished it were.

"I bet you have. You need people like that to keep the theoretical guys from inflating like helium balloons and floating away from reality," Dave said.

"Play nice, boys." Jack Porter sounded amused. Then his head swung toward Jerry and Steve. "Okay. You two got in, and—"

"Jerry got us in," Steve interrupted. "Give him the credit. You'd blame him if we were still stuck outside that door."

The security director plainly didn't want to give Jerry any credit. He muttered something that sounded like, "Elvish!" But then he eyed Jerry. "Do you think you can pull your trick twice?"

"I'll try. That's as much as I can tell you right now. I'm not the only player in the game, remember. Humpty Dumpty's playing, too," Jerry said.

"If you do get in again . . ." No, Jack didn't seem happy about dealing in uncertainties. "If you get in, what do you think you should do when you explore more of the interior?"

Slowly, Jerry answered. "Well, that yellow line on the corridor wall is interesting, because we didn't see anything else like it. Maybe we should follow the yellow brick line?"

"Brick?" Jack didn't get it. That made Jerry sad. He'd had the Oz books read to him, then read them himself. He'd seen *The Wizard of Oz* a bunch of times, the first several on a black-and-white TV that muted the difference between Kansas and Technicolor Oz.

Steve understood him. Dale and Dave did, too. Dale said, "I think Jerry has the right idea."

"I agree," Steve said. "Something that breaks a pattern needs to be looked at more closely than the elements that make up the pattern."

"Oz. You were talking about Oz." Jack sounded accusing. The light had gone on—more slowly than it might have, but it had.

"Who, me?" Jerry'd had a light go on more slowly than it might have, too. He wished he'd BSed about how he'd managed to get the starship to open up for him. Now that the CIA guys knew, too, they could beat the outer door the same way he had. He *thought* they could, anyhow.

"You'll carry walkie-talkies. With luck, they'll let you communicate with us after you get out of sight," Dave said.

"We'd have to take out our mouthpieces inside Humpty Dumpty to use them," Jerry pointed out. "Do you want us doing that? I mean, the temperature was okay and all, but we don't know if that was real air in there, even if it mixed okay with what we brought in when we went inside."

"We don't know about any bacteria or viruses it carries, either," Steve added.

"Okay. I didn't think that one through, obviously," Dave said. Jerry admired him for admitting it without fussing. The recovery director went on, "Well, we'll come up with something—unless we don't, of course."

"You really know how to cheer us up, don't you?" Jerry said.

"I try," Dave said. Jerry laughed. Dave wasn't and never would be the funniest guy in the world, but he did try. Considering what he could have been, that counted.

A copter landed on the helipad at the *Glomar Explorer*'s stern. It wore white American stars, not red Soviet ones. It looked sleeker than the chopper the *Chazhma* had carried. How much that mattered, Jerry had no idea. The Russian machine (people who knew such things had told him it was a Kamov Ka-25) seemed to do its job just fine.

Half a dozen men got out of the whirlybird. They carried suitcases and duffel bags. *Some of the B crew*, Jerry thought. He'd wondered if they would import a real sf writer to take his place, somebody like Heinlein or Asimov or Niven or Anderson. None of the people on the helipad looked familiar that way, he noted with a certain amount of relief.

Of course, that proved nothing. This would only be the first bunch of new people. Every time a helicopter set down, he'd have to worry.

The new men wandered off the helipad. Stewards took charge of them. They'd have to learn their way around, as Jerry had. He smiled: he liked that. He wasn't, or didn't feel like, a freshman anymore.

Doc Borden was one of the people who boarded the copter for the flight back to Midway, and presumably on to civilization from there. Jerry supposed that meant one of the newcomers was a doctor, too. The NSA guys who'd used Clementine to seize Humpty Dumpty also left the *Glomar Explorer*. The capture vehicle wouldn't have anything more to do this trip. The last departing man from the A crew was the engineer who'd had the mild heart attack. He'd done fine since then, but he'd probably want his own doc to look him over once he got to wherever he lived.

A voice from behind Jerry made him jump: "We still seem to be on the roster."

"You snuck up on me, man," Jerry accused Steve. "But yeah, for now."

"I was wondering if they'd bring out somebody like Carl Sagan, someone with a big reputation," Steve said. "And they may yet."

"You mean I'm not the only one who gets all hinky about shit like that?" Jerry said in surprise.

"Now that you mention it," Steve replied, "no. We all like to imagine we're unique and irreplaceable. It's an enjoyable fantasy. If you've got any sense, you know that's all it is. Somebody else can always step into your shoes and do as well as you did, or close enough for government work."

"Government work." The phrase tasted raunchy in Jerry's mouth, like lunch meat that had sat in the fridge three days too long. "Does it ever bother you that this is all government work?"

"This is the most exciting, important, worthwhile thing I've ever done in my life. If it weren't government work, how would it get done? Who else would have found the K-129, and Humpty Dumpty next to it? Who else would have laid out as much as it costs for a Moon mission to build this ship and haul Humpty Dumpty off the bottom? Flying men to the Moon is government work, too, by the way."

Jerry started to come back with something sharp, then realized he didn't have anything sharp to come back with. "Well, hush my mouth," he mumbled.

Steve didn't rub it in. He wasn't the type. He just said, "Think it through." That was a good idea any old time.

Even so, talking about something, anything, else also seemed a good idea right now. "Does President Ford know we've been inside the spaceship?" Jerry asked. No matter what Steve thought about government work, Jerry was damn glad he didn't need to ask about President Nixon anymore.

"I'm sure he does. I haven't asked Dale, but we wouldn't hold back on anything like that—especially when we got in and got out without losing anybody or doing any damage." The man from the RAND Corporation might be quiet, but he was cynical enough for all ordinary use.

"Makes sense." Jerry nodded, then chuckled, "I wonder if Dave wrote more innocent-text poetry to pass the word along."

Steve laughed, too. "I hope so! You know the code message that announced Fermi had got a chain reaction going in the pile at the University of Chicago, don't you?"

"Sorry, no." Jerry shook his head in embarrassment. "What was it?"

"'You'll be interested to know that the Italian navigator has just landed in the New World,'" Steve quoted.

"I can dig it!" Jerry said. "Echoes back to Columbus—and man, whoever came up with it sure wasn't wrong." His head swung toward the moon pool. "Different now. The new world's landed on us."

"So it has. So it has."

There were new faces in the messroom at lunch. Having seen only the same old ones for most of the past two months, Jerry found himself wondering how the men from B crew would fit in. The

A crew had worried all the time, first that they'd be able to raise Humpty Dumpty from the seafloor, and then that they'd be able to get inside once the spaceship lay on the leaky gates under the moon pool.

B crew didn't have to sweat any of that. They would deal with knowns, not unknowns. Except for one, of course. Nobody knew what would anger the aliens or robots in charge of the starship. If anything did, a new wreck would lie on the bottom of the Pacific. *I'm not even wearing seaboots,* Jerry thought.

After lunch, he went forward to the moon pool to look at the starship. Several people were always doing that. He saw three or four of the new men staring at it as if they couldn't believe their eyes. Had anyone briefed them on the true story till they got to Midway, or had they signed up like him, thinking they were going after the sunken Russian submarine?

One of the strangers came over to him and held out his hand. "Hi. I'm John Rogers. I'm John Rogers here, anyway," he said. He was about forty, suntanned and fit, and had a disarming smile. "I'm the new doctor."

"Nice to meet you. I'm Jerry Steinberg. Like you say, that's who I am here, I mean. I do oceanography and stuff." Even with somebody who was here, Jerry watched what he said. Sure as hell, the CIA had indoctrinated him whether it meant to or not.

Rogers pointed down at Humpty Dumpty. "That's the most astonishing thing I've ever seen in my life."

"I said the same thing. Everybody does," Jerry said.

"I believe it. What else can you say? Did I hear right? Did somebody really smart figure out how to get in there without blowing it up?"

"Somebody really smart? Nah." Jerry shook his head. "Matter of fact, it was me."

"You're kidding!" the doctor exclaimed. Jerry shook his head again. He knew he didn't look like much: a longhair with a beard, dressed the way he would have been on campus, with a T-shirt, bell-bottom jeans, and his sadly scruffy Blue Tips. John Rogers went on, "That's wonderful! How did you ever do it?"

"I got lucky," Jerry answered, and told again about the Tolkien connection. He wondered if he'd be telling the same story, maybe in the same words, at conferences fifty years from now. He also wondered if he'd ever be able to tell it to people not cleared to hear it.

"You know, I'd tell you you were making that up if I heard it anywhere else," Dr. Rogers said. "When I look at *that*"—he nodded down toward Humpty Dumpty—"I believe you. Nothing seems impossible right now."

"No kidding! If we can figure out even a little bit of what whoever made that can do, the world won't be the same," Jerry said.

"Just seeing it there makes the world not the same," Rogers said. "It tells us this isn't the only world with life on it. That's got to be the biggest news since Columbus got back to Spain with word of the New World."

"Bigger, I bet, but yeah," Jerry said, thinking, *Columbus again!* Next year, NASA planned to launch two Viking probes to Mars to see if life existed on the red planet. Those Vikings would try to learn whether Earth was unique in the universe or life sprang up whenever it got the chance. There in the moon pool lay the answer, shining as if scraped from the inside of a pearl oyster's shell.

"Are you going back inside?" The new man revised the question: "*When* are you going back in?"

"Steve—that's Steven, uh, Dahlgren—and I will take another shot whenever the mission director tells us to," Jerry answered. "I'm trying to get used to being part of a team, not doing my own thing whenever I feel like it."

John Rogers smiled. "What . . . thing were you doing before you wound up on the *Glomar Explorer*?"

"Grad student at UCLA, writing my thesis on whale songs," Jerry said. "This is a little different from that."

"I'll say. They didn't even tell me what they'd brought up from the bottom of the ocean till I got to Midway. Before that, I thought it was . . . I thought it was something else, anyway." Half a beat slower than he might have, he remembered to bow before the great god Security. He'd answered Jerry's unspoken question, though.

Jerry said, "Hey, I didn't find out what was really going on till I was a couple of days out to sea, either. They don't want news of this getting out," Jerry said.

"How can you blame them?" the doctor said.

"Can't." Again, Jerry wondered how much he meant that. Was Humpty Dumpty for the United States or for the whole world? Like

Hamlet's *To be or not to be?*, that *was* the question. Jerry still had no answer he liked. He didn't think he'd do anything like make a beeline for Jack Anderson's office the second he got back on the mainland, but he wasn't sure he wouldn't. As Watergate showed, sometimes the best thing you could do was shine a bright light on stuff.

Sometimes. *How bright a light* can *I shine?* Jerry wondered. Without evidence, Anderson would think he was a nut. So would any reporter in his right mind. Even with evidence, Jerry feared he'd have trouble getting anyone with good, hard common sense to take him seriously. Good, hard common sense argued against things like Humpty Dumpty. Which only went to show what good, hard common sense was or wasn't worth.

Dave Schoals eyed Jerry and Steve in the compartment that opened on to the moon pool. They had their protective suits on once more, all but the masks and mouthpieces. "Here we go again," Dave said, trying to ease the tension he knew was there.

"Here we go again," Steve agreed.

Jerry didn't say anything. His belt had a lot more weight on it this time than it had had when he and Steve first tried to get into the spaceship. No one then had really thought they'd succeed. Now that they'd done it once, they were supposed to do it again. He was equipped accordingly.

He had a scratch pad and three pens. He had his very own Insta-matic, with flash cubes and extra film. He had a flashlight, which could do double duty as a blackjack. He had a walkie-talkie—for emergency use only, everybody told him. And he had a big, fancy Swiss Army knife, with a whole bunch of tools that would probably be useless inside Humpty Dumpty and with a knife blade unlikely to scare off anything the flashlight couldn't deal with. Steve carried the same sort of gear. They also had balls of nylon twine, for find-ing their way out again.

"We'll have people ready to go in after you if you need help," Dave said.

"Far out," Jerry muttered, more sarcastically than not. They were doing what they could. He gave them credit for that. But he didn't think they could do anything that would save Steve and him if trouble came.

"Remember, you're looking for the way down to the engines—or the way up to them," Dave said. "Or the way to the control room, if there is one. Or to the crew quarters, if there are crew quarters."

"That sounds like kind of a lot on forty-five minutes' worth of air," Jerry said.

Dave gave him a dirty look. "Do what you can, that's all," he said. Jerry nodded back. That at least seemed reasonable. Seeing he wasn't going to have a mutiny on his hands, the recovery director nodded, too. "Whenever you're ready."

"We ready?" Jerry asked Steve.

"I think we are," the older man said. They both went to the watertight door. Dave touched each of them on the shoulder, as he had the last time. They stuck in the rubber mouthpieces and started the canned air going.

Dave undogged the door. "Luck," he said. Out they went. He closed and secured the door behind them.

The audience up top was there again, as if had been the first time. Approaching the entrance to Humpty Dumpty, Jerry worried less than he had before. If it opened, he wouldn't roast or freeze. That was something, anyhow.

Also not needing to fear that, Steve followed only a couple of steps behind him. A sailor had welded a steel hook to Clementine to give the explorers somewhere to secure their twine. Remembering Kip in *Have Space Suit*, Jerry made sure he tied his with a square knot.

He stood in front of the round doorway. For a moment, he thought about Anna. He thought about Tim Ishihara, whom he'd known since the third grade. He'd been best man at Tim's wedding. Tim would have done the same for him by now, only his got put on hold. Not being able to tell Tim the truth hurt almost as much as it did with Anna. One of these days . . . maybe.

Had he really thought like this the first time? Not in such detail; he'd had too many other things swirling through his head. But the idea had been there, down deep if not on the surface. It must have been, or the door would have stayed closed.

Or he'd just got lucky, and it wouldn't open now. Time to see. He pulled out the mouthpiece, said "Friend!" and put it back in as fast as he could.

Next thing he knew, the door had opened or vanished or done whatever it did. The way into Humpty Dumpty lay open again. He wondered if they'd caught the moment on film or tape. Not for long, though. Time to see what was what.

When he turned to Steve, the older man was making silent handclaps. Jerry scrambled up into the airlock, if it was an airlock. Then he helped Steve up and in, the way he had before. *Poor old fart isn't so spry anymore*, he thought sympathetically.

They went down that first corridor, paying out the nylon line behind them. Jerry wondered what Humpty Dumpty's proper attitude was. Was he walking on the floor, on a wall, or on the ceiling? Since everything glowed and there were no shadows, he couldn't tell.

The corridor didn't go very far before branching. The yellow line still shone on the wall or ceiling or floor to the left. Just beyond it was the opening that led to . . . whatever it led to.

Jerry pulled out the scratch pad. *Let's go left till we can see what that opening does.*

Steve nodded. Still one in front of the other, they walked along the corridor. Jerry photographed the twisting yellow line. He had no idea if those twists carried any meaning, but they looked as if they might.

There was the opening. Unlike the *Glomar Explorer*, Humpty Dumpty didn't seem to be divided up into airtight compartments. *Didn't seem to be* was probably the kicker, though. If the outer door vanished and appeared whenever it wanted to, why couldn't internal bulkheads do the same?

I'll go in. You wait here till you're sure it's okay, Jerry wrote. Half a second later, he added, *If you hear me scream, get the hell out.*

Go ahead, cheer me up, Steve answered. But he didn't say no.

Even I think I'm the expendable one, Jerry said to himself as he walked into the opening. It was partly that. It was also partly that he was younger, faster, bigger, and stronger than the man from the RAND Corporation. So here he was, boldly going where no man had gone before.

He wondered what he'd do if some mouse-sized six- or eight-legged *thing* scurried over his shoes. Besides piss his pants, anyway. Ships had rats, right? But that had to be impossible. Didn't it? What if it wasn't? What if the thing managed to hide somewhere on the *Glomar Explorer* before anyone caught it? What if it was pregnant, or about to lay eggs? What if it made rabbits in Australia look like good news by comparison?

What if you quit making like a writer and do your job? Jerry had to be stern with himself. He also had to fight not to keep looking at his feet.

Two openings lay along this corridor. The twisting yellow line ran past them. The one on the right came up first. When Jerry looked inside, he found he was likely walking on a wall, because everything in that chamber seemed ninety degrees out of true for him.

He took pictures of the . . . laboratory? He wasn't sure, but that was his first guess. He thought some of the gadgets on tall stands might be for heating things up. He didn't care to try to find out by experiment, though. Glassware—if it was glassware—lay in drifts on the wall that was now doing duty for the floor. Some had shattered, but more was intact. That said something either about how hard Humpty Dumpty had come in or how tough the alien utensils were.

Something tugged on Jerry's cord.

He whirled in horror. There stood Steve, looking as apologetic as anyone could with a mouthpiece hiding most of the expression on his face. *Didn't mean to scare you, but I want to see, too*, he wrote.

FUCK! Jerry underlined it for good measure. If some future scholar researching humanity's first contact with aliens wanted to get sniffy about his language, tough. As his heart slowed, he tried again: *Let's look across the corridor.*

That chamber made him change his mind about the first one. It looked more like a messroom than anything else, so maybe the first was more likely a kitchen than a lab. Again, though, everything was at a right angle to its proper arrangement, and quite a bit had gone topsy-turvy.

They're bigger than we are, Jerry wrote. He'd had the same thought on the other side of the corridor, too. The stands the stuff there were mounted on were definitely higher than humans would have made. The tables in here were also taller than people would have wanted unless they were perched on bar stools. Jerry didn't see any bar stools in the wreckage, or other kinds of chairs, either.

He and Steve both photographed the maybe-messroom. The older man wrote, *Shall we follow the yellow line?*

Sure. It's there. It's important, unless it isn't, Jerry replied. They went on. Jerry looked at his watch. They were still good on time, and they could leave a lot faster than they were exploring.

No mice. No snerps, or whatever the aliens would call their pests. Just the corridor and the yellow line. Another opening loomed ahead. The line led to it . . . and stopped. Jerry took more pictures. So did Steve. This was where things would happen, unless it wasn't.

If this is important, something may happen when I go in. Stay out till you know I'm okay. If I'm not, just get away, yes? Jerry showed Steve what he'd written. The older man nodded. Whether he meant it or not—they'd both find out. Jerry took a deep breath and went in, Instamatic in hand.

Three . . . things were on the wall that had been a floor. Two of them held the beings that must have crewed Humpty Dumpty. He could see them through the . . . things' clear domed tops. They reminded him more of centaurs than anything else. But they had what looked like feathers, not hair or bare skin. Their heads were more like owls than anything else that occurred to Jerry right away. Their eyes were open wide and yellow.

The third . . . thing had held one of them, too. Only bones and gunk were in there now. Whatever the other two did, this one had failed. Jerry gulped and started snapping photos.

Steve came in then. Jerry hardly noticed. Steve used his camera, too. Jerry had to change rolls to take more pictures. He stuck the exposed cassette in one of the pockets on his oversuit.

When he paused, he wrote, *Do you believe this?*

I'm seeing it. Either I believe it or I think it's a hallucination, the man from the RAND Corporation answered. *You see it, too, unless I'm also imagining that.*

Jerry would have joked about acid or magic mushrooms. He hadn't done them, but he knew plenty of people who had. He had a pretty fair notion of what they did. Steve seemed even straighter than he was. *And they said it couldn't be done!* he thought wryly.

After they'd both gone through more rolls and stashed film cassettes in various pockets, Steve wrote, *We'd better head back. About time, yes?*

Yes, Jerry agreed after checking his watch. He didn't want to leave, but he saw the need. And his mind was spinning in overdrive. Cold sleep? Some other kind of suspended animation? Could they revive those two centaurowls? Would doing that be smart or completely insane? He had all kinds of questions and exactly no answers.

Another one was what had gone wrong in the unit that didn't hold a perfectly preserved alien? Whatever else it was, it was another reminder that the beings who'd crewed Humpty Dumpty could screw up just like human beings. That might be worth remembering.

Reluctantly, he backed out of the chamber with the preservation units. He and Steve made their way up the corridor, rewinding their twine as they went. For all Jerry could tell, the airlock door would cleanly slice the nylon when it closed or reappeared or did whatever magic trick it did. But he and Steve didn't know that for a fact. The twine might make the door stay open just a crack, which might lead to Humpty Dumpty's air mingling with Earth's more than it had already, which might lead to . . . who the hell had any idea what?

Nothing dramatic happened on the way out. As he had before, Jerry left the starship first and helped Steve follow him. As before, the airlock door came back before he could see how.

Four men in suits and masks and air tanks waited not far away. Jerry wondered whether they were happy or sad they hadn't needed to charge in there on a rescue mission.

One of them spat out his mouthpiece. "You are all right?" he asked. He had a heavy German accent—he was the ex-U-boat engineer Jerry had heard about, one of the new men from the B crew. On the *Glomar Explorer*, he went by Manfred Krause. He seemed to like the handle—he said it was easier for Americans to pronounce than the last name he'd been born with.

Jerry shed his mouthpiece, too, and breathed in humid, subtropical air. "We're fine. We're great," he said, and gave a thumbs-up.

"What did you see?" Manfred asked.

"Wonderful things," Steve answered before Jerry could say anything. In a low voice, he added, "That's what Howard Carter said when they asked him what he saw in King Tut's tomb."

"Yeah." Jerry nodded. He knew that; he'd taken the history of ancient Egypt as an undergrad breadth requirement, and was prouder of the B he'd earned than many As in things that came easier for him. He'd never felt so intimidated as when the prof intoned, before both midterm and final, *You may write your bluebooks in English, German, or Arabic.*

Manfred said, "If all is good, then, come ahead for your decontamination check and cleanup."

Come they did. A guy in gear like theirs checked them for radioactivity, as had happened before. Then they took everything out of their pockets, peeled off the tape holding booties and gloves to their suits, and did the prescribed triple scrubdown. Jerry thought he came out of it smelling like a veterinarian's office (minus dog shit), but nobody on the *Glomar Explorer* gave a damn about his opinion.

Dr. Rogers went through the same routine of breathing over and spitting into culture medium, mouth swabbing, and cleanout at the other end as Doc Borden had before. After it was over, Jerry asked him, "Did anything weird grow on the culture medium from last time?"

"Not so far as I've been able to tell," the physician said. "That's good news, remember. You don't want to carry anything from another world that you may not have any resistance to."

"I understand that," Jerry said, as sympathetically as he could. The new guy was still getting up to speed.

Sure enough, Rogers repeated, "Anything from another world . . ." and let his voice trail away. After a moment, he picked up again: "You could have knocked me over with a feather when they told me about that on Midway. Up till then, I thought I'd be doing autopsies on Russian sailors, not on little green men." His laugh sounded nervous.

They aren't little green men, and two of them aren't dead. I don't think they are, anyway. Jerry kept his lips buttoned. The doctor didn't have need to know. People who did, people like Dale and Jack and Dave, would detonate like H-bombs if he talked out of turn.

Rogers's office had a tiny waiting room. A rent-a-frog sat in a chair reading an old *U.S. News & World Report.* When Jerry started to walk out, the diver said, "Why don't you wait here till the doc finishes with Mister Dahlgren, sir? Then I'll take you both to the director's cabin."

Why don't you? had to mean *You'd better.* "You talked me into it, Gator," Jerry said. The other man got his handle from a tattoo on his right forearm. A little farther up the arm was a nasty burn scar.

Jerry pretended to read a *Newsweek* even older than Gator's magazine till Steve came out of Dr. Rogers's sanctum. Then the two men who'd come out of Humpty Dumpty again followed the diver to Dale Neuwirth's chamber. Gator sketched a salute to the mission director. "Here they are, sir."

"Thanks, Gator," Neuwirth said, and then, to Jerry and Steve, "C'mon in."

He shut the door behind them and locked it. As before, Jack and Dave sat on the bed. Jerry noticed a stout trunk stashed in the space under the mattress. Did that hold some of the guns the CIA had insisted on having aboard? He wouldn't have been surprised.

Dale didn't turn on Bing Crosby this time. Instead, he started a tape recorder that sat on his desk. "Debriefing. Second entry to Humpty Dumpty," he said clearly. Maybe Gator stood on guard in the corridor, discouraging passersby. *He'd be good at it,* Jerry thought.

"What did you find inside the spaceship this time?" Jack asked.

Jerry and Steve looked at each other. Steve spoke first: "The most important thing we found is, there are two aliens preserved in some kind of suspended animation in the chamber the yellow line leads to. We have photographs."

"Ooh," Dave said softly. It was half a noise awe, half what he might've come out with had Steve punched him in the belly. Dale and Jack both looked as if they'd got clobbered, too.

Jerry added, "There used to be three of them. The life support on one failed. He's just bones and . . . and I don't know what. They look more like feathery centaurs than anything else, but they don't really look a whole lot *like* anything." Steve nodded.

"Photos will be ready in a few hours," Jack said. The *Glomar Explorer* might not boast a Fotomat kiosk, but one of the fancy containers held a developing plant that could double as one.

"Do you have any idea how to revive the two surviving . . . things, aliens, whatever they are?" Dale asked.

"Not really," Steve answered. "We would want to be very sure before we try that. It's not the sort of mistake we could fix."

"Other question is, do we want them awake?" Dave said. "That ship is stronger than anything we have, way stronger. Who knows what two aliens could do with it? Whatever it did to the K-129, I'd guess it did that without them. Jerry, would you say the dead one's been that way since before March 1968?"

"I don't know, but I think it's a pretty good guess, yeah," Jerry replied.

"How much before?"

"No way to tell." Jerry spread his hands. "Just no way. How fast the aliens decay naturally, temperature, germs involved, whatever chemicals it may have used when it went into suspended animation with the others . . . We don't know any of that stuff. What's the old line? *'The probability of predicting correctly in complete ignorance is zero.'*" He'd got the line from an *Analog* he'd read in high school. That made it old for him, anyhow.

"He's right," Dale said. "We need to do more work before we try anything we can't repair."

"I agree a hundred percent—I said so already." Steve gave the mission director a nod that seemed more than half a salute.

"Let's talk some more after the photos get developed," Jack said. "Then we'll all be more or less on the same page." Nobody said no, so the meeting broke up. Gator nodded to Jerry and Steve as they came out of Dale's cabin. Jerry nodded back. He would have done the same with any other guard dog.

Jerry heard some grim news at dinner that night, brought by one of the B crew newcomers. He didn't know who the man was; more unfamiliar faces sat at the table every day, it seemed. The engineer who'd had the little heart attack—Bob was his name—had flown from Midway to Honolulu to head home to the mainland. The connection was tight. He'd had to run to make it. He did . . . but moments after he fastened his seat belt, he had a big coronary and died on the spot.

"He was a good guy. I bet his family will miss him like anything," Jerry said. He knew people his age to whom death seemed unreal: something to worry about in the great by-and-by, maybe, but not now. He wasn't like that. He hadn't been since he was seven. Death was real, and death was forever. He'd noticed his friends who'd fought in Vietnam had the same attitude.

So did Stephen Dole. Jerry supposed years piling up could also give it to you. "Too young," Steve said, and then, "Anyone younger than I am who dies is too young by definition."

Said a different way, it would have been a joke. Steve sounded altogether serious. Jerry nodded and said, "I hear you, man." He sounded the same way.

After they ate, they headed for the Special Measurements container. Documents that had to do with the spaceship lived there. That included the photos Jerry and Steve had taken inside Humpty Dumpty.

Gator stood outside the door. "Hello again," he said. Jerry said hello back, but made sure he shielded the keypad with his body as he punched in the entry code just the same.

When he and Steve went in, Dale was there ahead of them, going through the photos they'd taken earlier in the day. Jack and Dave showed up together a couple of minutes later. For the next little while, people passed stacks of pictures back and forth.

"What's the scale on these critters?" Dave asked.

"They aren't as big as a centaur made from a horse and a person would be, but they're bigger than we are," Jerry said.

He eyed the prints with an odd, almost touristy, fascination.

They reminded him of where he'd been and what he'd seen, yes. But they were also what he'd remember of all that, because they were permanent and stable while what went on inside his head was subject to change without notice.

The higher-ups flipped through the photographs of the kitchen?/laboratory? and the messroom fairly fast. They were much more interested in the shots that showed the aliens and the clear domes encasing them. *And you're not?* Jerry asked himself. Himself had no good answer.

"Kind of convenient for us that one of them didn't make it. Gives a notion of how they're put together we couldn't get from just outside views," Jack said. Just when Jerry thought that was the most cold-blooded thing he'd ever heard in his life, the security director spoke again, in musing tones: "I wonder if they have souls."

Since Jerry wondered the same thing about people, he stayed quiet. But he reminded himself that nobody ever was all of one piece. He supposed that might even be true of Richard Nixon, however little he cared to admit it.

Dave pointed to a yellow oval inset into the base of one of the cabinets. "They all have this, I think," he said. "And yellow seems to be an important color with them, the way red is with us. If we gave one of those things a poke . . ."

Jerry had had the same thought. Now he downplayed it as much as he could: "We don't want to try anything till we know more."

"Agree. One way or another, we won't get a second chance," Steve said. Jerry nodded. They might kill the aliens, and then there'd be none. Or they might give them back control of their spaceship, and then there might be no more humans.

"Sure, sure." Dave nodded, too. But he sounded less convinced than Jerry wished he would have. *Am I just being paranoid?* he wondered. *But are you paranoid when they're really after you?*

"We won't do anything drastic until and unless we have clear instructions from the highest authority," Dale said. "That order got to me less than an hour ago. I missed dinner because I was decrypting it personally, as ordered. It's a good thing the galley can crank out something tasty no matter what time it is. But the order stresses that trying to activate Humpty Dumpty or trying to revive the aliens is as much a political decision as a scientific one."

"That's the way we do it, then." Jack Porter couldn't have been more respectful and obedient if he'd had a papal bull land in his lap. Dave nodded, too. When he had orders from people entitled to give them, that settled things for him. He got ready to follow them.

Back in the early 1940s, German officials had orders from people entitled to give them, too. Six million Jews wound up dead, including some men and women on both sides of Jerry's family. So did a whole bunch of Gypsies and homosexuals and people from insane asylums and anybody else the Nazis happened not to like. As far as Jerry was concerned, obeying orders just because they were orders was way overrated.

Theoretically, the USA agreed with him. Theoretically. Lieutenant Calley'd claimed he was only following orders when he led his troops to massacre Vietnamese villagers at My Lai. He'd got court-martialed and convicted anyway, and was still serving some kind of sentence. (Captain Medina, who was supposed to have given those orders, got acquitted. It made you wonder.)

"'The highest authority' here means the president, doesn't it?" Jerry asked.

Dale nodded. "That's correct. And what he says, goes."

He wasn't even a spook. But he'd worked for the United States his whole adult life. He'd see orders the same way Dave and Jack did.

It wasn't so much that orders to mess with Humpty Dumpty would be illegal or even wrong. They might not be. And politics did have to play a part. If not for the political struggle between the USSR and the USA, Humpty Dumpty might have lain on the ocean floor forever.

No, the real question was, did Gerald Ford know enough to give orders that made sense? Did anybody? *Do not call up that which you cannot put down*—the line from H. P. Lovecraft bubbled up inside Jerry's head. Eldritch horror wasn't his thing any more than Eldridge Cleaver was, but he'd read some Lovecraft and *Soul on Ice*.

"We will proceed with caution, then," Jack said.

"Extreme caution," Steve said. He'd been inside the starship, too. Photographs helped, but nothing matched real experience. Jerry enjoyed centerfolds as much as any other man, but a centerfold was no more like lying down with a real woman than a picture of a steak was like dinner at a steak house.

"Extreme caution, yeah," he said, thinking one more time of the extreme prejudice clause in his second nondisclosure agreement.

"We will proceed with caution, yes, and in accordance with the highest authority's directives," Dale said. That plainly satisfied Dave and Jack. It might even have satisfied Steve; not as if RAND didn't feed from the government trough. *What if the highest authority's directives don't match caution?* Jerry wondered. He didn't ask out loud. He knew useless when he saw it.

Back in the cabin later, though, he did ask Steve. He wasn't close to sure that was safe, but he had to talk to somebody. He piercingly missed Anna, though he'd never be able to tell her about any of this unless he wanted to learn more about "extreme prejudice" than he'd ever wanted to know.

Stephen Dole listened patiently. He did most of the time—and he'd gone into Humpty Dumpty, too. "It's a problem, no question," he said when Jerry ran dry. "They don't seem to understand that this is as much a you-only-get-one-chance situation as raising the starship was. If they make a mistake, chances are they can't go back and fix it."

"Bingo!" Jerry said admiringly. "I couldn't have put it that well myself. You oughta be a writer or something."

"Or something." Steve's smile was wry. "We've tried to tell them every way we know how. If they won't listen, what else can we do?"

"'You can lead a horticulture, but you can't make her think,'" Jerry said.

Steve gave him a curious look. "Aren't you too young to be quoting Dorothy Parker?"

"It's my fiancée's fault," Jerry said. "She's into that whole radio-celebrity thing. Dorothy Parker, Oscar Levant, all those crazy people. Oscar, he was a piece of work and then some."

"You've got that right. Up till a few years ago, he'd still show up on *The Merv Griffin Show*, places like that."

"Uh-huh." Jerry'd watched *The Merv Griffin Show* while he still lived at home because his father liked it. He didn't think he'd seen it once since he got his own place. "Anna gave me his autobiography. It's . . . interesting. 'I'm gonna memorize your name and throw away my head,' he told somebody. Hard to beat that."

"Isn't it?" Steve paused, then sighed. "If they won't listen to us, we can't make them, you know."

"I can't, not by myself. That's for fucking sure. Nobody would pay any attention to me if I tried. I'd just be some grad student who's messed up with acid and talking crazy talk. But what are they most afraid of right now? Publicity, that's what!" Jerry brought it out as confidently as Mr. McGuire had said "Plastics!" in *The Graduate*. "You're the world's leading expert on what goes into making planets with aliens on them possible, and—"

"No, I'm not. Not even close," Steve broke in. In his own way, different from Jerry's, he was also a modest man. "I could name a dozen people who—"

"Okay, fine. Have it your way." Jerry interrupted right back. "You're *one* of the world's leading experts on planets with aliens on them. If somebody like you said the CIA was doing strange things with a couple of them and with their starship, people would pay attention." He wanted to say, *The Russians would pay attention*. He didn't. He wasn't a Red, and didn't want Steve thinking he was. He was just somebody who believed in the balance of power. What lay in the moon pool seemed too important to belong to only one country.

The older man took off his glasses, polished them with a soft cotton handkerchief, and put them back on his nose. His look said he understood where Jerry was coming from. Gently, he answered, "You need to remember, son, I signed the same nondisclosure agreement you did."

"Did you sign it thinking you'd be looking at a couple of centaurs in suspended-animation tanks?"

"I knew the possibility was there. They showed me some of the pictures the *Halibut* took to help enlist me."

They trusted you a lot further than they did me, Jerry thought resentfully. But why wouldn't they? Steve already worked for RAND, and RAND and the CIA were in each other's pockets half the time. He wasn't a freaky, freaked-out, unreliable grad student. Muttering, Jerry said, "They can't swing this by themselves, dammit. They aren't big enough. Ford isn't big enough. Kissinger isn't, either."

"Well, I won't tell you you're wrong, but do you think Brezhnev and Gromyko are?"

"Hell, no, not by themselves. Added in with our people, maybe. But the way things are, it doesn't look like we'll get the chance to find out, does it?"

Steve puckered his lips and blew air out through them. "Remember the clause you noticed in the agreement? The one that talks about termination with extreme prejudice?"

"I'm not likely to forget it! I was remembering it earlier today, in fact."

"Okay. Good. If you think for even a minute that they don't mean it, you'd better think again. Anybody who talks out of turn about this, anybody at all, is a sudden fatal accident waiting to happen. He won't have to wait long, either. This game is for keeps."

"They wouldn't do that to you!" Jerry exclaimed.

"Of course they would. They'll do it to anybody. You said it yourself—this is too big for them. The only way they see to have any control over it is to keep it secret and hold on tight. If they can learn things from Humpty Dumpty without waking the aliens, or if they're positive the aliens can't take over the ship as soon as they wake up . . ."

Jerry stared at him. "You're as scared as I am."

"Who in his right mind wouldn't be? I think we're fine as long as we're on the ship. We can't talk to outsiders here. But unless they're convinced we're harmless, I'd be real careful once I got home. If you hear a car hit me while I was crossing the street or something, maybe you should try to disappear."

"Yeesh!" Jerry said. By sounding so calm and reasonable, Steve made it seem more scary, not less. *How far can I trust him, though?* Jerry wondered. If Steve reported him to Jack and Dale, wouldn't the man from the RAND Corporation buy safety for himself? Or was there any safety to buy anywhere? Was Steve trying to talk him into saying things that would justify punching his ticket for good?

Once you started down that rabbit hole of suspicion, how did you ever come out again? The dangers you imagined—the ones you thought you were imagining—might prove real after all. *Will I see CIA guys whenever I go outside from now on, the way John Birchers see Communists everywhere?*

"Hang on a second. I have something," Steve said. He opened a desk drawer, pulled out a bottle, and showed it to Jerry.

"Stolichnaya! Where'd you get that?"

"From Dale. He brought a lot of good Russian liquor aboard. I don't think he told the Agency about it, either. Instead of shooting it out if we got boarded, he aimed to try to bribe the Russian officers with it."

"No shit?" Jerry said. Steve nodded. Jerry went on, "We won't get boarded now."

"That's right. And Dale's a good Mormon, so he won't drink it himself."

"He is? I didn't know that." There'd been a Mormon family down the street from Jerry when he was growing up. He'd played with the kids. The dad, who'd joined the faith when he married, came over once in a while for a sly beer or cigarette with Hyman Stieglitz. Jerry thought the religion was odd, but it seemed to turn out pretty good people. Of course, there were those who said the same thing about Judaism.

"He is." Steve went into the bathroom, came back with his glass and Jerry's, and poured a good knock of vodka into each. After Jerry'd taken his, the older man made a toast: "May we live long and prosper!"

"You Trekkie, you!" Jerry said. They clinked and drank. The Stoli went down smooth as a kiss. A kiss . . . *I haven't had a kiss in way too long*, Jerry thought. *I mean, way too long.*

Steve got to the bottom of his glass before Jerry did. He didn't drink much ordinarily, but this hadn't been an ordinary day. He picked up the bottle by the neck. "Want a refill?"

"Do I ever!" Jerry thrust his glass forward. They drank some more, and some more after that. A little before midnight, the dead soldier went into the wastebasket.

People said vodka didn't give you a hangover. They said it wasn't the alcohol, it was the other stuff that flavored scotch or bourbon or gin that put the hurt on you. After half a liter of the Soviet Union's finest, Jerry woke up the next morning much the worse for wear. He groaned before he realized he'd done it.

"How are you doing?" Steve's voice floated up from the bottom bunk.

"I feel like dogshit," Jerry answered. "How about you?"

"Pretty much the same. Misery loves company, I guess. Maybe if I stand under a hot shower for a while . . ."

"Go ahead, man. It's a good idea, but I don't want to move yet."

When Steve came out of the bathroom, Jerry lurched in. He took two aspirins. Brushing his teeth got rid of some of the dead animals in his mouth. He cranked the shower up to just under parboil. When he came out, he swallowed two more aspirins for luck.

By the time he'd dried and combed his hair and got some clothes on, he felt better, if nowhere near good.

He wasn't ready to face food when he went to the messroom, but he poured down lots of sweet coffee pale with cream. Steve was being abstemious, too. Tapping his cup with a fingernail, he said, "Breakfast of champions."

"You know it," Jerry said. "Put it together with all the aspirins I had and it's got to be wearing a hole in my stomach right now."

"I haven't done that in a long time," Steve said, at least half to himself. "Not since a friend of mine had a stroke and died walking to an elevator at a conference. Whitey was forty-eight—no, forty-seven."

"Damn!" Jerry said. Forty-seven felt old to him, but it wasn't old enough to die, even if it was older than his mother'd got.

For years, he hadn't even been able to think about her, much less talk about her, without puddling up. He still sometimes wanted to. The wound had a scar on it these days, but he felt it now and then all the same.

He and Steve sat there under the fluorescent lights for a while, not saying much. Then Jerry remarked, "The steward who cleans up'll wonder where you scored that bottle."

"Probably." Steve tried a nod. It didn't seem to hurt him too much. "On a ship full of big mysteries, though, that's just a little one."

Before Jerry could answer, the chuntering roar of a copter settling down on the helipad made his head want to fall off. Steve flinched, too. Jerry said, "Never mind termination with extreme prejudice later. Somebody kill me now."

Steve looked around. Not seeing anyone obviously listening to them, he relaxed—a little. Not much above a whisper, he said, "Using that phrase out in the open isn't a great idea."

"Mm . . . I can see that. Sorry," Jerry said. People who'd kill you if you got out of line wouldn't like your saying they'd kill you if you got out of line, not even if you borrowed their euphemism.

"I wonder who's on the helicopter," Steve said. "I always do, whenever one comes in from Midway. I wonder if it's got my replacement aboard."

"You and me both, man. You and me both. I'm almost to the point where I'd sooner go home and try to forget any of this ever happened."

"Almost?"

Half embarrassed, Jerry gave back a careful nod. "Yeah. Those units, those yellow buttons . . . Kinda want to know how the movie ends."

"If it has a happy ending, for us and for them." Like Jerry, Steve didn't go into detail in a public space.

"Well, yeah." The aliens might die after people tried reviving them. That would be tragic, because humanity hadn't discovered any other sunken spaceships . . . as far as he knew, anyhow. Then again, the centaurowls might take control of Humpty Dumpty again. If they did, and if they were pissed off, that one ship might be able to beat everything America and Russia threw at it, even if you tossed in England, France, and China for good measure.

The happy medium was having them wake up and tell the CIA everything they knew, either of their own accord or because the Agency got . . . persuasive. That was what everybody hoped for. But hope came out of Pandora's box last for a reason.

After a little while, the helicopter took off again. The noise didn't seem quite so horrible this time. Jerry shoved back his chair and stood up. "I'm gonna get rid of some of this coffee before I wet my pants. Then I think I'll go forward and see what's happening with Humpty Dumpty."

"Fresh air," Steve said solemnly.

"Fresh air," Jerry agreed. It was supposed to be good for a hangover. As far as he could tell, nothing but time helped much. He didn't supposed fresh air would do him any actual harm, though.

Some faces he'd never seen before were looking down into the moon pool. They all had one thing in common: the look of utter amazement spread across them. If the men hadn't been reading science fiction since they were eight years old—and most of them probably had—they'd grown up hearing about flying saucers or UFOs or whatever the current label was. Now they weren't hearing about them. They were seeing one. It made a difference. *Yeah, just a little*, Jerry thought.

He walked to the rail that kept people from leaning too far forward and falling a long way to a hard bottom. He didn't stand close to any of the new arrivals. Talking with strangers was the last thing he wanted right now.

He peered into the moon pool—and stiffened, the way a German shepherd would if someone it had never seen hopped the fence and came down in its back yard. He wouldn't have been surprised if his hair frizzed out like an angry dog's, too. Two men were probing at Humpty Dumpty's nacreous shell, one with a hammer and chisel, the other with a blowtorch.

Rage burned away Jerry's hangover. He knew another grad student who'd been on LSD on a waterbed right near the epicenter of the 1971 Sylmar quake. "I was straight like *that*," Karl would say, snapping his fingers. "Adrenaline murdered the acid." Jerry hadn't been sure whether to believe him. He did now.

Swearing under his breath, he swarmed down ladderlike stairways till he got down to the bottom deck. He hurried to the chamber that adjoined the moon pool . . . and was not at all surprised to find Dave Schoals standing in there.

Jerry stabbed his index finger at the dogged doorway out. "What the fuck is going on in the moon pool?" he ground out.

Dave gaped at him. Later, Jerry realized he wasn't in the habit of barking at people who had a lot more seniority than he did—and not only barking, but barking with authority that declared he was entitled to answers. After Dave pulled his face straight, he gave him one: "We have orders to see if we can get samples of Humpty Dumpty's outer skin so we can find out what it's made of and whether we can duplicate it."

"Orders from who?" Most of the time, Jerry tried to talk grammatically. He was too rattled now to care.

"From the highest authority," Dave said.

"Oh, bullshit. Gerald Ford doesn't give a rat's ass what Humpty Dumpty's made of. Could be snips and snails and puppy dogs' tails for all he cares."

"What it is wouldn't matter. Knowing what it is and knowing whether it's anything we can match—that matters."

"Does making the ship notice us and maybe blow us away matter?"

"For God's sake, Jerry, be reasonable. You've gone inside it, remember."

"I had permission. It opened up for me. What if screwing with the hull weakens it so it can't fly or something? You think it won't know? You think it can't protect itself? Ask the Russians!"

"Dale thought the risk was small enough to be justifiable," Dave said.

"Fuck Dale, too."

Jerry would have gone on, but somebody—presumably the men who'd been messing with Humpty Dumpty's hide—rapped on the steel door. Dave let them in. "Any luck?" he asked, as he closed the door again and secured it.

"Not a goddamn bit," answered the guy with the hammer and chisel. He added, "Hey, Jerry."

"Hi, Woodie," Jerry said. The technician was—what else?—only following orders.

"What do you mean, not a bit?" Dave said.

"Chisel wouldn't bite." Woodie held it up. "It just slid, like. And Bert's torch didn't heat the shell even a little. We both struck out."

"Shit," Dave said, most sincerely. Jerry found himself relieved and happy at the same time. Ever since he first tried knocking on the airlock door, he'd wondered whether Humpty Dumpty was fully in contact with the world he lived in. You could lift it. You could touch it. But could you truly get a grip on it? Maybe not.

At breakfast the next morning, Dale bussed his tray and plate and silverware, then came over to the table where Jerry was eating. Nodding, he said, "Stop by my cabin when you get done, will you?"

"Uh, sure," Jerry said, but he was talking to Dale's back. The bite of sausage he was chewing seemed to lose flavor in his mouth. A friendly, casual order was still an order. He'd waited nervously for the other shoe to drop. Here it was.

"The condemned man ate a hearty meal?" Steve asked quietly. Jerry'd told him what had happened. He hadn't been thrilled to hear it, either.

"Nyeh—could be!" Jerry said in his best Bugs Bunny tones, which weren't too bad. One of his aunts knew Mel Blanc, but he'd never met the man of a thousand voices himself.

"For the record, I still think you were a hundred percent right," Steve said.

"Far out! That and a quarter'll get me a cup of coffee."

"They'll do whatever they do."

"That's what I'm afraid of." Jerry methodically finished his sausage and eggs and home fries. It *was* a hearty meal. He thought about getting seconds so he could dawdle over them and piss Dale off, but decided he was already in enough trouble. He climbed to his feet. "Wish me luck."

"You know I do." Steve crossed his fingers for a moment. Jerry wondered if that would do a Jew any good. He hoped so. Twisting the fingers even of two hands into a Star of David was next to impossible.

He disposed of his stuff, then went to the mission director's cabin. The door was closed. When he tapped on it, Dale opened it right away. "Hi. C'mon in," he said, still friendly and casual and still in command.

"Thanks." In Jerry came.

Dale shut the door behind him and waved him to a chair. He

sat down himself, steepling his fingers. "Dave tells me you aren't happy about the line of research we started yesterday."

"He's right." Jerry admitted what he couldn't very well deny.

"Even if experiments like that were ordered by the president of the United States?"

"*Especially* if they were. The president's five or six thousand miles away. He's never seen Humpty Dumpty. He doesn't know what it can do, and—"

"Neither do you," Dale pointed out.

"That's true, but I've got a lot more imagination than Gerald Ford does. And if Humpty Dumpty does something, it'll do something to me, not to him."

"Yesterday's experiments did no damage and provoked no reaction."

"Yeah, but you didn't know they wouldn't before you went ahead with them. What if they'd punched a hole in the shell or something?"

"That seems unlikely, in a ship that stayed at the bottom of the Pacific undamaged for an unknown but large number of years."

"Not undamaged. You saw the photos Steve and I took. Everything in there is all higgledy-piggledy, and one of those aliens is long, long dead."

Dale made an impatient noise: "Mff. You know what I mean. The ship is still structurally sound. The computers or whatever controls it in the absence of the crew are still operational. So is the weapons system that sank the K-129."

"It sure is," Jerry said. "What would it do to us, huh?"

"It didn't do anything," Dale said stolidly. "You can speculate as much as you want. That's fact."

"You had no idea it would work that way."

"I also had no idea it would work that way when Clementine grabbed Humpty Dumpty and when the pipe string hauled the spaceship up into the moon pool. Those encounters held much more potential danger than a couple of crewmen prodding at the outer hull. They caused no hostile action."

He wasn't wrong. Jerry hadn't looked at it like that. He decided he was lucky; if he had looked at it like that, he might have jumped off the *Glomar Explorer* and tried to swim back to the mainland. He said, "With something that powerful, do you want to take chances?"

"We've *been* taking chances," Dale said. "The highest authority thought, and I agreed, the possible reward justified the risk. We didn't learn what we wanted to, but we also didn't provoke or harm Humpty Dumpty."

No harm, no foul. Jerry didn't say it. The phrase wouldn't mean anything to Dale Neuwirth. He didn't live in Los Angeles, and wouldn't have listened to Chick Hearn doing Laker games since the team moved from Minneapolis. Jerry just shook his head.

The director sighed. "I didn't ask you to stop by here to convert you. I did my missionary work when I was younger than you are now, and I'm not sure I converted anyone then. But Dave and Jack and I did some talking last night, and we all agree it's time to send you and Doctor Dahlgren back to the mainland so you can get on with your lives and bring in some fresh people from the B crew for ideas about how best to exploit Humpty Dumpty."

Exploit. That was how Dale thought of it. Bound to be how the president thought of it, too. The biggest thing that might ever have happened to mankind, and they wanted to *exploit* it.

The next obvious question was, how did they know what Steve thought? Had he told them himself? Or did they have bugs in the cabins? By now, nothing the CIA did could surprise Jerry. The more he thought about it, the more likely the bugs seemed. Steve hadn't known he'd be going back to the mainland, too, or if he had, he sure hadn't let on.

Slowly, Jerry said, "I'm not asking for a trip home. I still think I can be useful here, if you'll let me."

"I'm sure Doctor Dahlgren will say the same thing. The attitude does you both credit," Dale replied. "We aren't angry at either one of you, believe me. If you ever need a letter of recommendation, if you ever need any kind of favor, get hold of one of us. We'll take care of you. And you won't suffer financially from what you've done here—I guarantee you that."

"You guys have paid me more than I thought I'd make for years and years. I'm not complaining about that. I never would," Jerry said.

The mission director waved his words aside. "Don't worry about it. Listen to me—I'm telling you what's what. Oh, and there's this." Dale went over to his desk, opened a drawer, pulled out a small piece of paper, and gave it to Jerry.

Jerry looked at it in confusion. "A post office box in Schenectady?"

"You're a writer. You're going to keep on writing. This is where you'll send your work for vetting before you submit it. You don't need to include a self-addressed stamped envelope. We'll spring for return postage, too. And I promise a quick turnaround—we're only looking for things that endanger security."

"Uh, thanks, I guess." Jerry folded the paper and stuck it in his wallet. He threw the dice one more time: "Can I do anything to get you to change your mind?"

"We value your contribution very highly. The list of possible outcomes you gave me was outstanding. And you were the one who brilliantly discovered the way into Humpty Dumpty. You'll get full credit for it, too," Dale said.

All of which added up to *no*. Jerry understood as much. He also understood that whatever credit he got would be in a classified report no one outside this extra-secret chunk of the CIA would ever see.

Sure enough, Dale finished with, "We're going to go in another direction now, see how that works out. If we find we need you later, we'll know how to get hold of you, right?"

"You're the CIA, for God's sake. Well, *you* aren't, but the people you work for are. If they can't find me, nobody can."

"True enough." Dale smiled, no doubt happy Jerry was being so civilized. Jerry would have screamed and kicked something if he'd thought it would do any good. He didn't, worse luck. Dale added, "Whenever you change your address from now on, drop a line to that PO box in Schenectady."

"Will do." Jerry got to his feet. There didn't seem to be anything left to say. Dale held out his hand. Jerry shook it. He opened the door and left, closing it behind him. He hadn't even got to the end of the corridor before Steve came around the corner. "I only wish I were surprised to see you," Jerry said.

"Jack told me Dale wanted to see me," Steve said. "So, it is what I think it is?"

"'*Never send to know for whom the bell tolls; it tolls for thee,*'" Jerry answered, feeling Donne to a turn. That English Lit class paid off again.

"Oh . . . hell," Steve said.

"Yeah. Fun while it lasted." Jerry hurried away. He didn't want anyone else seeing him on, or maybe over, the verge of tears.

He had himself together—he thought so, anyway—by the time he went forward to get a nearly last look at Humpty Dumpty. He couldn't, though; the tarpaulin stretched over the moon pool. Maybe a Soviet spy satellite was up there in the sky right now. Or maybe the powers that be didn't want anybody else seeing what they were up to with the starship. Jerry couldn't be sure, but he knew how he'd guess.

He walked back to his cabin and shut the door. Then he kicked the door to the steel locker where he stashed his stuff, as hard as he could. The door barely dented. His right big toe hurt like hell.

Swearing at the pain gave him an idea. He left the cabin again and limped down the corridor.

The tarp hadn't come off the moon pool for four days. That confirmed Jerry's suspicions. Whether he had them or not didn't matter anymore. He stood near the edge of the helipad, waiting for the copter that would take him away from all this. His suitcase sat by one foot, the hydrophone by the other. They were both heavy; he'd got sick of holding them.

Steve stood there, too, and four other guys who were going home. They acted overjoyed; Jerry and Steve were the glum ones.

"Did they search what you're taking home?" Steve asked.

"Sure." Jerry nodded. "I knew they would. I even helped. You?"

"Oh, yes."

Before they said anything more, one of them other men—he was a paramedic who'd worked with Doc Borden and Dr. Rogers— pointed southwest and said, "Here comes the chopper!" He sounded excited as hell.

Wind whipped Jerry's face as the Navy helicopter set down. The noise was appalling. Slowly, the rotors stopped spinning. Half a dozen men with suitcases and duffels got out. Jerry recognized one of them. If people on the *Glomar Explorer* thought *he'd* been a pain in the ass, they might not have seen anything yet. He kept quiet. They'd find out for themselves.

The newcomers walked by, their heads on swivels, trying to see everything at once. Then it was the turn of the men going home to board the helicopter. A petty officer stood by the little metal staircase that led up to the entrance. "Make sure y'all strap in soon as you sit down," he said.

Strap in Jerry did. The harness was more elaborate than an airliner seat belt or even the seat-and-shoulder belts new cars used (Jerry's beat-up Rambler boasted no belts at all). The petty officer climbed in right behind the passengers. He stowed the little staircase and secured the door, then sat up front with the pilot.

Being crewmen, they wore helmets. Jerry envied them as soon as the engine started up again. If being *near* a chopper was loud, being *in* one was. . . . For a few seconds, Jerry couldn't think of what it was like. Then he decided he knew now what the butter in a blender heard when a cook turned it up to high.

Up went the helicopter, just like that. Jerry craned his neck to keep the *Glomar Explorer* in sight as long as he could, but the ship soon disappeared behind the whirlybird. Part of his life was disappearing with it—a brief part, a strange part, but an important part. How important? He doubted he'd know the answer to that for years and years. Even when he did know, he doubted he'd be able to tell anybody.

Talking in the cabin was impossible. So was thinking, or nearly. The last time Jerry'd sat through so much noise, he and Anna were seeing Jethro Tull at the Forum. He'd enjoyed that more.

The flight back to Midway took about an hour. The island was actually two sandy islets, neither poking more than a few feet up out of the ocean. The eastern island was just sand, sand and gooney birds. Along with more gooney birds, the western island held the naval air station: a couple of runways, a few planes and copters, Quonset huts, and a more substantial building with a radar dish spinning on top of it.

Jerry had been at sea for a couple of months. Stepping down onto a surface that didn't move felt as strange and unnatural as the Hornblower books suggested. Without ever consciously noticing, he'd acquired reflexes he didn't know he had. His friend Tim drove a stick shift. Tim didn't have to think about that, either. He just did it. Jerry'd tried it a couple of times, but never enough to get smooth.

A young Navy lieutenant in tropical whites strode up to the helicopter. "If you gentlemen will come with me, we'll get you quartered, we'll provide you with transportation home, and you'll each be able to make two three-minute calls to the mainland to arrange for pickup and such. Any questions? . . . No? Follow me, then."

Quarters were half a dozen military cots in a Quonset hut. The noisy air conditioner that tried to cool the inside was fighting out of its weight. Jerry claimed a cot by plopping the hydrophone and his suitcase down on top of it. The other men marked their territory the same way. Once they had, the officer led them to the building with the radar set.

There, he played travel agent. Jerry and Steve were fourth and fifth in line, so they had a while to wait. In due course, Jerry's turn came. "You can probably take the two of us at once," he said. "We're both going to Los Angeles."

"You would be . . . ?"

"Jerry Steinberg and Steve Dahlgren." By now, Jerry was easy with his alias.

"Right," the lieutenant said after a glance down at his clipboard. "We'll have a flight for Honolulu departing at oh six hundred tomorrow. It's around eleven hundred miles—you should arrive before noon, Honolulu time. We're an hour behind that here."

"Five hours for eleven hundred miles?" Steve said plaintively. Jerry was thinking the same thing. Shouldn't it be more like two?

But the lieutenant—his name badge said FISKE—answered, "I'm afraid so. Not jetliners here. We use our recon planes: prop jobs. Not fast, not fancy, but they'll get you there. Los Angeles for the two of you . . . ? Yes, we can do that. There's a flight going out of Honolulu at sixteen thirty local time. Should get you there just before midnight Pacific time. Late, but not too late."

Tomorrow would be . . . Jerry had to think about it. Thursday. Days at sea melted into one another. Anna wouldn't be thrilled. She had to work Friday. So did Jerry's father. Sometimes you got stuck.

"We can make calls, you said?" he asked.

"Yes, that's right. We have a line to Hawaii that goes on through to the mainland. Connections are usually pretty good, but it isn't cheap, which is why we want you to keep it short," Fiske said.

"Gotcha." Jerry looked at his watch. It was a quarter after eleven. "Los Angeles would be . . . three hours ahead of us?"

"No, four. Midway doesn't use daylight savings time. Neither does Hawaii," the Navy man said. Jerry nodded. Anna would be in the middle of her afternoon when he called. That was good.

He waited for the three people in front of him to finish their calls. Then it was his turn. He knew Anna's work number as well as he knew the one for her apartment. Luckily, a card taped to the desk in front of the phone reminded him USE AREA CODE WHEN CALLING. So he dialed 213 first.

Some hisses and pops followed, the way they often did on long-distance calls. Then the phone rang, once, twice. Someone picked it up. "*Travel and Tourism*, Anna McGowan." She didn't quite sound in the next room, but he understood her just fine.

"Anna, honey, it's me, Jerry."

"*Jerry!*" she squeaked. "Oh, my God! Where are you?"

"Right now, I'm on Midway."

"Where the hell is that?"

"In the middle of the Pacific. The ship had some trouble, and they're fixing it here. But my thing is done. They'll fly me to Honolulu tomorrow, and I'll be back in L.A. like midnight tomorrow night. It's Hawaiian Airlines flight, uh,"—he had to check—"three six one. Can you pick me up?"

"I . . . guess so," she said. Her voice firmed. "Yeah, I can do it. If I run on coffee and fumes Friday, then I do, that's all. How *are* you?"

"I'm okay. I miss you. Have the Hughes people kept their promises?"

"Yes, they've been great."

"Glad to hear it." Jerry meant that. "Listen, babe, I gotta go— they don't want us talking long. I'll see you tomorrow night. Don't forget to bring my keys, right? Love you!"

"Love you, too. I'll remember. 'Bye."

"'Bye." He hung up.

Then he called his father. Hyman Stieglitz was an accountant, which meant he got very busy in the couple of months leading up to April 15, after which a lot of the air went out of his business. He answered the office phone right away: "Stieglitz Accounting and Tax Preparation."

"Hey, Dad. It's me. I'll be back in town Friday."

"Okay," his father said, as if he'd driven down to San Diego for a couple of days. "Do I need to pick you up or anything?"

"No, it's okay. Anna's gonna do it."

"All right." His dad accepted that as casually as he said it. "Want to have dinner Saturday night?"

"How about Sunday? Let me have a little chance to sleep and get caught up on things." *Let me have a chance to screw myself silly.*

He didn't say it. Hyman Stieglitz heard it anyway. Even across several thousand miles of bad phone lines, he sounded amused as he answered, "However you want. Call me Sunday morning and we'll figure out where. Did you get in enough work to make the trip worthwhile?"

"Dad, you wouldn't believe me if I told you." Jerry gave back the exact and literal truth.

"That's good. And the money was pretty decent. So all right, then—I'll see you Sunday." His father might have been talking with a client, not a son. Well, they could have been bellowing at each other, old bull and young banging heads, the way they had when Jerry was seventeen. Polite near-indifference seemed more peaceable, if not exactly better.

"'Bye," Jerry said with some polite near-indifference of his own. He walked out of the room with the phone connected to the mainland and nodded at Steve. "Your turn. If you live near where you work, you won't have a long trip home from the airport, either."

"I'm not real far away, no." Steve went into the telephone room, shutting the door behind him.

After that, there was lunch, and after that there was dinner. Both were Navy chow: plain vittles cooked even more plainly. After two months eating high on the hog on the *Glomar Explorer*, that kind of eating seemed like a war crime.

No TV after dinner. There hadn't been any before dinner, either. The Quonset hut didn't hold a set. A shortwave radio sat on a shelf near one end of the prefab building. That seemed to be Midway's main connection to the outside world. Jerry wasn't desperate enough for noise to want to listen to the BBC or Voice of America or even Radio Moscow. Neither was anyone else.

Everybody hit the sack early. If the flight took off at 0600, people would need to be up before sunrise for coffee and, with luck, breakfast. Jerry's mattress was thin and lumpy. He fell asleep as if coshed anyway.

The coffee was hot and fresh. Breakfast . . . biscuits and Danishes left over from the day before. It wasn't a taste treat, but it plastered over the empty places inside. Jerry wished he could have slept for another couple of hours, but he figured he'd make it through the long day ahead.

Along with the other A crew men, he lugged his gear out to the waiting plane. It was, he learned, a Lockheed EC-121 Warning Star, a machine more suited to carrying radar than passengers. With four enormous props, it looked like a leftover from World War II. It also looked as if it had a lot of miles on it.

Jerry figured it had made a ton of flights like this. It ought to be able to manage one more. He stowed his suitcase and hydrophone and plunked his behind down in a low, uncomfortable seat. The engines thundered to life. Soundproofing inside the fuselage? It was to laugh. The Warning Star made the helicopter quiet by comparison.

Four- or five-hour flight, too, Jerry reminded himself as the plane lumbered down the runway and, seemingly to its own surprise, hopped into the air. Next to him, Steve said something. Jerry cupped a hand to his ear to show he hadn't got it.

This time, Steve shouted: "Takes off like a gooney bird!"

"It does!" Jerry nodded to make sure the older man knew he'd heard.

Midway shrank and vanished behind the Warning Star. The ocean was . . . ocean. Jerry spent the flight being bored and deafened. He tried to doze, but the racket defeated him. Steve did sleep for a little while. Jerry didn't know how he could, but envied him.

Jets flew so high, they got above most of the weather. The EC-121 couldn't, so the journey was bouncy as well as noisy. Once or twice, the bounces made Jerry glad for his seat belt.

He couldn't complain about the landing, though. He didn't think he'd ever felt a smoother one. In the airport, he checked his suitcase at the Hawaiian Air counter after extracting *Have Space Suit—Will Travel* to re-rereread on the way back to Los Angeles. He carried the hydrophone through the terminal. He'd stow it in the overhead bin; he didn't want to expose it to the slings and arrows of outrageous baggage handlers.

A place in the airport sold saimin: Japanese noodle soup with pork and herbs and odd, interesting vegetables. Jerry bought a big Styrofoam cupful. It made an outstanding lunch. He knew they'd feed him dinner on the plane to L.A.

Steve got a burger and fries, which left Jerry obscurely disappointed. They found the gate where their flight to Los Angeles would leave, then settled down to wait. Somewhere in the middle of the afternoon, Jerry suddenly laughed. "What's funny?" Steve asked.

"I probably told you, Anna and I are going to Maui for our honeymoon."

"Yes, I think you did."

"And the *Glomar Explorer* was gonna go there, too, after it caught Humpty Dumpty. I was all worried about how I'd have to lie to her and make like I'd never seen Maui before. But the *Explorer* never got there, so I won't have that on my conscience, anyway."

"Good. Lying to people who matter to you chops holes in what you feel about each other. Lying to anybody is bad. Lying to someone who matters to you is worse."

"I was thinking the same thing. Don't have to worry about it now, though."

Half an hour before the scheduled boarding time, a woman's voice came over the PA system: "I'm very sorry, but Hawaiian Flight three six one will experience a small delay. The plane is having some minor mechanical issues, and we want to be absolutely sure everything is all right before we take off. Your safety is our foremost concern. Thank you for your patience."

The "small delay" stretched to an hour and a half. As Jerry finally filed on to the airliner, what kept going through his head was *Anna will kill me.* Picking him up at midnight was bad enough. If he came in at one thirty or two . . .

All he could do would be to apologize over and over. That might not cut it. Anna remembered screwups. This one wasn't his fault, but he'd be the reason she shambled like a zombie tomorrow.

After the plane took off, the pilot said, "Very sorry we're late departing Honolulu, folks. We'll try to make up as much time as we can in the air. Tailwinds will help some. Right now, best guess is we'll be on the ground in Los Angeles about twenty past one Pacific daylight time. If we can do anything to make that earlier, we will, believe me."

A few minutes later, a stewardess added, "We do feel bad about the delay. First drink in coach is free for everyone tonight."

So Jerry had a mai tai, complete with paper umbrella, with his vaguely tropical chicken dinner. For airline food, the meal was pretty decent. After dinner, they darkened the plane for the movie. It was *Mary Poppins*, which wasn't his speed. He turned on his overhead lamp and looked at *Have Space Suit—Will Travel* for a while.

After a while, he found he'd read the same paragraph three times. His body didn't quite know what time it was supposed to be, but did know he'd been up since what felt like forever. He killed the reading light, leaned against the bulkhead, and tried to sleep.

He didn't sleep well on planes—who did?—but managed forty minutes' worth of fitful doze. He wasn't sure he felt better after waking up. He still didn't know what time it should have been, and now he was more awake to realize he didn't know. He wondered if he'd sleep at all once he got back to his place.

He'd worry about that later. He'd worry about lots of things later. Classes at UCLA started on September 23. Since he was coming home now, he wouldn't need a fall quarter leave of absence after all. He'd have to let Professor Krikorian know he was back. *Monday*, he told himself. *It can wait till Monday.*

In the aisle seat, Stephen Dole was watching *Mary Poppins* with every sign of enjoyment. Maybe all his taste was in his mouth. Maybe he was using the movie the way Jerry had used his old, familiar book: to make time go by without thinking very hard. Jerry wasn't snoopy enough to ask.

The airliner droned through the night. It was a lot more comfortable than the Warning Star, and a lot quieter. Of course, this plane was made to carry passengers. On the Navy machine, they were only inconvenient freight.

The movie ended. Except for reading lamps here and there, the plane stayed dark. Somebody a couple of rows behind Jerry snored up a storm. A few people really did manage to sack out at 35,000 feet. Jerry tried to grab a little more shut-eye himself but had no luck.

After a while, the pilot said, "We're beginning our descent into Los Angeles, ladies and gentlemen. Local weather is clear—temperature at the airport is sixty-six degrees. We expect to be on the ground half an hour from now, just before one fifteen." He sounded proud of himself for not being quite so late as he might have been.

They circled over the South Bay so they could land into the wind. Some of those lights down there came from Jerry's apartment building, but he had no idea which ones. Coming back west, the plane flew low over the Harbor Freeway, then much lower over the San Diego—so low, he could almost read the green signs.

A hard bounce, another smaller one, and they were down. Bright lights came on inside the cabin. "Please remain seated with your belts in place and your seats in the fully upright position until we've taxied to the terminal," a stewardess said. California hadn't tumbled into the sea. Jerry was home.

Out of the plane and into the boarding area he came, hydrophone in one hand, *Have Space Suit—Will Travel* in the other. Some of the people waiting for their loved ones seemed ready to party, as if *they'd* gone to Hawaii. Others looked as tired as Jerry felt.

There was Anna! She looked tired, but threw herself into Jerry's arms so fast, he barely had time to put down the hydrophone. After they kissed, she looked up into his eyes and murmured, "Midnight, my ass."

"I'm sorry, babe. I didn't know. I couldn't. They had mechanical trouble in Honolulu."

"Yeah, I found that out . . . after I got here."

"I'm sorry," he said again. Yes, he'd need to abase himself for a while.

Maybe ten feet away, Steve was embracing a woman who looked a lot like Jerry's second-grade teacher. He'd liked Mrs. Simmons, not least because she'd let him stay in the classroom and read instead of going out to the disasters of kickball and sockball at recess.

Steve and his wife came up for air moments after Jerry and Anna did. Steve nodded to him. "Safe trip home."

"You, too," Jerry said. To Anna, he added, "This is Steve Dole. We worked together on the *Glomar Explorer.*" To Steve again: "My fiancée, Anna McGowan."

"Pleased to meet you," Steve said. They shook hands. He went on, "This is my wife, Beth. Beth, Jerry Stieglitz." He remembered Jerry's real last name, which was good. Jerry shook with her. Even her smile was like Mrs. Simmons's.

"Baggage claim," Anna said, in tones that brooked no argument.

To baggage claim they went. Because they were flying in from Hawaii, there was an agricultural checkpoint to deal with first. "Steve and I just walked through the Honolulu airport," Jerry told the inspector. "That's it."

"Where were you coming from, then?" the woman said.

"Midway. We're off the *Hughes Glomar Explorer,* the ocean-mining ship."

The woman looked dubious. But an older man who was examining a couple of other Hawaiian Air passengers overheard and said, "Pass him through, Grace. I dealt with somebody off that ship three days ago. They're legit."

"Okay." By the way Grace said it, she didn't think it was. She let them go on to baggage claim anyhow. That was all Jerry cared about.

Steve's bag came out right away. He and Beth said their good-byes and headed off to wherever she'd parked her car. Jerry and Anna stood there and waited. Time seemed to crawl on its stomach. "Just when you thought things couldn't get any better," Jerry said.

"I was gonna be death warmed over today. Now I'll just be death," Anna replied.

More and more passengers grabbed their suitcases and left. Jerry was starting to wonder whether he'd have to beard the Hawaiian Airlines baggage people in their den (and where their den was) when his suitcase came forth at last. He gratefully grabbed it, stuck the Heinlein inside, and straightened up again. "Let's get out of here."

Anna led him to her car. It was a yellow Toyota, small enough to make his Rambler seem like a Lincoln alongside it. He stashed the suitcase and the hydrophone inside the trunk, slammed it shut, and kissed her again.

She kissed him back . . . for about ten seconds. Then she pulled away. "Jerry, I love you, but I'm punch-drunk. And I have to get up at six fifteen, which feels like ten minutes from now. Save it for later, okay?"

This is a test. If you keep doing what you're doing, you flunk. "Okay," Jerry said, and managed not to sound too grumpy. That he was out on his feet himself didn't hurt. He'd also seen Anna play the same kind of game before. Recognizing it helped him handle it.

When he got into the car, he pushed the passenger seat all the way back. That gave him enough legroom. Even though the Toyota didn't seem much bigger than a tennis shoe, it had more headroom than some standard-sized American machines.

The parking attendant was dozing in his booth, but woke up when Anna's headlights hit him. She paid him. The bar swung up. She drove out and headed east on Century.

Not much traffic at the airport: two in the morning was ebb tide. There was even less as they moved away. Jerry approved; this wasn't a great part of town. Hawthorne, where he and Anna had their apartments, was better, but not a whole lot.

She drove him to his place. She did have his keys with her, too. She used the one that opened the gate to the parking under the building. After she pulled into his space, she gave it to him, along with the apartment key and the one that opened his mailbox in the front lobby.

He took his impedimenta out of the trunk. She'd got out with him, so he kissed her again. He thought about trying to steer her upstairs, then thought better of it. Instead, he said, "I'll see you. We both need to crash."

"Jesus, do we ever!" The way Anna said that made him realize he'd passed another test.

She slid into the car, backed out of the space, and made for the exit on the far side of the building. He followed; the stairs up to the ground level started from the driveway. He slowly climbed them, and the ones that led up to his apartment.

When he opened the door, the place smelled musty. Nobody'd been in and out much lately: just Anna fetching the mail every couple of days. He turned on a light. What she'd brought in lay on the coffee table. A manila envelope meant he'd had a story rejected. He'd get mad about that later.

Now . . . Now he opened the suitcase and took out *Have Space Suit—Will Travel*. They'd flipped through the pages before he left the *Glomar Explorer*. They hadn't thought to take off the dust jacket, though. To make sure they didn't, he'd helpfully held the book while they went through it. He took the jacket off now. He'd taped a photo of Humpty Dumpty inside the front panel, and one of a centaurowl inside the back panel.

They were here. They were safe. He'd made sure. He could relax, as much as he'd ever be able to relax now. He yawned. Relaxed or not, he was exhausted. Everything could wait till the sun came up. He shed his shoes, belt, and the stuff he had in his pockets, collapsed on the bed, and fell asleep.

Jerry woke at half past ten. He still felt beat up and jet-lagged. Anna, of course, had been awake for hours, and was making money at her job. Jerry tried to decide whether he needed breakfast or a shower more. The shower won. It felt great. So did putting on clothes that weren't the ones he'd been wearing over and over since June.

Breakfast . . . Breakfast was more complicated. The cupboard and fridge were bare. He didn't have his car yet. The closest place where he could get food was Pizza Plus, a couple of blocks south and one west from his place. They were good, but in the morning when he didn't have the munchies?

Pizza or go hungry? Pizza won. He walked over, and walked in while they were still opening up. The guy behind the counter gave him the stink eye when he ordered a large with the works, but twenty minutes later he had it. He took it back to the apartment, wolfed down three slices, and stowed the rest in the refrigerator for dinner.

He also made coffee, of a sort: he had Folger's instant, sugar, and Cremora. It tasted like hot mud, but it was hot, caffeinated mud. That was what he needed.

Once fed and energized, he went through the mail Anna'd brought in. He threw a lot of it in the trash—junk was junk, and junk two months old even junkier. There was a letter from the phone company saying they'd cut off service if he didn't pay his bill. Like any other human institution, the CIA failed to think of everything. *Tomorrow*, he told himself. *After I get my wheels back.*

The rejected story had come back from *Analog*. It was a near miss; the letter with it offered encouragement and suggested a couple of tweaks that didn't seem too horrible. Ben Bova didn't promise he'd look at it again if Jerry made the tweaks, but he wouldn't have written that kind of letter if he didn't want to . . . would he?

Bank statements showed he had money in his savings account, more than he was used to. It came from the Summa Corporation.

Jerry needed a moment to remember that was the Hughes subsidiary fronting the *Glomar Explorer.*

After that? After that it was Friday afternoon. Everybody he knew was still working. Even if someone by chance had got time off, whoever it was would have to come here. Without a car, Jerry couldn't go anywhere much. They called Los Angeles' buses the Retarded Transit District for a reason.

What did you do when nothing was going on? Jerry took a nap. Peewee from *Have Space Suit* would have approved. Peewee was a genius, too. Jerry wished he were. He was plenty smart enough, but knew too well that that wasn't the same thing. He also knew he was running on fumes. So he slept some more.

He woke up around five. He might have slept longer yet if he hadn't rolled back into a fresh drool spot on the pillow. He finally felt caught up on sleep, at the price of being out of phase with the rest of the West Coast. That would eventually straighten out. In the meantime . . .

In the meantime, he turned on the oven so he could heat up the rest of his pizza. Anna had made noises about buying a microwave oven to do that kind of thing in seconds. She hadn't done it yet; they cost close to five hundred dollars, more than twice what Jerry'd paid for his electric typewriter. One of these days.

After he ate, he washed the few dishes he'd made. He did that every day. His father was kind of a slob at home. He'd promised himself he'd do better when he had his own place. So far, he hadn't made himself too big a liar. The major exception was the blizzard of papers on the dinette table. Even that was organized chaos. He kept telling himself it was, anyhow.

He looked at that blizzard differently now, though. Whale songs were still interesting, sure. But they didn't seem so totally fascinating anymore, not next to centaurowls and spaceships. The only problem with that was, he didn't have anything to do with centaurowls and spaceships at the moment. And that was nobody's fault but his own.

At a quarter past six, he called Tim Ishihara's apartment. A woman's voice answered: "Hello?"

"Hi, Cheryl. It's Jerry. Is the man home yet?"

"Jerry!" Tim's wife exclaimed. "When did you get back in town?"

"This morning, hideously early. My carcass has no idea what time it's supposed to be."

"I've done that," Cheryl Ishihara said. She raised her voice: "Tim! Jerry's on the phone!"

After a moment, Jerry's buddy came on the line. "Hey, man," he said. "So they finally had enough of you, did they?"

Like a lot of friends, they insulted each other as naturally as they breathed. That crack, though, cut closer to the bone than Tim could know. Jerry needed a moment before he could say, "Damn right they did," without sounding as if he meant it—which he did.

"Were you just along for protective coloration and money, or did you get something worthwhile done?" Tim asked.

"You wouldn't believe me if I told you," Jerry said—one more truth spoken in jest. "Listen, any chance you can drive me down to Long Beach tomorrow so I can get my car back? Without it, I might as well be in jail."

"Yeah, I can do that," his friend said at once—Tim was a friend indeed. "What time you want me to get you?"

"Whatever's easy for you. You're doing me the favor."

"Ten o'clock okay?"

"That'll work. I owe you one, man."

"No sweat. See you then. Listen, I gotta go. Cheryl's waving lamb chops under my nose," Tim said. Jerry thanked him again and hung up.

Then he called Anna. The first thing he said when she picked up the phone was, "How you doing, honey?"

"I'm dead," she answered. "I made it through the day. I had enough coffee to keep me pissing like a racehorse, and I probably won't sleep tonight the way I ought to. But I got through it. How about you?"

"I don't know what time it's supposed to be," he answered, realizing not mentioning how hard he'd crashed had to be the smart play. "Tim's gonna take me down to Long Beach tomorrow morning, so I'll have my wheels back. See you tomorrow night?"

"Sure," she said, and then, "Good for you. If you'd wanted me to come over there tonight, I would've hit you with something as soon as I walked in. A brick, probably."

"I kinda figured that." Jerry'd had enough sleep that he remembered how long it had been since he'd lain down with Anna. After so long, he told himself, one more day wouldn't make that much difference. A particular part of himself didn't want to listen. Even so, he said, "We'll both rest up tonight as much as we can. I'll call you tomorrow when I'm back with the car."

"Okay. *Cut that out!*" she said. Jerry realized the sharp cry was probably aimed at the King of Siam, not at him. Sure enough, Anna muttered, "Stupid cat. Listen, I'm gonna go. Pretty soon I'll collapse, that's all."

"Love you, hon."

"Love you, too. 'Bye."

Left to his own devices, Jerry watched the Angels finish hammering the Milwaukee Brewers. They were still as lousy as they had been when he sailed on the *Glomar Explorer*. With Nolan Ryan pitching, though, they were . . . better, anyhow.

After the game ended, he carefully took the two photos he'd lifted out of their hiding place. He peeled the tape off them. Would anyone who hadn't been there believe they were what they purported to be? He hardly believed it himself, and he'd watched it happen. But they might make people ask interesting questions, anyhow.

Or nobody might ever see them again. You just never knew.

Jerry was standing on the sidewalk in front of his building when Tim pulled up. He'd gone out at ten to ten; he'd known his friend would be five minutes early, and he was. Jerry slid into the car. They shook hands. Tim Ishihara was no more than five eight, and on the chunky side: he and tall, lanky Jerry made an odd pair, but they'd been tight for years and years.

Before Tim drove off, he pointed to the taped-up manila envelope Jerry'd set on the floorboards between his feet. "What you got there?"

"Some stuff. There were . . . hassles on the ship. Can you hang on to this for me, put it in the safest place you can think of? Don't look at it or anything—believe me, you don't want to know. Don't tell anybody about it, either. I mean *anybody*. Give it back to me if I ask for it. Otherwise, just hold it."

Tim didn't hesitate. "Sure, I'll do that. Hell, I'll stash it in the safe at work. Nobody'll get it outa there." He had a tech job in aerospace over in Redondo Beach. As he stepped on the gas, he said, "You all right? This sounds kinda heavy."

"I *think* everything is okay. I'm just staying on the safe side, like. If I'm wrong, well, you'll know. Do whatever you think is best then."

Tim turned onto Rosecrans and headed east toward the Harbor Freeway. Jerry remembered the freeway pushing south past the elementary school where the two friends met. It seemed a million years ago, but it wasn't. His mother had already died by then.

Slowly, Tim said, "You mean, if anything happens to you?"

"Nothing's gonna happen to me." One more time, Jerry tried not to think about termination with extreme prejudice. One more time, he didn't have much luck. It was too much like trying *not* to think about a blue monkey. Even as that thought ran through his mind, he realized he'd got it from one of Manly Wade Wellman's Silver John stories. Science fiction and fantasy had started warping his life long before Stephen Dole first showed him photos of what they weren't yet calling Humpty Dumpty.

Tim took one hand off the wheel to scratch an ear. He still wore his hair short. He'd grown sideburns, but that was as far as he'd gone along those lines. But for them, he still looked the way he had in high school. "I hope you know what you're doing," he said.

"Me, too," Jerry said: an admission, he realized too late, that he wasn't telling everything he might have.

The rest of the ride to the south passed mostly in silence. Only after the Long Beach Freeway divided and they went to the harbor instead of into downtown Long Beach did Jerry tell his friend how best to get to Pier E. Tim pulled into the parking lot where Jerry's Rambler had been sitting since June. Jerry hoped like hell they'd remembered to turn the engine over every now and then.

He and Tim walked to the security perimeter that had protected the *Glomar Explorer*. The ship was long gone; the perimeter remained. Tim whistled softly. "Razor wire? They weren't kidding around, were they?" he said.

"Not even a little bit," Jerry said.

A man with a pistol on his hip came out of the little guard shack as Jerry and Tim drew near. "Do something for you guys?" he asked. He would have said "Do something *to* you guys?" in the same tone of voice.

"I'm Jerry Steinberg. I'm just back from the *Glomar Explorer*. You people have my car keys," Jerry said.

"Hang on." The guard ducked back into the shack for a moment. When he reemerged, he had the keys and a clipboard. "Show me some ID, please."

Jerry produced the driver's license from the apartment on Ocean Boulevard. The guard looked it over, nodded, made a checkmark on the sheet in the clipboard, and gave him the keys. "Thanks," Jerry said.

"No problem," the guard replied. Since he had the proper papers, he'd earned the proper respect.

As he and Tim went back to the lot, Tim said, "Steinberg?"

"Yeah, well . . ." Jerry shrugged. "Everything they say about how security-crazy Howard Hughes is, it's an understatement." Which was true, if you substituted a secretive spy agency for a reclusive gazillionaire. Or, for all Jerry could prove, even if you didn't.

"Crazy enough to get people fake licenses?" Tim said. Jerry just shrugged again. He hoped Tim wouldn't push it. His friend didn't; he had the same kind of politesse as the King of Siam.

There was the Rambler. It was dusty, but all the tires had air in them. Jerry opened the driver's-side door. Hot air poured out. He rolled down the window. To Tim, he said, "Hang around till I make sure it starts, okay?"

"I was going to. I'll give you a jump if it doesn't." Tim sounded offended he could have imagined anything else.

Jerry slid behind the wheel. When he turned the key, the motor fired up right away. "Ignition! Liftoff!" he said.

"Cool. Want to go somewhere and have lunch?"

"Did you see that Greek place a couple of blocks back? That might do it. They had 'Breakfast' on the sign, so they should be open."

"Sounds like a plan," Tim said.

The Greek place wasn't fancy—what harborside joint was?—but it gave a lot of food for not a whole lot of money. Tim had chicken in avgolemono sauce; Jerry got the keftedakia plate. He bought. Tim grumbled, but only for form's sake. He'd driven Jerry here; he deserved some reward.

"You heading back up now?" Tim asked as they walked out to their cars.

"One more errand to run down here," Jerry answered. "You

saw my fake ID—forget you did, man. That never happened, okay? Anyway, I need to get my real one back."

Tim Ishihara looked at him. "You want somebody around?" He didn't say *in case they hit you over the head with a pipe*, but getting it didn't take much reading between the lines, either.

"Everything oughta be cool." Jerry didn't want company. He also didn't want to drag Tim in any deeper, although with that envelope, his friend was already in too deep.

"Okay. I sorta have to figure you know what you're doing. I only wish I had some evidence to go with that."

"My ass and your face," Jerry said sweetly. They both laughed. As long as they were woofing on each other, things couldn't be too bad. They could pretend things weren't, anyhow.

Tim drove off toward the freeway. He'd head back to his place in Lawndale, to his wife, to peace and quiet. Jerry started in the same direction, but he couldn't go home yet. He just hoped the CIA was still renting that apartment on Ocean. Without documents that proclaimed who you were, how could even you tell?

He found the white stucco apartment building with the blue roof, and also found a parking space. He walked in through the gateless entrance and went to apartment 127. The door opened almost as soon as he used the coded knock. The tough guy standing there wasn't somebody Jerry'd seen before. "If you're selling something, we don't want any," the fellow growled.

The mad demon that infested Jerry's brain made him wish he had *Watchtower* tracts to shove at the (probably) CIA man. Since he didn't, he just said, "I'm off the *Glomar Explorer*. I'm here to get my real license and my credit card and my Social Security card back."

"Oh." The man looked at him differently. "What's your name—your real one?" Jerry told him. The guy checked a list, nodded to himself, and stepped aside. "C'mon in." He turned. "We got another one, Vic."

For all Jerry could prove, Vic hadn't moved from behind that table in the past two and a half months. He held out his hand. "Lemme have the documents we gave you back in June." Jerry handed them over. Vic nodded to himself. "All here—good." He looked up. "Have any trouble with 'em?"

"No. I didn't use them much, but they worked when I did."

"Good deal. That's what we want to hear." Vic opened his cash box with a key and flipped through envelopes till he found the one with *Steinberg* so neatly written on it. He took out Jerry's authentic documents and gave them to him. "Here you go."

"Thanks." Jerry checked to make sure they really were his before he put them in his wallet. Vic chuckled, for all the world as if the idea that the CIA might play identity games with him was the funniest thing in the world. Jerry stuck the wallet in his pocket and got the hell out of there.

When Anna let Jerry into her apartment, the King of Siam took one look at him, then bolted into the bedroom and hid under the bed. The beast hadn't seen him for a couple of months, which made him a stranger and a presumptive cat-killer. If you looked at it the right way, it was funny. If you didn't, the way the King of Siam saw Jerry was too much like the way Jerry saw the CIA. He did his damnedest to look at it right.

He kissed Anna, which took his mind off other things while he was doing it. "Hey, babe," he said. "How are you?"

"I'm tired. I'm way better than I was yesterday, though—I'll tell you that."

"I *am* sorry." Jerry'd known he would keep paying for his late flight.

"It wasn't your fault." From Anna, that was no small admission. She took back half of it a moment later: "No matter whose fault it was, I was a mumbling idiot at the office."

"It was screwed up all the way around. You want to go to Tres Hermanos and get something to eat?" Jerry said. They both liked the Mexican place on Prairie.

"And a margarita. Maybe three margaritas, one for each brother," Anna said. Jerry nodded. Tequila wasn't his favorite, but Tres Hermanos served Dos Equis, too. He liked that fine.

He had enough beer with dinner to be extra careful driving back to her place. Luckily, it wasn't far. The King of Siam had come out when he realized he had the apartment to himself. Since Jerry walked in with Anna, the cat decided he might be an acceptable human being after all.

Then his very own person shut him out of the bedroom while Jerry stayed in there with her. That was insulting enough to provoke a couple of irate meows. The cat must have realized the people weren't paying any attention to him, because he shut up after that.

"Oh, honey," Jerry said. "*Oh*, honey. I missed you *so* much."

Anna poked him in the ribs with a sharp fingernail. "Did you miss me or did you just miss *this*? You could play with yourself in the shower and get *this*."

He'd done that. He was damned if he'd admit it. "It's not the thing. It's the company." He meant most of that, anyway. And he did his very best to show her how sincere he was.

His very best must have been good enough, because she didn't hit him when he was ready to go again right away. He thought he got her where she was going once more, too, but he was less sure than he had been the first time. That made him decide against trying for round three just then.

She got up, used the bathroom, and let in the King of Siam. Instead of hiding under the bed, the cat jumped up onto it. Jerry held out his hand. The Siamese sniffed it, then suffered himself to be scritched.

"We need a new wedding date," Anna said. Spoken by a woman wearing bare skin, the words were more inspiring than they might have been otherwise.

Jerry nodded. "I've been thinking about that, too."

"You have?" Anna sounded amazed.

"Uh-huh. How does the twenty-fourth of November sound? It's the Sunday before Thanksgiving. If I remember straight, the sections I'm gonna teach this quarter are on Thursday and Friday, so I wouldn't even need anybody to cover for me while we go on our honeymoon."

For the first time since he'd come home, she kissed him instead of the other way around. He'd heard somewhere that the person who started a kiss was the one who really needed it. He didn't know if he totally agreed with that, but it made more than a little sense.

When they broke apart, she said, "I love you! That's just the day I was looking at myself! I checked with the temple. They had it open, so I booked it."

"Good deal," Jerry said. Anna was an even more half-assed Protestant than he was a Jew, so they'd planned a Jewish wedding. She made noises about converting. If she decided she wanted to go through with it, that was fine with him. If she didn't, that was fine, too. He asked, "Can we still get Rabbi Burstein?"

"I called him. He's free," Anna answered. People who looked at Jerry, with his long hair and his beard, sometimes said he looked like a rabbinical student. People who looked at Shlomo Burstein, with his bald head and his long, tangled gray beard, said he looked like a rabbi. Jerry wasn't so sure about that. He thought Rabbi Burstein looked more like God's older brother.

"Then we're good." Jerry kissed her now. This one went on longer than the last one had. Down deep in his throat, he said, "I think we're pretty good." Stroking her was more fun than it was with the King of Siam.

"I should have told the cook at Tres Hermanos to put saltpeter on your rice and beans," she said darkly. He knew she'd got that from *Auntie Mame*, because he'd found it there, too. He had no idea whether saltpeter did what people claimed it did. A moment later, she said, "Really?"

"I don't know. Let's find out," he answered.

He managed it, too. That surprised him almost as much as it delighted him, at least until Anna said, "Once we're married, you'd better not go away for months at a time. I'm not sure I'd live through the reunions."

Thanks a lot. Jerry got just enough of where she was coming from to keep from saying it out loud. Fighting at reunions wasn't in the recipe for happiness, either; he could see that. They weren't always in perfect rhythm about what went on in the bedroom. He kept hoping more time together would get them better synched.

She asked, "So what did you actually do while you were out in the middle of the Pacific for four years?"

Lying at a loving reunion wasn't a great plan, either. He knew that. It wasn't that she wouldn't believe the truth; she read science fiction and fantasy, too. But telling her the truth would put her in the same kind of danger he'd put himself in when he smuggled those two photos out of the Special Measurements container. He was willing to take his own chances. He didn't want her to have to.

Then what about Tim? he asked himself. That somehow felt different. The difference between a loved one and a friend? Between a woman and a man? Maybe he just thought Tim was better at taking care of himself.

"Hello?" Anna said. "Did *all* your brains fall out that time?"

"Felt like it," Jerry answered with dignity, wishing she were as happily torpid as he was. He went on, "I really didn't do a whole lot. I was one more research project on a research ship. Engine

THREE MILES DOWN   163

noise and things kept me from getting the kind of data I wanted. But I sure got the kind of money I wanted."

"That was good," she agreed. "Seems almost like they wanted you more for cover than for what you could really do, though."

No, she didn't have a college degree. Yes, she was plenty smart anyhow: more than smart enough to see the obvious. "Next time you're at my place, I'll show you a manganese nodule," he said. "I've got one in my suitcase, maybe the size of a golf ball. We all do—souvenirs, you know. They came in the sludge along with the bigger ones the mining unit was really after. I don't know how much money the Hughes people spent on the project and on security, but having me along was chump change to them. Less than chump change."

As with Tim before, except for tagging Howard Hughes instead of the CIA, he wasn't even lying. And Hughes made perfect camouflage for the Agency. Anna proved it: "He's nuttier than a Mission Pak fruitcake. He has been for years. Everybody knows that."

"Hey, I'm not gonna argue with you, babe. He threw money at me when he didn't have to. If that doesn't make him crazy, what would?" Jerry said.

"Good point," she said, puncturing him and getting the last word at the same time. If only she didn't sound so much as if she meant it . . .

He'd intended to spend the night at her place. He liked sleeping with her, even when it was only sleeping. He put up with sleeping with the King of Siam, who sometimes decided an exposed ear was something that needed killing. Now he decided going back to his apartment made a better idea. Assuming he was entitled to stay was liable to piss her off.

She didn't ask what he was up to or tell him to stop when he began getting dressed. That made him figure he was probably doing the right thing. She needed to get used to his being around again, too. "We're both still getting our act back together," he said.

"And getting *our* act together back," she said, which also wasn't wrong.

From her place to his wasn't more than five minutes. He thought hard all the way down 139th Street. Everything would be fine for a while. He'd lifted the photo of Humpty Dumpty and the one of the aliens inside from the middle of sequences of similar pictures.

Nobody would notice they were missing right away. You'd need to count the prints or compare them one by one with the negatives before you'd realize a couple had walked with Jesus.

Not with Jesus, Jerry thought as he pulled into his building's driveway. *I'm only a distant, distant cousin.* He was smiling when the security gate swung up to let him in, but not by the time he got out of his car.

Jerry dialed the number his old house had used since he was eight years old. They called it a three-two number now, not a DAvis number, but it was still the same number no matter what they called it. The phone rang twice. Then his father picked it up. "Hello?"

"Hi, Dad. It's me."

"Oh, hi, Jerry," Hyman Stieglitz said, as if the call were a surprise. Then he got himself back in gear. "Where do you want to go tonight? The Tijuana Inn okay?"

"Anna and I had Mexican food last night," Jerry said.

"Did you? All right. How's Helen Yee's sound, then?"

"That'd be great," Jerry said. When he was a kid, Gardena had boasted only two Chinese restaurants. Helen Yee's was the good one. There were more Chinese places around now, and it seemed kind of old-fashioned, because it hadn't changed a bit. But the food was still tasty. "What time?"

"Six o'clock work for you?"

"How about a quarter to?" Jerry said. If his father went along with that, he ought to be there by six straight up.

"Fine," his dad said. "See you then." He hung up. So did Jerry.

Helen Yee's actually worked out pretty well. It was on Rosecrans a little west of Western, about halfway between the house where Jerry's father still lived and his apartment. The lot just east of the restaurant had always intrigued him. For as long as he could remember, it had held a Quonset hut like the ones on Midway, what he thought were drop tanks, and other war-surplus junk.

He pulled into the parking lot right at five forty-five. One glance told him his father's big Olds wasn't there yet. He walked into the restaurant. He was enough of a regular that the woman behind the register smiled at him and said, "Hello! You aren't here with your lady friend?"

"Not today. My dad and I are having dinner."

"Ah. Table for two anyway, then." She plucked menus from a stack and led him to one. The place wasn't crowded. A waiter brought a pot of smoky tea and two small, handleless cups.

Hyman Stieglitz strode in at two minutes to six. For him, that was making good time. Jerry waved. His father came over. They shook hands. "How you doing, kiddo?" his father asked, as if he were still nine.

"I'm okay. Still don't know what time zone I ought to be in, but I'll get over that. How are *you*?" Jerry asked the last question with some concern. Not having seen his dad in a while reminded him the old man was, well, old. He looked weary. And his clothes and probably his skin carried the ingrained stink of a million cigarettes. Smokers didn't know they smelled bad, but everybody else did.

"I'm fine," he said as he sat down. He put on a pair of reading glasses for the menu. Laughing sourly as he did it, he added, "Time's a real son of a gun, you know?"

"Yeah." Jerry nodded. Being on the *Glomar Explorer* with the old guys had rubbed his nose in that. So had Bob the engineer, who'd dropped dead after hustling to catch his plane home.

His father snorted. "Fat lot you know about it. When I was your age, I was in a foxhole somewhere between Rome and Milan, and the Germans were throwing mortar bombs at me."

"Yeah," Jerry said again, and then, "You don't usually talk about the war."

"Not a lot *to* talk about. I didn't want to be there. Nobody wanted to be there, not even the Krauts. I mean, they needed beating, God knows, but it wasn't fun or anything. People who're happy because they fought in it, those stupid *mamzrim*, don't remember what it was like. Nobody who ever smelled a dead body's got any business being proud of making like a soldier."

That was more than he'd said about World War II than any other time Jerry could recall. It also reminded him of how veterans his age talked about Vietnam. Before Jerry could ask him to go on, the waiter came by to take their orders. They both chose the number two dinner. The waiter scribbled on a notepad and went back to the kitchen.

Hyman Stieglitz sipped tea and looked down at his hands. He seemed as surprised he'd opened up a little as Jerry was. After a moment, he asked, "What was it like while you were on the ship?"

"Like a hotel, more than anything else. Hughes has more money than they know what to do with," Jerry answered—once more, the truth, as long as you substituted the *Glomar Explorer*'s actual owners for the ones it belonged to on paper. He tried to steer his father back to the days before he'd been born: "What was the ship you crossed the Atlantic in like?"

"Horrible scow. Liberty ship. Couldn't make ten knots if you threw it off a cliff." Plainly, his dad didn't have fond memories. "Bunks four and five high, maybe eighteen inches between them. Crappy food. Nobody wanted to eat anyway, 'cause it smelled like puke all the time—the ocean was rough and we got seasick. The heads . . . You don't even want to think about the heads." He paused. "Let's not talk about that. Here come the soup and the appetizers. How can you enjoy appetizers with no appetite?"

The soup was egg drop, something Jerry only had at Chinese restaurants. The spoons were similarly distinctive. The first mouthful took him back in time. He'd loved egg drop soup when he was little, and he still did. The appetizer platter hadn't changed, either. Fried shrimp with the batter curled around to make them circles. Pork ribs in a sweet-and-sour glaze. Foil-wrapped chicken, his least favorite part of the platter. Egg rolls. Egg foo young.

"I hope this place is still here when your kids can enjoy it," his father said.

"That would be good," Jerry answered, though Anna was dubious about children. He was dubious about them himself; he didn't think he'd make a great dad. He added, "We've got a new wedding date—the twenty-fourth of November."

"I was going to play golf that day," his father said, so straight-faced that Jerry believed him for a moment. Hyman Stieglitz smiled crookedly; he knew he'd scored a hit.

You got beef with broccoli and exotic, steaky mushrooms, along with chicken fried rice and shrimp chow mein. The shrimp there were much smaller than the ones that glorified the appetizer platter. A bowl of fried noodles let you soak up sauces or just eat something crunchy if you felt like that. Jerry'd always pigged out on them when he was little. Now he made sure he cleaned his plate first.

"I'll bring dessert in one minute," the waiter said as he put dirty dishes on a tray. Jerry nodded. His father lit a cigarette. He always did right after dinner. A couple of other people in the restaurant were smoking, too. Jerry thought it was gross, but what could you do?

The waiter came back with a little lacquerware tray that held fortune cookies, almond cookies, and the bill. Hyman Stieglitz took that. "Hey, I was gonna pay," Jerry said. "I've even got money for a change."

"Don't worry about it. I'm not broke." His father opened his fortune cookie. "*Good luck is heading your way.* That'd be nice. What's yours say?"

Jerry cracked his cookie, too. "*You will succeed despite difficulties.* How does it know I'm in grad school?"

"Magic. Ancient Chinese magic, probably from a cookie factory in Oxnard." Jerry'd lived with his father till he got his bachelor's degree. Since then, he'd tried to forget how much of the way he thought came from his old man.

His father put a ten, a one, and a couple of quarters on the tray. As they walked out together, Jerry said, "Thanks, Dad. You really didn't have to do that."

"I know. I wanted to, though. What are those difficulties you'll succeed in spite of?"

What would he do if I told him? Jerry asked himself, and immediately answered his own question: *He'd land in the CIA's crosshairs, too, that's what.* Tim was now, no matter how much Jerry didn't like it. *Three men may keep a secret, if two of them are dead.* If he knew what Benjamin Franklin had said, so would the Agency.

No more than half a second slower than he should have, he said, "Too much work. Not enough time. Not enough money—the time on the *Glomar Explorer* helped there, anyhow."

"Good. You should have a little something socked away before you get married," his father said. He'd been ten years old when the market crashed in 1929. He'd worked on and off from the following summer on, and studied in scraps of time he'd carved out somehow. The Depression scarred him for life. As much as anyone could be, he was a self-made man, and sometimes thought Jerry's generation soft and spoiled. He might not be religious, but he passionately believed in suspenders *and* belt.

"I do my best, Dad, honest." Young man and older went their separate ways.

XII

Monday morning, Jerry called Professor Krikorian. "So you're back, are you?" his advisor rumbled. "Now you can tell me about how we're going to get all our metal from manganese nodules from now on, right?"

"Not exactly," Jerry said. "The machinery still has some kinks in it."

"Good," Hagop Krikorian said, which surprised Jerry. "Even if it didn't, I wouldn't like it, not even a little bit. Strip-mining is bad enough on dry land. On the ocean floor, where all the sediment you kick up goes into the water and circulates? You have to be crazy!" He added something in what might have been Armenian.

"Yeah." Jerry hadn't really thought about that. He realized he should have. He also realized the professor had less to worry about than he feared, since that wasn't really a mining machine the pipe string had lowered to the bottom. He couldn't say anything about what it was, especially over the phone. He did say, "The gadget didn't work as well as they wanted it to. I'm not supposed to tell anybody much, but I can say that."

"Breaks my heart," Krikorian said. "Did you get any decent recordings out of it, at least?"

"Afraid not. Engine noise and machinery noise kind of ruined things. I did get more money than I would have from a year of TAing, though."

"Grad school is a miserable business. You think it's bad now . . ."

To Jerry's relief, Professor Krikorian didn't launch into more tales of how rotten things had been in his day. That let the current sufferer say, "Can I bring the hydrophone up to campus today so I don't have to worry about it in my apartment anymore?"

"Sure. Bring it here. I'll be in the office till about four."

"I'll be there inside an hour. When I come, will you give me the form authorizing eight units of directed study from you?" In something straight out of *Catch-22*, Jerry had to be an enrolled student to serve as a teaching assistant. That killed more than half a month's paycheck by itself.

"Yeah, sure. We'll dot the i's and cross the t's." Krikorian sounded as disgusted with university foolishness as anyone to whom it didn't apply very well could. Then again, he had his own bureaucratic barbed wire to cut through.

Jerry put the hydrophone in his car and drove up to UCLA. He paid to park on campus, to save himself from having to lug it very far. There were free spots around the university to grab, but you had to show up early and you had to be willing to walk.

He delivered the instrument and collected his form. He was glad his advisor didn't pump him for details about the *Glomar Explorer*'s supposed nodule vacuum. He had none, not for a fictitious device.

Escaping Professor Krikorian let him go over to Murphy Hall, the building that ran the university. He turned in the form. He paid the fee that went with it. He didn't need to worry about his check bouncing, the way he had at the start of a couple of anxious quarters. He'd never actually had one come back, but those escapes came too close for comfort.

Missions accomplished, he went home. He enjoyed driving the San Diego Freeway when it wasn't rush hour. To him, it was what driving should have been all the time. You were here, you needed to get there, and you did. Not much traffic to worry about, only the new and ever more ignored fifty-five-mile-per-hour speed limit.

After he pulled into his parking space, he went to the lobby to see what the mailman had wrought. There were ads for local restaurants and an auto-parts place, plus a bank statement: it was the second of the month. He set a hand on his heart to hold in the excited palpitations, then climbed the stairs to his place.

Most of the mail went straight into the trash. He almost tossed the statement, too. It wasn't as if he'd written any checks in August except the one settling his overdue phone bill, and that wouldn't have cleared yet. But he was trying to get back into the regular swing of things, so he opened it.

No, no canceled checks in the envelope. There was the record of the payment for his second month on the *Glomar Explorer*. And, below that, there was a listing for another deposit to his savings account, this one in the amount of $57,211.92. It had gone into the account about when he was waking up Friday.

His eyes popped. He jerked straight upright, as if somebody'd jabbed him in the ass with a hat pin. Adrenaline iced him down, the way it had right after he got rear-ended. He felt as if he'd just picked up the BANK ERROR IN YOUR FAVOR—COLLECT $200 card in a Monopoly game.

But not $200. $57,211.92. "Bullshit," he muttered as he came back to earth. That kind of money didn't fall from the sky. Even with inflation going crazy and gas up around sixty cents a gallon, you could live for three years on that kind of money, and live pretty decently, too. Maybe even four.

You could if they let you keep it, that is. Fat chance! He'd watched computers in action out in the Pacific, and seen the future brought to life. Here, he had to be back in the all-too-fallible present. Some electronic "brain" somewhere must have screwed up.

He went into the bedroom, ready to call Bank of America and give them a piece of his mind. But he stopped before he picked up the phone. Some things needed to be done in person. He wouldn't get the runaround that way. He wouldn't get so much of it, anyhow.

Down to the car, bank statement in hand. The branch he used was on Gardena Boulevard, closer to the house where he'd grown up than to where he lived now. It was his folks' bank, too. He'd had his own account there since before his mother died; his father hoped to get him used to saving money. That had worked out the way Dad wanted, sure enough.

Fifteen minutes later, he stood in line at the bank. Five minutes after that, he walked up to a teller. "Yes, sir? How can I help you today?" the Japanese-American woman asked. She was maybe five years older than he was, so he hadn't gone to school with her, but he would have bet she came out of Gardena High, too.

He showed her the statement, pointing out the insane item. "This can't be right," he said. "What do I have to do to get it fixed?"

A vertical line appeared between her eyes as she frowned. "That is . . . a lot of money," she said carefully. "Let me check it for you, okay?" She took the statement and disappeared with it. Jerry imagined alarm bells ringing and cops aiming pistols at him.

She came back a few minutes later. "This seems to be correct, Mr. Stieglitz. We received a certified check from the Summa Corporation for deposit to your account, the same way we did with the two smaller payments before. You are familiar with the Summa Corporation?"

"I am, yeah." Jerry knew he sounded dazed. Summa meant Howard Hughes meant CIA front. But why the hell had the CIA suddenly dropped a not-so-small fortune into his lap?

The teller said, "If somebody paid me that much money, I bet I'd look happier than you do right now."

"I'm still kind of getting used to the idea," Jerry said. She slid the bank statement across the counter at him. He took it, looked at it one more time to make sure those numbers were still there, and walked out of the bank building.

A secondhand bookstore with a good sf section was only a few doors down from the B of A. Jerry usually went in when he found himself here. Today, he just got in the car and headed back to his apartment. His head buzzed like an out-of-control electric motor all the way there.

What had Dale said while he was canning him? Something to the effect that Jerry wouldn't hurt for money because he'd got involved with Azorian and Midlothian. He didn't remember the exact words, but that was what it amounted to.

He put the Rambler in park, turned off the engine, and pulled the hand brake. Not hurting for money was one thing. This, this right here, was something else again. Throwing a stack of greenbacks like that at him?

"Why, in God's name?" he said as he got out and locked the car. As soon as he asked the question that way, he saw the likely answer. What did they think they were buying with so much money out of the blue? What could it be but his silence? *We'll make you happy*, they had to be saying. *Now you keep your mouth shut and make us happy, too.*

He looked around the quiet parking garage before he headed for the stairs. No hit man lurking behind a Ford Pinto. Wouldn't rubbing him out have been cheaper than bribing him? Maybe not. Always the risk that the cops might uncover more than the Agency wanted them to, or even that the gunman would wonder why he'd plugged a harmless grad student and start poking around. Money would do the job as long as Jerry played along.

He'd thought about the Bank Error card before. To the CIA, that was what fifty-seven grand and change added up to: Monopoly money. They might not print it themselves, but they sure knew the people who did.

"Crazy. Fucking crazy," he said, and went on up to his place.

The next day, he got a letter in a Summa Corporation envelope. It had been postmarked the Saturday before in Honolulu. That gave him a running start at guessing who'd actually written it.

When he opened the envelope, the letter inside also proved to be on Summa Corporation letterhead. It was handwritten, though, which he couldn't imagine any real corporation big shot doing. He had no trouble reading Dale Neuwirth's script.

Dear Jerry, the mission director wrote,

> *As I told you when you were leaving the project, everyone here was delighted with your cleverness and resourcefulness, which played a vital role in our successes up to this point. Talk is cheap, though, and sometimes a more material show of appreciation can be welcome. Accordingly, it was my pleasure to award you a bonus equivalent to two years' salary. This amount, minus deductions for federal and state taxes, should have been deposited in your bank account by now. You've earned it, believe me. And, as I also told you before, you have only to ask if I can be of any further assistance. Sincerely—*

Dale's signature followed. He wrote *Neuwirth*, though that surely wasn't his real last name. Jerry wondered what that name was in fact, and also wondered whether he'd ever learn it. He had his doubts.

He did abstractly admire the letter. No one who read it could have any idea what kind of project he'd been working on or what he'd done that the boss man so appreciated. The most even Sherlock Holmes would deduce was that it was something special, to have earned such a generous bonus.

He wondered if they'd bribed Steve the same way. It occurred to him that he could call the older man at the RAND Corporation and ask him. Half a second later, it also occurred to him that that wouldn't be Phi Beta Kappa. Bonus or no bonus, from now on he had to figure the CIA was keeping tabs on him. Talking about Azorian on the phone, even with someone else who'd worked on it, might be dangerous. Talking about Midlothian or Humpty Dumpty might be worse than dangerous.

Up to the apartment he went, letter in hand. He stopped halfway up the stairs to the second level. "Huh!" he said thoughtfully. That hesitancy—hell, that fear—about talking too much on the phone must already have taken root in his mind. Otherwise, why hadn't he told Anna about the money when he talked to her last night?

He started up the stairs again. When she came over, or when he went to her place . . . He shook his head. If they could bug his phone, they could bug his apartment, too. And hers.

"Christ," he said as he unlocked his door. If he went on thinking this way, he'd end up as paranoid as Richard Nixon. Understanding fear of persecution from the inside out might prove useful to him as a writer. Any new experience might. All the same, he could have done without this one.

On Thursday, he went up to UCLA again to put in an interlibrary-loan request for a Japanese journal with a study of humpback migration patterns. The article was in Japanese, but it had a summary in English that would give him the gist. And maps showed the same oceans, regardless of language.

Interlibrary loans all went through the Research Library at the north end of campus. It would have been nice if he could have done this through the Biomedical Llibrary in his preferred part of the sprawling university, but no such luck.

At UCLA, science, engineering, and mathematical types mostly hung out in the southern part of the campus. The north was for English majors, would-be historians, students of foreign languages, and others even less likely than marine biologists to land jobs after graduating. There *were* more girls up there, but that was only of theoretical interest to him these days.

He walked past Bunche Hall on his way to the library. Every one called the building the Waffle. The red-brown granite on the south-facing side was punctuated by a grid of square, dark windows. It had been the Social Sciences Building when he got to UCLA in 1966. They rechristened it for the diplomat two years later and put his bust, his name, and, below it, 1904– near the elevators. Bunche's birth year was set asymmetrically under the name. That had pissed Jerry off: it was as if they were waiting for Bunche to die. When he did, near the end of 1971, symmetry was restored.

When Jerry turned in the request form, the woman who took it said, "You understand, it won't come in right away. Three weeks if you're lucky, six if you aren't."

"I know," he answered resignedly. "I've done this before. I'm just glad I'll get my hands on it sooner or later."

She nodded. "That's the right attitude. Interlibrary loan is marvelous, but sometimes people expect too much of it." Even librarians got excited about what they did.

Instead of driving straight home after finishing his morning errand, Jerry took the Santa Monica Freeway west from the San Diego. Ten minutes later, he was in Santa Monica and the freeway was ending. Not far from where it did, the RAND Corporation had its headquarters. The curving gray stone walls, the sheer size of the building, and where it was declared that RAND wouldn't be out begging on the sidewalk with a tin cup and sunglasses any time soon.

A single entrance channeled visitors to a reception area. "What can I do for you today, sir?" asked a man about Jerry's age when Jerry came up to his desk.

"My name is Jerry Stieglitz. I'd like to talk with Doctor Stephen Dole for a few minutes, if that's possible."

"About what?"

"Some business we were both doing this summer."

"Let me check." The man picked up a phone and punched in a number. He spoke briefly, then hung up and again acknowledged that Jerry was there. "Yes, he'll see you, Mr. Stieglitz. How do you spell your last name?" When Jerry told him, he typed it on a square of cardboard and put that in a plastic holder. He spoke into the phone again before handing Jerry the badge. "This is your visitor's display. Please show it as you walk through the hallways. Your escort will be here in a moment."

Jerry pinned the badge to his shirt. He wondered whether different days had different-colored holders so you couldn't use today's next Tuesday. RAND seemed to take security as seriously as the CIA did.

The escort was a black woman a couple of years older than he was. She had a badge, too. It bore her photo and the name Angela Simmons. "Come with me, please," she said, and led Jerry past the receptionists.

An elevator ride to the third floor, a walk down a corridor that could have belonged to a prosperous corporation anywhere in the

world, a stop at a door with Steve's name and "Director of Communications" on it. Angela Simmons knocked. Steve opened the door.
"Hi, Jerry," he said, and then, to the woman, "Thanks for bringing
him up, Angela."

"You're welcome, Doctor Dole," she said. "I'll wait here to take
him down again."

"Okay." Steve waved Jerry in, then shut the door behind him.
The office also could have belonged to any prosperous corpora-
tion anywhere. Steve sat down behind his aircraft carrier of a desk,
Jerry in front of it. "What can I do for you?" the older man asked.

"I was up at UCLA turning in a book request. Long as I was
close by, I figured I'd stop in and see if you wanted to have lunch.
It's getting close to twelve." As Jerry spoke, he pointed to corners
of the room where walls met ceiling. How did you suggest a place
might be bugged without yelling, *Hey, this place might be bugged*?

He'd never been great at charades, but Steve got the message.
"Sure, we can do that," he said. "Did you see that place just when
you were getting off the freeway?"

"The one with the penguin outlined in neon on the sign?"

"That's it. It's called the Penguin Coffee Shop."

"No kidding? I figured they'd name it the Hyena or something."

Steve chuckled. "You haven't changed, have you?" He and Jerry
went out together. Steve told Angela, "We're going to have lunch
together, so you can do whatever else you need to. I'll get him outside myself."

"However you want, Doctor Dole." She nodded to him, then to
Jerry, and went on her way.

Once they were out in the open air, Jerry shed his badge. So
did Steve. The man from the RAND Corporation asked, "Do you
really think they're listening to what goes on inside my office?"

"I don't know. I think they could be. It's harder out here." Jerry
still wondered whether Stephen Dole reported back to the CIA,
too. But Dale had fired Steve right after he got Jerry, so that seemed
unlikely. And Steve was already in the know; Jerry could talk to
him without putting him in more danger than he was in already.
He had to talk to *somebody*.

"Okay." By the way Steve said it, he might have been humoring
a nut case. "Go on."

"Did something funny happen with your bank account right after
you got back to L.A.? Did you get a letter from Dale telling you

what a good boy you'd been without saying a word about how or why you'd been a good boy?"

Steve missed a step. After he caught himself, he answered, "Yes and yes, respectively." He didn't sound as if he thought Jerry was crazy anymore.

"They're bribing us to keep our mouths shut," Jerry said.

"They sure are. As far as I'm concerned, it's going to work, too. They could be killing us to keep our mouths shut." Steve said nothing more till they got to the corner across the street from the Penguin Coffee Shop. As he punched the button on the streetlight pole and waited for the Walk signal, he added, "Isn't this a cheerful thing to talk about on the way to lunch?"

"Well, yeah," Jerry said. The light changed. He and Steve crossed the street and walked into the restaurant. It was full; they had to wait ten minutes before they got a table. Jerry ordered two pieces of fried chicken and fries. Steve chose the cheeseburger.

"Enjoy the money," the older man said. "That's all—just enjoy it. It's a nice piece of change for me, but I'm already doing all right. For you, still in grad school and about to get married, it'll mean a lot more. What does Anna think about it?"

"I haven't told her yet. I'm still trying to work out how. What could I have done to deserve that kind of money when I was just along for window dressing?"

"Ah. Yes, there is that. I haven't said anything to Beth, either, to tell you the truth. The less anybody outside knows, the better."

"You got that right!" Jerry said, and then, a moment later, "Have you heard anything about what they're up to out there?"

"Not a word," Steve replied. "If we're out of the program, we're *out* of the program. They may be pressing ahead as hard as they can, or they may have decided to be cautious after all. I have no idea."

"I just hope we don't find out the hard way."

Before Steve could answer, the waitress came with their lunches. "Remind me who had coffee and who had Coke," she said.

"Coke here," Jerry said. She set the glass in front of him along with the chicken—she knew he got that. Then she gave Steve his food and went off to deal with more hungry people.

After she'd disappeared, Steve said, "If you hadn't lost your temper with Dave, we'd probably still be out there." He took a big bite from his cheeseburger.

"I've thought about that. You think I haven't?" To keep his temper now, Jerry gnawed on a drumstick. It was good fried chicken—not great, but good. After a moment, he went on, "But you know what? I bet we wouldn't, not for long. They would have done something else stupid. If I didn't blow my stack, you would have."

"It could be," Steve admitted. "They were talking in ways that made me nervous, and when they started testing structural integrity. . . ." He shook his head. "You weren't wrong. That went way over the line. I might have been more restrained telling them about it, though."

"Yeah, yeah. I've thought about that, too. But when I got a look at them going ahead and doing it, I saw red," Jerry said. He ate some fries. They were top notch. "If you'd talked to them, they might even have listened a little. You aren't the weird hippie kid, you know? You're an *authority*."

"The only authority they listen to is the highest one," Steve said. "People like you and me, we're just tools to them. They use us as long as they need us, then toss us when they don't anymore. Now they know how to get inside, so they think they can run with the ball themselves."

"Uh-huh." Jerry thumped his forehead with the heel of his hand. "If I hadn't told them how I did it . . ."

"You were part of the team then. You thought you'd stay on it longer than you did. Can't say I blame you. I thought the same thing. The next question they'll want to make sure of is, are you an honest politician?" Steve cocked his head to one side, plainly wondering whether Jerry knew what he was talking about.

As a matter of fact, Jerry did. Anybody who'd read as much Heinlein as he had pretty much had to. "'An honest politician is one who stays bought,'" he quoted.

Steve smiled. "There you go. You may be the weird hippie kid, but you've got an old man's head on your shoulders."

"Nah. I've read a lot of stuff and I remember too goddamn much of it, that's all."

"I think we just said the same thing with different words."

When the waitress came by again, she said, "You guys sure cleaned that up. Either one of you care for some dessert?"

"Let me have a slice of cherry pie, please," Jerry said.

"Peach for me," Steve added.

"Coming up." She took their plates and hurried off.

When she brought back the slices of pie, she also set the check on the table. "I've got it," Steve said.

"Thanks," Jerry answered. He wasn't broke. He was further from broke than he'd ever been in his life, in fact. All the same, he didn't argue. Steve had made it clear he'd been a long way from broke for a long time. Buying lunch at a coffee shop wouldn't mean he'd miss paying the rent.

They headed back toward the RAND Corporation headquarters. When Jerry started to peel off to go to his car, Steve set a hand on his arm. "Remember the honest politician," the older man said earnestly. "I mean it. You have no idea how much out of your weight you'd be fighting. Don't do anything silly. You won't regret it later—you won't *have* a later."

"Believe me, man, I get it," Jerry said. Stephen Dole didn't know he'd lifted those two photos. But his having them didn't make Steve wrong. If the CIA could rub him out before he got to use them, or could make sure everybody thought they were hoaxes, the Agency still won and he still lost.

With a sigh and a shrug, Steve went off to the entrance. Jerry walked to the Rambler. There was only one of him, and a hell of a lot of CIA. If he ever did decide not to stay bought, he couldn't afford any mistakes. Assuming, of course, that deciding not to stay bought wasn't the first, inevitably fatal, mistake.

On Saturday night, he and Anna saw *Blazing Saddles* for a second time at the Crenshaw, a movie house that specialized in showing yesterday's hits tomorrow. He had no idea how the place stayed in business, but it had sat at the corner of Crenshaw and Compton Boulevard for as long as he could remember, and no doubt longer than that.

He still didn't say anything to her about the two years' bonus. For one thing, he had yet to come up with a way to make it sound plausible. For another, he didn't want to touch the money unless he absolutely had to. Having it felt wrong, as if by taking it he remained complicit in whatever the CIA wound up doing. And the less Anna knew about all that stuff, the better—for her.

Then, on Sunday, Gerald Ford pardoned Richard Nixon. Jerry watched and listened with his mouth hanging open while the new president let the old president off the hook. If any flies had been buzzing around inside his apartment, they could have flown right on in. He didn't believe what he was hearing. No, that wasn't right. He didn't *want to* believe what he was hearing.

After Ford vanished from his small black-and-white screen, commentators came on to explain what the pardon meant. Jerry turned off the TV. He knew too well what the pardon meant. "Fuck a duck!" he said. "The fix is in! Is it ever!"

Not two minutes later, the phone rang. It was his father. "Hell of a country we've got here, isn't it?" Hyman Stieglitz sounded as disgusted as Jerry felt.

"Sure is, Dad," Jerry said. They'd quarreled plenty over politics. His father had thought Vietnam was worth fighting about a lot longer than Jerry had—Jerry's unkind guess was, because his dad wouldn't have to carry a rifle this time. But they'd never argued about Richard Nixon. His father'd thought Nixon was a bastard longer than Jerry'd been alive.

"Let this be a lesson for you," Dad said. "See if you can wind up rich and famous. A guy like that, he'll get away with anything. His rich, famous friends, they'll make goddamn sure he doesn't have to pay for it. *Disgusting,* that's the only word I can think of."

"Dad, you oughta go on TV!" Jerry exclaimed.

"On TV? How come?" His father sounded suspicious, and well he might have. Jerry'd zinged him often enough, or maybe too often.

Not this time, though. "Because you were reading my mind, that's why. If you can do it with everybody, you'll be one of those rich, famous people yourself."

"Ha! Fat chance! Besides, you ever take a good look at your old man? If anybody's got a *punim* meant for radio, you're talking with him right now."

"Everybody says I look like you," Jerry said, realizing too late he'd given his dad the chance to zing him this time.

And his dad did, though not so hard as he might have: "I figured that was why you grew the face fungus, to keep people from noticing."

"Thanks. I love you, too," Jerry said.

"I'm sure," Hyman Stieglitz said dryly. "Anyway, I just wanted somebody to vent my spleen with for a few minutes. I'll let you get back to what you were doing."

"I was cussing at the TV, and it isn't even on. I killed it right after Ford finished saying what a swell old boy Nixon was."

"Swell old boy, huh? Well, you got that right, anyhow. So long, kid." His father hung up.

Jerry wanted somebody to vent his spleen with, too, so he called Anna. She'd been reading instead of watching the boob tube; she didn't know what President Ford had done till he told her. "That's terrible!" she said. "I always thought Ford was honest. Not too smart, but honest."

"Not too smart, is right." Jerry wished she'd sounded more outraged, but knew he ought to count his blessings. Her father was a construction worker; he and his wife were both rock-ribbed (rock-headed, Jerry thought) Republicans. He was lucky she didn't go with them.

"What can we do about any of it, though? It's back in Washington, and it's not like Ford'll do anything different with taxes or with the Russians because he gave Nixon the Get Out of Jail Free card." Anna proved she thought in Monopoly, too.

"I guess," Jerry said. Would Ford do anything different with Humpty Dumpty because he'd pardoned Nixon? Nixon knew about the spaceship, of course. Whether he knew about explorations inside it, Jerry couldn't have said. He'd already left office by then. Would Ford and Kissinger have kept him in the loop? They might have. Being stupid wasn't Nixon's problem; being crooked was.

"We'll see who the Democrats nominate in seventy-six and we'll worry about it then," Anna said.

"Yeah." Jerry didn't want to argue with her, not when she wasn't wrong. And thinking about the election in 1976 made him think about the Bicentennial in 1976. Less than two years away now. People had already been talking about it for a while: mostly people who hoped to make money off it.

It was pretty special, though. How many democracies lasted two hundred years? He knew a lot less history than oceanography, but you didn't need to know much to realize the answer was *damn few*.

"*Blazing Saddles* was funny." Anna changed the subject with a lurch. "I don't know if it was funnier than *The Producers*, but it was funny."

"You don't see a comedy twice if it isn't funny," Jerry said. If she'd had enough politics, okay, she had. And it let him avoid admitting he hadn't seen *The Producers* in a theater, only in chopped-up bits and pieces on TV. Movies weren't the same that way. Better than nothing, but not the same.

"Especially not at the Crenshaw. Mom and Dad would take me there for cartoons and for dinosaur movies. A million screaming kids, and the smell of buttered popcorn as thick as cigarette smoke is other places," Anna said. Her parents smoked, too.

"I was there for some of those, too," Jerry said.

"I wonder if we were ever there for the same ones."

"Probably." They were only a year apart. They'd grown up in the same suburb. It would have been more surprising if they hadn't been in the same place at the same time every once in a while.

Jerry thought so, anyhow. Anna said, "A Sign It Was Meant To Be." He could hear the capital letters thumping into place.

He answered, "I'm glad it was." He might not have been the most socially adept human being in captivity, but he didn't miss the right response there.

Anna let out a squeak. "The dumb cat just knocked something over in the kitchen. I'll call you back. 'Bye." She hung up without waiting for a good-bye in return.

The phone did ring again a minute later. Jerry grabbed it. "Hi, sweetie."

"Well, hello, beautiful." It wasn't Anna. It was Tim Ishihara. Laughing, he went on, "I didn't know you cared."

"Believe me, I don't." Jerry's ears felt like a forest fire.

"That's what you say. Hey, I know I'm irresistible." Naturally, his friend didn't want to let him off the hook, not when he'd hooked himself. Then Tim asked, "Were you watching TV just now?"

"Afraid I was."

"What do you think?"

"I think it sucks. How about you?"

"The same, man. The same. Other thing I think is, if you're a fat cat it doesn't matter what you do. They threw Nixon out of the White House? Big fucking deal. He'll write a book full of bullshit about how it wasn't his fault, and then he'll laugh all the way to the bank. Wanna bet?"

"You really think I'm that dumb?"

"Since you're asking . . ." Tim said. They both laughed this time. Sometimes you had to. If you didn't, you'd pound your head on a table or against the wall till your forehead bled or your brain fell out through your nose. Tim added, "Don't we live in a great country?"

"Oh, at least," Jerry said. "It's better than most other places, but it sure isn't as good as it ought to be."

He wondered what the centaurowls would think of the United States of America. How long had they lain at the bottom of the Pacific? Since 1964? 1954? 1554? 1554 BC? He had no way to know. He also had no way to know whether Dave or one of the other CIA guys had pushed one of those big yellow buttons. Maybe they were trying to talk with an alien right now.

If they were trying to wake the centaurowls, they'd be smart to rouse only one of them and keep the other as hostage for good behavior. Jerry was sure they didn't need him to tell them that. All the spy games they'd played since the end of World War II would have taught them those lessons.

"We're trying to get better, but there sure as hell are times I wish we'd try harder," Tim said.

"You and me both. I think everybody our age does," Jerry said. *And no matter how hard we try, we'll still look like savages to those things inside Humpty Dumpty. Dangerous savages, maybe, but savages.*

"You think we'll be any better when we're old enough to run things? I don't. The guys who get in power, they get in power 'cause they make you think you can trust 'em, but you can't trust any of those assholes. Not a fuckin' one." Tim spoke with great conviction.

Jerry'd thought *he* was cynical about politics. Tim left him in the dust. "You do defense work, too," he said.

"The Russians aren't better'n we are. They're even worse. You know that."

"Yeah." Jerry did, too. But were they enough worse to be kept away from Humpty Dumpty and whatever it could teach mankind? Was America so much better that it alone deserved to control so much power? He still worried about that.

XIII

You can't trust any of those assholes. After Tim said the words, Jerry thought they'd be engraved on his soul forever. It didn't work like that. Life kept getting in the way.

Instead of writing to see whether Ben Bova would look at a revision of the story that had come back while he was out in the Pacific, he took his courage in both hands and called the Condé Nast offices in New York. Before long, he found himself connected with the editor of *Analog*. After introducing himself, he said, "Excuse me, but if I make those changes you suggested, would you consider it again?"

"Of course I would! Why do you think I wrote you *that* letter?" Across 2,500 miles of phone line, Jerry could hear the editor smile; he must have asked the right question. Bova added, "No guarantees, of course. I have to see what you do with it."

"Oh, sure. I understand that," Jerry said quickly.

"It's good to hear from you," the editor said. "I was kind of disappointed when I didn't for so long."

"I've been on a research project out in the Pacific. I couldn't get my mail for a while," Jerry said.

"Is that what it was? I should have realized. You wrote me before that you were doing studies on whale songs. That must be fascinating!"

"It is," Jerry answered, amazed that Bova remembered the cover letter from the story he'd sold the year before. He wondered what the editor of *Analog* would think if he told him about the spaceship and the aliens.

John W. Campbell probably would have believed him. Of course, Campbell had believed in Dianetics, too, and in the reactionless Dean Drive, and the allegedly psionic Hieronymus Machine, and using astrology in weather forecasting. By everything Jerry could see, Ben Bova's head was screwed on a lot tighter. Which wouldn't be an asset, of course, when the truth was so bizarre.

Whatever psionics the current *Analog* editor had weren't enough to let him pluck secrets from Jerry's mind. He said, "Make the changes and let me have another look. If I don't buy it, I bet somebody else will."

"Okay. Thanks again." Jerry said his good-byes and got off the phone. A bit slower than he might have, he realized Bova'd given him another good piece of advice. You started with the top markets, sure. But if you didn't sell there, you sent your brainchildren to magazines with less prestige and less money. Getting paid at all beat getting zilch for what you did.

Fired with enthusiasm, he made the changes that afternoon. Two days later, he needed to go up to UCLA. He took the revised story along and fed nickels into a xerox machine in the Biomedical Library. The copy went into a manila envelope addressed to that PO box in Schenectady. He wanted to send it straight back to *Analog*, but he wasn't going to make the CIA pay attention to him when he didn't have to.

On the way home, he stopped at the post office on the corner of El Segundo and Hawthorne Boulevard. A friend of his, a guy named Alex Wilkins, worked there, though not at the windows.

"First class, please," he told the clerk. He paid the freight and collected a receipt. When you wrote for money, things like postage were deductible. The clerk tossed the envelope into a plastic tub.

Jerry left. Somebody else brought a package to the window. *The exciting, romantic life of a writer*, he thought. As he left the post-office parking lot, he got an idea that might make the story about the skeleton in seaboots come to life . . . if a story about a skeleton could do that.

The piece intended for Ben Bova came back to his apartment in eight days. Whoever'd read it in Schenectady had stuck a three-by-five under the paper clip. *No security issues. Typo at the top of page 5*, he or she had written. Jerry fixed the mistake and put the story in the mail for New York City.

Then he forgot about writing for a while, because classes started at UCLA. He was TAing two sections of Introduction to Oceanography, a class whose enrollment outdid some minor league teams' average daily attendance. Most of the people in the course didn't give a damn about oceanography, of course. All they cared about was four units of credit, preferably with a B or better.

"My office hours are Tuesdays from nine to eleven," he informed both sections at their first meetings. "I can tell you right now that I won't be there on the twenty-sixth of November."

Naturally, someone in each section asked, "Why not?"

"Because I'm getting married on the twenty-fourth," he answered.

That shut them up, except for one class-clown type who exclaimed, "You mean you'd rather go on your honeymoon than hold office hours?" Everybody laughed, including Jerry.

He fiddled with the story about the skeleton in boots. He fiddled with his dissertation, too. He knew he should be working harder on it, but he didn't feel the drive he had before John P. knocked on his door and changed his life forever.

He wondered what they were doing on the *Glomar Explorer*. It gnawed at him, the way his father said a tooth did when it was starting to tell you it needed a root canal. He'd never had one of those. He'd never even had a permanent tooth pulled; his wisdom teeth came in straight, which made his dentist call him a lucky son of a gun.

He also wondered how the man he figured was his replacement was doing on the ship. He'd read some of Jerry Pournelle's stories, mostly in *Analog*. He'd heard him talk, too, at signings at A Change of Hobbit. Pournelle was way to the right of him politically; as far as that went, he'd get on fine with the CIA guys. But he didn't suffer fools gladly. He could be—he often was—loud and sarcastic. Jerry Stieglitz wondered what the fellow who shared his first name would have to say about trying to scrape bits off Humpty Dumpty's shell. Something anyone in the way of it would remember a long time, he suspected.

No, Dale and Dave and Jack might not have much fun with Pournelle. They wouldn't have to listen to him. They were in charge, and he wasn't. But they'd have to hear him whether they listened or not. When he got going, the whole ship would hear him. So would the gooney birds for a couple of miles around.

Along with everything else that was going on, Jerry started moving stuff out of his apartment and into Anna's. Her place was bigger and her building allowed cats, two reasons the move was going in that direction. He'd known for a while he would be doing that. Putting boxes in the trunk, driving over, and carrying them inside, though . . .

"This is really gonna happen," he said as he set another box of paperbacks down on the living-room floor.

"Yeah." Anna sounded as doubtful as he did. He supposed all the twos on the verge of becoming one felt that way. She went on, "It'll take a while before everything all gets blended together and it's not you and me anymore but just us."

"Tim and Cheryl are making it work." Jerry's friend and the lady he'd married were his type specimens for how to do it right. He tried to put the reason why into words: "They don't get on each other's nerves, you know?"

Anna sniffed. "I'm not sure they have any nerves."

"Hey, be nice." There were times when Jerry wondered whether getting married, or at least getting married to Anna, was the smartest thing he could do. True, he wouldn't need to worry about where he'd get laid if he did. They could talk to each other, too. And they trusted each other.

But they both had strong views about how things ought to work, and those views weren't always the same. She spent money as fast as it came in, for instance, where he socked it away whenever he could. She liked to go out and shop and hang with other people more than he did, too. If they argued about stuff like that now, wouldn't it get worse after they tied the knot and were together all the time?

He thought he could have dealt with all that, though. Now . . . *Between the idea / And the reality / Between the motion / and the act / Falls the Shadow.* Old Thomas Stearns had got that one right. Jerry knew the Shadow's names, too, knew them only too well. Azorian. Midlothian. Humpty Dumpty. Centaurowls.

All that flashed through his mind in some small fraction of a second, because it was very clear by the time Anna answered, "They're all right. They're good people. I'm not interested in a lot of the things they are, that's all."

"Okay." He knew he wouldn't get any more out of her. He was surprised he got that much. She was trying to make him happy, the same way he did with her. That had to mean something. If they kept pulling toward each other, wouldn't they wind up meeting somewhere in the middle? Wouldn't they?

Ben Bova bought the story for *Analog*. Jerry threw the check into his savings account. He mailed the story about the skeleton in seaboots to Schenectady. It came back with another note under the paper clip: *This is no security risk. It is spooky.* Then he sent it to *Fantasy and Science Fiction.* Ed Ferman promptly sent it back. His note read, *Creepy, but not up my alley. Good luck with it elsewhere.* Jerry sent it off to *Fantastic.*

He wished he were putting as much energy into his thesis. He had the data. He had everything organized. He'd lost something that might have been more important, though. He didn't care anymore. Centaurowls again.

But days went by, whether he cared or not. Wedding rehearsal. Bachelor party, not that his was especially wild. Tim and Alex took him out for dinner and drinks. Then they went to a strip joint and watched the girls up on stage wiggle.

"Cheryl know you're here?" Jerry asked Tim.

"Oh, sure."

"She gonna give you a hard time?"

"Nah." His buddy shook his head. "She says it doesn't matter where I get my appetite as long as I eat at home."

"Does she?" Jerry was jealous. Anna looked daggers at him, or sometimes daggered the back of his hand with a fingernail, if she noticed him noticing anyone else.

"Not gonna catch me getting tied down like that. I just flit from flower to flower like a bee," Alex said. He'd drunk more than his friends had. Jerry was glad he lived only a few blocks from the strip club.

Tim said, "Hey, you know the bees that do the flitting are females, don't you? Sterile females, too."

"What? No way!" Alex looked comically dismayed. He turned to Jerry. "Tell him he's full of it, man."

"Sorry. He's right. Worker bees *are* females, and they can't lay eggs."

"Well, shit. See if I'm gonna make like a bee, then," Alex said.

"But you're already buzzed," Jerry observed, and from then on the night of the bachelor party became The Night Alex Got Buzzed.

Jerry rented a ruffled shirt and a tux. Luckily for him, the black tie that came with the outfit had clips to hold it in place. He could deal with an ordinary necktie, but he'd never tied a bow tie in his life. He discovered the best way to put on a cummerbund was to fasten it in front and then turn it around. Women did that with bras all the time, but men didn't have to worry about it much.

The wedding went off fine. Everybody who'd stand at the front showed up at the temple hideously early so the photographer could do his thing. Charlie McGowan, Anna's father, looked less at home in a yarmulke than Tim Ishihara did. He tried his best to be gracious, though. "I hope you kids are as happy as me and Sally," he said.

"Thanks, Mister McGowan," Jerry said. He didn't like the way Anna's folks shouted at each other, but this seemed the wrong time and place to point that out.

Rabbi Burstein did indeed look like some close relative of the Creator's. He ran things as if he'd done a million weddings, which of course he had. When Tim put the cloth-covered glass representing the Temple on the platform upside down in front of Jerry, the rabbi unobtrusively knocked it sidewise so Jerry could be sure of breaking it when he stomped it.

After the reception, the new Mr. and Mrs. Stieglitz drove to the Hilton near the airport. They'd leave for Hawaii the next morning. Meanwhile . . .

Anna let out a little squeal when Jerry picked her up and carried her into the room. A dozen roses in a vase on the nightstand and a bottle of champagne in an ice bucket near the bed awaited them. Jerry read the card by the flowers. "Tim did it," he said.

"That was sweet!" Anna exclaimed. "Shall we drink some?"

"What are you talking about, some?" Jerry paused. "Well, maybe some at first. Can't get too smashed to make things official."

"I don't know *what* you could mean," Anna said.

They drank some bubbly. The bed was wide and inviting. They became officially man and wife. They finished the bottle. Jerry always got happy when he drank enough champagne to feel it. Tonight was no exception. It didn't seem to hurt his performance, either.

"You brute," Anna said after the second round.

"Oh, at least," he answered lazily. "This is what a honeymoon is for, right?"

"That's what the men say." She walked into the bathroom. Jerry decided keeping his mouth shut might be a good idea. They both fell asleep in short order, so that took care of itself.

Next morning, the first course of breakfast was two aspirins. Coffee in the hotel restaurant also helped. They drove down Century to the airport. Everything there went as smoothly as Jerry could have hoped. So did the flight to Honolulu.

As they were touching down, Anna said, "Won't you be glad to see more of this place than just the airport?"

"I guess," he answered. "But the inside of one hotel room is pretty much like the inside of another one, right? . . . Hey!" She'd poked him in the ribs.

Greeters called "Aloha!" as passengers got off the plane. They hung leis around people's necks. Jerry imagined he was supposed to feel Hawaiian. He felt more like a tourist who was supposed to feel Hawaiian.

Then he exclaimed, "I got lei'd in Honolulu!"

"Not yet, you haven't, Buster," Anna said. "And if you keep doing things like that, you won't, either." She poked him again.

They took a cab to their hotel: another Hilton, a big glass-and-steel box rising near the beach. Honolulu wasn't Los Angeles, but it was a good-sized city. And the weather! In the L.A. area, the South Bay, with its sea breezes, had the best climate, not too hot in summer, not too chilly in winter. Along with Santa Barbara and San Diego, it was about as good as you could get on the mainland. Next to Honolulu's perfect mildness, it took a back seat.

Their room was on the fifteenth floor. Jerry could see the beach and the blue Pacific (not the gray-green Pacific you'd see from a Los Angeles beachside hotel). When he looked way to the left, there was Diamond Head. Anna snapped pictures with an Instamatic just like the one he'd used inside Humpty Dumpty.

To keep from thinking about that, he grabbed her. "We just got here!" she said.

"What else are we gonna do right now?" he asked—reasonably, he thought. So they did that before they went down to dinner.

They did other things, too, though. They spent some time on the beach—not a whole lot, because Anna was fair enough to burn fast. They walked into the ocean. Seawater that wasn't cold freaked them both out: Angelenos weren't used to it. They took a tour bus around Honolulu and Pearl Harbor. They saw the old royal palace and went out on a boat to the *Arizona* memorial.

That sobered Jerry. Looking down at the water there, he could see a shimmering rainbow oil sheen on the surface. It still came up from the battleship the Japanese had sunk almost seven years before he was born. He wondered if Humpty Dumpty'd been down on the bottom of the Pacific by then. He wondered if he'd ever know.

And they took another tour bus to give them a look at more of Oahu. Once you got away from the city, the place was even more preposterously gorgeous. The bus stopped at the Mormons' Polynesian Cultural Center. The Mormons claimed the Hawaiians and other Polynesians were close kin to American Indians. Jerry thought that was utter nonsense, but the exhibits and shows were interesting anyhow.

Then they flew to Maui. Their hotel, on the outskirts of Lahaina, was on the island's west coast. Jerry rented a car and they drove along the northern and eastern shoreline to the village of Hana and the seven sacred pools just beyond. Like the trip up Pacific Coast Highway from Los Angeles to San Francisco, the drive was beautiful and wearing at the same time. Beaches of white sand, gold sand, black sand. Jungle. Waterfalls. A narrow, twisty road where the driver had to pay attention every second. Jerry was sure Anna saw things he didn't, because he focused on where the next bend was and what might be coming around it.

The hotel room had a view of the Pacific and, in front of it, a golf course. That was green, but everything on Maui was green. It failed to fill Jerry's heart with delight. Tim and Alex both played golf. He liked them anyway.

The hotel room also came with its own geckos: little lizards that scurried around after bugs. Jerry caught two on successive days and turned them loose on the small balcony outside. Watching one scurry straight up the stucco wall told him how they'd made it to the fourth floor.

When he and Anna walked into Lahaina, he looked the harbor over to see if the *Glomar Explorer* was there. The ship wasn't. That didn't surprise him. No, they wouldn't want to risk exposing Humpty Dumpty to the world till they were ready. If they were ever ready.

"I don't want to visit here," Anna said, as they got on the plane that would take them back to Honolulu. "I want to *live* here!"

"Yeah, well, you could do worse. I don't know how you could do better, though," Jerry said. "Only drawback I can see is, everything's more expensive than it is on the mainland."

"Worth it," she said, and he couldn't very well disagree.

At the gate to the flight that would take them back to the mainland, Jerry eyed the passengers who'd board with Anna and him, wondering if any of them were returning from the *Glomar Ex-*

plorer. He didn't see anybody he recognized. Maybe everyone from the A crew was long since back. Or maybe those people were still out there at Site 126–1 off of Midway, doing whatever they were doing with and to Humpty Dumpty.

He and Anna landed in Los Angeles a little before midnight. It was in the mid-fifties and cloudy. It wasn't raining, but it felt as if it might. It felt like the start of December, in other words. In Hawaii, they called the rain "liquid sunshine." Not here. As they walked to Jerry's Rambler, Anna said, "Let's go back!"

"Would be nice," Jerry said, but he kept walking. So did she.

At the apartment, the King of Siam hid from both of them. Anna's mother had fed and watered him and cleaned the cat box while they were gone. A week away was plenty long enough for him to decide they were invaders from Rigel, not proper humans at all. The invaders, though, knew where the kitty treats were and how to make inviting noises. The road to the King of Siam's heart ran straight through his stomach. He came forth to claim his reward.

After some treats, he admitted the apparent strangers might be friends after all. He let Anna fuss over him and even put up with Jerry scratching him under the chin. Chances were he wanted to play, too, but that wouldn't happen. The humans needed to crash; they went back to the real world in the morning.

"It's late," Anna said—blurrily, because she was brushing her teeth. She spat and rinsed. Then, more clearly, she went on, "Not as late as when I got you in the summertime, but still late."

"Everything worked on this plane," Jerry said. "Let's go to bed, okay?" That was too obviously a good idea for her to badmouth it. Go to bed they did.

Anna's alarm clock went off like a bomb at 6:15. It woke Jerry, too; with that hellish racket, he thought he would have had a hard time staying dead. He didn't need to be up so early, of course. He tried to go back to sleep while she dressed and fixed breakfast and got ready to head out the door.

Since he couldn't sleep, he climbed out of bed to kiss her good-bye. He was in the sweatpants he'd worn on the ship, with a different ratty T-shirt. She wore business attire, already ready for the office. She didn't say anything about that, but he could tell she was thinking pretty loud.

"Hope the traffic isn't too bad," he said: an Angeleno's prayer to the gods for good fortune. "Love you, Missus Stieglitz."

"Love you, too, Mister Stieglitz," she said, and then she scooted out the door. The King of Siam eyed Jerry. Jerry could read his mind, too. *You're still here. Amuse me, human.* So Jerry did.

He took some of his things out of boxes and put them into drawers, when there were drawers, or on high shelves that Anna couldn't reach, when there weren't. He'd shoehorned most of his bookcases into the place Anna and he now shared. His sf, fantasy, and references were here. The rest of his books lay in other boxes in his dad's garage.

He went through his file cards, trying to pick up where he'd been on his dissertation and where he wanted to go with it. In fact, he had a good idea about both. That wasn't the problem. He wanted to be back on the *Glomar Explorer,* either keeping the CIA from going crazy and doing too much with Humpty Dumpty or, alternatively, trying to talk with the centaurowls if he couldn't keep the spooks from going crazy . . . and if the aliens lived through revival.

Sooner or later, Professor Krikorian would want to see what he'd been up to lately. A story about a skeleton in seaboots wouldn't thrill him. He'd want data, and charts, and analysis. Before John P. banged on his door, Jerry would have been eager to give them to him. He just couldn't get excited about it now.

He had breaded pork chops and a diced onion going in a pan on top of the stove when Anna came in. The range here was electric. He liked gas better, but he could manage with what the apartment had. He wasn't a great cook. Neither was Anna, though they could both cope. Since he'd been home and she hadn't . . .

"I could get used to this," she said, after an appreciative sniff.

"I'm supposed to spoil you, right?" he said.

"Works for me." She came over for a kiss, so she meant it.

He did the dishes after dinner, too. She wouldn't till the pile filled the sink. He might eventually get her to change her ways. Or she might get him to change his. Or he might wind up doing a lot of dishes because she wouldn't.

"Waste of time," she said now.

"Nah." He shook his head. "That's drying. Washing's okay. You can see you're making progress. And my mind kind of goes blank to the sound of running water. I've had story ideas while I wash. In the shower, too."

On Tuesday, he got up with her for his nine o'clock office hours. The earlier he made it to UCLA, the better his street-parking chances. When he checked his mail slot in the department office for anything that might have come in while he was away, the secretaries fussed over him and made him show off his ring. It was a plain gold band, but he did anyway.

That night, Anna put up a Christmas tree. It was just a little one, plastic, that sat on the end table between the couch and the wall. She hung a few ornaments on the branches and mounted a plastic gold star on top. "No tinsel?" Jerry asked.

"No way," she answered. "The cat thinks aluminum foil is a food group." Jerry glanced over at the King of Siam. As far as he could tell, the Siamese thought everything was a food group.

Jerry'd never lived in a place with a Christmas tree before. It made him feel stranger than he'd thought it would. He dug in his boxes till he unearthed the menorah the temple had given him for his bar mitzvah. He found candles at the local Alpha Beta and lit the first one on the night of Sunday, the eighth. He hadn't bothered while he lived alone. Now he felt the need to remind himself he was Jewish.

And he gave Anna *Bridge of Sighs*, the latest Robin Trower album. "Happy Chanukah!" he said.

She looked flustered, not an expression she wore very often. "Thanks, but I don't have anything for you yet," she said.

"Don't worry about it," he said. "You do your holiday, I'll do mine, and we'll all be happy."

"Mrp," she said, but she seemed more happy than not.

The next Sunday was the last night of Chanukah. Jerry and Anna got his dad a big bottle of Chivas Regal. Then they took him to Helen Yee's. "You guys didn't have to do any of this," Hyman Stieglitz said. His present for Jerry was a herringbone tweed jacket with suede elbow patches, so he could look like the professor he was less and less interested in becoming. He'd got a cashmere sweater for Anna.

"We didn't do it because we had to," Jerry said.

"We did it because we wanted to," Anna finished for him. "And the sweater is beautiful. So soft!" It was a brighter green than she usually wore. Jerry thought she looked nice in it. He wasn't so sure she agreed. But she was polite at the restaurant, which was all that mattered.

"I never shopped for a daughter-in-law before," Jerry's father said. Jerry hadn't thought of it that way, but his old man was right.

Jerry had a couple of weeks off between quarters. Christmas and New Year's fell on Wednesdays. Anna's company, in its infinite generosity, didn't even give the people who worked there Christmas Eve or New Year's Eve. She called down curses on the CEO's head that would have made Cthulhu or Nyarlathotep blanch but didn't faze the businessman one bit.

Christmas Day was at Anna's folks. They had a big real tree, which to Jerry smelled like an overgrown pine air freshener. They also had two large dogs, who sniffed him even more suspiciously than usual. Maybe they could smell that he was Jewish, and didn't like it. Or maybe they noticed he had cat hair on his clothes . . . although Anna did, too, and they fawned all over her.

Charlie McGowan handed Jerry a Miller. He dutifully drank it, even if it tasted thin and sour to him. They all exchanged presents. Everyone exclaimed and made the right thank-you noises. Jerry suspected at least as much hypocrisy as gratitude was on display. He didn't say anything about it. Little by little, as he got older, he was learning to stick his foot in his mouth less often, anyhow. He knew what Christmas spirit was supposed to be.

He didn't say much on the ride back to the apartment, either. "You didn't have a good time," Anna said when they were almost there.

"Did you?"

That made her pause. She prided herself on being relentlessly honest. At last, she answered, "They were trying their hardest."

"I know they were." That was part of the problem; the older McGowans' best wasn't real good. There was one more thing Jerry didn't say.

Anna sighed. "They're my parents. They love me the best way they know how. I love them, too, or I try. They're just . . ."

He was driving. He took his right hand off the wheel for a moment to set it on her shoulder. Then he gave his full attention back to the road. *All in the Family* bubbled up in his mind, as it often did when he spent time with Anna's folks. It was the most popular show in the country, but he and Anna hardly ever watched it. They didn't need to. They lived it.

And it came to pass that 1974 gave way to 1975, and fall quarter to winter quarter: world without end, amen. *Fantastic* bought Jerry's story about the skeleton in seaboots. "That's four sales now!" he said when the acceptance letter came instead of the manila envelope. "Maybe I really can make this work!"

"All put together, how much have you got paid for them?" she asked.

He did some mental arithmetic. "Uh, a little more than eight hundred dollars."

"That's probably not enough to live on," she said, which was, for her, diplomatic. She wasn't wrong, either.

"You don't write short stories to live on. You write them to get better at writing, or because the idea isn't big enough for a novel. Novels, you can make a living writing novels. There are people who do."

"How many?"

"Not a whole lot. Most writers keep their day jobs. Heinlein, Clarke, Asimov, de Camp, Andre Norton . . . You can do it."

"Make damn sure you're one of those people before you quit your day job," Anna said.

"I will. I would anyway." Of course, Jerry was sitting on a different kind of bestseller, not science fiction but nonfiction. If the CIA didn't murder him before he published. If they didn't murder his editor or his publisher to keep their secrets secret. If . . . all kinds of interesting things.

He and Anna got more used to living with each other, and to putting up with each other. Or sometimes not. She complained that he squeezed too much toothpaste from the middle of the tube. "Do you have to?" she asked.

"I don't even notice I'm doing it," he said, feeling like a character in a Tom Lehrer song. "Is the world gonna end if I screw up once in a while?"

"No," she said, in a way that could only mean *yes*. So he tried to remember not to commit that particular sin. And sometimes he did, and sometimes not so much.

He had gripes of his own. Sure enough, he found himself doing the dishes almost all the time. Yes, he hated dirty dishes much more than she did. Yes, he was home more than she was. He still muttered to himself when she kicked back while he cleaned up.

One of his winter quarter sections had a couple of very pretty girls in it. He would have been delighted if they'd been as smart as they were good-looking; he liked smart women. But they both bombed quiz after quiz and lived down to every stereotype about blondes.

They were friends. They hung out together—*the blind leading the blind,* he thought. In his mind, he tagged them the Bobbsey Twins.

When he told Anna about them, the first thing she asked was, "Will you flunk them if they keep being stupid?"

"Of course I will," he said, surprised. "Why wouldn't I?"

The look she gave him said there were more things in heaven and earth than were dreamt of in his philosophy. It also said he was still wet behind the ears, which annoyed him—at least until she answered, "Because men are shitheads, that's why. You never had anybody flash a hundred-dollar bill at you and say he hoped you'd be nice, did you?"

"Uh, no. You have?"

She nodded. "Uh-huh. A couple-three years ago, not long after we got together. I told him to stick it up his ass. My boss was pissed the magazine didn't get the ad buy."

"You never said anything about that before."

"Well, now I have. I don't come out with everything that's on my mind, unlike some people I could name."

She means me, Jerry realized. He almost started laughing, but didn't for fear of not being able to stop. If she knew some of what he knew . . . the CIA was liable to rub her out, too. So she could think he blabbed all the time if she wanted to.

Of course, the other reason she didn't come out with everything that was on her mind was, she expected him to know without being told. So it seemed to him, anyhow. If he had to ask her what she wanted, she stopped wanting it. It wasn't even slightly an accident she was a cat person.

He did wonder every now and then if their match was made in heaven. Then again, he wondered if anybody's was. If you both worked and plugged away at things, couldn't you patch up the cracks before they got too bad? He hoped so.

If you both worked and plugged away at things, sure. But what if one of you, or maybe two of you, didn't feel like it anymore? One question he never asked her was, *Hey, how do you think the marriage is going?* He was afraid she might tell him, and she *was* relentlessly honest.

She didn't ask him any questions like that, either. She might have thought everything was fine. Or, like him, she might have thought not looking right at things was better than examining them too closely. She might have been right, too.

He kept making feckless lunges at his thesis. At the end of January, he gave Professor Krikorian a chapter . . . and a week later his advisor admitted he'd misfiled it. "You have a carbon or a xerox, don't you?" Krikorian asked.

"Um, no," Jerry said unhappily, vowing never to make that mistake again as long as he lived. Writing the damn chapter once had been hard enough. Twice? He didn't want to think about twice.

"It'll turn up," Professor Krikorian said. Jerry had to hope he was right.

Some people got drunk when things like that happened. Jerry went up to the student union to check out the new sf in the bookstore. He bought a Niven story collection that would keep him from worrying about the AWOL chapter or his own fiction for a few hours.

It was a Friday afternoon. He should have hurried back to his car so he could beat some of the rush. Instead, he paused at the newspapers outside the doors. One of the *Times* headlines above the fold was **US REPORTED AFTER RUSS SUB.**

"Oh, fuck me," Jerry said. A guy going in gave him a funny look. He didn't care. He dug a dime out of the coin pocket on his jeans and got a paper. *Where am I going again?* he wondered. *And what am I doing in this handbasket?*

XIV

J erry sat down on the brickwork supporting a planter and tore through the story. It had holes, bad ones. The reporters thought the lost Russian sub lay at the bottom of the Atlantic, not the Pacific. *I saw the Atlantic and the Pacific / And the Pacific wasn't terrific* jangled through Jerry's head. And both submarines the story identified as possible targets were nuclear powered, which the K-129 wasn't, and had gone missing after 1970.

Nor did the photo of the Soviet submarine on the front page look much like the one Humpty Dumpty actually sank. But the photo right next to that one was of the *Hughes Glomar Explorer*.

So the guys from the *Times* had got a lot of things wrong. But they got the most important one right: the *Glomar Explorer* wasn't an ocean-mining ship. It was built to raise a sunken sub.

After a moment, Jerry shook his head. The reporters had missed *the* most important thing. The story didn't say a word about spaceships or flying saucers or any of that sci-fi nonsense. Either the men from the *Times* hadn't peeled down to that layer of the onion or they had but didn't believe what they'd found. They might have decided it was bullshit meant to throw them off the sensible, logical Cold War story they'd begun to unravel. And who could blame them if they had?

How much did any of that matter, though? Azorian wasn't a secret anymore. Maybe Midlothian still was . . . for now. But what if the two men from the *Times* kept prodding and poking? Even more to the point, how many other people were or would start looking for answers?

Still almost as much in shock as he had been after Steve showed him the photos of the Midlothian object, Jerry walked to his car. He got on the southbound San Diego Freeway as usual, but instead of staying on it he took the westbound Santa Monica to the city of Santa Monica and RAND Corporation headquarters.

As before, he asked to speak to Stephen Dole. As before, Steve agreed to see him (his Friday visitor's badge was purple where the

Thursday one had been blue, which confirmed that speculation). And, as before, his escort was Angela Simmons. "Oh, hello," she said, smiling. "I remember you."

"Likewise." He smiled back.

"It's nice you made friends with Doctor Dole while you were working together," she said, as they walked down the corridor to Steve's office.

"I'm glad I was lucky enough to get to know him. He's a heck of a smart man. He's got his head on tight, too, if you know what I mean."

"I sure do." She nodded.

Steve came out of his office while Jerry and Angela were nearing it. "Hey," Jerry said as they shook hands. "Can I buy you some coffee over at the Penguin place?"

"Sure," Steve said, and then, to Angela, "He's mine from now on."

"Okay, Doctor Dole."

Jerry and Steve made small talk till they left the building. As soon as they were out in the open air, Jerry asked, "Did you see today's *Times*?"

Steve had been grinning. Instantly, a wary mask fell over his face. "I'm afraid I did."

"I'm afraid, too. How long till everything unravels?"

"I'm the wrong person to ask." Steve spoke slowly, choosing his words with obvious care. "John P. would have a better idea of how many reporters know anything, and of how much they know. But I can keep an eye on *The New York Times* and *The Washington Post* here. Can you do the same?"

"Yeah, at least some of the time. The UCLA Research Library has a periodicals room where the out-of-town papers are only a day or two old. I'm not on campus every day, but I guess I can arrange to be."

They walked into the Penguin Coffee Shop. It wasn't crowded; the lunch rush was over, while the dinner rush hadn't started yet. Jerry wondered if he'd sleep tonight after late-afternoon coffee. Then again, he also wondered if he'd sleep tonight any which way.

"One good thing, anyhow," he remarked, after the waitress brought them their brew.

"Tell me. I could use some good news. When things like this start coming out in the open . . . Well, look what happened to Nixon."

"It's not all out. They didn't say anything about you-know-what." Jerry laughed sourly. "Of course, who would believe them if they did?"

"There is that. There certainly is," Stephen Dole said. "No one who hasn't been through some things believes them, no matter how true they may be."

"What do we do if everything starts coming out?" Jerry asked: the question uppermost in his mind at the moment.

Steve paused to sip coffee. Then he said, "The best thing we can do is make sure those people understand it's not coming out because of us. They wouldn't be very happy if they thought it was."

"I know." Jerry thought about the photos in the manila envelope he'd passed to Tim Ishihara. In there with them was an account of what he knew about Humpty Dumpty, how it had been found, and how it had been raised. He also thought about termination with extreme prejudice. He'd never believed the CIA was kidding about that. He really didn't believe it now. "I just wanted to make sure you didn't go out the door in a hurry or something this morning and miss it."

"Thanks. I mean it. Thanks! It's good to know somebody cares," Steve said. "And you were right before, I think. Way better not to talk about any of this on the phone or where too many people can listen in."

"Uh-huh." Jerry set money on the table and stood up. "I better get back. If I'm not there when Anna comes in, she'll wonder why."

"Okay." Steve rose, too. "The fewer people who wonder anything about this, the better."

"Amen!" agnostic-leaning-toward-atheist Jerry said, most sincerely.

He did get back to Hawthorne before Anna came home. It helped him less than he'd thought it would. When she walked through the door, the first thing she did was toss the *Times*'s front page on the couch so the story about trying to raise the Russian submarine was face up.

She pointed at the photo of the *Glomar Explorer*. "That's the ship you were on, isn't it? One of the guys in sales with me noticed it and gave it to me."

"Yeah, that's the ship," he said—denying it would be worse. "I saw the story, too, up on campus. All I can tell you is, it wasn't going after subs while I was on it." That was true: just barely, but it was.

And Anna, of course, didn't believe it. "Don't bullshit me. I hate when people do that. I especially hate it when somebody I think I can trust does it." She pointed at the paper again. "Are you gonna try and tell me that story's a lie?"

A lot of it was, or at least wrong. Jerry could see, though, that insisting on that would only get him in deeper. So he said, "Babe, they built the *Glomar Explorer* in Philadelphia. They sailed it all the way down around South America, 'cause it's too wide to fit through the Panama Canal. Then they brought it up again, to Long Beach. Whatever the hell they did out in the Atlantic, nobody said word one about it to me." He blessed the *Times* reporters for screwing up the ocean where they thought the *Glomar Explorer* did its dirty work.

"Really?" The way his wife studied him made John P. seem like a rank beginner. But Jerry thought her voice held a little uncertainty. He sure hoped so.

"Really." He went over to a bookcase and plucked the manganese nodule from it. "This no-shit came up from seventeen thousand feet in the middle of the Pacific." The nodule no-shit came from half that depth off the California coast, but he was into it now. He went on, "I didn't expect the Spanish Inquisition as soon as you came in."

"No one expects the Spanish Inquisition!" Anna exclaimed, and some of the tightness eased from his spine. If she was doing Monty Python shtick with him, she couldn't be too mad or too sure he was lying. They'd both fallen crazy in love with the Flying Circus when KCET, the L.A. PBS station, started running it, about the time Jerry got back to the mainland.

"The soft chair! The comfy cushions!" Jerry said. Yeah, he'd got away with it.

Unless he hadn't. At dinner, Anna said, "If that ship did that kind of stuff, probably half the people on it worked for the CIA."

All the people on it worked for the CIA. Including me, Jerry thought. Aloud, he answered, "Nobody said so. Nobody tried to recruit me. Nobody had horns or kept tucking a spiked tail down his pants leg or anything. They were just . . . guys. You met that Steve Dole."

"Who knows what he does when I'm *not* meeting him?" Anna said darkly. Jerry told himself to put *Habitable Planets for Man* someplace where she wouldn't see it. If she noticed Steve's name on the spine, she was liable to wonder why a guy who wrote about life on other planets was out in the middle of the Pacific scouring the seafloor for manganese nodules.

After he did the dishes, he started nuzzling her neck and nibbling at her ear. "Cut that out!" she said, brushing him away like an annoying bug.

"What? You don't think it's an ear-ogenous zone?"

She made a horrible face. "Cut that out, too! Seriously, wait till morning. I'm tired. If you're not tired, I don't know what's wrong with you."

He didn't feel like waiting till morning; he felt like it right then. But fighting about sex could get even uglier than fighting about in-laws. He nodded and said, "Okay." There was a certain luxury in slowly and lazily fooling around on a Saturday morning. And if he felt he compromised more often than she did, he would have bet she thought the opposite.

What he mostly did that night was wonder how the CIA would handle the leak. He knew it hadn't come from him. They might not be so sure. If they'd ever noticed that their run of photos didn't exactly match their run of negatives . . . So far, they didn't seem to have. He had to hope seeming matched reality.

Or he had to do something. As long as those photos sat in an envelope with no one studying them, they didn't mean much. Of course, taking them out and showing them to somebody, to anybody, was the quickest way he could think of to finish the story of his own life while it was still only a novella.

To keep from thinking about that, he took another stab at working on his diss. He even got into it, more than he had for a while. He was sitting at the Smith-Corona and making some sense of frequency patterns when Anna kissed him on the back of the neck.

Caught by surprise, he jumped. Then he tried to grab her. Laughing, she skipped away. "No fair," he said. "You were the one who said, Wait till tomorrow."

"You looked so cute, though," she answered, laughing still. "Like everything was a million miles away. I thought I'd give you a wake-up call."

This had happened before. If he pushed it, she might go on saying no. Or she might give in and show she resented giving in. She didn't get that, once she pulled him out of writing, he had trouble getting back to where he'd been. The other possibility was that she got it but didn't care. Jerry preferred not to think about that.

He looked down at the sheet in the typewriter again. For all he could remember about where he'd been going, it might as well have been written in Cherokee. Sometimes he could start it up by putting one word after another till the whole thing got rolling again; a critic he admired called that method "shitting rocks." Sometimes even shitting rocks didn't help. This was one of those nights.

"Fuck," he said softly, and gave up. Maybe tomorrow would be a better day. He hoped like hell tomorrow would have a better morning, anyhow.

He headed for the bedroom. Before he got there, the King of Siam did a flop-and-roll at his feet. After a couple of months living there, he'd become an acceptable human being. He squatted down, rubbed the cat's stomach, and scratched the sides of his mouth. The King of Siam condescended to purr to show that his loyal subject was doing something right.

"What kind of drugs are you feeding him? I can hear that in here," Anna called. She was what she was, the same way the King of Siam was what he was. Jerry was, too, though at the moment what he felt like was a dog in a cats' world.

Sunday morning, Jerry and Tim went to a park off El Segundo to play catch and hit fungoes, and goof around. Alex often joined them, but he was down with a cold.

"Spring training," Jerry said when Tim picked him up. The Angels were working out in Palm Springs. The Dodgers, whom Tim liked more, got ready in Florida, the way they had since they played in Brooklyn.

"I wish!" Tim said. Jerry laughed ruefully. They were both klutzes; that was part of why they were friends. Alex made a better athlete than either of them. His glasses were even thicker than Jerry's, though, so it didn't matter much.

Nobody else was at the park when they got there. It didn't seem to get used a whole lot. Jerry wondered why. It was a perfectly good park, with a couple of diamonds, basketball and handball courts, and a sandbox with a jungle gym. Whether anyone else was or not, he was glad it was there.

Any scout who watched the two of them work out would have

gone off shaking his head, and probably toward the closest bar. Jerry had a good time throwing and hitting and running around anyway. He hated dropping balls, but he knew too well that that came with the territory for him. He admired the guys who made baseball look easy all the more because he knew too well it wasn't.

"That was exciting," he said, after they'd both had enough. "Not good, but exciting."

"No shit." Tim looked up at the sky.

Jerry's gaze followed his friend's. A gull glided by; they weren't very far inland. It made Jerry think of the gooney birds he'd seen while he was on the *Glomar Explorer:* a smaller model, but the same basic design.

Then Tim said, "My security clearance came up for renewal this past week."

"Yeah?" Jerry nodded. He was one of Tim's references. A couple of years earlier, somebody'd phoned him and asked how long he'd known his friend and whether he was sure Tim was loyal to the United States.

"Yeah. At my interview, they were asking questions about you."

"Were they?" Ice walked up Jerry's back. "Like what?"

"Like how reliable I thought you were. That was what they said, reliable. Like whether you could be counted on to keep your commitments."

"What did you tell them?"

"I said of course you were. You're my buddy. What am I going to say to the spooks?" Tim Ishihara sounded offended he'd asked.

"Thanks, man." *A friend in need is a friend indeed* ran through Jerry's head. "Did they . . . ask about the envelope?"

"I don't know what's in it, so I can't say for sure, but I think so." Tim chuckled harshly. "Which is funny, 'cause when they were sitting there grilling me they were no more than ten feet from it. They wanted to know if you were a careful custodian of government property. Sounds pretty weird, doesn't it?"

"Sounds like what happens when people who don't know how to write do it anyway."

"Yeah." His friend eyed him. "That ship you were on, it wasn't just out there mining the ocean, huh?"

So he'd seen Friday's *Times,* too. Jerry stuck to as much of his story as he could: "It didn't do anything else while *I* was on it.

What happened in the Atlantic before it got to Long Beach, I can't tell you."

"Okay." Tim left it right there.

Jerry realized he could have put that better. Or maybe he couldn't. Did Tim think he meant *I don't know what it did in the Atlantic* or *I can't talk about what it did in the Atlantic*? Tim respected secrets—respected them more than Jerry did, for sure. Jerry said, "I think before real long I may need that envelope back."

"Let me know so I can get it out and bring it straight to you. I don't want to leave it at my place. I've got the feeling that'd be dumb," Tim said.

"Will do. Um . . . don't mention it on the phone, y'know?"

"I won't. I already thought of that. How much trouble did you get yourself into?"

"More than I wanted to, that's for sure."

"I believe it." Tim hesitated. "Would knowing what it is do me any good?"

"No. Christ, no!" Jerry was a halfhearted Jew. Tim was an equally halfhearted Buddhist. Most of the Japanese-Americans Jerry knew were Baptists, but Tim's dad hadn't bothered to convert. Both of them said *Christ!* and *Jesus!* all the time anyway, because they lived in a Christian country. Jerry went on, "For one thing, you wouldn't believe me if I told you. For another, what you don't know, nobody else can make you tell him."

"That doesn't sound real good."

"It isn't. It's liable to get worse, too." Jerry wondered how much worse. They still weren't sure about him. They wouldn't be sniffing around the edges of what he'd done if they were sure. They'd stick him in a soundproofed room somewhere and work on him with hot things and sharp things and pointy things.

"All right. Thanks for playing straight with me, anyway. Whatever happens to me, I don't want anything bad coming down on Cheryl, know what I mean?"

"Afraid I do. I haven't said a word to Anna, either, and I'm not going to. The less she knows, the better off she is."

Tim digested that. Then he said, "Maybe we should head on home."

"Maybe we should. I'm sorry I got you into this to begin with."

"Fuck that. We're friends." Time sounded sure and serene. Jerry feared he wouldn't have done nearly so well with their roles reversed. The old riff on the Kipling poem also crossed his mind: *If you can keep your head when all about you / Are losing theirs, chances are you don't understand the situation.*

When he walked into the apartment, he set down his bat and glove and threw his Angels cap onto the couch like a Frisbee. The King of Siam plainly didn't know whether to attack it or run away. Anna wrinkled her nose and pointed toward the bathroom. "To the showers, Pete Rose!"

"You think I stink now, you should have seen me chasing fly balls," he replied with dignity. Anna laughed, so he supposed he broke even, anyhow.

The quarter dragged on. During the last week of instruction, students in Jerry's sections who'd spent the time since January doing nothing swarmed to his office to find out how to get As just the same. He did what he could for them, knowing what he'd probably do to them when he read their finals. That had saddened him in his first quarter TAing. He was hardened to it now.

And, one morning when he didn't have to be on campus, he visited the Bank of America on Gardena Boulevard. He took out $8,500 in cash. If he had to disappear in a hurry, he wouldn't be paying for things with a check or his credit card, not unless he wanted to yell *Here I am!* at the top of his lungs.

It was funny, in a black way. The CIA had dropped a small fortune on him to make sure he kept his mouth shut. He might end up using a chunk of it to fly under their radar. Or he might put it back later if he was worrying about nothing.

He wished he thought he was.

He wondered whether the bank would hassle him for taking out so much cash. But, by luck, he dealt with the same teller he'd had when he wondered about the money to begin with. "Hello again!" she said and didn't ask him anything except what kind of bills he wanted and, after she gave him the fat envelope, "Would you like our guard to go out to your car with you?"

"That'd be terrific. Thanks!" he said.

The guard's name badge said he was Paul. He was a black man in his forties; he wore a Stetson and a pistol on his hip. He walked with a limp. "Sorry I'm not quicker," he said, his voice deep and also slow. "Stopped somethin' in Korea a long time ago."

"It's okay. Take it easy. I'm not in a hurry," Jerry said.

When Paul got a look at the Rambler, he said, "You oughta buy yourself some better wheels with that there money."

"Maybe I will." Jerry tried to give the guard five dollars. Walking had to hurt him.

But Paul waved the money aside. "Bank pays me good enough. This, it's just part of my job."

Tuesday morning at eight o'clock the following week, Jerry sat with the other TAs to proctor the final and to gather up his sections' bluebooks. He did some of them in his office. The pile he didn't finish there, he took home. Grades were due back forty-eight hours after the exam ended, so he had till Thursday at eleven.

He worked on the finals till Anna came home. One of the Bobbsey Twins flunked; the other got a D+. They were cute, but they were stupid. Or, if you looked at it another way, they were stupid, but they were cute.

"Did the prettier one get the D?" his wife asked when he told her.

"As a matter of fact, no. She didn't know *anything*. She didn't even suspect anything," Jerry said.

"What a *shame*." Anna sounded as brokenhearted as Jerry thought she would.

Perhaps as a reward for his not cutting pretty girls any slack, she fixed dinner herself: ground beef, taco seasoning, and rice. Homemade Hamburger Helper. Anything but exciting, but pretty much harmless. Jerry washed the dishes, though. That had hardened into routine.

Then he settled down at the table and started grading more finals. More than half of him hoped Anna would come by and kiss him on the back of the neck again. It made him mad when he was working on his dissertation. Now he would have welcomed any excuse to stop for a while.

Anna stayed away. She and the King of Siam were doing whatever they were doing in the back of the apartment. Jerry yawned. A few minutes later, he yawned again, wider this time. If he drank coffee now, he wouldn't sleep at all tonight. He turned the radio on to KNX. Listening to the news station might keep him alert. He'd done that a lot as revelation followed revelation during Watergate.

He didn't pay much attention to the stock market report or the sports news. The local car crashes and shootings didn't interest him, either. But KNX was a CBS affiliate, and hooked in with the network's national and foreign correspondents. They did that stuff better than anyone else in town.

On a 5–4 vote, the Supreme Court had decided plays enjoyed the same First Amendment protection against obscenity charges as books, newspapers, and movies did. That seemed reasonable to Jerry. So did the British government's recommendation of a Yes vote on joining the Common Market.

But Vietnam was gurgling down the drain. Refugees were fleeing from the highlands to the coast, hoping to escape oncoming North Vietnamese forces. The latest North Vietnamese drive seemed aimed at splitting South Vietnam in half. Jerry shook his head. Too many people he knew had done and suffered too much for too little.

Meanwhile, the Socialist Workers Party claimed the FBI was harassing it, which the FBI probably was. And Henry Kissinger and Andrei Gromyko were talking about the Middle East again.

Jerry set another exam on the pile of ones he'd finished. He was more than halfway through them now. He hoped he'd get done by one in the morning, though two seemed more likely. As he reached for the next bluebook, part of him wished Kissinger and Gromyko were meeting to discuss Humpty Dumpty. Kissinger knew about it, of course. But he wouldn't say anything. Not a chance in the world.

Then the KNX newsman said, "As long as we're talking about American-Soviet relations, some of you may have heard Jack Anderson's show on another radio network earlier tonight. Anderson expanded on and corrected reporting in the *Los Angeles Times* from last month. The *Hughes Glomar Explorer,* he says, was indeed trying to raise a Russian submarine last summer, but in the North Pacific, not the Atlantic. No submarine was raised. He calls it a 'boondoggle,' and says the secrecy surrounding the project was 'simply the cover-up of a failure—three hundred and fifty million dollars literally went down into the ocean.'"

The newsman coughed and said, "Excuse me": live radio. He went on, "Anderson added that some rumors about the *Hughes Glomar Explorer*'s mission were 'absolutely unbelievable, and had to be intended to deceive.'" He paused. "We'll be right back, with traffic on the ones, after these messages."

Jerry turned off the radio. He was awake now, by God! He wondered if he'd ever dare to sleep now. No matter how hard the CIA guys had tried to bury it, word about the *Glomar Explorer* was out. Word about Humpty Dumpty, too. Jack Anderson didn't believe that; he was a thoroughly rational man, rooted in the world as he knew it.

Outer space? Flying saucers? Aliens in suspended animation? That was crazy stuff, nothing else but. It was to sensible people like Jack Anderson, anyhow.

What did you do, though, when the crazy stuff turned real? Jerry's dad had had to deal with that after the United States dropped A-bombs on Hiroshima and Nagasaki. People took A-bombs and even H-bombs for granted now, but in 1945 they would have seemed straight out of science fiction. And in 1945 science fiction had been way more disreputable than it was now.

Who'd tipped Anderson off? What would happen to him now, and to his informant? Those were fascinating questions, weren't they? So was another one that occurred to Jerry. *What happens if they think I talked with Anderson?* Whatever happened, it wouldn't be good.

He wanted to get up and pull back the curtains so he could see if anybody was sneaking around outside. Being a rational man himself, he could see that that wouldn't help, even if someone was. After a moment, he did it anyhow. Hadn't he just reminded himself that rationality was overrated?

If an assassin was out there, Jerry gave him a perfect shot. He didn't see anybody, and no one fired at him. Logic said nobody was there. How much you listened to logic . . .

He let the curtains fall back into place. Nothing would happen right this minute. Maybe nothing would happen at all. He could still hope nothing would. He could hope not, yeah, but he couldn't make himself believe it anymore. The CIA might not murder someone for talking to a reporter about the K-129. For talking about Humpty Dumpty? That was a whole different business.

He *hadn't* told Jack Anderson about Humpty Dumpty, of course. But, while *he* knew that, the CIA didn't. *Termination with extreme prejudice.* He'd signed on the dotted line. If they condemned him, he had no appeal.

The condemned man went back to the table and finished grading finals. What were you supposed to do when the world came to pieces around you? You tried to make things as normal as you could.

Just this side of two in the morning, he put the last exam on the finished pile. He set down the red pen and rubbed his eyes. Then he got to his feet to go to the bathroom and brush his teeth before trying to sleep. He was tired. Sleepy? Sleepy was a different story.

Full of piss and catnip, the King of Siam intercepted him in the hallway. Why was the human up at such a funny time? Why else but to play with a Siamese? Jerry played a little, halfheartedly, then did what he needed to do.

Anna snored softly in the dark bedroom. Jerry slid into bed without waking her. That was good; she wouldn't grumble in the morning. He lay on his back, staring up at the cottage-cheese ceiling he couldn't really see. After a while, sleep ambushed him the way the imaginary hit man hadn't.

"I thought you'd sleep late instead of getting up with me," Anna said, as they ate breakfast together.

"Yeah, well . . ." He shrugged. "I'm awake. I'm moving. I'll turn in my grades, then come home. If I need a nap, I'll take a nap."

"You can do that." His wife sounded somewhere between jealous and resentful. Even when she got the chance, she couldn't nap for hell, not unless she was really sick.

He kissed her hard before they both headed out the door. He didn't want to let her go. A quickie right then would have been wonderful. He thought so, anyway. She plainly didn't. He made sure the door was locked before they went down the stairs.

"See you tonight," she said.

"Love you, hon," he answered. Her car was under the building, his out on the street. He looked back at her once before she got to the stairway down to the parked cars. She didn't look at him. She was already thinking about the work ahead, or else just running on automatic pilot.

Up to campus he went, and walked into the department offices as they were opening. When he turned in his grade sheet, the department chair's administrative assistant exclaimed, "Good Lord! Did you sleep at all last night?" (The department chair herself wasn't here yet, of course, and probably wouldn't be for another couple of hours.)

"Little bit," Jerry answered, shrugging.

"Well, you can enjoy the break now, anyway," the AA said.

"Thanks, Marcia. See you next quarter." Jerry didn't stick around.

He'd done what he had to do. Now he could go back to the apartment and do nothing for a while.

The southbound drive was slow. Because he'd gone up so early, he was still in the middle of rush hour on the way down. As he had driving to UCLA, he listened to KNX in hopes of hearing more about what Jack Anderson had had to say.

Naturally, the news station talked about everything else. And then, when Jerry was almost down to the airport and thinking about sliding over so he could get off the freeway at El Segundo, the newsman said, "RAND Corporation executive Stephen H. Dole was shot and killed outside his Santa Monica home last night a little past eight. Police are investigating the crime as a botched robbery—the killer, perhaps alarmed at the sound of the gunshot, fled without taking anything of value from the victim. No description of a suspect is available."

"Oh, sweet fucking Jesus Christ!" Jerry said. He hadn't wanted to believe these days would really come. But he also didn't believe Steve Dole had died in a botched robbery: not for a second, he didn't. Which meant they were bound to be looking for him, too. They wouldn't give him a big kiss when they found him, either.

Which meant . . . He'd thought about what he might do if these days came. Now he had to try to do it. He feared the odds were stacked against him. He had to try just the same. It wasn't as if he owed the CIA anything anymore.

Instead of leaving the San Diego at El Segundo, he kept going till Redondo Beach Boulevard, then headed west instead of east. Twenty minutes later, he pulled into the lot in front of the small skyscraper where Tim worked. He'd had lunch around here with his friend a few times; he knew where visitors' parking was.

As with the RAND Corporation, you couldn't just walk through the halls here. He asked the receptionist, "Would you buzz Tim Ishihara and tell him Jerry's in the lobby, please?"

"Hold on for one minute," she said. After she made the call, she told him, "He'll be right down."

"Thanks," Jerry said.

Tim came out of the elevator. Jerry had intended to ask him to go back up and retrieve the manila envelope from the safe where he'd stashed it. He turned out not to need to; his friend already had it. Tim held it out to him, saying, "Here you go, man. You show up at this time of day, I figure you're gonna want this."

"You're a lifesaver!"

"Am I? Way it looks to me, chances are I'm messing up your life, not saving it."

"No." Jerry shook his head. "With this, I've got a chance to fix things. Without it, I'm dead." He knew how literally he meant that, too.

By Tim's expression he had a fair idea himself. "Luck, buddy," he said. They shook hands. Jerry wanted to hug him, but didn't. He hurried out to the parking lot instead.

He didn't want to go back to his apartment. He did it anyway. He parked across the street from the building, not underneath. If anyone was waiting, he guessed it would be there. If the hit man was already inside his place, he'd made his last mistake, that was all.

The only one waiting inside had four legs. The King of Siam must not have expected him—the cat acted glad he'd come in. Jerry rubbed his tummy and scratched him under the chin. Then he threw clothes, a Dopp kit, and the envelope he'd got from Tim into the little suitcase he'd carried onto the *Glomar Explorer*.

He had his hand on the doorknob when he hesitated. He needed to tell Anna *something*. If he disappeared without a trace, what would she do? Call the cops, what else? That was the last thing he wanted now. He grabbed a sheet of paper and wrote in large, looping letters: *Family emergency up north.* (He had cousins in Tacoma. He couldn't stand them, but he didn't think she knew that.) *Heading that way. Don't know when I'll be in touch. Will call when I can. Some private stuff, so don't tell anybody. Love you a lot. XOXOXO—Me.*

He stuck the note on the kitchen counter, where she couldn't miss it. Down the stairs he went, and out. Nobody called to him. Nobody shot at him. He stuck the suitcase in the Rambler's trunk, then slid behind the wheel. When he turned the key, the car started. With a sigh of relief, he drove north.

At El Segundo, he turned right. He kept looking in the rearview mirror. As far as he could tell, no one was following him. He took El Segundo east to the Harbor Freeway and got on, heading north.

XV

At the four-level interchange, he drove east on the San Bernardino Freeway. He hadn't gone very far before noticing he was low on gas. He got off the freeway at Atlantic, in East L.A. Boyle Heights, his father would have called it, but nobody much younger than his dad said that. In those days, this part of town had been Jewish and Japanese and Mexican. It was mostly Mexican now.

Jerry filled the Rambler at a Chevron station, muttering at paying sixty-two cents (well, actually 61.9) a gallon. Next to the station, a barber pole snaked its way to infinity. Eyeing its endless spiral, he had an idea. He didn't like it, but he didn't like anything about what he was doing. He asked the man who'd pumped his gas, "Can I park over there at the edge of your lot while I get my hair cut?"

"Sí, Señor. go ahead," the fellow answered.

Two of the three barbers in the shop looked Hispanic, too. The third guy was black, his head shiny and shaved like Yul Brynner's. Jerry didn't have to wait; they waved him to the middle chair. "What can I do for you today?" the black man asked.

"Can you cut my hair just kinda regular, know what I mean?" Jerry said. "I've got a job interview tomorrow."

"Sure can. Want me to shave your beard, too? Extra three bucks."

"Do it." Jerry knew he sounded bitter and disgusted, the way he should have. He felt bitter and disgusted, too. But if he wasn't going to be easily recognized from here on out, he couldn't fool around.

Forty-five minutes later, the barber waved to the mirror and said, "What do you think?"

"Christ! I just graduated from high school!" Jerry exclaimed. The black man laughed. Jerry felt his newly naked chin. It seemed smoother than he remembered after shaving himself. The barber's straight razor was *sharp*.

He paid the tab (and it wasn't *Shave and a haircut—five cents*, worse luck) and went out to his car. Heading back toward the freeway, he drove past a liquor store. In front of the place sat a dirty white Corvair of about the same vintage as the Rambler. A cardboard sign in the car's window said FOR SALE—$1000 and gave a phone number.

"All right!" Jerry said. Driving a car the CIA knew about had been one of his biggest worries. If he was driving something else, though . . .

Perhaps not coincidentally, the liquor store had a telephone booth by the door. Jerry drove around the corner. He got out of the car, went to the trunk, and loaded up his wallet as unobtrusively as he could—it was that kind of neighborhood. Then he walked back.

He stepped into the street and stared at the phone number till he had it memorized. As soon as he did, he fed a dime into the pay phone. It gave him a dial tone, which wasn't guaranteed. He called the number.

One ring, two . . .

"Hello?" The guy on the other end had an accent, but not a heavy one. Jerry'd gone to school with people who talked the same way.

"Hi," he said. "I'm in the phone booth by your Corvair. I'm interested."

"Oh, yeah? Okay, I can be there in like fifteen minutes. My name's Rodolfo. Who're you?"

"I'm Jerry." Jerry wished he'd given a false name, but he hadn't.

"Okay, Jerry. See you soon." The line went dead. Jerry hung up. The phone went *click-chunk* as it finished swallowing his dime. He went into the liquor store and bought a Coke. Sugar and caffeine would help keep him going.

Rodolfo showed up on a bike, which he chained to a lamp pole. He was about thirty-five, squat and strong looking, his hair retreating at the temples. After they shook hands, Jerry asked, "How many miles? I couldn't read the odometer through the side window."

"Ninety-two thousand—not quite ninety-three," Rodolfo said. "Still runs pretty good—you wanna drive it a little, see for yourself?"

"Yeah." Jerry tried not to think about *Unsafe at Any Speed*. If he hadn't done what he needed to do with the Corvair inside a week, he'd probably wind up dead in some way that had nothing to do with the kind of car he was driving.

Rodolfo unlocked the door and waved for Jerry to get in. He had to move the seat back before he'd fit; he was six or eight inches taller than the man who wanted to sell. Rodolfo slid in from the curb and handed him the key. Before he started the car, he checked the odometer for himself. It said 92,741.6, so Rodolfo'd told the truth about that, anyway.

He turned the key. Like a VW Bug, the Corvair kept its engine in the rear. It was still noisy. "Air-cooled, you know," Rodolfo said. "You don't gotta worry about the radiator boiling over or nothin'."

"I remember that, uh-huh." Jerry had to look to see where the controls were. He didn't reach for them automatically, the way he did with his own machine. He released the parking brake, put the Corvair in drive, and pulled out onto Atlantic.

It drove like . . . a car. It didn't have much pickup, but neither did the Rambler. If it broke down on the way, he'd worry about what to do then. "What you think?" Rodolfo asked when he parked in front of the liquor store again.

"I'll buy it," Jerry said.

"*Bueno!* I brung the pink slip with me, in case." Rodolfo pulled it out of his wallet and unfolded it. Then, suddenly cautious, he added, "You got the money?"

"You bet." Jerry took out his wallet, too.

While he counted greenbacks, Rodolfo filled out his half of the change-of-ownership form at the bottom of the pink slip. He said, "Lemme see your license for a minute."

Jerry'd expected that. He gave Rodolfo the grand, waited while he counted it, then pulled out two more fifties and said, "You just did."

It fazed Rodolfo not a bit. "Like that, huh? Okay, man, you do your half." He passed Jerry the pink slip and a pen. Jerry named himself Gerald Smeltzer. A California driver's license carried a letter and seven digits. He turned the *M* on his license to an *N* and added one to each number. The address he put down was just as fictitious.

He separated it from the rest of the document and handed it to Rodolfo, whose last name, he saw, was Jimenez. "You mail it to the DMV," he said. "I'm gonna be on the road."

"Hope it goes good," Rodolfo said.

"Me, too," Jerry answered. "Glad I saw your car."

"Your car now. Me, I'm heading home." Rodolfo snapped his fingers and dug out his key ring. "Almost forgot—here's your trunk key, too."

"Thanks. I wondered if it was the same as the ignition." *Wouldn't not having it have been fun?* Jerry thought.

Rodolfo unlocked his bike and pedaled away. Jerry drove the

Corvair around the corner. He parked behind his Rambler. He had to remind himself the new car's trunk was in front. He took his suitcase and the cash out of one car and put them in the other. He had a little tool kit with the tire-changing gear. He used a screwdriver to remove the Rambler's plates and put them in the Corvair's trunk, too. He also removed the registration from the glove compartment. Then he locked the car again.

Eventually, somebody would tow the Rambler away. Eventually, in spite of what he'd done, people would figure out it belonged to him. Eventually, the DMV would realize the info on Rodolfo's change-of-ownership form was bullshit of the purest ray serene. With luck, those *eventuallys* would come too late to matter. Without luck, he'd be too deceased to care.

One more thing to do before he hit the road for real. He checked the Corvair's oil. He was pleased to find it had plenty. The oil on the dipstick even looked clear and clean. So this might work. "It might," he muttered.

He got back on the San Bernardino Freeway, heading east.

A lunch stop in San Bernardino. A stop for gas and a long leak in Blythe: he'd had more coffee with lunch. Over the Colorado. Jerry knew he was in Arizona by the saguaros on the far side of the river. He was careful to keep to the double nickel from then on. Arizona cops had an evil reputation for ticketing cars with out-of-state plates doing anything even slightly illegal. He took no chances.

By the time he got to Phoenix, night was falling. He laughed at himself for thinking of it that way. He'd never cared for the Glen Campbell song.

He spotted a neon sign on a tall pole so you could see the big red letters from the interstate: MOTEL. That worked for him. He exited and made for it on whatever this cross street was. The clerk gave him a room key and change from the twenty he passed across the counter.

Half a block farther down the street was a Denny's that also sported a tall sign. He ate dinner there. It wasn't great. It wasn't terrible. It was food. He figured he'd have breakfast there tomorrow, too.

The room was, well, a room. The walls were thin; he could hear the TV next door through one of them. He hated that, and turned on his room's TV in self-defense. He took off his shoes, but fell asleep in the rest of his clothes.

Next thing he knew, it was 5:07 a.m., Phoenix clock radio standard time. His watch said it was an hour earlier. He changed it; he was on mountain time now, not Pacific. Then he tried to sleep some more, tried and failed. He turned off the television and hopped in the shower to help get himself all the way awake. Then, being without shaving cream, he shaved with lather from the bar of motel soap. Life with a beard was much easier.

He checked out before six. As he walked out of the lobby, he grabbed a road map of Arizona from a case full of brochures for tourist attractions. He took it into the Denny's with him and studied it while he ate bacon and eggs.

The I-10 went south to Tucson and then southeast. The I-17 went north to Flagstaff, where it met the eastbound I-40, which would take him to Albuquerque. Flagstaff was up in the mountains. It might be snowy. He didn't want to drive in snow if he could help it. The I-10 it would be. He'd go as long as he could.

Away he went. He stopped for gas in Tucson, and bought a cheap little road atlas of the United States so he'd have at least some idea of what the hell he was doing. "Where you headed?" asked the man in the small building next to the pumps.

"Just driving. Kinda like *Easy Rider*, only without the drugs and the motorcycles." Jerry looked out at his Corvair and laughed self-consciously.

"Still fun. Wish I could come along." The gas station guy sounded wistful.

That it might be fun hadn't occurred to Jerry. All he'd thought about was staying in one piece. He drove away with a new attitude. It lasted half an hour, maybe even forty-five minutes. After that, the drive turned back into work.

Lordsburg, New Mexico, made a lunch stop. He ate at a Burger King, where he knew exactly what he'd be getting. He stopped again for gas and the bathroom, then kept going till he came to El Paso. He found a motel near the interstate and had dinner at a Mexican place across the street. Mexican food in El Paso wasn't the same as Mexican food in Los Angeles, but it was good. And the Dos Equis he washed it down with was heavenly.

As he had the night before, he crashed early and woke early. The

Mexican restaurant wasn't open yet, so he got scrambled eggs and sausage from the Golden Arches down the street. Then he hit the road again.

Texas was miles and miles of miles and miles, even more so than the I-5 boogie through California's Central Valley. No one, locals or out-of-staters, paid any attention to the energy-saving speed limit. Jerry stayed in the slow lane on the I-10 and then the I-20. If people wanted to pass him, they could pass him. He passed trucks going even slower than he was. There were some.

Despite hurrying less than most people, he made Fort Worth before quitting for the day. That was around six hundred miles, not too bad if you were a lone driver. When he got to his motel room, the nightstand clock told him he'd traded mountain time for central somewhere east of El Paso.

He bought a steak for dinner, and enjoyed it. As he went back to the hotel, he realized he didn't have to stay in cheap joints like this. He had plenty of bread for nice hotels. After one more step, he shook his head. He was willing to spend money to do what he had to do. He wasn't willing to spend more than he had to.

"Well, shit," he said out loud—no one was close enough to hear him. "I really *am* my father's son." It had been true all along, of course. He'd never realized it so intensely before, though.

Back in the room, he sent the telephone by the clock a longing stare. He wanted so much to call Anna and let her know he was okay. Even more, he wanted to hear her voice. He shook his head. He'd figured his phone was tapped back at the place he'd had by himself. The CIA wouldn't have suddenly lost track of him when he moved in with Anna after they married.

The most he could hope for was that they kept on not knowing where he was. If they had the note he'd left, they'd be looking in the wrong area. But if they traced a call, he was toast.

You can't make any mistakes. Not even one. Calling home is a mistake, he told himself firmly. Calling Tim or Alex or his dad was also a mistake. Professor Krikorian, too. The CIA guys had talked to his advisor before they ever met him.

That left . . . nobody. He wasn't an outgoing person, which put it mildly. He didn't have a whole swarm of friends. Even if he did, the Agency might monitor all of them. Not only could he not make mistakes, he couldn't take chances.

His back gave a reproachful creak when he got into the Corvair the next morning. The car wasn't as comfortable as the Rambler—either that or he'd spent too goddamn much time in it lately.

Away he went, heading east and a little north. The country changed. This wasn't the Southwest anymore; this was the South. It was greener and wetter than he was used to. It wasn't the jungle paradise of Hawaii, but it wasn't desert, either. Somewhere near Hot Springs, Arkansas, he tried out the Corvair's windshield wipers for the first time.

He bought gas in Hot Springs. He bought new wiper blades, too. He'd forgotten to check them when he bought the car from Rodolfo. "These here, they're shot t'hell an' gone," said the attendant who put on the new pair.

"Yeah, I found that out," Jerry said. The man gave him an odd look, but didn't ask any questions.

With wipers that actually did something about the rain, Jerry drove on. In Southern California, every rain seemed a separate natural disaster. People didn't know how to drive in wet weather. They went too fast and they tailgated. Here, they were used to water falling from the sky. They spread out, took their time, and got where they were going.

Jerry made another stop just before crossing from Arkansas to Tennessee. Memphis was where he was going. But he bought an umbrella before he got there. "Bet y'wish you hadn't left yours at home," said the fellow who sold it to him.

"Bet you're right," Jerry answered. It was still coming down pretty hard.

Crossing the Mississippi amazed him. A river half a mile wide? The one they had in Los Angeles was dry eight or nine months a year, and encased in a concrete straitjacket so it wouldn't make trouble. So much fresh water flowing freely or lying around in lakes and ponds freaked Jerry out.

He found a motel on the outskirts of Memphis, just off the I-40. The only way he could be sure what town he was in was by the phone book in the nightstand drawer. All the places where he'd stayed the past few days blurred together in his mind. Motels by the highway were America at its most homogenized.

The barbecued pork sandwich he got at the joint next to the motel, like the Mexican food in El Paso, showed restaurants varied from place to place. It was good, but the sauce wasn't what he thought of as barbecue sauce. When he said so, the waitress answered, "Where you from? Not around here, not by how you talk."

"San Francisco." He lied without hesitation.

"California? Really?" She looked and sounded jealous. She was short and blond and pretty, which made him think of Anna. "What're you doin' here, then?"

"Passing through." That was honest enough.

"I believe it. If you're from there, you wouldn't want to stay here, even if you like the barbecue. California? That'd be somethin'." She studied him. "You stayin' at Stanley's place next door?"

He nodded. "That's right."

"Well, I'm off my shift in another hour, if you want to talk or somethin'."

She didn't mean *talk*. Jerry'd never run into a come-on so direct. Was she a pro, or just hoping some of that exotic California stardust would rub off on her? If he'd been single, he thought he would have found out. He was tempted anyway, tempted enough to wish he had less common sense. After a second, though, he held up his left hand so she couldn't miss the ring. "I better not," he said.

"Doesn't worry plenty o' guys any," she said. When he just shrugged, she turned away. "You'll never know what you're missin'." She put enough hip action into her walk to give him a hint.

Feeling squelched, he squelched back to the motel. Knowing he might have had company made the plain room seem even lonelier than it would have anyway. He took care of biological pressure the way he had on the *Glomar Explorer*, but Heinlein had been dead right in *Time Enough for Love:* that was lonely, too.

He was glad the blond waitress wasn't on yet when he had breakfast at the place next door. He ate, checked out of the motel, and got on the interstate again. The Corvair kept running. He wondered whether the Rambler would have done the same. He'd never know now. But he would have bet there was an APB out for that car.

California was long from top to bottom, narrow from side to side. Tennessee was the other way around. He drove more than five hundred miles to get from the southwest corner of the state to its northeastern tip. Bristol City wasn't much of a town, but it had the usual assortment of places to stay and places to eat when you pulled off the highway.

He got a room. He went to the closest place and ate a pork chop and mashed potatoes. The food wasn't nearly so interesting as it had been the night before. Neither was the waitress. That might have been just as well.

Out of Tennessee and into Virginia. The farther east he went, the more traffic there was. He'd crossed the country in six days. He knew he might have pushed harder, but he didn't care. He might have killed the car. He also might have got busted, which was the last thing he needed.

He came into Washington, DC, just in time for rush hour. It wasn't as bad as getting stuck on the San Diego Freeway when a wreck closed three lanes, but it wasn't much fun, either. And he knew where he was going on the San Diego. Here, he groped his way along.

No motels by the off-ramps now. No swarm of not-too-fancy places to eat. This was a real city. He drove along, looking for a hotel of the plainer sort. It took him a while to find one; this part of town seemed pretty fancy. You didn't plop a green space as big as Rock Creek Park down in the middle of a ghetto.

At last, he saw a place that might do. All the parking was by valet. He grabbed his suitcase and cash and gave the black guy in the maroon uniform a buck to stow his car, then went in to register. Even a plain hotel here cost more than he'd expected it to. He booked his room for three nights, adding, "I may stay longer. It depends on how my business goes."

"That's fine, sir," said the black woman at the registration desk. The staff looked to be mostly black. The guests walking through the lobby were all white. That saddened Jerry without surprising him.

He looked around for the case that would hold brochures and maps. There it was, on the wall by the concierge's stand. He plucked a city map from it before going up to his room. The room was nicer than the ones he'd used on his cross-country journey, but of the same kind.

He got the hotel's address from a notepad on the dresser. A moment later, he found it on the map. He used the pen that had lain next to the pad to make a dot in the right place. Then he looked to see where he'd be going in the morning.

1125 Sixteenth Street NW. He'd memorized that after finding it on one of his visits to the UCLA Research Library. The map told him the address lay between M and N Streets. It wasn't very far away, either; he hadn't come to this part of town by accident.

Down to the restaurant for a steak and a Michelob, which was the best beer they had. Then back to the room again. He sprawled out on the bed. "Damn!" he told the ceiling. "I made it!" He figured he'd earned the right to be surprised. The Corvair had run like a champ. The CIA hadn't caught up with him.

Tomorrow . . . Tomorrow, in Roger Zelazny's immortal words from *Lord of Light*, the fit would hit the Shan.

He dressed for the occasion, as best he could with what he'd quickly thrown into the suitcase. He had a blue dress shirt. He had a pair of brown cords. They weren't dress slacks, but they weren't jeans, either. He had shoes that weren't Blue Tips and socks that weren't white. And he had the tweed jacket his father had got him for Chanukah. When he looked at himself in the mirror, he had trouble recognizing the serious-seeming young man who looked back.

"Good," he said, and went downstairs.

He had both manila envelopes with him. After the valet brought his car, he put one on the front seat and the other with the spare tire in the trunk, where the engine should have been. He hoped his cash would be safer in the car than in his room, where the cleaning lady might snoop through his stuff while he was gone.

He also had the city map. He'd memorized his route, but he wanted to be able to work out where he was if he had to detour because of an accident or construction or something. He thought of it as being a suspenders-and-belt man. His father probably would have said it sounded familiar.

"There it is!" he said, when he got where he was going. The building was four stories tall, and looked to date from the early years of the century.

Finding it was one thing. Finding somewhere to park was something else again. When he finally did, he had almost a ten-minute walk back. A fence made of black steel spears, each taller than a man, protected the grounds. Bushes beginning to flower grew in front of it.

But the gate was open. Jerry paused, took a deep breath, and walked in. A bronze plaque by the entrance said EMBASSY OF THE UNION OF SOVIET SOCIALIST REPUBLICS and, below that, the same thing in Russian. A red flag with a gold hammer and sickle in the top left corner flew from a pole mounted on the roof.

Jerry went up the stairs and into the embassy. An attractive

young woman sat behind a reception desk. On the wall in back of
her hung a big portrait of Leonid Brezhnev, all jowls and scowl and
bushy eyebrows. The portrait had to be meant to flatter, but it still
made the Soviet boss look like one tough bruiser.

The receptionist, by contrast, was good-looking enough for Jerry
to notice no matter how nervous he was. "Yes, sir? What can I do for
you?" she asked. She had a slight Slavic accent. Being pretty didn't
mean she wasn't with the KGB. Probably the opposite, in fact.

Another deep breath. "I'd like to speak with Ambassador Dobrynin for a few minutes, please." He'd learned the ambassador's
name the same way he'd learned the embassy's address.

The receptionist frowned. "What about?"

"I can't tell you that. But it's important. It's very important,"
Jerry said. Then he repeated it in Russian.

One of her eyebrows lifted. In the same language, she answered,
"I can't send up any stranger off the street, you know."

"*Da,*" he said sadly. Falling back into English, he went on, "Let
me have a piece of paper, please." She tore a sheet off a scratch pad
and slid it across the desk. He printed *Azorian* on it, then *Midlothian* below it, and, after a moment's hesitation, *Humpty Dumpty*
below that. "Take this to him, please. If he doesn't want to see me
after he gets it, I'll leave quietly, promise." *What'll I do in that case?
Cut my throat, I guess.*

She considered. Then she waved him to a chair. "Sit there and
wait." She didn't take the paper upstairs herself. A young man in
a black suit that would have been the height of style in 1963 did.
Jerry sat and waited and worried.

Fifteen minutes later, the man in the black suit came back. He
spoke to the receptionist, too quietly for Jerry to make out what he
said. The surprise with which she eyed him afterward, though, was
unmistakable.

She sent Jerry a peremptory *Come here!* gesture. When he did,
she said, "Go with Georgi Pavlovich here. He will take you to the
ambassador." To Georgi Pavlovich, she added in Russian, "He
speaks our language."

"I'll remember," the man in the black suit said, also in Russian.
He switched to English for Jerry: "You will come with me, please."

"Thanks." Jerry came.

They went up two flights of stairs. Halfway up the second, the
Russian said, "It is unusual for ambassador to see someone who

comes in off street." He nodded to himself, savoring the word. "Unusual, yes." Jerry didn't say anything.

The ambassador's office struck Jerry as being halfway between a business executive's and a professor's at an Ivy League university. Everything on the desk was modern as next week. The bookcases were wooden, though, and many of the books in Russian, English, and French looked old. Another portrait of Brezhnev, smaller than the one downstairs, hung above them.

Anatoly Dobrynin was about fifty-five, with a wide bald dome, and what was left of his hair curly and gray. Jerry knew he must have seen him on television, but hadn't remembered what he looked like. Beside him sat a younger, foxy-faced man with reddish hair. The man in the black suit murmured to the ambassador, probably warning that Jerry knew some Russian. Dobrynin nodded. Jerry's guide disappeared, closing the door behind him.

After shaking hands, Dobrynin said, "This is Major Bronstein. He is assistant military attaché here." Studying Jerry, the ambassador went on, "You know some . . . extraordinary things."

"Yes, sir. I'm afraid I do," Jerry agreed.

After a glance at his boss for permission, Major Bronstein said, "What we need to hear is. how do you know them?" His English held almost no accent.

Jerry's stomach knotted. *This is where the treason starts*, he thought. But it wasn't, not really. He'd convinced himself it wasn't. The CIA would have a different opinion, of course. He said, "I was on the *Glomar Explorer* when we raised the Midlothian object. The other name for that, the newer name, is Humpty Dumpty."

"We have hints of this, but only hints," Bronstein said. He looked like somebody Jerry knew or had seen, but Jerry couldn't think of who. He continued, "What is this Midlothian object?"

"For one thing, it's what sank your submarine, the K-129, in 1968." Jerry opened the envelope he'd got back from Tim Ishihara. He took out the photo of Humpty Dumpty in the *Glomar Explorer*'s moon pool and slid it across the ambassador's desk to Dobrynin and Bronstein. "For another, it's this. It's a spaceship— not a human spaceship—that lay three miles under the Pacific for I have no idea how long, till it came to life when it sank your sub. The United States was looking for the K-129 when we found Humpty Dumpty right next door."

The ambassador and his aide (Jerry would have bet the foxy-faced man was KGB, though he might have been GRU) stared at the photo. Major Bronstein asked, "Why should we not think this is disinformation, aimed at making us seem like idiots if we act on it?"

There it was, the rational world rising up to kick Jerry in the teeth. He said, "Steve Dole is dead because the CIA didn't want you guys to get any word of this. Only reason I'm in one piece is dumb luck. If you don't want to get dealt in to whatever people can learn from that spaceship, go ahead. Laugh at me. And *yob tvoyu mat'*."

His Russian TAs and profs had all warned him never to say that: telling somebody *Fuck your mother!* was a good way to start a fight. Bronstein looked comically amazed. As he did, Jerry realized he reminded him of Danny Kaye. Ambassador Dobrynin said, "You say you were on this ship that was a CIA project?"

"That's right." Jerry nodded.

"They would have checked you politically. You would have passed. You were not a sympathizer with the Soviet Union."

"That's right, too."

"Why are you here, then?"

"Because some things are too big for one country to grab hold of all by itself. Here, take a look at this." He took the other photograph, the one of the centaurowl in its suspended-animation apparatus, out of the envelope and passed it over to the Russians. "This is one of the, the beings that crewed the Humpty Dumpty. It's . . . I don't know, maybe frozen. Not dead, anyhow. I'm not sure whether I took this picture or Steve Dole did. Maybe it's still there this way. Maybe the people on the *Glomar Explorer* have tried to wake it up since I left. Maybe they've managed to. Maybe they've killed it instead. I have no idea."

Anatoly Dobrynin and Major Bronstein examined the second photo. Slowly, Bronstein said, "This could be a movie special effect. Trick photography."

"Yeah, it could be," Jerry said. "But if I were making this shit up—excuse me—wouldn't I invent something a lot less crazy than aliens from outer space?" He took out his account of his time on the *Glomar Explorer* and gave it to Bronstein. "This is what happened, or as much as I could remember when I was writing it."

The major read it. As soon as he finished a page, he passed it to the ambassador. They needed twenty minutes or so to finish. Then

Dobrynin said, "I have a question. This Humpty Dumpty, you say it destroyed a Soviet submarine cruising five kilometers above it, a submarine that had no idea it was there. Yet it let you Americans seize it and bring it up to the surface. Why would it do this?"

"I don't know. Obviously. But I've thought about it a lot," Jerry said. "My best guess—and that's all it is—is that it could sense the K-129 had nuclear weapons aboard, and it didn't like that. The *Glomar Explorer* is just a ship. No proof, only a possibility."

Dobrynin and Bronstein glanced at each other. Almost at the same time, they both shrugged. Major Bronstein tapped the photo of Humpty Dumpty with his index finger. "You say this is what you were concealing from Soviet reconnaissance?"

"Uh-huh. We knew when your spy satellites would be coming over. We made sure you couldn't spot this. You'll probably have pictures of the moon pool from before we brought up the spaceship, but not from afterward. This is why."

"He's right about that," Dobrynin said to Bronstein in quick Russian.

"They would have covered it for a sub, too, or however much of it they brought up," the assistant military attaché answered in the same language. Jerry was more sure he wasn't supposed to understand than that he really had.

Dobrynin set a thick-fingered hand down on the photographs and on Jerry's account. "We may keep these? I may possibly need to refer to them when I speak to people in authority in the United States."

"Yes, you can do that." A certain pang accompanied Jerry's nod. Without the photos and what he'd written, would he really believe he'd ever seen and done these things? Pictures and writing made memory concrete.

"You mentioned Doctor Dole's death. We knew of this, but did not connect it to anything involving the *Hughes Glomar Explorer*," Major Bronstein said. "Do you think you are in danger yourself?"

"Probably," Jerry said. "He got killed right after Jack Anderson talked about the *Glomar Explorer*. They took us both off the ship when we showed we weren't happy about how they were trying to get specimens from Humpty Dumpty's hull. As soon as I heard he was dead, I came east. I didn't stick around waiting to be a target."

"How did you cross the country safely?" Bronstein asked with what sounded like professional curiosity.

Jerry shrugged. "I got my hair cut and my beard shaved. I used cash. No phone calls—my wife will be going nuts. And I had a car they didn't know I had."

"Ah." Bronstein eyed him. "You may be an amateur, but this is sound tradecraft. I think that is the English word, *tradecraft*."

"It is." Anatoly Dobrynin pursed his lips and blew air out through them. "When I talk to Henry, I will tell him to tell his people that they must leave you alone. This is a precondition, and the Soviet Union will be most displeased if the United States violates it. If you are telling us the truth here, you are doing something most important. As you say, not just for a country but for mankind."

"If you are telling us the truth," Major Bronstein echoed.

"Thank you, sir," Jerry said to Dobrynin, ignoring the assistant attaché. His mind was slightly blown that the ambassador would casually call the U.S. secretary of state by his first name. He went on, "Yeah, that's about it. If we can figure out how Humpty Dumpty works, we've got no one knows how many worlds out there waiting to be found. Worlds! With life on them! Intelligent life, too—that second photo I showed you proves it. Well, so does the ship we found. There's something for everybody, not just for one country or one way of doing things."

"Would you like to stay here at the embassy until I have made my telephone call?" Dobrynin asked. "You do not have to. You are not a prisoner. But you may feel safer here than with your own countrymen."

"Yeah, I'll do that. Thanks again." Jerry was sure the ambassador wasn't offering from the kindness of his heart. He thought Jerry might possibly be useful to the USSR. He wasn't wrong, either.

Bronstein said something in Russian, too fast for Jerry to follow. Anatoly Dobrynin translated for him: "He says your willingness to remain makes you more deserving of being taken seriously."

"Sir, take people seriously because of their evidence, that's all," Jerry said. Maybe this would turn out all right after all. Maybe, after Henry Kissinger laughed his ass off, Dobrynin would throw him to the wolves. All he could do now was wait.

XVI

They stashed him in a room with a comfortable chair, a bookcase, and yet another portrait of Leonid Brezhnev. They gave him hot tea in a glass: sugar, no milk. Except for the glass, that was how he drank it; his father's family came out of Byelorussia. They gave him a pastrami on rye, too, obviously ordered from outside. It was good.

He checked out the books the case held: Brezhnev's collected works, translated into English. Curious, he pulled one out . . . and quickly found Marxist-Leninist theory wasn't his thing. He put it back on the shelf before his eyes glazed over.

The volumes were handsome, and plainly expensive—hardbacks with gold leaf edging on the pages and fine white paper that looked as if it would last five hundred years. And if anybody worked his way through even one of them in all that time, Jerry would have been amazed.

He stuck his head outside, and was not astonished to find Major Bronstein standing in the hallway. If RAND didn't let unescorted strangers wander its corridors, the Soviet embassy wouldn't. Sheepishly, Jerry said, "Can you take me to the men's room, please?"

Bronstein smiled. "Of course. Come with me." Jerry did what he needed to do. When he came out, the assistant military attaché escorted him back. Bronstein didn't ask any questions. Jerry would have liked it better if he had. The Russians were playing it cool. If Henry Kissinger convinced Dobrynin that Jerry was spouting nonsense, they'd throw him out on his ear and forget about him. If the secretary of state couldn't do that . . .

After a while, Jerry looked at his watch. Three hours had gone by. It only seemed like seventeen years. Time flew when you were having fun.

He wondered if the chair was comfortable enough to sleep in. When all this ended, he wanted to sleep for a year. Of course, he'd sleep forever if it ended badly.

Then Major Bronstein walked in. "The ambassador wishes to speak with you," he said.

Jerry got up. "Okay." And either it was or it wasn't.

Bronstein led him back to Anatoly Dobrynin's office and stood aside to let him go in first. Even as Jerry was wondering what that meant, Dobrynin looked up at him and said, "Henry does not like you very much."

"No? I mean, he doesn't?"

"Sit. Sit," the ambassador said quickly, and Jerry sank into the chair he'd used before—sure enough, his legs didn't want to hold him up. Dobrynin waited till he'd settled himself, then went on, "No, he does not. He thought that, in spite of the damaging stories from Jack Anderson and Seymour Hersh, his people had succeeded in keeping the Midlothian object a secret."

"Seymour Hersh?" Jerry echoed.

"His piece ran in *The Washington Post* the morning after Anderson spoke on the radio."

"Oh. I didn't know about it. Sorry. That was the morning I hit the road."

"He admits, because he cannot very well deny any longer, that the United States has this alien spaceship, this Midlothian object, this Humpty Dumpty," Dobrynin said. "He says he is sorry for concealing it. I say he is sorry the way a robber is sorry for getting caught. I told him so. He laughed. To him, it was funny."

"But we're going to share what we learn from Humpty Dumpty with you? We're going to let you help investigate?" Jerry wanted the movie to have a happy ending.

He didn't get one. He discovered the movie wasn't over yet, because the Soviet ambassador somberly shook his head. "He told me we were entitled to nothing from the Midlothian object, nothing at all. He said the United States salvaged it from international waters, and under international law had the right to keep for itself what it found. Under international law, as I understand it, this position may possibly be justified."

"So you're going to let him, Russia's going to let him, get away with that?" Jerry couldn't believe his ears.

But Dobrynin held up a hand like a cop halting traffic. "I did not say so, young man. It is more complicated than that. Also, it is more dangerous. In 1945, your country used two atomic bombs against Japan. You had this new, very strong weapon. *You* had it. The Soviet Union did not. You could have used the threat of it, or the thing itself, to force concessions from my country. I was just entering the diplomatic service at that time. The concern was very great."

"We didn't do anything like that, though," Jerry said.

"You did not. That is to your credit. Still, you could have, and we would have been powerless to resist. Comrade Stalin understood this very clearly." Anatoly Dobrynin held up that meaty hand again. "I have not many good things to say for Stalin. He was harsh and brutal. But he had proper care for the security of the USSR. We used a maximum project to create our own nuclear bomb. By 1949, we succeeded. My country could speak again to yours as an equal on the world stage. We did not have to let ourselves be dictated to or bullied. Are you with me so far?"

"Yes, sir." Jerry hoped so, anyhow.

"Good. I do not know how much of the history you take in, but that does not matter. You see what is important is the balance of power, or you would not have done what you did. From 1945 to 1949, the balance of power was tilted. The USSR stayed free and independent only because the USA let it stay that way. After 1949, my country stood on its own two feet once more. We will not exist on American sufferance again. The Midlothian object gives you the potential to claim such power over us. This is intolerable. We will not permit it."

Jerry liked the sound of that not even a little bit. In his mind's ear, he heard alarm bells ringing. He heard civil-defense sirens wailing. He heard fifty thousand high school teachers yelling *"Drop!"* In his mind's eye, he saw a million high school kids diving under their desks and kissing their asses good-bye.

"What will you do, then?" he asked.

"I do not make policy. I carry out policy made by the general secretary and the Politburo. I have sent my government a report on the news you brought, and on my conversation with the American secretary of state," Dobrynin said. "I have informed them of how important and how urgent I think this is. I hope a peaceful solution will be possible."

"You . . . hope?" Jerry realized his mind's ear and eye had known what they were imagining. He wondered if he would go down in history as the guy who started World War III. He didn't think it was likely. If World War III started, nobody'd be left afterward to write history.

"That is correct. We will not let ourselves be surpassed. We are content with a share of whatever may be learned from the Midlothian object. America deserves credit for finding and raising it. But your view of things is the correct one, Mister Stieglitz. The Midlothian object is too important to be the sole property of one nation."

Would you say the same thing if Russia had it? Jerry wondered. He doubted it. In that case, Dobrynin would be playing the Henry Kissinger role, with Kissinger doing his impression of the Soviet envoy. People were people.

People *were* people, yeah. They were all pretty similar, no matter where they came from. That was why whatever came from Humpty Dumpty deserved to belong to everybody, not just to the USA.

"Oh. Henry did agree to one thing," Anatoly Dobrynin said. "He promised me the CIA would not retaliate against you for what you have done."

"Do you believe him?"

"I do—because I made it very plain how important this was to me," Dobrynin replied. "You have done all mankind a service. The Soviet Union does not forget."

"Thank you, sir," Jerry said. He had the feeling the diplomat meant *the USSR* when he said *all mankind*. Right this minute, that was okay with him.

"If you do not trust the secretary of state's assurances, you may stay here at the embassy. No one can reach you here," Dobrynin said. "I would suggest you stay here for some little while anyhow, to make sure all the people in the Agency learn what Henry has agreed to."

"That's . . . probably a real good idea. I'll take you up on it, and thanks one more time," Jerry said.

"The least I can do. Now we hope all turns out well. I am not a praying man. If you are, this is a good time to do it."

"I'm not, either, Ambassador. From the way you talk, I kinda wish I were."

Major Bronstein took Jerry back to the room with Leonid Brezhnev's collected works. As he had before, Jerry tried to read some. And, as he had before, he bogged down. He noticed the beautifully printed books were dusty. No, nobody else cared about them, either.

After a while, the man in the outdated black suit looked in and asked, "You would like dinner?"

"*Da, Georgi Pavlovich. Bolshoye spasibo,*" Jerry answered. He still had no idea of the Russian's family name. First name and patronymic were plenty for politeness.

"*P'zhalista,*" the embassy man said, and then, in English, "You speak good. Well? Well." He made the right choice.

"Thanks." Jerry knew how far from true it was. But even a little was better than nothing.

His pastrami sandwich had been brought in. Dinner plainly came from the kitchen here: salmon in a creamy dill sauce, boiled potatoes, and cabbage gussied up with tomato sauce and peppers till you almost forgot it was cabbage. It was all good. So was the California Chablis that came with it. Jerry drank a glass, then half a glass more. After that, he stopped.

Georgi Pavlovich took away his dirty dishes. Jerry wondered how you said *Flunky, first class* in Russian.

After the man left, there he was, alone again with Leonid Brezhnev's literary output. He could have gone out into the hall and talked with Major Bronstein, but he didn't. Talking with the major would have been interrogation, not conversation. Like the CIA pros on the *Glomar Explorer*, Bronstein struck Jerry as a man who couldn't not do his job.

So he sat there and got bored instead. A little before nine o'clock, Bronstein came in and said, "The ambassador tells me to assure you that your safety outside the embassy has been guaranteed. Everyone who needs to know of the American secretary of state's promise to Anatoly Fyodorovich is informed and has assented."

"Thanks very much. I'll go back to the hotel, I guess." Jerry stood up and stretched. Then, not quite idly, he asked, "*Nu, vus makht a Yid?*"

That wasn't Russian, but Major Bronstein understood it anyway. From his looks and name, Jerry'd thought he would. "Being a Jew is interesting, the same as it is most places," Bronstein answered, luckily, in English. Jerry had only fragments of Yiddish. His folks had used the *mamaloshen* when they didn't want him to know what they were talking about. That gave him a great incentive to learn, of course, but his father spoke the old-country lingo much less after his mother died.

Out into the cool Washington night he went. He tried to look every which way at once while walking to the Corvair. The CIA might have promised to leave him alone, but the local muggers probably weren't in on the deal.

Unmugged, he got the car, drove back to the hotel, and went up to his room. Okay, Henry Kissinger said the CIA wouldn't murder him. If you couldn't believe Henry Kissinger, you . . . were like a large part of the world. But Jerry figured Kissinger wouldn't waste much time or effort lying about anything as trivial as he was.

Which meant he could (probably) let other people know where he was. He picked up the phone and called home. It was getting on toward half past six on the West Coast. Anna ought to be back from work.

"Hello?" she answered after the fourth ring. Chances were, that meant he'd caught her either fixing her dinner or eating it.

"Hi, babe. It's me."

"Jerry? Oh, my God! Where are you? How are you? What have you been doing? How are Bruce and Barbara? Oh, my God! Are you okay?" Questions poured out of her, as well they might. She even remembered his cousins' names.

"Honey, I'm in Washington," he said.

"I know *that*. Tacoma, right?" She sounded impatient.

"No, not that Washington. Washington, DC."

"Washington, DC? What the hell are you doing there?" Anna paused for a moment. Then she said, "Oh, my God!" one more time, now on an entirely different note. "It's that stupid fucking ship you were on, the one that went after Russian submarines. Is the CIA after you? Did they kidnap you or something?"

She might be melodramatic, but she was a long way from dumb. "It has to do with the CIA, yeah, but they're not after me anymore, not after I got here and did what I had to do."

"*Anymore*? What *were* you doing? Why didn't you tell me about any of this?" Anna demanded. Those were all reasonable questions, too.

Jerry answered the last one first: "I didn't tell you anything because the less you knew, the safer you were. I was in a bad spot. I didn't want you there, too. I'm still not gonna tell you what it was all about over the phone. I figure the CIA's been listening to me ever since I got back to the mainland. To you, too."

"That's illegal!" She sounded furious.

He nodded, though she couldn't see him. "It sure is. They do it anyway. They do all kinds of shit that's illegal." He almost told her about what had happened to Steve Dole. At the last second, he held back. It would only alarm her and make her angrier. And he wasn't in danger of getting bumped off anymore, not if he could rely on Henry Kissinger's word.

How's that working out for South Vietnam? he asked himself. Himself loudly told him to shut the hell up.

"When are you coming home?" Anna asked.

"I don't know yet. Stuff here isn't finished. And I drove, so it'll take a little while."

"What did you do for money? Do we have any left?"

Those were also sensible questions. "I managed. And we have more than you think." When Jerry told her how much more, she let out a startled squeak. He said, "I kept quiet about it because I couldn't explain it without explaining a bunch of other stuff, too. And I was always afraid I might need to use some of it for something like this."

"We really need to talk when you do get home," Anna said—ominously, Jerry thought.

"Yeah. I know. I got in deeper than I thought. I didn't find out how deep till I was already on the *Glomar Explorer*. That was too late for me to do anything about it. You may find out on the news, though."

"What does that mean?"

"You'll see. Or else you won't." Jerry yawned. "Sorry, babe. You've got no idea how worn out I am. Listen, if you need to get hold of me . . ." He gave her the hotel's name, the phone number, and his room number. "With any luck, I'm gonna crash. I love you."

"I love you, too. But I'm not sure I know you at all."

"Right this minute, I don't know me, either. I did the right thing, though. That's pretty important just now. I'm going to go. 'Bye." He hung up.

He put on his sweats and T-shirt (*the House of Slob*, he thought, not without pride) and brushed his teeth. It was a little after ten: late, by the hours he'd kept on the road. He *was* worn out, but he was also wired on adrenaline. He took *Have Space Suit—Will Travel* out of his suitcase. If anything could relax him, familiar words might.

Fifteen minutes late, Kip and Peewee were prisoners at the Wormfaces' base on Pluto. Things looked bad for the good guys.

Jerry was about to turn another page—he couldn't read Heinlein and not keep turning pages—when somebody banged on his door.

He jumped. He dropped the book. Even as he went to the door, he thought he knew who it would be. When he peered through the little wide-angle peephole, he found he was right. There stood John P., with a younger, bigger guy behind him.

"What do you want?" Jerry asked without opening up.

"Just to talk. Promise." The senior CIA man held up his right hand as if taking an oath.

Jerry considered. They'd been faster about tracing the call than he'd thought they could be. But he'd figured they'd do it. Now that they knew where he was, they could take him out whenever they pleased unless he planned to stay in here forever. Sighing, he undid the dead bolt and security chain and opened the door.

John P. scowled at him in disgust. "You motherfucking son of a bitch."

"Hey, I love you, too." Jerry stepped back and to the side. "C'mon in."

"You look better without the hair and the hippie whiskers, I will say," John P. added.

"Bite me," Jerry said without heat. "You came here to talk about how I wear my hair, you can goddamn well leave."

"Do you have any idea how much damage you've caused your country? I mean, any idea at all?" the CIA man demanded as his muscular henchman closed the door.

"No. Neither do you, unless your people have got a lot further with figuring out how Humpty Dumpty works than I think they have."

John P. waved that aside. "We did the heavy lifting. Literally—*we* did. Why do you think the fucking Russians deserve a piece of the pie?"

"They're human beings?" Jerry suggested. "They have scientists? Smart scientists, even? Plus the big one, of course—you assholes were gonna rub me out. Your turn now. How come you *don't* think they deserve it?"

"They're Russians. They're a pack of murderous Commie bastards." To John P., it was as obvious as *The sun will come up tomorrow.* He added, "If I had my druthers, we'd fry you like a pork chop, the way they did with the Rosenbergs."

Jerry just barely knew who the Rosenbergs were. Spies for the

Russians, who'd been executed when he was tiny; that was about all. "Why don't you ask Steve Dole how he feels about it?" he said.

"I had nothing to do with Steve Dole's death. The Agency had nothing to do with it," the CIA man said quickly.

"My ass. If you mean you didn't pull the trigger yourself, okay, I believe that much. The rest is just crap. He and I talked about what it would mean if one of us came down with a sudden case of loss of life. You think I couldn't read the signs, man? I was next, first chance you found. So don't talk to me about how murderous the Russians are, okay?"

John P. just glared at him. The younger man who'd come into Jerry's room with the CIA bigwig shifted his feet, ever so slightly. Jerry didn't *know* he was tacitly admitting anything, but would have bet that way.

He went on, "This is bigger than countries. It'll change the whole world."

"Exactly," John P. said. "It *will* change the whole world. And the United States needs to set the agenda on how."

"We haven't done so real great at that, have we? How long do you think Saigon's gonna last?"

"Not very long." The CIA man's admission surprised Jerry. John P. went on, "And what happens afterward, there and in Cambodia and Laos, will be one of the ugliest things since Mao won in China."

He was much too likely to be right about that. Even so, Jerry said, "Not like our hands are clean. Some of the generals who've run South Vietnam, Franco, South Africa, all the tin-pot dictators in South America . . . C'mon, man. You know all this way better'n I do."

"Democracy," John P. said. Jerry laughed in his face. The other CIA man stirred again, this time like an attack dog waiting for *Sic 'im!* John P. ignored him, continuing, "You think we're bad, wait till you find out about your new friends."

"Oh, I know about them. Bet your balls I do. But you guys were gonna kill me," Jerry said. "Like, what can they do that's worse than that?"

He thought he'd asked an unanswerable question. But John P. said, "They're liable to start a thermonuclear war. If you live through it—which isn't likely—you can put that on your conscience. Jesus, when I make a mistake I don't do it halfway." He looked disgusted again, whether at Jerry or himself Jerry couldn't say. Then he turned. "Come on, Andy. Let's get the hell out of here."

Out they went. Andy tried to slam the door, but the pneumatic gadget at the top foiled him. The door clicked shut instead of banging.

Jerry sank into a chair. His legs didn't want to hold him up anymore. His hands shook, too. He'd never done confrontations worth a damn.

He still wasn't sleepy, either. He started to pick *Have Space Suit—Will Travel* up off the rug, then looked at the nightstand clock. It was a few minutes before eleven. Somebody would be showing news at the top of the hour.

A couple of stations were, in fact. Both opened with the same robbery and shooting at a liquor store. Yellow journalism was alive and well on color TV. It had been alive and well on black-and-white TV, too.

But then a newsman with almost-long hair sprayed firmly into place said, "In foreign affairs, Secretary of State Henry Kissinger has received what he described as an 'alarming call and note' from Soviet Ambassador Anatoly Dobrynin. Sources speaking off the record say this has to do with the *Hughes Glomar Explorer*, the so-called ocean-mining ship that's been in the news a lot lately. Some of the other things those off-the-record sources say seem too bizarre to be believed."

He went on to talk about a bad crash on the Beltway that afternoon. Jerry didn't know whether to laugh or to scream. No one wanted to believe any of this. It seemed too much like sci-fi.

What did you do, though, when sci-fi turned real? People had been asking that question since the first V-2 fell on England, since the A-bombs incinerated two Japanese cities, since Sputnik beeped across the sky, and since Neil Armstrong walked on the moon. One of Jerry's best moments ever had been watching Robert A. Heinlein talk about that live with Walter Cronkite. A not-so-good moment followed: remembering that Wernher von Braun, who'd pioneered the V-2, had also had a big hand in the moon-landing program. What was Mort Sahl's line? *I aim for the stars, but sometimes I hit London.*

He left the news on till it ended, hoping they'd say more. They didn't, though. He was watching the ABC affiliate here. He thought about getting up and switching to the Peacock and Johnny Carson. Before he could, a voice-over guy said, "Here is an ABC News special report, live with Harry Reasoner." Jerry didn't change the channel after all.

On came the ABC News anchorman. Jerry thought of him as Walter Cronkite Lite; he'd been Cronkite's backup at CBS for years before moving to ABC, and he had the same kind of measured, reasonable delivery. Now Reasoner sat in front of a picture of the *Glomar Explorer* in Long Beach harbor.

"What *did* this ship find when it sailed into the North Pacific to try to raise a sunken Soviet submarine?" Reasoner said. "Whatever it was, learning of it was enough to make Leonid Brezhnev's veteran ambassador virtually threaten war with the United States unless his country is included in examining and exploiting it. More than one source has told ABC News that the answer may literally be out of this world."

So the real story was finally starting to come out. Jerry wondered whether Harry Reasoner's sources were American or Russian. Reasoner had a fairly good notion of what had gone on while Humpty Dumpty was being raised, but he could have got that from either side.

"I know this will sound incredible to many of you," he said. "It sounds incredible to me, too. But it seems believable to both the Soviet Foreign Ministry and the State Department. And the peace of the world may depend on their ability to reach a mutually satisfactory arrangement." Then he proved he was indeed a TV man: "We'll be back after these messages."

Jerry endured the commercials. In due course, Reasoner returned. He said, "I am informed that there has been an ongoing dispute among the specialists on the *Hughes Glomar Explorer*, and in the highest echelons of the U.S. government, over how aggressively to investigate this, this object from another world. Thus far, I hear, caution has for the most part prevailed."

"Thank you, Jesus!" Jewish Jerry exclaimed. However ABC News had got that, it was something he hadn't known himself.

"Whether and to what degree the United States will let the USSR share in this astonishing discovery remains to be seen. So does what the USSR will do if its demands are refused," Reasoner said. "On that, at the moment, depends the future of the world, and whether the world has a future. Thank you, and good night."

More commercials. Jerry turned off the TV. He finally did pick up *Have Space Suit—Will Travel*. As he did, he wondered what Heinlein thought of today's news—and how much of it he already knew.

When Jerry went down for breakfast, Major Bronstein sat in the lobby reading *The Washington Post*. **SPACESHIP THREATENS WORLD PEACE!** the headline shouted. For a moment, Jerry wondered how the Russians knew where he was. But somebody could have tailed him as he walked to the parking lot. Somebody could have followed him back to the hotel.

Bronstein saw him, too. The Soviet officer put down the paper and came over with his hand out. "Good morning, Mister Stieglitz."

"Good morning." Ruefully, Jerry added, "Guess my tradecraft wasn't all it could've been last night."

"You got here. You completed your mission. And now, will you eat with a friendly adversary?"

"Sure. Will you tell me your name and patronymic? I'm Jerry Gymanovich." Jerry pronounced his father's name Russian style; without the *H* sound, the Russian language substituted a *G* for it.

"You know our customs," Major Bronstein said with a smile. "I'm Yakov Moiseyevich." A lot of Jews in the USSR wore Russified names. Not Bronstein. Jerry wondered how much harder that had made his life.

A black attendant poured coffee for both of them. Jerry ordered bacon and eggs. Yakov Bronstein got ham and eggs. They smiled the wry smiles of Jews who didn't keep kosher. Jerry said, "Is it really going to be that bad?"

"Well, I don't know." Bronstein plainly chose his words with care. "It may be that bad. We do not aim to be closed out of learning from the Midlothian object. The ambassador has made that very clear to your secretary of state. So has Foreign Minister Gromyko. Anatoly Fyodorovich told me Kissinger told him the foreign minister had never before spoken to him that bluntly. So where we go from here is up to the United States."

"Is Kissinger still saying it belongs to us because we found it in international waters?" Jerry asked.

"He is. He seems less insistent than he did yesterday—he has discovered we are serious," the major said. "He has also discovered we have put our military forces on alert and are beginning necessary preparations for whatever may come."

Jerry was saved from answering when their breakfasts came. He ate for a little while. Then he said what was still on his mind: "Good Lord!"

"Is this not the effect you wanted to create?"

"I wanted both sides to study Humpty Dumpty. I didn't want to blow up the world!"

"We also want both sides to study it." Bronstein steepled his fingers. "No one wants to blow up the world. But what we want to do and what we find ourselves doing, these are not always the same thing. If our interests are flaunted—no, excuse me, flouted—we will defend them."

Jerry ate some hash browns. He didn't see anything to say to that. The attendant came by with his coffee pot and raised an eyebrow. Jerry nodded. The man refilled his cup. "Thank you very much," Jerry told him. He raised the eyebrow again. He might not have been used to getting treated as a person rather than a convenience.

"I have looked at your work and your writing," Bronstein said. "I understand why your government recruited you for the *Hughes Glomar Explorer*. I also enjoyed the stories."

"Flatter me some more," Jerry said. Major Bronstein laughed, altogether unembarrassed. Jerry was pleased anyway.

"You are welcome to stay at the embassy. Even to request asylum," Bronstein said. "We recognize the debt we owe you."

"No. I didn't do it for you. I did it for everybody. I don't have any use for Communism myself. Sorry to be rude and everything, but that's where I'm at."

"I understand. You may be safer under our roof, though."

"Ambassador Dobrynin told me the CIA wasn't after me anymore." Jerry didn't mention that John P. had said the same thing. Either the Russians already knew about last night's visit or they didn't.

Yakov Bronstein's sorrowful look told him he was in over his head, and hinted at how far in over his head he was. "I was not talking about the CIA. They are professionals. But sooner or later your name will come out. Your whole country will know you were the one who told Russia about the Midlothian object. What kind of life will you have then?"

"Urk," Jerry said, most sincerely. He'd thought things through till he got to the Soviet embassy—if he got to the Soviet embassy. Whatever happened next would just happen. But *And they lived happily ever after* only worked in fairy tales. In real life, things were messier.

A thermonuclear war? His name mud from sea to shining sea? Yeah, quite a bit messier.

"Think about it. You will be received as a friend if you visit us again." Bronstein set money on the table. He said, *"Zei gezint,"* and left.

Jerry got up, too. He asked a valet to fetch his car. "I just need to get something out of the trunk. You can put it back again once I'm done," he said.

"Yes, suh," the man answered. Jerry tipped him the same as he would have any other time. He was sure nobody ever got rich fetching other people's cars for them.

He breathed a sigh of relief to find that his envelope of cash hadn't walked with Jesus. That would have messed him up but good. *Should have thought of it last night,* he scolded himself. He took the envelope back to his room and checked it there to make sure the Agency hadn't substituted cut-up newspapers or something. Nope—still Federal Reserve notes.

Then he turned on the TV. He skated from station to station, the way he had during the Watergate hearings. Commentators were speculating as hard as they could. *Better to specu late than never,* Jerry thought vaguely. Of course, these might be the last days of the late, great Planet Earth for real.

He put the DO NOT DISTURB sign on the door. He didn't go down for lunch. Breakfast would keep him running till dinner, and the fewer people he saw, the better off he figured he was. In the middle of the afternoon, somebody handed John Chancellor a note. Chancellor glanced down at it, then eyed the camera again. "We've just learned that President Ford will address the nation at nine tonight—six Pacific time."

Being a California guy, Jerry was used to important speeches at six. Nine seemed late to him. It did give him time to eat, though, and to take a shower. He turned on the TV a little before nine. In California, Anna would be driving home from work. He wondered if she'd be listening on the radio.

At nine on the dot, there was Gerald Ford. In spite of pardoning

Nixon, he looked like a decent man. Was it LBJ who'd said Ford had played too much football without a helmet? Jerry thought so.

"Good evening, my fellow Americans. I have spent most of the day conferring with Soviet General Secretary Brezhnev over the Washington–Moscow hotline," Ford said. "What you've heard and read about over the past few days is true. The United States has raised from the bottom of the Pacific a spaceship from another planet circling another sun, built by intelligent creatures who are not human beings."

The TV showed photos of Humpty Dumpty in the *Glomar Explorer*'s moon pool, photos of the spaceship's interior, and photos of the centaurowls in their protective units. Jerry wondered if he'd taken any of them. He thought so.

"The United States discovered this spacecraft. We brought it up. But General Secretary Brezhnev is concerned that, if we alone learn its secrets, we will gain an unfair advantage over the rest of mankind. I did my best to convince him that we would never act in that way. Unfortunately, he was not altogether reassured.

"Because he was not, and as a token of American goodwill toward the USSR and towards all the nations of the world, I have agreed to allow a Soviet team of scientists and specialists to join the Americans currently studying what has been known as the Midlothian object. We will fully share what we have learned to this point with the USSR, and everything the American and Soviet teams discover together from now on will also be equally shared.

"The United States takes this action in the spirit of world peace and mutual understanding between nations. If humanity succeeds in unlocking this spaceship's secrets, worlds beyond count may be there for the taking. That is my deepest, most sincere hope. Thank you, and God bless the United States of America. Good night."

In a way, Jerry admired the speech. Gerald Ford had made *Let us in, too, or we'll blow up the world* seem mild and friendly. That wasn't easy. And Ford must have been sure the Russians weren't kidding, either. He never would have yielded ground unless he was. If you didn't already know what was going on, you'd hardly realize he was backing down.

Jerry jerked when the phone on the nightstand rang. He hesitated before answering. Had some reporter found out who he was and where he was staying? "Hello?" he said warily.

"A spaceship? You were working on a *spaceship*?" That was no reporter—that was his wife.

"Hi, hon. Good to hear from you," Jerry said. "Yeah, I was, but I couldn't tell you."

"Well, of course not! I get that!" Anna said.

The night before, she'd wondered if she really knew him. Now he wasn't sure he would ever understand her.

He was not surprised to find Yakov Bronstein waiting for him in the lobby again when he went down to eat breakfast the next morning. *The Washington Post* the assistant military attaché was looking at had photos of Humpty Dumpty and a centaurowl under the headline **WE ARE NOT ALONE!**

"*Dobry den, Yakov Moiseyevich,*" Jerry said.

"Good morning." Bronstein stuck to English. His was certainly better than Jerry's Russian. "Would you join me once more? The ambassador has asked me to ask something of you."

"Has he?" Jerry wondered whether this was the hook, about to snag him so the Russians could reel him in. They'd done something for him: they'd kept him alive. If they thought he owed them something in return, they wouldn't hesitate to go after it. The CIA wouldn't have, either; Jerry was sure of that.

"That's right," the major said lightly. "Let's get some food, and then we'll talk."

"How can I say no?" Jerry replied. They walked to the restaurant. A woman who wore a big Afro led them to a table. The attendant with the coffee nodded to Jerry, ever so slightly, as he filled their cups.

Major Bronstein made small talk till they'd nearly finished eating. Then he said, "You are wondering what Anatoly Fyodorovich wishes of you."

"Oh, I may be, just a little bit," Jerry said.

The Soviet officer studied him, head cocked to one side like an inquisitive sparrow. He looked more like Danny Kaye than ever when he did that. After a moment, he chuckled. "You have an interesting sense of humor. I saw it in your writing, too. You might almost belong to my country, not your own."

"I don't. I don't want to, either."

"I understand that. I respect it. What I said is still true. And you speak our language."

"Not very well."

"Few Americans speak it at all. And this matters for what Ambassador Dobrynin has in his mind."

"What *has* he got in mind?" Jerry asked, as of course he was meant to do.

"The Soviet Union will be sending a team to join in research on the Midlothian object. You will have heard last night that your president has agreed to this?"

"Oh, sure. Most of the people in the country heard him say so, I bet. But what's it got to do with me?"

"Anatoly Fyodorovich has suggested that you go out to the *Hughes Glomar Explorer* as a member of the Soviet research team." Major Bronstein still looked like Danny Kaye to Jerry: an animated Danny Kaye cat blowing a feather off its nose. "I think this is an excellent idea myself, a most excellent idea."

Jerry peered down at the table. He was sure he'd find his jaw lying there. He'd felt it drop, long and hard. "You're kidding, right? You've got to be making that up."

"By no means," Bronstein said. Jerry understood him, though no native speaker ever born would have come out with *By no means*. The Soviet major went on, "For one thing, as I told you before, I understand why the CIA chose you in the first place. You have the training and the imagination to belong with such people, whatever country they come from."

"I'm only a goddamn grad student," Jerry said, as if that explained everything. To him, it did.

Yakov Bronstein ignored him. "You also have some insight into the way the aliens think. If you did not, you would never have realized how to persuade their ship to open to you. That was not artisanship. That was genius. What is genius except doing what is unexpected but correct?"

That was dumb fucking luck, nothing else, Jerry thought. He almost said so, but something about Bronstein's expression made him hold back. The major still looked uncommonly like a canariophagous cat. Instead of po-mouthing himself, Jerry asked, "What aren't you telling me?"

Bronstein's smile broadened. As he had with Ben Bova, Jerry'd managed to find the right question. "Anatoly Fyodorovich also thought it might be . . . amusing to give the CIA a finger in the eye by having you return to the *Hughes Glomar Explorer*," the assistant military attaché replied. "Poetic justice, I think you say in English?"

"Poetic justice. Yeah, we say that." Jerry smiled, too. It occurred to him that Dobrynin didn't just want to give the CIA a finger in the eye. He aimed to poke the whole United States. At another time, under different circumstances, that might have bothered Jerry more than it did now. "You know what? I'd love to do that, not just to get even with people but to have the chance to find out what's what with Humpty Dumpty. If the ambassador can get your government to say yes, and if your government can get my government to say yes, I'm in."

"This is wonderful! And I do not think there will be any difficulties," Major Bronstein said. Jerry wondered how wonderful it was. Anna probably wouldn't be happy with him. At least this time, though, he wouldn't have to lie to her. That was . . . something, anyhow.

"There are no guarantees, you know," he said. "We may look at Humpty Dumpty from now till the cows come home and never figure out how it works. You think if you landed a 747 outside the Colosseum, the Romans could learn how it flies?"

"No, but if they saw it in the air they would know flight was possible. That might set them thinking in new directions of their own. And if they could teach Latin to the pilot and the engineer, who knows what they might find out?" Bronstein said.

"You oughta be the guy who writes sf, not me," Jerry told him.

"I do other kinds of things." The major didn't go into detail. Chances were he couldn't, not without committing treason.

"Well, anyway, thank you. I don't think I said that yet. And please thank the ambassador for me. I know I'm incidental in all this, but I want him to know how grateful I am."

"I will pass it along. You may be sure of that." Yakov Bronstein eyed Jerry one more time. "You do not give yourself enough credit. This can be a serious failing in a man." He set money on the table and strode out. Jerry stared after him.

He started for home. The Corvair ran. He had to admit he'd got his money's worth from Rodolfo Jimenez. Sooner or later, he figured he'd have to straighten out the lies he'd told on the change-of-ownership form. That would likely cost him some bucks. Since he had them for a change, he didn't let it worry him.

Coming west, he could call Anna every night when he chose a

motel. Talking to her was a relief. So was the feeling that he wasn't driving into uncertainty anymore. He'd done what he'd set out to do. He hadn't expected to know what that was like till he finished his dissertation. Now he didn't much care if he ever finished it.

He wanted to call Tim Ishihara, too, but held off. Most of the things he wanted to tell his friend needed to wait till he saw him in person. He had to assume the CIA could still listen to Tim's phone. They didn't know Tim had held on to that envelope for him and lied to them about it. He didn't want his friend to get in trouble for any of that. Sometimes the best thing you could say was nothing.

He thought about calling his dad, too, but that could wait till he got back.

In eastern Arkansas, not far west of Memphis, his oil light came on. He pulled into a truck-stop garage and explained the problem. They put the car on the rack. The mechanic who looked underneath said, "You got an oil seal that's crappin' out on you. Two fresh quarts of oil, ten bucks for the part, seventy-five bucks labor, an' sales tax."

The labor charge was as close to literal highway robbery as made no difference. Jerry didn't even flinch. "Fix it," he said. Having money didn't mean no problems came your way. But it sure as hell meant you could make them go away if they did.

When he got back into the Los Angeles area, he made a couple of extra stops before he went to his apartment. The first was off Atlantic in East L.A. Sure as hell, the Rambler still sat there. Maybe it would even start when he turned the key. This wasn't the kind of neighborhood where people called the cops to get an abandoned car towed.

Then he drove down to Long Beach, to the white apartment with the blue roof that pretended to be on Naxos, not Ocean Boulevard. He used the coded knock on the door to the apartment the CIA used. Sure, they might have pulled out by now. But they were probably still moving people on and off the *Glomar Explorer*, so they also might not have.

A large, muscular man opened the door and looked him over. "Whatever you're selling, we don't want any," he rumbled.

"Oh, shut up," Jerry said sweetly. "I don't need to talk to you. I need to talk to Vic."

The guy's demeanor changed. "Who are you?"

"Jerry Stieglitz."

"You're—him?" The CIA man's balled into fists. "I oughta—"

Jerry wagged a finger. "That's a no-no." He overplayed for all he was worth.

It worked, too. The man stood aside. "Do what you're gonna do." He spat in front of Jerry's feet, but that was all he did.

Vic eyed Jerry with a curiosity not far removed from Major Bronstein's. He asked, "What the hell are you doing here?"

"You still have the fake license and credit card and everything I gave you when I came back to the mainland?"

"Even if I do, what do you care? And how come I should give a shit about what you care?"

"It may be handy not to be Jerry Stieglitz for a while, and to be able to *show* people I'm not him. And you should give a shit because you bastards owe me one. You murdered a friend of mine like you were squashing a tin can with a tank. Only reason you didn't get me, too, is that I bailed before you could. I haven't talked to the *Times* or anybody about that yet, but I can."

"Not if you have an accident first," the CIA man with the thick arms said from behind him.

"Forget it, Zach," Vic said. "He'll have some kind of dead-man setup so it all comes out if anything happens to him. He wouldn't show up here if he didn't." He sounded cynically revolted.

Jerry didn't, not unless the Russians would take care of it for him. He said, "Damn straight," anyway. Zach muttered something that wasn't an endearment.

Vic said, "Okay, kid. You got a deal. The plastic'll even work." He dug out the envelope with Jerry's false documents and handed it to him. "Now get the hell outa here."

Outa there the hell Jerry got. As he drove away, he checked the rearview mirror to see if anyone was tailing him. He hadn't done that in Washington, but he was trying to learn. He didn't spot anybody before he swung on to the Long Beach Freeway again and headed north.

He got back to the apartment a little before five. The King of Siam seemed to recognize him, which was a pleasant surprise. Then he stopped in his tracks and said, "Fuck!" He'd missed teaching his first spring quarter section. He scribbled a note on a scrap of paper—*Call Krikorian*—and stuck it by the phone. Tomorrow morning. His boss wouldn't be in the office now.

His father would. April 15 was only a couple of weeks away.

This was the time of year when Dad went bonkers, only to have his business go into hibernation after the deadline passed.

Jerry made the call. The answer was quick: "Stieglitz Accounting and Tax Preparation."

"Hi, Dad. It's me."

"Hi, Jerry. Let me call you back in five minutes. I'm with a client."

"Sure. 'Bye."

The promised five minutes stretched to twenty. Jerry wasn't surprised. His dad always underestimated how long things would take. In due course, the phone did ring again. "Sorry," Hyman Stieglitz said. "Chris there was trying to do some strange things on his Schedule C."

"Okay." Jerry knew Schedule C was where you noted income and expenses if you were self-employed, but no more. He hoped to be fully initiated into its mysteries one of these days, but he hadn't been yet.

"How much were you involved in the strange doings on that ship you went on last summer?" his dad asked. "Aliens? That would have been right up your alley."

"Yeah. That's why they hired me, only I didn't know it till I was already on board," Jerry said.

"You should have been flattered to land such an important slot so young."

"I was. I am. Looks like I may be going back there again pretty soon. Now that the Russians know about it, things are opening up some." Jerry didn't talk about how the Russians knew about it.

"Who'd have thought a spaceship might come so close to starting the great big war? Korea, Berlin, Cuba, Vietnam—those you could see, and *alevai* see your way around them. But this? This came out of the blue!"

"Did you ever think there'd be proof of intelligent life on other planets?" Jerry couldn't resist the dig.

His father just snorted. "The way things are these days, I'm not so sure there's intelligent life on *this* planet."

"You know what, Dad? You've got something."

"What I've got is Joe Yanai coming in in five minutes with a boxful of receipts and statements he wants me to add up for him. I charge him twice as much as I would if he did the preliminary work himself, but it doesn't stop him. It doesn't pay me enough for the *tsuris*, either."

Jerry said his good-byes. He'd gone to high school with Joe Yanai's daughter, Faye. She'd been one of the other handful of really smart people in their class. She'd dealt with that better than Jerry, though he hadn't realized it at the time. There were a lot of things he hadn't realized at the time. Looking back on his high school self, he'd been kind of a prick.

The Agency still thinks I am, he thought with a certain amount of pride as he went to the kitchen. When he opened the refrigerator, he saw steaks. He grinned. Anna knew he'd be back, so she'd put out something he liked. There were mushrooms in the veggie drawer, too. He sliced them thin and put them on the steaks so they'd broil along with the meat. He was a better cook than she was, but he'd learned that trick from her.

She came in at twenty past six. "I knew you were home, 'cause you picked up the mail, and—" She stopped, staring. "You cut off your hair! And your beard!"

"'Fraid so. I didn't want people to recognize me while I was going east. Do I get a kiss anyway?"

"That might be arranged," Anna said and then, afterward, "You're scratchy. Your mustache would tickle, but now you're scratchy. You'd better shave again before you even think about sticking your face between my legs."

"If I don't fall asleep on you, babe, you got a deal." Jerry turned on the broiler. "First dinner, then who knows what?"

"We'll both find out. God, it's good to see you!" She squeezed him.

He squeezed her, too. "It's good to be seen. Oh, Lordy, is it ever good to be seen."

Jerry phoned his advisor a little past nine the next morning. As soon as Professor Krikorian realized who was on the line, he said, "Now I know why they really wanted you on the *Hughes Glomar Explorer*!"

"Yeah, well, they lived to regret it," Jerry answered.

"Did they? If it's something you can tell me, did you have anything to do with our little adventure with the Russians last week? Has that got anything to do with why you missed your class day before yesterday?"

Like Anna, Hagop Krikorian could add two and two and come pretty close to four. "The fewer questions you ask me about any of that stuff, the better off we'll both be," Jerry said.

"I think you just told me what I wanted to know."

"I didn't tell you anything." Jerry snapped his fingers as he thought of something else. "Oh! I may need to give up my TAship for this quarter. It looks like I'll be going out to the *Glomar Explorer* again." He didn't mention that it wouldn't be as part of the American team, any more than he had with his father.

"That's very good for you. Congratulations! If you are going to give up the assistantship, please do it now, though. I'll have an easier time finding a replacement close to the start of the quarter than I would four or five weeks in," Krikorian said.

The request was reasonable. It annoyed Jerry anyway; it reminded him how grad students were easily replaceable parts in the university's giant mill. "Uh, I'd guess I'd better," he said. The Russians didn't think he was an easily replaceable part: one more thing he didn't mention.

"All right. I'll get the paperwork started." The professor hesitated, then asked, "You *are* still planning to finish your thesis?"

"Yeah. I am," Jerry answered without enthusiasm. Becoming an expert on centaurowls instead seemed a lot more interesting. So did making a go of it as a writer, if he could swing that. So did almost anything that didn't involve faculty meetings.

So before very long he'd need to go up to UCLA and deal with whatever forms he had to fill out and sign because he was leaving the TAship. He didn't know what they were, but he was sure Professor Krikorian or somebody in the department offices or at Murphy Hall would be able to tell him in great detail. He was also sure he wasn't going up there today. After driving back and forth across the country, he was damned if he wanted to hop on the San Diego Freeway again.

He played with the King of Siam. Then he lay down on the couch to read. The cat hopped up on his stomach and purred and shed hair on his shirt while he scratched it. They both fell asleep, the King of Siam curled into a croissant just north of Jerry's belly button. He felt better after the nap, but he needed to use the john. The King of Siam's hooded blue stare said he did not approve of being ousted from his nice, warm cat mattress.

After Jerry did the dinner dishes that evening, he called Tim Ishihara. "Hey, I'm back in town," he said when his friend picked up the phone.

"Yeah, I buzzed you last week. Anna said you were up north—something to do with your cousins," Tim said. "Everything work out okay, I hope?"

"Pretty much. Feel like hitting some fungoes Saturday morning?"

Tim laughed. "That's what I called you about then, only for last Saturday. Sure, let's do it. Show the Dodgers and the Angels what they're missing."

"What we're missing, you mean—talent."

"I got good looks. What more do I need?" Tim said. "Pick you up at eight thirty?"

"See you then."

Jerry stood on the sidewalk in front of the apartment building with ball, bat, and glove. Tim pulled up right on time. "Holy crap, man!" he exclaimed when he took a look at Jerry. "You got trimmed!"

"Protective coloration," Jerry more or less explained.

They headed for the park off El Segundo where they pretended to be better than they were. Jerry was going to warn Tim if his friend asked any questions about what he'd been up to. He didn't know if the CIA could plant a mike and a radio transmitter in a car; he also didn't know if they couldn't. Better to take no chances.

But Tim, after a "How ya doin'?" when Jerry got in, said very little till they got to the park. Working in aerospace, he was trained to think about security, where Jerry'd had to learn on the fly. Then, as they started to play catch to loosen up, Jerry's friend asked, "So how'd you like doing the I-5 all the way up? I haven't been much past Sacramento myself."

"I didn't drive up the coast," Jerry said.

"Yeah?" Tim sounded altogether unsurprised. He broke off a better curveball than either one of them usually managed. "You were sure goin' somewhere last time I saw you. Had to do with that goddamn envelope, huh?"

"You got it." Jerry tried a curve of his own. It didn't do much. His elbow asked him what the hell he thought he was up to. "Anyway, I headed east instead. Wound up in DC."

"Did you?" Tim held up a hand before Jerry could answer. "Don't tell me what was in the envelope. I don't wanna know. As long as I don't know, I don't break any oaths by lying if they ask me about it. I may even pass a polygraph, 'cause I'll be sure I'm telling the truth when I play dumb."

"Gotcha," Jerry said, and caught another pretty decent breaking ball. He sent a not-too-fast fastball back. His elbow liked that better.

They hit fungoes for a while. Jerry made one over-the-shoulder catch he was proud of and dropped a towering pop a seven-year-old should have caught in his sleep: about par for the course. Tim was just as erratic with the ones Jerry hit. Then Tim asked, "Where in DC did you wind up?"

"The Russian embassy," Jerry answered, and waited for the sky to fall.

But all Tim said was, "*Did* you?" He eyed Jerry, very visibly thinking. "You have something to do with all the fun and games between the Russians and Kissinger? And with Ford's speech and all that?"

"Oh, maybe a little," Jerry said.

Tim knew how he talked. They'd hung around together since they were seven or eight; Tim was the brother Jerry didn't have. "I wondered. I kinda thought so, to tell you the truth. I knew you were out on that ship. And if you were out there, you were there to work on the waddayacallit."

"The Midlothian object," Jerry supplied. "Yeah. Only after we saw it for real and not just in photos, we called it Humpty Dumpty."

"Oh, yeah?" Tim laughed. "That's pretty good, from the pictures I've seen. Did you . . . see the aliens, too?"

"Uh-huh. Steve Dole and I, we were the first two people into the spaceship."

"Were you? That's . . . something, man." Tim thought some more. "Steve Dole? I know that name from somewhere."

"*Habitable Planets for Man*," Jerry said. Like a lot of aerospace people, his friend thought about what humanity might get up to if its reach ever stretched beyond the solar system.

"There you go! Must have been something, working with a guy with that kind of firepower," Tim said. "What's he like for real?"

"He's, like, dead." Jerry's voice went hard and flat. "He got killed in a 'robbery' the night before I came to get the envelope from you.

I didn't park the car under the building when I went back to my place to grab some stuff before I took off."

Tim Ishihara studied him. "You aren't kidding?" Jerry shook his head. Tim asked, "Who bumped him off? The KGB?"

"Three letters, but those aren't the right three. Word about the *Glomar Explorer* and the Russian sub and even the spaceship was starting to leak out. Even the reporters who heard that didn't believe it, but guys who ran things got scared somebody from the other side would. So . . ."

"Huh," Tim said. "Is that why you talked with the Russians, then?"

"Partly. I figured it was the best chance, maybe the only chance, to save my own ass. But c'mon, Tim! A spaceship! A *starship!* Aliens, for God's sake! I thought that was too important to, well, everybody for us to get greedy about it. And we were." Jerry waited anxiously. Along with Anna's and perhaps his father's, Tim's good opinion mattered more to him than anyone else's.

His friend didn't say anything for close to half a minute. Then his head went up and down, once, twice. "Yeah, I don't see how you had much choice. If they're after you like that, you do whatever you've gotta do." He made as if to point a camera at Jerry. "Who's gonna play you when they make the flick?"

"Fuck that shit!" Jerry exclaimed in sincere horror. Tim laughed his head off. Jerry didn't think it was funny, not even a little bit. But he did a little thinking of his own. Things being as they were, the CIA might not do anything to him if he didn't send the manuscript of the story of his time with Project Azorian to Schenectady before he tried to sell it. Didn't contemplating murder render a nondisclosure agreement null and void?

People would want to read a story like that. They'd want to know how Humpty Dumpty got discovered, how the *Glomar Explorer* raised it to the surface, and how humans made contact with the centaurowls . . . if humans could do that without killing the two survivors and without letting them retake control of their ship. If he wrote the book, he thought he could sell it. If it did well, somebody might play him in a movie after all.

"Hey, I've got another question for you," Tim said.

"Shoot."

"How come nobody stopped your car when you were driving east? They knew your license number and everything."

Jerry told him how he'd acquired the Corvair after he lost his long hair and beard. Tim cracked up again. Jerry finished, "The Rambler's still there, too, or it was when I checked it coming back into town."

"You wanna go pick it up? You can leave the Corvair there instead. If you told a bunch of lies on the change-of-ownership form, they may never even trace it back to you."

"I'm not sure the old car'll start. It'll have been there more than two weeks."

"I've still got the jumper cables in the trunk. We can throw 'em in the Corvair, and we'll use 'em on the Rambler if we need to."

"Let's do it," Jerry said.

Tim drove back to Jerry's apartment. "There's the Ralph Nader special," he said, seeing it on the street, so he remembered *Unsafe at Any Speed*, too. He parked behind the Corvair. They made the necessary transfers. When Jerry started the car, his friend made a face. "Noisy bastard."

"I know. Air-cooled engine."

"That's right. I forgot. What kind of performance does it have?"

"About like the Rambler: zero to sixty in twenty minutes. Maybe eighteen if I'm going downhill."

Sarcasm aside, forty minutes later they were in East L.A. Jerry turned off Atlantic and on to the side street where he'd left his car. "There it is," Tim said. "Nobody else wants it."

"Yeah, yeah." Jerry took the Rambler's plates out of the Corvair's trunk and put them back on. Then he got in and turned the key. He could tell right away the battery was low. But he thought it might start. It might . . . It did. Blue-gray smoke farted from the exhaust.

Tim banged on the window. He was holding the jumper cables. Jerry rolled down the glass. "Sometimes you'd rather be lucky than good," Tim said.

"Better believe it. You wanna pace me on the way back in case I have trouble?"

"I was gonna," his friend replied.

"Good deal. Thanks, man," Jerry said. Tim waved that away and went back to his own car. They both turned onto Atlantic and headed back to the San Bernardino Freeway.

On the San Bernardino and on the southbound Harbor, Jerry worried that the cops would pull him over because of whatever bullshit story the CIA had given them. But a CHP cruiser and one from the LAPD zoomed by without paying any attention to the Rambler. Had the CIA pulled the APB? Had there never been one at all? He didn't believe that, any more than Tim had.

Things around the building were slow on Saturday. He put the Rambler by the curb where the Corvair had parked. Tim pulled in behind him. Jerry got out and walked back to the Corvair. "You're a lifesaver. All kinds of ways," he said, from the bottom of his heart.

"Aaah, no big deal. Listen, I'm going home. I've been gone so long, Cheryl'll think the Dodgers signed me and sent me to Double-A." Tim started for his own set of wheels.

"She may be crazy—I mean, she puts up with you—but no way she's dumb enough to believe that," Jerry said.

Tim flipped him off. They both laughed. His friend drove south, toward Rosecrans. Jerry watched him go for a few seconds, then turned and walked into the apartment building.

Monday morning, Jerry went up to UCLA to finish the paperwork for pulling out of his TAship. As Professor Krikorian gave him the forms to sign, the oceanographer said, "I wish you the best of luck with what you're doing. It would be a shame to lose you, though. You're one of the best students I ever had."

"Uh, thanks," Jerry mumbled. *Why the hell didn't you ever say anything like that till I was bailing out?* he wondered. Maybe his advisor had almost as much trouble making like an ordinary human being as he did himself.

He delivered the papers to Murphy Hall. The academic affairs secretary there took them without the slightest sign she cared whether he stayed or went, lived or died. Sometimes UCLA was a wonderful place. Sometimes it was a frozen desert. Jerry kept an eye peeled for police as he drove home. Otherwise, he was glad to be leaving.

He was washing the dishes after dinner when the phone rang. "I got it," Anna said, and went back into the bedroom. She came out again a moment later, a slightly sandbagged expression on her face. "It's for you. It's Anatoly Dobrynin."

"Jesus!" Jerry turned off the water and dried his hands on a dish towel. Then he ran for the bedroom. He almost sat on the King of Siam, who lay near the edge of the bed. Grabbing the phone, he said, "Hello? Mister Ambassador?"

"Good evening, Mister Stieglitz." Yes, that was Dobrynin, not some practical joker. "I hope you are well? I am afraid I startled your wife."

"It's okay, sir. Yes, I'm fine, thanks. What can I do for you?"

"You told Major Bronstein you would be willing to be part of the Soviet research team going to the *Hughes Glomar Explorer* to help investigate the so-called Midlothian object. This is still true?"

"It sure is," Jerry said.

"Khorosho. Ochen khorosho." Dobrynin chuckled. "'Excellent,' I should say, but you know some of my speech, so you will understand. This team will land in Los Angeles Wednesday. They fly on to Hawaii on Hawaiian Airlines flight 286, leaving Los Angeles International Airport at nine forty-five p.m. that day. You can be on that flight with them?"

"Yes, I can do that. I will do that." Jerry repeated the flight information back and wrote it down.

"Very good. A ticket on that flight will be reserved in your name," Dobrynin said. He coughed once or twice. "The major did not discuss this with you, but we of course will pay you to work on this project. Tell me what the CIA gave you."

"Two thousand nine hundred and thirty-three dollars a month," Jerry answered automatically. He guessed he'd remember that figure as long as he lived.

"This is also what I understood before," the ambassador said, and Jerry realized he'd passed an honesty test. Dobrynin went on, "We will raise this by fifty dollars. We want no one in the world to accuse us of being tightfisted. And you live in a capitalist society. Money is to you more important than in a socialist society of workers and peasants."

"Uh, thank you very much." Jerry had the bad feeling he'd be making six or eight times as much as his fellow Soviet team members. He hoped to God they never found out about that. Socialist society of workers and peasants or not, they'd hate his guts. In their shoes, he would hate somebody like him, too.

"It is a pleasure to be of service to someone who has been of service to all mankind," Anatoly Dobrynin said. Again, he didn't mention the USSR: not overtly, anyhow. "May your investigations bear fruit for the whole human race. Good luck go with you. Good-bye."

"Good-bye," Jerry managed. The ambassador hung up. So did he. Anna came in. She still looked astonished. "What was that all about?" she asked. Jerry told her. "Wednesday?" she said. "Damn! I was just starting to get used to having you around."

"I was just starting to get used to being around," Jerry said. "The cat'll forget who I am again by the time I get back."

"The cat? What about me?" Anna said.

He hoped she was kidding. When he reached for her in an experimental way, he found she was. That was nice, even if the King of Siam got insulted when they chased him off the bed. Didn't they understand they were there to do what *he* wanted? Not well enough, not right then.

The next two days went by in a blur. He drove to the Bank of America on Gardena Boulevard and then to the Sumitomo Bank on Redondo Beach Boulevard, moving the money he'd got from the Summa Corporation out of his older personal account and into the one Anna and he shared now. And he took his father his W-2's, his wife's, and the 1099s from his writing.

"Figure out where we are with this stuff, please," he said. "If we owe money, let Anna know so she can write a check. I bet she can forge my signature on the return, too."

His dad laughed. "That happens with a lot of the couples I do taxes for. As long as there's no hanky-panky in the numbers, you don't need to worry."

"Pretty much what I thought," Jerry said. "Oh—charge us whatever you would for anybody else with the same return."

His father shook his head. "Blood is thicker than money, even if not everybody thinks so. And, thank God, I don't need it that bad. On the house."

"Thanks, Dad." Jerry set a hand on his father's shoulder for a moment. "You're a mensch, you know?"

"I try. I don't always make it, but I try. You aren't doing too bad yourself, kid."

Jerry had his suitcase packed and dinner almost ready when Anna got home Wednesday evening. He left the dishes in the sink after they finished eating. She'd wash them, or else she wouldn't. He wouldn't be around to get upset if she didn't.

They headed for the airport. She stopped in front of the terminal Hawaiian Air flew out of. He kissed her. "I love you, babe," he said.

"Love you, too. Wake up one of those weird aliens for me."

"Ha! I wish!" Jerry took the suitcase out of the trunk and walked into the terminal. Sure enough, his boarding pass waited at the counter. He checked his luggage and went to gate 51, where the plane would leave.

There were the Russians! Those dozen or so men sitting together couldn't be anyone else. They were paler than Californians, and wearing sports clothes straight from 1959. Most of them were smoking. Nervously, Jerry walked over to them. *"Dobry den, tovarishchi,"* he said.

XVIII

When the plane landed in Honolulu in the wee small hours, Jerry felt sorry for the Soviet scientists. All they'd see of Hawaii was the airport. He was glad they all spoke English, some quite a bit better than he spoke Russian. That made sense; they'd need to work with their American counterparts. But Ambassador Dobrynin and Major Bronstein had been right—the Russian he did know, and his willingness to try with it, helped ease his way with his new colleagues.

The Russians and Jerry got off the airliner in a group. Nobody draped leis around their necks or shouted "Aloha!" at them. Jack Porter, the security boss on the *Glomar Explorer*, stood near the entry gate with a sign: SOVIET DELEGATION. Four or five other guys in casual clothes almost as outdated as the Russians' waited behind him. They'd be shepherds, watchdogs, minders, whatever you wanted to call them.

Nikolai Kalyakin seemed to be the seniormost Russian. He was in his fifties, an astronomer by training, and by interests a man who would have got on well with Steve Dole. He was short and stocky, and had lost the last two fingers on his left hand. He wasn't the only visibly injured man in the group; the USSR had had a rugged World War II.

Kalyakin pushed his way forward now. He introduced himself to Jack Porter. "Very glad to meet you," he said in good English.

"And you," Porter answered. He took a piece of paper from a pants pocket. "I have a list of the men in your party, sir. Before we head for baggage claim, I'm going to read it out so I can see who's who." And he did. Each Soviet scientist nodded or raised his hand like a schoolboy when his name was called. When the CIA man got to "Stieglitz, Jerome," he took a good look at Jerry and said, "I didn't recognize you for a second."

"Everybody tells me that." Jerry was thinking about letting his whiskers grow when he got to the *Glomar Explorer*. His hair would take longer, but he figured he might grow it out again, too.

After the Russians had their suitcases, Porter and his comrades led them to the area where cargo planes landed and took off. No one examined the Russians' luggage; after a moment's puzzlement, Jerry realized that would have been done in New York City or L.A. or wherever they landed in the United States. His suitcase would have got the once-over, too.

They filed aboard a military transport. It was a jet, not a Warning Star; the prop job wouldn't have carried all of them. The seats were military issue: no more roomy or comfortable than they had to be. Next to what the Hawaiian Air airliner had had, they were pathetic. The Soviet scientists took them in stride. Jerry wondered what flying on Aeroflot was like.

It was still dark when they landed on Midway. Counting the dogleg to Hawaii, Jerry'd come more than 3,500 miles, and the Russians, of course, much farther than that. But they'd almost kept up with the sun's motion instead of going against it as they would have heading east.

"No photography on Midway," Porter said as they taxied to a stop. "On the ship, you can do as you please—that's been agreed. But not here. Everybody understand?" Nikolai Kalyakin translated for his less fluent colleagues. They all nodded.

Sailors with flashlights guided the new arrivals straight to the mess hall. They parked their suitcases by a table and lined up for trays of Navy breakfast chow. Jerry remembered how disappointed he'd been with the food here after eating high on the hog on the *Glomar Explorer*. It didn't seem too bad now.

Most of the Russians went back for seconds, and a couple for thirds. "So much!" one of them said to another.

"So good!" his friend added. Jerry wouldn't have gone that far. Again, he suspected the Soviet scientists had different standards of comparison.

"We may rest now?" Kalyakin asked Jack Porter. How weary and jet-lagged were he and his fellows? If they'd left from Moscow, they'd come more than halfway around the world.

But the security chief shook his head. "First helicopter leaves at sunrise, second one forty-five minutes later. Once you get aboard the *Glomar Explorer*, you people can take all the downtime you need. Till then, I'm sorry, but no."

If Jerry had been Nikolai Kalyakin, he would have raised hell. The astronomer just sighed, nodded, and turned Porter's words into Russian. None of the other scientists fussed, either, though they must have been dead on their feet. They were bound to be used to having security personnel tell them what to do.

One of Porter's subordinates read the names of who'd go out on the first flight and who on the second. Jerry was on the first. So was Kalyakin. He gave low-voiced instructions to an engineer named Vitaly Yushchenko, who'd fly to the *Glomar Explorer* on the second chopper. *Keep your half of the guys in line till we get back together,* was Jerry's guess.

Along with half a dozen Russians and a couple of CIA men, Jerry boarded the Navy helicopter and strapped down. The sun was just coming up. Away from the base, the gooney birds began to stir. Kalyakin pointed at them. *"Al'batrosov!"* he said, which probably meant Russian had borrowed the name from English.

The whirlybird's engine roared to life. Jerry'd thought he remembered how horribly noisy it was in the cabin, but he turned out to be wrong. He gritted his teeth so hard, he hoped he didn't break one. The helicopter hopped off the ground and flew across the Pacific.

Midway's two islets were just specks that soon vanished. All was seawater and raucous racket. The Russians stared down at the vast blue ocean. Now they could see it, which they hadn't been able to do between Los Angeles and Midway. Somewhere out there lay Site 126–1, unless they'd moved the *Glomar Explorer* after Jerry lost his place there.

An hour later, he spied the ship. The copter bounced once when it touched down on the helipad. Jerry grabbed his suitcase and jumped out. It was very strange: he hardly felt he'd been away.

Dale Neuwirth stood near the edge of the landing platform. Jerry wondered whether to shake hands with him. After a moment, he did, more as a façade for the Russians than for any other reason. Dale sounded warm enough when he said, "Good to see you, Jerry, and good to have you back again."

"Good to be back," Jerry said. "I wish Steve could be here, too."

Neuwirth's lips skinned back from his teeth. "That was not my idea, and I didn't know about it till after the fact. I wish it hadn't happened. Some people on the mainland went a little bonkers."

"Yeah, a little. They almost bonked me, too," Jerry answered tightly. Still, he gave Dale credit for coming closer to admitting what had happened than John P. had. Then he noticed Kalyakin and the other Russians were hanging back to let him talk with Dale. He waved them up. "Here are our new colleagues," he said to Dale, and introduced them one by one.

"Very pleased to meet you, gentlemen," Neuwirth said, and shook hands with all of them. "I'm sure your contributions will be invaluable to us." He waved them forward. "As soon as we all get off the helipad, the chopper can take off." He had to pause while it did; he couldn't shout over it. Then he went on, "Here are the stewards, who will give you your cabins and guide you to them if you need that. Jerry, if it's all right with you, I'm going to put you back in cabin 116. Doctor Parker has had it to himself for a couple of weeks, since the last personnel rotation. A roommate won't do him any lasting harm."

"Okay by me, yeah," Jerry said. "I know where it is, anyhow."

"It'll be kind of a 'Jerry-built' cabin," Dale said with a small chuckle. "That's his first name, too."

"Is it? That should confuse things." Jerry looked around to make sure the Russians were being properly taken care of. Seeing that they were, he got a key to the cabin from a steward and headed for the cabin to throw his stuff into one of the lockers inside.

Instead of just using the key, he knocked on the door. "Who's there?" The voice from within easily pierced the metal.

"Jerry Stieglitz." Nobody'd told Jerry he had to be Steinberg this time around, even if he had the papers to show he was.

The door opened. The man on the other side of it was in his early forties, as tall as Jerry and thicker through the shoulders, with red-brown hair, bushy sideburns, and a mustache. He scowled at Jerry. "You're the son of a bitch who told the Russians what we're up to," he growled.

"I sure am," Jerry agreed cheerfully. "I'm also your new roomie, or that's what Dale told me. And you're Jerry Pournelle. I've heard you talk a few times. The CIA gave you a phony name in Long Beach, too, huh?"

"Yeah, they did." Pournelle looked as if he wanted to stay angry but couldn't quite manage it. He stepped aside. "Don't stand there blocking the passageway. C'mon in, for God's sake. Why in hell did you do such a horrible thing?" Now he sounded more curious than furious, too.

"For one thing, I don't think it was so horrible. For another thing, it was my best chance to keep from getting murdered. Which locker you using?"

"The one on the right. What d'you mean, murdered?"

"As in killed. To death." Jerry started putting his clothes in the empty locker. While he was tossing in socks and underwear and hanging up shirts and pants, he told the sad story of Stephen Dole one more time.

"I heard that was a robbery," Pournelle said. Jerry just shook his head and explained why he didn't think so. Pournelle looked troubled. "Damn! That's terrible if it's true. I knew Dole. Ferociously smart man."

"I saw that from his book. Found out for real when I worked with him."

"You were the one who figured out how to get into Humpty Dumpty to begin with, weren't you? You aren't so dumb yourself, I bet."

Jerry shrugged. "That hardly matters now." He eyed Pournelle. "Have you been one of the go-slow people when it came to trying to wake the aliens? I know somebody must have been, or they would have done more after they threw Steve and me out on our ears."

"No, you aren't dumb, not even slightly." Pournelle had a habit of shouting even when he stood near you; Jerry remembered that from listening to him back in Los Angeles. He continued, "Yeah, I'm not in a hurry about it. We're liable to damage them, or else they're likely to damage us. I kind of had to raise my voice to Dale a couple of times to get the point across."

"Has anyone had any luck in the control room or with the engines?" Jerry asked.

"We know where they are. We think we do, anyhow: behind airlock-type doors we can't open," Pournelle said. "That stuff the centaurowls build with, it may look like mother-of-pearl, but mother-of-pearl, is it ever tough."

Jerry laughed. "Anybody who does W. C. Fields can't be all good."

"I may not be all good, but I'm pretty damn good," Pournelle said with a laugh of his own. "And you aren't too bad yourself, kid. Now I remember seeing that story of yours in *Analog*. Felt real. Can't ask for more than that."

"Thanks," Jerry said, astounded. "I've sold another one there."

"Good for you! Easier to do it once than twice, believe me. If you can sell regularly, you'll build yourself a nice career."

THREE MILES DOWN   265

"If we make it through this. Maybe. I hope." Jerry hesitated, then went on, "But if we can't get at the controls or the engines, we are gonna have to press those big yellow buttons pretty soon, aren't we?"

"Unless you or the Russians figure out how to reach them, yeah, I'm afraid so. Either that or sink Humpty Dumpty even deeper than it was before. It's piss or get off the pot time, sure as hell."

"What do you want to bet we and the Russians both have missiles with H-bombs aimed at this ship right now?"

"I won't touch that one. I'm sure they do and we do. That'd end everything in a hurry, anyway—unless the aliens can shoot down the warheads or make it so they don't work," Pournelle said.

"I think the aliens worry about nuclear weapons, or at least the ship does." Jerry explained his idea about why Humpty Dumpty might have sunk the K-129 but suffered itself to be brought to the surface by the *Glomar Explorer*.

"Huh!" Pournelle said. "That makes a fair bit of sense. I don't recall hearing it from anybody else, either."

"I thought of it after I got shitcanned," Jerry said. "Not something I can prove, not without asking one of the centaurowls, but it seems to be the way Occam's razor slices."

"Yeah, it does. I first thought you had sense when Neuwirth showed me your list of scenarios. Now that I've met you, and now that I remember your *Analog* story, I see I was right—even if you do like the Russians too goddamn much."

"I don't *like* them for beans. But they're here, whether we like them or not. We've got to deal with them. We've got to deal them in, too. Word about the *Glomar Explorer* was already coming out, remember. So was word about Humpty Dumpty, even if the news guys couldn't believe it."

"Some people are too rational to cope with reality," Pournelle said.

Jerry nodded. "That's pithy—and I'm not even lithping." Pournelle looked as if he'd bitten down hard on a lemon. From then on, they got along with each other pretty well.

The men on the *Glomar Explorer* had made some progress since sending Jerry and Steve back to the mainland. "We know what the atmosphere is like inside Humpty Dumpty now," Dave Schools told him. "Eighty-two percent nitrogen, seventeen percent oxygen, one percent argon and neon and what have you. Pressure is just a skosh higher than ours, so the oxygen level is that much closer to what we've got here."

"How could the pressure difference persist if it opens up when you say 'Friend'?" Jerry asked.

The recovery director shrugged. "You find the answer to that one, you win the Nobel Prize. People can go in and out, but the local atmosphere stays in and ours doesn't mingle with it."

"That's . . . pretty crazy, man," Jerry said.

"No kidding," Dave said. "Oh, we go in there without air connections now, too. We put in a cage of white mice, left 'em there with food and water for several days. They did fine in there and after we took 'em out. So we did the same thing with a monkey, to check a biochemistry closer to ours. He did all right, too. He breathed the air and didn't come down sick or anything, even after we got him out. When we were sure he'd stay healthy, I tried it myself. Except for growing an extra pair of legs and feathers, nothing happened to me, either."

"Right." Jerry couldn't help smiling; it was the kind of joke he might have made himself. Dave was okay . . . for a career CIA man. How much had he known about the hit on Steve Dole, and about whatever preparations the CIA had made for Jerry? Had he and Jack approved all that? Had they suggested it?

Jerry would have asked him, only he was sure whatever answer he got would be what Dave wanted him to believe, not the truth. He'd thought about Wernher von Braun not so long before. Von Braun had been a capable man serving unsavory bosses, too.

"I'm allowed to go into Humpty Dumpty with the Russians, then?" Jerry asked.

"With the other Russians, you mean?" Dave said.

That did it. Jerry's temper was more fragile than he'd thought. "Fuck you," he said. "You try and murder somebody, all of a sudden you find out he's not your best buddy anymore. And then you act surprised and snotty? *Fuck* you! I'm ten times the American you'll ever be."

Dave Schoals went red. Jerry suspected the CIA guy could clean his clock if he wanted to. But all Dave said was, "You have the same privileges we do. That's been agreed to. So yes, you and they can go in as you please. And . . ."

He stopped for so long, Jerry said, "And?"

"Fuck you, too."

Jerry blew him a kiss. By Dave's expression, he didn't know whether to laugh or be disgusted. He compromised with a sweeping get-away-from-me gesture. Jerry did. An hour or so later, he and Nikolai Kalyakin went up to Humpty Dumpty's round entry door. It was closed, which meant no one—no one human—was inside. Kalyakin had a 35-millimeter camera on a strap around his neck. It wasn't a Russian model, or even a Zeiss from East Germany, but a Japanese Nikon.

"May I be one to open door?" the astronomer asked Jerry.

"Sure, go ahead. Think friendly thoughts before you speak, remember."

"I shall do this." After concentrating, Kalyakin said, "*Dryzha!*" Jerry was sure he couldn't have brought out the vocative of *dryg*— friend—on a Russian test, but he recognized it when he heard it. Kalyakin addressed the airlock as if it were a person. And he looked childishly delighted when it opened as if a person were operating it.

He went in ahead of Jerry. Yes indeed, the people on the *Glomar Explorer* had done more exploring since Jerry left the ship. He'd had to study almost as hard as the Russians to catch up. One of the chambers they'd found seemed to be the crew quarters. At least, it held three things that might have been centaurowl beds and a jumble of junk that had the look of personal effects, if you weren't exactly a person.

Kalyakin took some pictures. "I see no photos here," he said. "This is strange. No memories of loved ones or of favorite places? What kind of beings were these aliens?"

"Good point. I wish I had an answer, but I don't," Jerry said.

"Is permitted to touch and pick up these artifacts?" Kalyakin asked.

"Nobody told me it wasn't. We aren't supposed to take anything out of Humpty Dumpty without letting people know, though."

"All right. Thank you." The Russian lifted something that looked like a slightly thicker clipboard backing. One side was clear glass or plastic, and cracked. The other seemed to be made of the same tough stuff as the starship hull. "What you think this may be?"

Jerry shrugged. "Maybe it's a super-duper computer." He thought of the state-of-the-art Honeywell machines in the Control container. "Or maybe it's just a tray they ate dinner from. No way to tell, not for us."

"You are right. One day, maybe we know." Kalyakin carefully put the whatever-it-was back where he'd found it. He lifted a couple of other incomprehensible objects, examined and photographed them, and set them down again. "No idea what any of this is, but so fascinating!"

The astronomer also photographed the two centaurowls in suspended animation and the remains of the one whose gear had failed. He looked into some of the other chambers. And he eyed the two airlock-style doors the Americans had found after Jerry got booted off the ship. One apparently led toward Humpty Dumpty's projections, the other toward the dimples at the far end of the spaceship's long axis.

"To say 'Friend!' does not make these open?" he said.

"I guess not, or they would've gone through them." Jerry's thought about those two doors was *The lady or the tiger?* Except they were both liable to have tigers behind them. What might he think of or say to make them disappear so he could find out? He thought of traveling across the galaxy. He said, "Warp Factor Seven, Scotty!"

It didn't work. It did make Nikolai Kalyakin laugh. "This is from your show *Star Trek*. I know of *Star Trek*. I have never seen, but I know of," he said.

"Maybe when you get back to the American mainland, you'll have the chance to watch some." Jerry pitied Kalyakin. Here he was, a man who'd devoted his career to the idea of life on other planets, and he'd never seen *Star Trek*? That seemed almost unimaginably sad.

"If we cannot find way through these doors, we perhaps have to try to wake up aliens and find out what they can tell us. Will tell us," Kalyakin said.

"Yeah." Jerry nodded reluctantly, but he did nod. "That scares me. It scares me a lot. But we'll never learn anything if we don't."

"This is how I see things, too. Also my superiors," Kalyakin said. Jerry wasn't surprised; he didn't think the Russian would come out with any views Moscow didn't approve of. Kalyakin went on, "Now that the two most powerful nations on Earth meet this challenge together, we have better chance of success."

"I sure hope so." Jerry couldn't help thinking of the Romans and the 747 again. Or maybe it would be more like New Guinea natives paddling out to a battleship dead in the water with engine trouble. They'd have no idea what fourteen-inch guns could do . . .

"When we agree to try, we must inform both governments of exact moment of effort," Kalyakin said. "They need time to make, ah, certain preparations."

"Must we? They do?" Jerry didn't like that. Here was the talk he'd had with Pournelle, coming to life for real. The generals would want to be sure they had people with their fingers on the launch buttons, just in case. If something went wrong, they'd try to erase the evidence. And maybe they would, and maybe not.

The lady or the tiger? Jerry thought again. The question seemed even nastier this time around.

But Kalyakin took it seriously. "We must, I think," he said. "This is dangerous step. Everyone recognizes step is dangerous. If step proves to be mistake, we must do all we can to fix mistake. If all we can do is not enough . . . In that case, mistake is bigger than we thought."

"Do you already have permission from your government to go ahead and try to wake the aliens, or do you need to get in touch with Moscow so people there can give you permission?" Jerry asked. Learning Russian had also involved learning something about how Soviet society worked. He'd seen very clearly that the Russians used way more top-down control than Americans did.

"I have permission to ask authorities for permission when I think time is right," the astronomer answered. "I have talked with Doctor Neuwirth, your American leader here, about this matter. He has same arrangement, or one very much like ours."

"That's interesting," Jerry said. So much for the Americans being less top-down than their Soviet counterparts. Well, it wasn't as if this wasn't important. No less than the general secretary, the president would want to make the final decision. Jerry found another question: "Did Dale pull out some of the liquor he has in his cabin?"

"He did. He told me why he had it, too. He is clever man." Nikolai Kalyakin smiled. "I drank some. I drank not much. However clever is Dr. Neuwirth, he belongs to odd religion that does not let him use liquors. Maybe he is virtuous, but how can he be happy?"

"I don't know. I don't drink to get drunk—not very often,

anyway—but a little every now and then is nice. Takes the edge off the day, if you know what I mean."

The way Kalyakin looked at him said he was almost as naive as the Mormon mission director. Jerry had the feeling days in the USSR needed a lot more edges taken off them than days in the States did. His eyes went for a moment to Kalyakin's mutilated hand. How much did you need not to think about what might happen to you when you charged into battle against the Nazis?

His father might have been able to answer the question. He couldn't. Till now, he hadn't really thought about how lucky that made him.

"We will do what we can do," the astronomer said. "If our luck is good, we revive an alien and he is friendly. If our luck is not so good, we die a few minutes later, but it is quick and we know nothing of it. If our luck is very bad . . . They tell me you are man who writes *nauchnaya fantastika*."

That meant *scientific fantasy* or *fantastic science*. Jerry needed a second to get it. "We say *science fiction* in English."

"Science fiction, yes. Thank you. You can for yourself imagine what may happen if our luck is very bad."

"I've done that more than once. Probably everybody who's had anything to do with the *Glomar Explorer* has," Jerry said.

"Yes, probably," Kalyakin said. "It is thought that cannot help coming up. But so is thought of all we can gain if we succeed here. Sometimes is necessary to gamble."

The other choice, as Jerry Pournelle had said, was sinking Humpty Dumpty somewhere like the Marianas Trench and hoping no one ever figured out how to bring it up from there. But somebody would surely try, and, with the better technology the future would have, might well do it. Then the problem would start all over again.

If it happens, let it happen while I'm here to see it, Jerry thought. He sighed, but he said, "Yeah, sometimes it is."

Jerry found himself at the meeting that officially decided things because Nikolai Kalyakin invited him to sit in as part of the Soviet foursome along with himself, Vitaly Yushchenko, and a spaceflight doctor named Pyotr Shuvalov. On the U.S. side of the table were Dale Neuwirth, Dave Schoals, Jack Porter, and Jerry Pournelle.

They all looked less than thrilled to have Jerry there. That, of course, would also have been a big part of why Kalyakin asked him to come along.

His presence turned out not to matter much. As often happened, the meeting just formalized what everybody had already decided: they were going to try to revive one of the centaurowls. They did settle on a date and time there—Tuesday, the fifteenth of April, at noon Midway time.

"You'll have the chance to pass this on to your government, of course," Dale told Kalyakin.

"Yes, of course," the Russian said. "What do we do in case something goes wrong? We need to plan now."

"I'll speak to that," Jack said. "We have military rifles on this ship."

"*Bozhe moi!*" Vitaly Yushchenko exploded. "Why?"

"For the same reason we brought liquor aboard: to defend the ship in case Soviet sailors boarded us," the security director answered.

"Liquor is better notion," Yushchenko said.

"Yeah, I think so, too," Jack said. "But we have them. Armed men will be in the chamber when we attempt the revival. They'll try to disable or kill the centaurowl if it wants to take control of the ship. If that fails, you and we will both have lines out to warn our people on the bridge to warn our governments. And they will do what they do, and may God have mercy on our souls." He crossed himself.

"And if even two thermonuclear missiles don't solve things, the rest of the planet will put up the best fight it can," Jerry Pournelle added.

No one said anything about that. Saying something would just have called attention to the difference between *the best fight it can* and *a good enough fight*.

Instead of saying anything about Pournelle's comment, Dale remarked, "April fifteenth is the day American taxes are due. I hope my wife's taking care of that."

"It is thirtieth of April for us," Kalyakin said. "I hope what we do here is not too much taxing experience for us. You say that—taxing experience?"

"Yeah, we say that." Jerry wanted to applaud. He admired anybody who could make a pun in a language he didn't grow up speaking. It was a bad pun, but then, most puns were bad puns. He'd made enough of them to know.

The Americans and Russians both readied and tested the phone lines that would connect the people in the suspended-animation chamber with the bridge and ultimately with Moscow and Washington. Whatever Humpty Dumpty's hull was made of, it blocked radio signals. The Americans had found that out, Jerry learned, not long after he and Steve left the *Glomar Explorer*.

Jerry Pournelle was designated the American responsible for shooting the alien if it caused trouble. He got one of the AR-15s stowed in Dale's cabin. "More firepower than I carried in Korea," he told Jerry. "I was a punk second lieutenant, and I had a punk second lieutenant's piece: an M1 carbine. Deadlier weapon than a flyswatter, but not a whole lot."

"Okay." Jerry's interest in firearms was only writerly. He'd played with cap pistols and toy rifles when he was a kid, but he'd never handled a real gun.

Nikolai Kalyakin chose Vitaly Yushchenko as the Russians' rifleman. "I would do it myself, but man with rifle should have two good hands." He wiggled the surviving fingers on his left hand. "I was wounded near Lake Balaton in Hungary in 1945."

"My father fought in Italy. He was up close to Milan when the war ended."

"We were allies then. And now again," Kalyakin said. Jerry nodded. Neither mentioned the thirty years in between. Hitler had been deadly dangerous to both the USA and the USSR. No one knew if the centaurowls were, but no one could deny they might be.

Two unarmed Americans and two unarmed men from the Soviet team would go into the suspended-animation chamber with the riflemen. Dale picked Jack Porter to accompany him. Dave Schoals did not take that well. He asked Dale for one of the vodka bottles from the formerly secret stash, and hurt himself with it.

And Nikolai Kalyakin chose Jerry. "Are you sure?" Jerry said when the astronomer told him over dinner. "Won't everybody else on your team hate you if you do that?"

"They will hate me even more if I take one of them—all of them except that one, I mean. If they want to hate you . . . well, I can manage that. And you deserve to be there, same way you deserve to be here on ship. You found way into Humpty Dumpty. And you

were first to see centaurowls. Centaurowls—is word I like." Kalyakin paused for a bite of filet mignon. He followed it with one from
his lobster tail.

Jerry ate some lobster, too. He realized the astronomer headed
the Soviet delegation not just for his seniority and scientific bril-
liance. He was also a shrewd practical politician. If his comrades
blamed Jerry, they wouldn't blame him.

Kalyakin ate more steak. "Is food on ship always so good, or do
you have special things now because Russians are here?" He understood Potemkin villages, all right. Well, a Russian would.

But Jerry answered with the truth: "It's always been like this."

"I guessed it was so," Kalyakin said with a sigh. "In Great Patri-
otic War, soldiers who saw countries in Western Europe saw they
were richer than the *rodina*, the motherland. I saw this in Hungary.
Men who fought in Germany said it was so rich, they wondered
why Nazis also wanted what little we had. And United States, I
know, is richer than Germany ever was."

Enough to eat, a tolerable place to live, a car of his own . . .
Listening to the man from the Soviet Union reminded Jerry how
much he took for granted. The freedom to tell a senior CIA man
Fuck you! was bound to be one more thing Kalyakin would be
jealous of, if he could imagine it at all.

"Next to the centaurowls, we're all a bunch of ignorant barbarians," Jerry said, remembering his vision of New Guinea natives
rowing out to a battleship.

"Is bound to be true." Kalyakin sighed again. "If we learn from
them, before long we are not so ignorant, not so much barbarians."

"I hope you're right." Jerry imagined humans suddenly bursting
into whatever interspecies society there was in this part of the galaxy. Wouldn't the races that had been part of it for a long time look
down their noses—if they had noses—at the upstart bumpkins
moving in and lowering planetary real-estate values? Jerry didn't
know they would, but it sure seemed likely to him. Hadn't Japan
needed to thump the czar in the Russo-Japanese War before the
other great powers, all of them white, grudgingly began to admit
her to their club?

"I hope so, too," the Russian astronomer said. "If I am wrong,
Earth remains in danger even if the centaurowls here prove
friendly."

Somewhere in the USSR and somewhere in the USA, soldiers

would be making sure the missiles in their silos were ready to launch and the warheads atop them would blossom into thermonuclear fire above a particular patch of ocean. Did Humpty Dumpty's sensors know anything about that? What would the starship do if those missiles flew? Jerry could only wonder and worry.

Tuesday came. At a little past eleven, the American and Soviet delegations entered Humpty Dumpty, trailing their telephone lines behind them as they walked to the suspended-animation chamber. Carrying rifles, both Jerry Pournelle and Vitaly Yushchenko looked serious and military. And well they might have; they'd both seen their share of hell on earth.

"Which one are we going to wake up?" Pournelle asked when they went in.

"One closer to doorway. Is easier to reach yellow button for this one," Kalyakin said. Dale Neuwirth didn't try to tell him no. Maybe they'd settled it ahead of time. Maybe Dale just thought the astronomer's words made good sense.

Kalyakin and Jack Porter spoke into their phones, each making sure he had the connection with his government he needed. Kalyakin nodded to show he did. Jack gave a thumbs-up. Everybody was as ready as humanly possible, and hoped the humanly possible would prove ready enough.

Then Pournelle asked, "Who pushes the button? Who gets the credit—or the blame?"

"Should be Stieglitz," Kalyakin said. "He is American on Soviet delegation, part of both. And he found way into spaceship to start with. Who better?"

By the look on Dale's face, and Jack's, they didn't want the USSR's delegation there at all. Want it or not, they had it. Dale, as was his way, managed to be gracious: "One small push for man, one giant leap for mankind. Let's see what happens."

"Okay," Jerry said in a small voice. Dale had borrowed Neil Armstrong's first words on the Moon. If this went well, it would make what Armstrong had done seem not just a small step but a baby step. If it didn't . . . He tried not to think about that.

He eyed his watch. At noon exactly, he reached up and pushed the raised yellow area as hard as he could. *Something* happened; he could feel it. Pournelle and Yushchenko pointed their rifles at the centaurowl inside its glassy half-dome.

Silently and without any fuss, the half-dome disappeared the way the airlock door had when Jerry said *Friend!* He hoped that meant the centaurowl wasn't suspended anymore but back in the real world, the world of time.

Did its beak quiver, ever so slightly? He wasn't sure—he might have been imagining things. But then the centaurowl blinked. When its yellow eyes opened again, they moved until they met his. Then their gaze steadied, and the two very different beings regarded each other for the first time.

ABOUT THE AUTHOR

HARRY TURTLEDOVE is an American fantasy and science fiction writer who *Publishers Weekly* has called the "master of alternate history." He has received numerous awards and distinctions, including the Hugo Award and four Sidewise Awards for Alternate History. Turtledove's works include the Crosstime Traffic, Worldwar, Darkness, and Opening of the World series; the standalone novels *The House of Daniel* and *Fort Pillow;* and many short stories, including more than a dozen available on *Tor.com*. He lives in Los Angeles with his wife, novelist Laura Frankos.

Twitter: @HNTurtledove